THE ORDER
OF THE
ETERNAL SUN

Also by Jessica Leake

Arcana

THE ORDER
OF THE
ETERNAL SUN

A NOVEL OF THE SYLVANI

JESSICA LEAKE

Talos Press

Talos Press books may be purchased in bulk at special discounts for sales promotion, corporate gifts, fund-raising, or educational purposes. Special editions can also be created to specifications. For details, contact the Special Sales Department, Skyhorse Publishing, 307 West 36th Street, 11th Floor, New York, NY 10018 or info@ skyhorsepublishing.com.

Talos® and Talos Press® are registered trademarks of Skyhorse Publishing, Inc.®, a Delaware corporation.

Visit our website at www.skyhorsepublishing.com.

10 9 8 7 6 5 4 3 2 1

Library of Congress Cataloging-in-Publication Data is available on file.

Cover design by Jason Snair

Print ISBN: 978-1-940456-42-3
Ebook ISBN: 978-1-940456-43-0

Printed in the United States of America

For my mom, who has been my biggest fan since day one—and who should probably get paid to be my publicist for all the marketing she does for my books!

ONE

London, England, 1908

I'VE learned two things fencing with Monsieur Giroux: go immediately for the kill and never let your guard down.

Today, I am failing miserably on both counts.

I tighten my grip on my foil sword and lunge, my black skirt swishing against my knees. Monsieur Giroux retreats, and before I can advance on him again, he lunges. The blunt tip of his foil touches the red appliqué heart sewn onto the chest of my blouse, and I let out my breath in a rush.

"*Touché*," he says and pulls his mesh mask off. I do the same, and I feel my hair tumble down my back. He eyes me appraisingly, his slim mustache twitching. "You are distracted, Miss Sinclair."

I glance at my sword, chagrined. "My apologies, Monsieur."

"Always, your mind must be on the match at hand. If I retreat, you must already be advancing. If I advance, you must already be retreating. Yes?"

"Yes, Monsieur," I say, but I can already feel my mind slipping away again—far away from the polished marble floors beneath our feet and the tall columns around us. The sunlight spills in from the wall of windows, splashing onto my white sleeves. Energy swells within me, its golden warmth spreading all the way to my fingertips.

I drag my attention back to Monsieur Giroux, who is now scowling. "Your apology is meaningless if you do not correct the behavior," he says. "Ready?"

I pull my mask back down over my face and nod. "Ready."

"*En garde*," he calls, and we both sink into our defensive stances: knees bent, right foot forward, left foot back.

I advance, leading with my right foot, gliding across the floor. It is not enough. He lunges, landing the tip of his foil in the middle of my chest.

"*Touché.*" This time he rips off his mask. "I would not be upset if I hadn't seen you do far better."

"Then perhaps I could be of assistance."

I freeze at the sound of the painfully familiar voice. We both turn.

Monsieur Giroux's pinched mouth spreads into a smile, but I am left standing rather dumbly, my heart pounding.

"Monsieur Thornewood," Monsieur Giroux says. "How good it is to see you."

They clasp hands, Monsieur much happier now that his favorite pupil has arrived.

"Hello, James," I force myself to say. I should have known he'd come to town for my debut ball. Memories of the last time I was with him threaten to overwhelm me: the feel of his lips on mine, the strength of his arms around me, the pain that sliced through me when he said he had no interest in me romantically.

"Hello, Luce." His gaze meets mine, and I give in to a compulsive urge to smooth the skirt of my fencing uniform. "It's so good to see you."

His dark hair is mussed as though he has just been for a drive, and his grin is as boyish and charming as ever. A flush creeps up my neck. Last I'd seen him, I'd been a smitten sixteen-year-old girl.

"To what do we owe the pleasure of your company?" Monsieur Giroux asks, dragging my attention back to the present.

"My brother has sent me on an errand—as usual," he says, "though this is one I was quite happy to do." He pulls out a polished wooden box he had tucked under his arm. He opens it to reveal two daggers nestled on a bed of black velvet. "He has asked that I school you in self-defense, Lucy, and since you can't very well walk around town carrying a sword, a dagger is the best way to go about it."

The challenge of learning a new weapon is admittedly appealing, but I cannot think of a more uncomfortable situation than having James teach me. As merely standing in the same room with James has me blushing, I can't imagine how my body will betray me when he is instructing me.

"An excellent idea," Monsieur says before turning to me. "Perhaps a little practice with something that can actually maim you might finally capture your attention."

"Daydreaming again?" James asks.

His eyes are warm with his teasing, and I dart my gaze away. I focus on the contents of the box instead. The hilt of one dagger is encrusted with a smattering of jewels—small diamonds and an emerald the size of a marble. The other is much plainer, but still lovely, with a filigree pattern tooled into the blade. "The daggers are quite . . . beautiful," I say hesitantly, "but why did he ask you, James? Surely that is insulting to Monsieur Giroux."

Monsieur snorts. "I should say not. I despise short blades. They lack the graceful dance of swordplay." He points to the foil sword still in my hand. "If you will kindly hand that over, I will put it where it belongs. And Mademoiselle Sinclair," he says after I've handed over the sword, "I will expect you to be fully present and prepared when next we meet."

"Yes, of course, Monsieur," I say, vowing to myself that I will be. Ordinarily I am eager to fence—the movements remind me of dancing, and I do so love to dance—but today it seems I have no control over my mind. "I apologize again for my distraction."

"Very good, then. Monsieur Thornewood, be sure to come fence while you are in town. You and Mademoiselle Sinclair always did make excellent partners."

"I'll be sure to make the effort," James says with a smile that I struggle to return.

Monsieur Giroux nods. "I will plan accordingly then." With a bow to us both, he says, "*Adieu.*"

Silence descends upon us the moment Monsieur leaves, and I have to fight the urge to wring my hands. It hadn't always been this way between us. There was a time when we got along famously. But that was before he returned to Oxford, before I was painfully reminded of just how young and naïve I was. His parting words of two years ago drift through my mind:

I cannot tell you how flattering it is to know you care for me, Lucy, but truly, I don't deserve your admiration.

A gentle rejection, but a rejection nonetheless.

After a moment or two of silence, James clears his throat. "To answer your earlier question, he asked me because I'm rather good at it." He hands me the dagger with the emerald on its hilt.

The weight of the dagger is heavier than I anticipated, more substantial than the light, flimsy foil. I touch a finger to its blade and can feel even through my glove how sharp it is. I frown. "Surely this is too dangerous?"

He twirls his own blade in one hand, his familiarity with the weapon evident. "Perhaps, but it's less dangerous than being caught by a member of the Order of the Eternal Sun with no means of protecting yourself. Colin has decreed you should carry a dagger everywhere with you beginning immediately, which means you don't have time to practice with training blades."

I feel the color drain from my face. It's been three years since the brotherhood had posed a threat to my family; three years since my sister Katherine barely escaped having her power drained. In my mind, I can see Katherine telling us everything she'd learned about them: well-connected men and women who delved in the dark arts, who could take our arcana—the power that is our life's blood—by force, using it to prolong their lives like their own personal Fountain of Youth.

James steps closer. "Shall I give you a lesson on the basics?" A smile touches his lips.

I hesitate. *Find a means to escape,* my head tells me, while the rest of me longs to stay. For the truth is, in spite of everything, I've rather missed him.

"Very well," I say, "but only for a little while. My celebratory ball is this evening, after all."

"Ah, yes. I'm looking forward to it." James reaches out and adjusts my grip on the dagger, his hand warm on mine. My whole body stills. "Your presentation at court went well, I take it?"

Stop blushing, I tell myself firmly, cursing my fair skin. "Yes, very well."

"I'm glad to hear it. I would have been there, only . . . it's a terribly dull affair," he says with a wide grin I used to know so well.

I laugh in spite of myself. "I suppose an endless procession of ladies clad all in white may be a tad dull, but I found it exciting to be presented to the king and queen."

He raises his eyebrows imperiously. "Ah, but if they only knew who they were being presented to, my otherworldly friend, perhaps *they* would have bowed to you."

My eyes widen. "Don't tease me so. What a terrible thought."

He laughs, obviously delighted at my discomfort. "Very well—enough teasing. Shall we begin?"

"If you insist," I say, the feel of the dagger in my hand still unfamiliar.

"The most basic thing to learn is that a dagger shouldn't be used for stabbing—" he pauses to mimic the downward motion. "But rather for slicing across an opponent's targeted area." He makes a smooth slicing motion in the air. "Doing so will give you a much greater chance of actually connecting with your opponent and wounding him. I believe a demonstration is in order."

He sinks into a defensive position, and reluctantly, I mimic him. "Good," he says with a nod. "I'll start by showing you everything in slow motion." He steps forward and arcs the blade just in front of my chest.

Unfamiliar with my short blade, I am at a loss as to how to block his attack. Consequently, I stand rather uselessly as he pretend-slices me with his dagger. "And how am I to stop you?"

"Excellent question," he says. "That's where feinting and dodging come in. But first, I want to see you try to attack me."

I copy his movement, arcing my blade in front of his chest, but he shakes his head. "This isn't a sword, Luce. You're much too far away." He reaches out and pulls me closer. I stiffen.

Again, I arc the blade across his chest, this time only a mere inch away. "Close enough?" My sarcasm earns me an arch of his eyebrow.

"Well done," he says. "On to feinting and dodging. Feinting is important in confusing your opponent; dodging is necessary to avoid being cut. Try that last move on me again, only faster."

I frown. "Are you quite sure?"

"Quite."

I step forward and slice with my blade in one smooth movement. Even so, he dodges away from it, pivoting on his back heel fluidly. I am grudgingly impressed. "Ah, yes," I say, "I see how that would be better than physically blocking the attack."

"Are you ready to give it a go?"

"If you swear you won't wound me. I wouldn't want blood on my dress later tonight."

He smiles. "Then you'd better dodge my attack."

His attack is sudden, but my reflexes are sharp. Despite his speed, I dance agilely out of the way. Again and again we practice our attacks until it begins to resemble true combat. A bead of sweat trails down my spine, my long-sleeved blouse absolutely stifling.

Just when I believe I've almost become rather proficient, James feints to the left and immediately attacks to my right. I try to dodge but am not fast enough. But before his dagger can pierce my skin, he spins behind me and pulls me to his chest. It is hard and unyielding against my back, and I let my breath out in a rush. Instantly, I'm transported to the last time his arms were around me, holding me close as he kissed me tenderly.

"You have excellent defenses, Lucy," he says. "You must learn to use them."

His natural charm is pulling me in like the moon does the tide, so I do the only thing I can do: retreat. I push away from him harder than I intended to and spin to face him. "Thank you for the lesson today, James," I say breathlessly—more from my heightened emotions than from physical exertion. "But I really must insist we stop for the day."

"Of course," James says. "Please allow me to give you a lift home in my motor car, it will be—"

"No, that won't be necessary," I interrupt. "A carriage is already waiting for me."

He looks a little taken aback, as though surprised by my abrupt tone. *Does he even remember the last time we were together?* This thought alone embarrasses me more than anything else, and I redouble my efforts to extricate myself from the situation.

"Lucy, I—"

"Thank you again for the lesson," I say. "I shall see you later this evening."

I walk away before he can respond and pray that a few hours will be enough time to learn not to be so self-conscious in his presence.

After my mentally and physically draining instruction with James, I collapsed on my bed as soon as I returned to Lord Thornewood's townhouse.

Now, refreshed and freshly bathed, I can think of no better way to relax than to draw: the soothing sound of a pencil scratching across paper, the lead sliding smoothly across the fibers, the smell of crisp paper. Some people journal with words to help remember events in their lives; I journal with my drawings.

Before I arrived, Colin thoughtfully had an oversized escritoire moved into my room so I could draw in solitude if I so chose. Ordinarily, I enjoy drawing in the presence of my family, but with James possibly roaming the rest of the house, my room seems a much safer choice.

I pull down the writing panel of the desk and spread my big leather-bound sketchbook upon it. I can feel my arcana quivering just beneath the surface of my skin, waiting to be called forth, but I hold back for the moment. I let my mind wander to the night of my debut, to the opulent throne room where I was presented before the king and queen.

My presentation lasted only a few minutes—only a short procession and a few curtsies, really—but I could have wandered around the richly decorated throne room for hours. If I hadn't been sure the royal guards would forcibly remove me, I would have carefully examined every inch of it.

I think of the intricate details of the room: the leaf filigree upon the molding, the detailed plaster frieze of the War of the Roses bordering the ceiling, the glittering crystal chandeliers. Arcana flows over my hand and down to the paper as I sketch, turning my casual drawings into vivid images. I have a natural affinity for drawing, but it's my arcana that truly breathes life into my sketches with color more vivid than any paint. The filigree shimmers in its golden hues as though I'd transported a sample of it onto my paper. The soft light of the chandeliers glows from the center of the paper, illuminating the sketch of the plaster frieze—just one piece of the whole that represents the War of the Roses. The throne room is the color of crimson, but strangely, it doesn't seem garish—only impressive, as I'm sure it's meant to.

Soon, my muscles relax, and all thoughts of James get pushed to the back of my mind. I draw more and more of the room until the creamy paper is filled with vivid sketches—details of the room, but also random pieces of jewelry I admired, or even an elaborate up-do a countess wore.

When the sketches begin to overlap each other, I turn to a fresh sheet of paper. A smile touches my lips as I think of my grand entrance, even as soft flutters of residual anxiety fill my stomach. I will draw my favorite scene: curtsying before the queen as my family looks on behind me.

But as I set pencil to paper again, a strange compulsion overtakes my hand. No longer do I see the crimson walls, the golden chandeliers, the soaring ceilings of the throne room; instead, my head fills with detailed images of a ruin of stones. My jaw set in determination, I try to wrest control of my thoughts, but the rune remains.

Without conscious decision, my hand returns to the paper and draws the stones exactly as I see them in my mind: gray and pitted by centuries of wind and rain. All rough-hewn edges, they make a crude bridge, though this particular bridge leads to nowhere. They have an almost eerie quality, as though one can sense they are much more than a simple rock formation.

They are, of course. This is the gateway to Sylvania.

Years ago my sister stood in this very spot. Her blood—our blood—had the power to open the portal.

"What are you trying to tell me?" I whisper, though I'm not sure to whom my question is addressed. This isn't the first time this has happened—where I set out to draw one thing and end up with this rock formation instead.

The stones shimmer before me, and I concentrate harder, blocking out the sensations of my body: the soft rug beneath my feet, the press of the desktop against my arm, the pencil gripped in my fingers.

Flashes of light, so brief it's hard to believe I see them at all, appear the longer I stare at the stones on my paper. In those flashes are brilliant colors, tempting me to look closer. They seem so much more vibrant than the colors I'm used to; verdant shades of green, reds and blues richer than any gemstone, and silver—silver everywhere.

Another flash, and its brightness burns an image on to the inside of my eyelids: a grand lady, her hair lit up by the sun, her form willowy and regal at once. I hold my breath and hardly dare to blink.

The sound of a door opening near me fractures my concentration, and the vision before me begins to waver.

"Luce?" my sister Wren says from my doorway, and the flashes of color, the regal lady, everything but the stones I have drawn with my own pencil, disappear.

For a moment, I can only sit blinking dumbly at her.

She comes over to my side with a soft rustling of silk. With her hand upon my shoulder, she peers down at my drawing. "The portal? I must say, it's a lovely rendering, though I'm not sure why you'd feel the urge to draw it."

I glance up with what I'm sure is a sheepish smile, though I do not find anything but curiosity in her expression. A relief, that, since the portal wasn't exactly a pleasant memory for my sister. "It was a strange thing—I set out to continue my drawing of my debut, but I was overcome with this . . . compulsion, I suppose, to draw these stones instead."

"Very strange indeed," she says, touching the tip of her finger briefly to the largest stone. "It must be the Sylvan part of us that wants so badly to see our mother's realm."

I think of the flashes I saw, the otherworldliness of the colors and images, but something holds my tongue. Did I truly see Sylvania? Or was it simply my artist's mind bringing to life my sister's descriptions of it?

"I still dream about it sometimes," Wren says, her tone turned wistful. "Of the fox and the portal and the brief little glimpses I saw through the runes." She flashes me a quick smile. "Not all my memories of that time are bad, after all."

My stomach twists as some of the fear of three years ago resurfaces. I try never to think of her near death at the hands of the brotherhood of men hell-bent on destroying us. Only the knowledge that our secret was still safe allowed me to sleep at night. At least, I'd believed that right up until James had interrupted my fencing instruction today with a dagger. "Wren," I say hesitantly, "surely if all the members of the Order knew the truth about us, they would have come for us long ago."

She tilts her head to the side slightly. "I agree, of course, but what makes you say that?"

I retrieve the ornate dagger from its hiding place in my vanity. "James gave me this today—he said Colin asked him to train me in self-defense. Did you know of this?"

She shakes her head. "No, but neither am I surprised. Really, Luce, it isn't a bad idea. I just hope it wasn't terribly uncomfortable for you."

Heat creeps up my neck. My sister knows only part of the truth—that I'd confessed my feelings to James, never that he'd kissed me. "It was rather awkward, I must admit."

She winces. "Truly? Well, then I'll have Colin find someone else."

"Oh, no," I say, surprising myself, "you don't have to do that. I must learn to be comfortable around him again. It just all came as a surprise—the idea I might need self-defense against the Order. I suppose I've been blindly hoping we would never face such danger again. It's been three years, after all."

She gives me a small smile. "Something I've tried many times to remind Colin of. Still, he remains suspicious. I'm afraid he may become rather overbearing during the course of the season. You wouldn't believe how intensely he scrutinized every guest invited to your debut ball. Attendees at court aren't even subjected to such rigorous censure. In fact, he was such a bear to the Lord Chamberlain yesterday during your debut at court that I thought for sure he'd be thrown out."

I laugh at her exasperated expression. "I must have missed it. What did he want from the poor man?"

"A list of everyone who would be in the palace that day. He wanted to be certain no members of the Order would be in attendance."

I shoot her a look of confusion. "But how would he know who to look for?"

"Precisely," she says.

I stifle another laugh. "I *do* appreciate his concern, though."

She snorts. "We'll see what you have to say after this ball. He's insisting I use dance cards, though you know I find them tedious."

My sister may be exasperated with her husband, but I do understand. Not everyone is who they seem, and not everyone can be trusted. Truly my brother-in-law means well. He was willing to trade the seclusion of his country estate for his London townhome just so I can receive their considerable support during my debut.

Even so, I know rejoining London society will be something of a hardship for them both.

"Never fear, though," she continues. "I'm quite determined to make this the event you've always dreamed of."

I glance around at my richly furnished bedroom, my armoire filled with expensive dresses, skirts, jackets, and a wide assortment of accessories—everything from shoes of the softest kid leather to elaborate hats. I have only to walk out of my room to find my lady's maid hovering nearby, or stroll downstairs to find a veritable feast prepared for every meal.

"I think it's safe to say you've already accomplished that. My every need has been anticipated here."

"I'm relieved to hear it," she says with a smile. "Now, as usual, I've gone off on a tangent and quite forgotten to ask you if you've seen Izzie. The little darling has evaded both her nanny and me—all because Nanny wants to give her a bath."

I smile at the mention of my mischievous niece. I adore that child as though she were my own. I've always had a maternal streak, but there's just something about Izzie's personality that I love. She's only two, but she's quite opinionated already. It rather makes me long for one of my own. "No, but you were right to search for her here. So many times have I found her rummaging through my art supplies. I shall have to start her drawing lessons soon."

Wren heaves a sigh. "I wish you would. Perhaps that would be a more constructive outlet for her—better than hiding anyway." She moves to my wardrobe and peeks inside. "Just checking," she says with a laugh. "All right—I'll continue my search elsewhere then."

"Would you like my help?"

She shakes her head. "Oh, no. Finish your drawing. I'm sure she'll make her way to your room eventually anyway. Just call if you see her."

I agree and then turn back to my drawing with a frown.

After turning to a fresh sheet of paper in my sketchpad, I take a moment to clear my thoughts of everything but my debut. The fact that my drawings seemed to have developed minds of their own of late has caused no small amount of anxiety—and I have the gnawed-on pencils to prove it—but I'm determined to wrest control.

Again, I picture the beauty of the throne room, the rich colors, even the smells and sounds. In answer, my arcana surges into my pencil, transferring each detail of the throne room onto paper: the vibrant colors, the gold-and-velvet thrones, the elaborate crystal chandeliers, the ornate molding. I fill in the edges of the drawing, leaving white space in the center to add all the many people in attendance.

Once I have a satisfying rendition, I add several music notes to the corner of the page. A lively tune by Johann Strauss had been playing at the time, and I know whenever I hear that particular opus, I will remember that night.

The symphony plays in my mind until I can hear the quick bow strokes of the violins combined with the almost playful sound of the flutes. When I touch the notes, energy surges to the tip of my finger, ready to give life to the music I can hear so clearly in my mind. I smudge the notes into the fibers of the paper, releasing my energy at the same time.

Music surrounds me, and it's as though I'm standing in the throne room once again. With my own symphony playing gently in the background, I add the people: lords dressed in full court dress of midnight black velvet, the Royal Guard dressed in crimson regimentals, ladies in heavily jeweled satin gowns of every color. The king had been regal in a scarlet coat adorned with countless medals, some large enough to dangle from his chest. The queen, elegant in gold, her train so long I had to take care not to step on it when I curtsied before them.

I narrow my eyes in concentration as I decide on the exact shade of gold of Queen Alexandra's train. Was it as bright as the filigree adorning the throne room? No, more of a rose gold. My arcana pulls the true color from my mind and adds it to the drawing, turning Queen Alexandra's gown to vivid life.

My own gown was an absolute dream, done in ivory and gold, with delicate cap sleeves and an impossibly long train. I think of the detailed gold embroidery, of how the gown made me feel as regal as a queen, and a desire grips me then, so strong my fingers tighten around my pencil. I wish I could go back to that night, to that one beautiful moment.

And with only that mere breath of a thought, arcana surges down my arm, spilling onto my paper in a glittering dance of light. The fine hairs on the back of my neck rise. The colors seem to shimmer and rise above the fiber of the papers, like sunshine reflecting on a pool of water. The more I stare, the dizzier I become. It feels as though my eyes are crossing, and I blink several times to fend off the uncomfortable sensation.

The drawing swirls around and around until I'm sure I'll be sick. I cannot pull my eyes away. A terrible tugging, like I'm being forcibly dragged, grabs hold of the center of my body. A flash of light as bright as lightning illuminates the room, and I cry out in surprise and pain. My eyelids slam closed.

When I open them again, I'm no longer in my room.

TWO

WITH a chill of suspicion seizing my senses, I take in the scene around me. Crimson silk wall coverings, golden chandeliers, and a symphony playing an opus by Johan Strauss. The throne room at Buckingham Palace.

Debutantes dressed all in white process in, one after the other. With a little squeak of fear I dodge out of the way, but they pass through me as though I am nothing but air. Elegantly dressed lords and ladies line the perimeter of the throne room, but none spare me so much as a glance. Never before has a vision of my drawing been so vivid. It's almost as if I've traveled back in time.

How could this have happened? Not only did I not consciously summon energy, I never drew a rune to allow me to enter the drawing.

"Can anyone hear me?" I ask aloud, standing directly in front of a lady in a glittering sapphire gown, but no one reacts.

A shivery feeling creeps up my spine, and I glance up. I let out my breath in a rush as I see...myself. The soft white feathers in my hair complement my gown with its yards of train and glittering golden embroidery. I can only stand agape as I watch the me of last night curtsy before the king and queen. With my drawing as the conduit, my memories have come to life, escaping from my mind in startling accuracy.

My breaths come faster as I watch myself outside my own body. Apprehension bleeds rapidly into fear. The use of arcana is a heady thing, and that's when one is in control. Here, I have an astounding lack of control.

A couple moves toward me, oblivious to my presence, and I stumble out of the way. I force my eyes closed for a moment, trying to reason with myself. All the other times I've entered my own drawings, part of my consciousness has remained in the present time. I need only picture my room in London, and I should return. I think of the small wooden chair, the smooth feel of my escritoire, the chaotic mess of all my drawing supplies.

I wait for the uncomfortable tugging sensation, for any sign I am about to return.

Nothing happens.

I open my eyes. Buckingham Palace still lies before me. Panic grabs hold of me like a vise as a question resounds in my mind: what if I cannot return?

I wring my hands as I take in the scene. As the people before me shift again, a gentleman catches my attention. He stands not far from the throne, his expression guarded. His eyes are arresting—a clear toffee color and shaped in a way that suggests an Eastern influence. What's more, his dark hair and bronzed skin assures he would be impossible to miss, yet I cannot remember him. Could this mean I am not trapped within my own memories?

Again, a prickly fear that I have no control over this arcana creeps over me.

The beautiful gentleman seems to take notice of me, a look of perplexed interest crossing his face. He moves toward me, and I hold my breath. Surely he cannot see me? After all, everyone else in this bizarre vision has treated me as though I am no more substantial than a ghost.

Very faintly, a voice calls out to me, and I stiffen. I strain to hear the voice; it sounds as though it comes from a great distance.

"Auntie!" the childish voice calls again, and I turn all around to find the source of it.

"Izzie?" I say.

The tugging sensation follows another bright flash. I scarce have time to draw breath for a scream before it's over again. When I open my eyes, the familiar sights of my room greet me: the barely contained chaos of my drawing supplies strewn over every available surface, my wooden trunk, my bed with its plush linens.

My niece holds onto the edge of my bed, her plump face awash with worry. "Auntie?" Izzie asks, her bottom lip quivering.

"Izzie, darling," I say as I open my arms to her for an embrace, "I cannot tell you how relieved I am to see you." She toddles forward and presses her chubby cheek against my chest.

I close my eyes and just hold her for a moment, my own cheek resting atop her dark curls. My whole body feels weighted down, as though my limbs have suddenly become infused with lead. Never have I felt so weakened. Proof, then, that whatever happened to me drained my energy. Was this how Katherine felt when she performed powerful arcana? I recall terrible memories of when she healed that hateful Eliza from a would-be fatal riding accident. I wince, trying to push the memories away. I try to never think of that time—when Colin brought my sister back from the woods, her body limp in his arms, as though her soul had already left this world. In that moment, my heart had been made of glass, and it shattered the moment I saw her.

The ghost of that pain assaults my chest now, and I give my sister's beautiful daughter a gentle squeeze. "Izzie, just now, was I . . . was I here with you?"

She gazes up at me with clear blue eyes, and I hold my breath. She nods. I let out that same breath in a rush. I cannot deny how much it relieves me to hear I didn't disappear—at least physically.

"But Auntie," she says, her head tilted to the side quizzically, "what was that big room?"

My heart pounds harder. "Big room . . . what do you mean?"

"The big red room with all the pretty people."

"Isidora?" Katherine calls from the hallway, a note of worry in her voice. She lets out an exaggerated sigh when she sees the two of us. "Thank goodness. I should have known you'd be in here." Something in my face must give away how utterly exhausted I am because she says, "Lucy, are you ill? You look terribly pale."

"No, not ill," I say with great hesitation in my voice. I shoot another worried glance at Izzie before remembering the drawing lying open on my desk. Of course—the big red room. She'd seen my drawing. The one I'd been trapped in.

"What is it?" Katherine demands, her face tense.

16

My words tumble out of me as they always do when I'm terribly nervous. "I was finishing my drawing just now, before Izzie came in. I'm not sure how it happened, but I was transported into it—though I did not consciously use arcana."

Katherine's eyebrows draw together. "And you are sure you didn't plan to transport yourself? Perhaps you even had a fleeting thought—enough to bring forth energy?"

"No, I'm quite sure of it. I remember feeling a surge of energy, but I was surprised at its appearance. I never intended to use arcana."

Izzie looks back and forth between us with wide eyes the mirror image of her mother's.

"Dare I ask what it was you were drawing?" Katherine asks.

I point to my book of drawings as Izzie takes great delight in sorting through my box of pastels. "As you can see, I was in the middle of recording my presentation at court."

Katherine lets out a breath. "I must confess, I'm relieved it was your debut and not the gateway. I just worry—drawing the gateway when you have little control over your arcana seems rather risky."

Her words are intended to discourage me, but unfortunately, they have the opposite effect. What *would* happen if I lost control during a drawing of the gateway? Would I finally see the visions of Sylvania clearly?

I stare at my book of drawings as though it might suddenly offer an explanation. "I'll be sure to use caution in the future."

"Or at the very least, alert me should you want to try again." She puts her hand on my shoulder. "You still look pale, and I'm sure this horrid city doesn't help. We should go for a ride in Hyde Park to let the sun replenish your lost energy."

"Oh, but I couldn't," I say, noticing that more than an hour has already passed. "I must get ready for the ball tonight."

Katherine waves her hand in a dismissive gesture. "The ball can wait. We cannot have you fainting away."

I shake my head. "No, I know you and Colin care very little for society's edicts, but consider how it would look if I'm not even there to greet the guests who are arriving in my honor. I'll just go outside in the garden for a spell; I'm sure it'll be just the thing to perk me up."

"You're too kind-hearted, little sister," Katherine says. "If you are feeling weak, then I'd rather do what we must to help you feel better."

"I'm well. I *am*," I insist when she fixes me with a skeptical stare.

Katherine nods after a moment—and whether it's because she believes me or because she's decided to let it go for the time being, I'm sure I don't know. She pulls Izzie into her arms as though sensing my anxiety. "Come, little one. Auntie Lucy needs to go rest in the garden." To me she adds, "Send for me if you find the garden's light to be insufficient."

"I saw the queen, Mama," Izzie says as Katherine carries her out of the room.

"You did? How lovely, darling."

I smile at the exchange before moving to follow Wren's advice. Already I can feel the bone-weary fatigue settling over me, as though I've spent the whole day fencing. My drawing catches my eye, and as I move to put away the sketchbook, I'm cautious in the handling of it. I place it gently in my trunk, and it suddenly occurs to me. In my excitement to tell Katherine about my newfound ability, I neglected to mention the fact that I was trapped there until Izzie called me back.

However did I manage to return?

Free of the confines of the house, I let out my breath in an appreciative rush as the sunlight touches my skin. Its warmth is so delicious that I immediately plop myself down in the little patch of grass with my face tilted skyward. Roses and jasmine scent the air, and I smile contentedly as the sun brings energy back to me in a rush headier than a full night's rest.

My fatigue over using so much arcana fades away, and my thoughts return to my drawings. Wren seemed to be right in fearing I was losing control, although, in the first instance, it almost seemed as though my drawing—or the portal?—was trying to tell me something. I think of the grand lady I saw, and it makes me wonder if I truly saw her, or if it's my admittedly overactive artist's imagination.

Perhaps even more frighteningly, the second instance of being pulled into my own drawing is something that's never happened before. Over and over again I think of my actions before being trapped, and each time I'm at a loss as to how it happened. No rune had been drawn, and my arcana hadn't been consciously summoned. For years now, my abilities have grown stronger, but always I've been in control. What was different about *this* time?

A shadow falls across my face, and I startle. I turn toward the source and find James standing over me, wearing a hesitant smile.

"Forgive the intrusion," he says, "but you left so quickly after our lesson, and Devi said I would find you out here. I hope I didn't completely wear you out."

I start to stand and he holds a hand out to help me. After only a moment's hesitation, I take it. "I would be lying if I said I hadn't been, but I've since recovered."

"That's a relief. We can't have the debutante exhausted during her own ball."

A small smile touches my lips. "I'm never too tired for dancing."

"I hope you will save a dance for me, then," he says.

I glance away at the flowers and shrubs—anything but his face. "Of course."

"Has my brother been treating you well?"

I nod and force myself to finally meet his gaze. "He has. My every need has been anticipated."

James tilts his head, watching me. "I don't remember our conversations being this . . . incredibly stiff and polite before."

My eyes widen, and a surprised laugh escapes me. I'd forgotten how James never hesitates to speak exactly what he's thinking—etiquette be damned. Unfortunately, I am a peacekeeper. Katherine is the one who isn't afraid to speak out—even if it's a painful truth. What am I to say? *You kissed me, led me to believe you cared, but cast me aside as soon as the summer was over.*

Yes, I think to myself, closing my eyes in frustration, *that's exactly what I should say.*

"You must forgive me," I say instead. "My mind must be on all the things I must do before the ball this evening. In fact, if you'll excuse me, I really should get dressed."

He takes out his pocket watch and glances at it. "It will take you three hours to get dressed?" His tone is wry.

"I'm a slow dresser." I take a step toward the door, but James stops me. I turn toward him reluctantly.

"Lucy, I hope . . . I hope we can be friends."

"Of course. Why shouldn't we be friends?" I force a smile.

Coward, I berate myself.

He takes a step back, his smile not quite as bright. "That's a relief, then."

"Do excuse me," I say and move past him, the words I should have said trapped behind clenched teeth.

I return to the house and head straight for my room.

Once inside, I close the door behind me and lean against it. *Well done, Lucy,* I think derisively. I'd been given the chance to resolve things, but instead, I'd held my tongue. Of course, the last time I'd confessed to him exactly how I felt, he'd been quick to turn me away. The scene replays in my head, and I grit my teeth as embarrassment hits me like a wave.

"I don't know what I shall do when you return to Oxford," I'd said to him. "Who will I fence with?"

"You're quite right there. Everyone else is afraid of you," he said.

I laughed. "Don't tease me."

He reached out and tugged a strand of my hair. "I'll miss you, too, Luce." And then, before I even realized what he meant to do, he had leaned in and kissed me. The first was sweet, gentle. The second was hungrier.

"I love you, James," I said, my lips swollen from his kiss.

Abruptly, he pulled away. "I cannot tell you how flattering it is to know you care for me, Lucy, but truly, I don't deserve your admiration."

The very next day, he'd left for Oxford.

I'd allowed myself a single night to cry burning tears of humiliation before swearing I would never speak to him again.

Of course, such a thing was impossible considering James is Colin's brother.

THREE

AN unmistakable beauty can be found in the sensory array at any ball: the vibrant colors of elegant gowns, the glittering chandeliers, the lilting music of the symphony, the smell of hundreds of roses and peonies creating a sweet perfume. As this is my debut ball, custom dictates I must be presented to each guest, so I have yet to enjoy any of it. Katherine, Colin, and I stand in a receiving line just outside the ballroom in the gallery. Magnificent paintings of past earls and countesses hang above us, done in rich and somber colors. My gaze continually drifts to the painting directly across from us: two dark-haired boys with an enormous wolfhound between them. As I stare at the beautiful details of the painting, my mind wanders.

I think of my awkward meeting with James in the garden and wince. At least he'd proven a good distraction from my astounding lack of control over my arcana. Once I'd returned to my room from speaking with James, I'd packed up everything in my trunk to keep from being tempted into drawing again—at least for the rest of the night.

Strange, too, that my sweet little niece had such an impact on me as to return me back to the present.

Katherine nudges me subtly with her elbow, and I glance up to find an elegantly dressed lady smiling at me as though waiting for a response.

"How do you do?" I say in a rush, a flare of heat traveling to my cheeks at my blunder. I don't even know the lady's name.

After she shakes my proffered hand and enters the ballroom, Katherine leans toward me. "Are you all right? You seem distracted."

Before I can answer, Colin says, "No doubt she's grown weary of standing here—as have I." He lifts his hand toward the guests still waiting to be introduced to me. "Thank you so much for coming. I would like to present my sister-in-law, Lucy Sinclair."

The guests nod and murmur greetings to me, but their bewildered expressions make it clear they aren't sure what to make of Colin's announcement. Having expected to be presented to me by the earl and countess personally, I can understand why being introduced en masse like that might be disconcerting. But then, Colin has always cared very little for the rules of society. Beside me, Katherine sighs.

He holds out an arm to both Katherine and me. "Now, if you will please accompany us into the ballroom."

The guests follow, still casting confused glances at one another.

Though the ballroom is already crowded with finely dressed ladies and gentlemen, Colin cuts through the crush as easily as the prow of a mighty ship sails through calm water. He leads us to the relatively quiet area of the ballroom where Papa has been waiting, and I'm momentarily taken aback by the pride shining in Papa's eyes.

"You look beautiful, Lucy," Papa says. "I cannot believe it's already time for your own debut. Your mother would be beside herself with joy."

I slip my hand into his big, warm one. "I wish she were here, too."

He gives my hand a squeeze, his eyes a bit red.

"Robert!" Katherine exclaims from behind me, and I turn. Dressed in his navy blue full dress uniform, my brother looks more dashing than ever. Katherine shakes her head, a wide grin on her face. "You told me you couldn't get away."

The giddy excitement I have at seeing Robert for the first time in more than a year bursts forth as I wrap my arms around him.

Robert chuckles and kisses my forehead. "I'm so sorry I'm late, Luce. My leave began much later than anticipated." He takes a step back. "But don't you look beautiful."

"And you're handsomer than ever," I say with a wide smile. "You certainly need not apologize for being late. I'm only glad you're in town at all."

"I'm so happy to see you," Katherine says, placing her hand on his arm.

He leans forward and gives her a kiss on her cheek. "I've missed you, too, Wren."

Papa's smile is a bit watery, and I know he is missing Mama terribly. He puts his hand on Rob's shoulder. "It's wonderful to have us all here together."

I am smiling so hard my cheeks hurt, but then James joins us, and I suddenly have a fascination with the gleaming parquet floors at our feet. I will myself to stop being embarrassed in his presence, but all I can think about is his stolen kiss and my ardent confession. Katherine will be sure to notice my continued unease around him, which can only be disastrous considering she knows nothing of the kiss, and both she and Colin will be . . . furious? Disappointed? I'm unsure, and I'd really rather not find out.

"You did well coming to me to keep your secret," James is saying to Rob as I drag my attention back to the conversation at hand. "We managed to surprise them, which is a lot more than Colin would have done for you," he says with a grin in his older brother's direction. "He can't keep a secret any better than a lady's maid. He tells Katherine everything."

Katherine laughs, but Colin only shakes his head at their teasing.

The last few notes of the prelude the symphony has been playing drift away, signaling the dancing will soon begin. "Should we move closer to the dance floor?" I ask, eager to join in.

Colin takes a step forward. "Just a moment, Lucy, if you please," he says, holding up a card with gilded edges attached to a white satin ribbon. "I have your dance card here."

"Oh yes . . . thank you," I say hesitantly.

"Oh, Colin," my sister mutters under her breath.

He ties it onto my wrist and steps back. "There. As you can see, it's already filled, so there's no need for you to seek out any dance partners tonight."

I glance down at the card. On one side is a list of the types of dance, and on the other is a list of names.

Waltz	Robert Sinclair
Quadrille	Sir Henry Hawthorne
Waltz	James Wyndam
Quadrille	Robert Sinclair
Waltz	Lord Colin Thornewood
Quadrille	Lord Edward Sinclair

All the names are written in Colin's bold handwriting. "How did you know Robert would be here?"

"I didn't," Colin says, "but I knew your sister would fill in a name if I didn't."

No doubt she wouldn't choose only family, either. Well, all except one. "Who is Sir Hawthorne?" I ask.

Colin smiles. "Sir Hawthorne is the gentleman over by the window holding court." I follow his line of sight to an older, rather portly gentleman making sweeping arm gestures to a small group of people surrounding him. His mustache is bushier than Papa's. He's also closer to Papa's age than my own. I open and close my mouth several times, unsure what to say.

"I told you she'd be upset," Katherine says, glaring at Colin and Papa in turn.

"Do not be cross, darling," Colin says. "We discussed this. We're not taking any chances this time."

"Very true," Papa says firmly. "Making a match is the last thing we need to concern ourselves about. Lucy should enjoy the Season, but she's much too young for marriage."

"We wanted to give her the chance to enjoy the dances without worrying about some young lord pushing his suit," Colin says to Papa.

After they've discussed my fate in front of me as though I'm either a small child or someone who is very deaf, I clear my throat. "I appreciate everyone's concern, but it's only a dance. In the future, I'm sure I can find my own partner without any assistance."

"There," Katherine says, "you see? No more meddling." She turns to Robert. "Go on and dance with her, Robert. You're first up on that ridiculous dance card my husband insisted upon."

Robert makes a big show of bowing in front of me and offering his arm. I take it with a smile.

"They mean well," he says when we are far enough away that they cannot hear.

"Oh, I'm sure they do."

We take our places on the dance floor, and Rob takes my hand in his. As the first lilting notes of the waltz begin, we join the other dancers in twirling about the floor. I may not be dancing with a dashing suitor, but still, I feel my heart lift. Rob smiles down at me, and it reminds me of when we were small. He helped teach me to dance, patiently spending hours with my governess and me, until I learned each of the steps. I tell him so, and his smile widens.

"You were such a sweet little thing. Robbie, you called me. You were the only one I'd let call me that."

I laugh. "Are you saying I'm no longer sweet?"

"I'm saying you're no longer *little*. Don't think I missed the way you looked when James joined us." His eyes meet mine knowingly. "Care to explain, little sister?"

I glance away. "Surely you don't want to hear about all that. Tell me of officer's training at Cambridge."

"Shooting practice, marching, rigorous physical exercise. There. Your turn."

"I believe this dance is about to end," I say. I stare at the symphony and will them to cease playing.

"He's a playboy, Luce," Rob says, his expression more serious. "He's my friend, but I've seen a different side of him than you have."

Finally, the last few strokes of the violin signal the end of the waltz, but Rob continues to watch me, waiting for a response.

"There's nothing to explain," I say reluctantly. "I had a schoolgirl's infatuation with him two summers ago and made the mistake of confessing that to him. Now, I find I'm embarrassed to be around him."

He offers his arm to escort me off the dance floor, but his steps are painfully slow. "There must be more than that."

I grit my teeth for a moment. Rob will never rest until he extracts every detail from me.

"Very well, I shall tell you, but you must promise not to breathe a word of it to Wren or Colin."

He nods once. "I promise."

"He kissed me, and then I foolishly told him how I felt, but he turned me away and hurried back to Oxford."

Rob lets out his breath in a sympathetic sigh. "Shall I rough him up for you?"

I let out a horrified laugh. "No, of course not. I harbor no ill-will toward him." Rob glances down at me with a single eyebrow raised. "Well, only a *little*. I'm sure it won't be long before the memories never even enter my mind."

"My offer still stands," Rob says, but he thankfully keeps his voice hushed as we return to Katherine and Colin. Katherine laughs at something Colin says, and her mirth lights up her eyes. "Returned safe and sound," he says louder to Colin.

Katherine rolls her eyes, but Colin smiles. "Glad to hear it. If you'll come with me, Lucy, I'll introduce you to Sir Hawthorne for the quadrille."

"Colin," Katherine says, "surely you won't continue to have her uphold her dance card?"

"It's fine," I say. "It would be very rude indeed if I left Sir Hawthorne in a lurch."

Colin kisses Katherine's cheek. "There, you see? All is well." He offers his arm to me. "Shall we?"

He leads me to the portly gentleman he'd pointed out earlier.

"Hi-ho, Lord Thornewood," Sir Hawthorne says in a booming voice. When nearly everyone around us turns to gape, I have to resist searching for a hole to disappear into. "I haven't seen you in so many years, I'm surprised I recognized you so quickly. Though that arrogant look you always wear is very difficult to forget." He claps Colin on the back and turns his attention to me. "Ah, and who is this? Surely not your wife?"

"This is the Honorable Lucy Sinclair. My sister-in-law," Colin says with an unimpressed tone that suggests either he is masking his reaction to this outspoken man or he is used to his idiosyncrasies. "This is her celebratory debut ball, if you'll recall. Lucy, this is Sir Henry Hawthorne."

"What blinding beauty," he says as I curtsy. "Shall I compare thee to a summer's day? Thou art more lovely and more temperate."

He delivers these Shakespearean lines as though he is upon a stage, and I shoot an accusing glare at Colin. It is quite obvious that what he considers an "interesting" dance partner is very different from my own definition.

"You are very kind, my lord, but I dare say I cannot compete with the beauty of nature."

"So humble! Truly," he says to Colin, "she is a treasure."

Colin favors me with a rare smile. "She is indeed."

"I hope you will agree to a dance with me, my dear Miss Sinclair," Sir Hawthorne says, his watery blue eyes lighting up in an almost boyish anticipation.

"You needn't ask, sir, your name is already written on my dance card," I say, not unkindly.

"Capital!" he says, rocking back and forth on his heels. "Come, my fair lady," Sir Hawthorne's voice booms across the ballroom. "We will dance until the floor blurs underneath our intrepid feet."

With a strangled laugh, I take his arm.

Once we are in line for the dance, my mood improves considerably. The music is a stirring Scottish air, one which always brings a smile to my face. And, amidst the other dancers, Sir Hawthorne is not nearly so conspicuous. Everyone's talk and laughter has contributed to the din around us to the point where even his deafening voice is of little consequence.

As we twirl in and out of the other dancers, I can only be thankful this is a line dance and not a waltz. I shudder to think of how loud his voice would be spoken directly in my ear. Now, our conversation is sporadic and, therefore, of a rather dull nature.

"This music is very lively," he says as we briefly join hands.

"Yes, very much so," I say.

"The refreshments are very good as well," he says the next time we pass each other.

"I'm glad to hear it."

And on it goes until I begin to pity anyone else around who might inadvertently hear our exchange. When at last the dance is over, I curtsy to him in a hurried manner and scurry away like a hare fleeing from a starving fox.

"Quite the partner your brother-in-law chose for you," Rob says with a grin when I reach his side. "It's a wonder you're not deaf."

I rub my forehead. "You heard that, did you?"

He snorts. "Lucy, my dear sister, I'm sure the whole ballroom heard it."

"Yes, yes, it was all very embarrassing," I say, waving my hand at him in a vague cease-and-desist gesture, "but we shouldn't mock him. I truly think he has difficulty controlling the volume of his voice."

Rob bursts out laughing—the kind of laughter that draws stares and answering smiles, even though no one else knows the source of his amusement. "Your kindness does you credit," he says after his laughter has died down to a mere sparkle in his eyes.

"Has anyone offered you a drink, Lucy?" James asks, coming up behind us. I watch in surprise as Rob's jaw tightens, and for one terrible moment, I'm afraid he'll say something. "I'm next up on your dance card, but I'm perfectly amenable to escorting you to the refreshment room instead."

"Actually, I would much rather dance," I say. Dancing is probably the best option; it will take away Rob's opportunity to say anything to James, in any case—at least for now.

"I'll be over here," Rob says as I take James's proffered arm, ". . . watching."

James looks as though he isn't sure whether to be concerned or laugh, and I have the sudden urge to cover my face with my hands. What have I done to deserve all the men in my life becoming completely insufferable?

As we take our places for the waltz, James gives my hand a little squeeze. "You look beautiful tonight—you always do."

"Thank you. You look absolutely charming—as usual."

He shrugs. "It seems to be what I'm best at. Colin scares people, and I charm them." He indicates his older brother with a nod of his chin. Colin leans against a wall, swirling a glass of wine, his expression aloof. I search the crowd for my sister, for they are rarely apart for long, and find her dancing alongside us with Papa.

I smile at the two of them, happy she coaxed Papa onto the dance floor.

"But of course," James continues, "I'm also a master of the waltz." He punctuates his statement by twirling me vigorously around, and a burst of laughter escapes me.

He keeps the pace as fast as the tempo, and we are soon soaring across the floor. In truth, he is a splendid dancer, just as he said.

And whether it's the movement of the dance or the beautiful music, I find much of the awkwardness I've experienced around him lessens.

"I hope you will forgive me, Lucy," James says halfway into the waltz. "I wasn't fair to you. In truth, I often lie awake at night thinking about how abominably I treated you."

I shoot him a pointed look. "You lie awake at night agonizing over it, do you?"

"Perhaps that was a *slight* exaggeration," he hedges, "but I do sincerely regret making you feel any less than a beautiful woman and one of my greatest friends."

Something inside me sighs in relief. "Of course you're forgiven." I hold his gaze so he knows I mean it.

He grins, his eyes twinkling. "Friends?"

I nod. "Friends."

The tension in my shoulders melted away, suddenly leaving me exhausted. I should have spent more time in the sun when I had the chance. We pass the doors to the terrace, and I cast a longing look at the calm, empty balcony beyond. I know from my dance card that the intermission won't be for another couple of dances, but I long for a moment to myself. Of course, that will involve extricating myself from my dance card obligations.

"James," I say with my sweetest smile, "would you mind doing me a favor?"

Free now that James agreed to tell both my brother and Colin that I became almost incurably parched and would be spending the next two dances taking refreshments, I hurry to the terrace doors.

Dim light from the ballroom windows illuminates the terrace as I leave the crowded room. I move to the railing and draw a deep breath. The night air is perfumed with scents from the garden below, a welcome change from the usual smells of London.

I glance over my shoulder at the ballroom, golden light spilling onto the terrace floor. The scene within would be simply divine on canvas. The gowns of the ladies' are vibrantly colored—like jewels. The effect is like stained glass on the dance floor, the color broken up by the gentlemen's dark coats. I can almost feel the paintbrush in my hand, smooth against my palm.

A tingling sensation flows into my fingertips. With a start, I realize I have unconsciously summoned my energy. I frown at my hands, concern prickling in my mind as I wonder if this is what happened earlier. Memories of myself trapped in a dream world of my own creation bombard me, and I try to shake free from the unpleasant thoughts. If I paint this scene later tonight, will I be transported yet again? Perhaps if I am more cognizant of my flow of energy while painting, I will be able to control it better. There is only one way to know.

Movement from the corner of my eye startles me. I hadn't realized anyone else was here. I turn to go, afraid I've caught some overly affectionate couple unawares.

"You needn't leave on my account," a voice calls out softly, and I stop. And stare.

Frozen, I can do nothing but stare as the beautiful man from my vision of my Court presentation steps out of the shadows.

FOUR

You must forgive me if I frightened you," he says, and I am struck by his clipped pronunciation.

"No, indeed," I say, finally finding my voice again. "I was only surprised." *How are you here? Do you recognize me as well?* I want to ask all of these things, but I cannot.

We stare at each other for a moment, etiquette forcing an uncomfortable silence upon us. Rarely does a lady encounter a gentleman without someone to make introductions, and thanks to Colin's impatience, if this man was in my receiving line, I was never introduced to him.

With a short bow, he says, "Please allow me to introduce myself. I am Alexander Radcliffe, Earl of Devonshire."

My words freeze on my lips. An earl. For some reason, disappointment chases on the heels of my surprise. This was no mysterious man conjured by my vision—this was a nobleman I had overlooked during my debut. "A pleasure, my lord," I say. "I am Lucy Sinclair."

Surprise flits across his face. "Ah, then this"—he gestures to the ballroom behind us—"is in your honor?" I give a short nod. "Congratulations on your debut." He takes a breath, watching me intently for a moment. "Forgive me, but have we met before?"

I think of the vision of the Court, of his beautiful tawny eyes. "No, my lord—at least, not formally. Were you at Court yesterday?"

"I was, which is what makes my question so terribly rude." He shakes his head in a frustrated sort of way. "Of course I should remember you."

His look is one of such chagrin that I immediately regret my white lie. "Please do not trouble yourself over it. I have very common features."

"That is a grossly inaccurate statement, Miss Sinclair. Indeed your decidedly unique appearance is why I feel such embarrassment over my blunder. For how could I forget a lady so beautiful?"

I have never been especially quick-witted when it comes to the flirtations of gentlemen. I suppose it is because I've never been able to determine if they are serious or merely empty platitudes. So instead of flirting boldly back or demurely accepting his praise, I suddenly become interested in the state of my feet and as silent as stone.

After a few moments of this awkwardness, he says, "I've made a perfect muddle of things now, haven't I?" He sighs. "This is why I exiled myself to the balcony. I'm afraid my ability to blend in well with polite London society is sub-par, to say the least."

"Oh, but that's not true at all, my lord," I say in a rush, afraid I've offended him.

"Please, you must call me Alexander. I've only just inherited this title, and I am by no means ready to be addressed so formally." He pauses as though unwilling to elaborate, but something in my expression must change his mind because he continues in a hesitant tone. "I have spent most of my life in India, you see."

"India! How fascinating. I have always longed to see it."

He relaxes into a warm smile. "You actually sound as if you mean it."

"I do! Of course I do. I've heard the jungles there are breathtakingly beautiful—like nothing we've ever seen before."

A smile filled with nostalgia lights up his face. "They are; the gardens here cannot compare to the vibrant colors you'd find in India. But I spent most of my time in the mountains where it was cooler." His expression turns sheepish. "Forgive me for doubting your sincerity—I so rarely encounter enthusiasm or even understanding when others learn I was neither born nor raised in England."

I would like to say that I don't take his meaning, but I do. The members of high society despise nothing more than someone different from themselves. And I would know—my family was nearly ruined by the revelation of how different we are.

"You needn't apologize. I am sincere in my interest, but I must confess my geography must be woefully lacking—I had no idea there were mountains in India."

"Indeed—the Himalayas. I made my home at the foothills, where the trees colored everything green and the cool mists blanketed the landscape."

"Goodness, I can picture it just as you say. Such a scene would make a lovely painting."

True interest alights in his eyes. "Do you paint then?"

Having his full attention is a heady thing, and my words stumble from my mouth. "I—yes. It's a particular hobby of mine."

"There is nothing so beautiful as life immortalized in art," he says.

The reverence in his tone tells me he is an art connoisseur if not an artist himself. I'd love to discover more, and I only wish I could remain out here with him for the remainder of the evening. He is more fascinating and delightfully candid than anyone I've encountered thus far—especially since Colin has been maintaining control of my dance card.

Before I can say another word, my sister appears in the doorway.

"Lucy, forgive me, but I—" Wren says. Alexander turns, and my sister's eyebrows rise in surprise. "Oh," she says.

"Katherine," I say, a blush stealing over me. I feel as though I've been caught doing something I shouldn't, though we've only been conversing these past few minutes. "May I introduce Alexander Radcliffe, Earl of Devonshire?"

"How do you do?" Wren says as she and Alexander shake hands.

"A pleasure, my lady," he says, tightness at the corners of his mouth the only indication he is not entirely comfortable. I suppose he anticipates her censure.

"Likewise, I'm sure," she says. "Lucy, I'm terribly sorry to be interrupting, but Colin sent me to make sure you were all right." Her lips curve upward in a slight smile. Colin's overprotectiveness has turned into a bit of a joke between us.

But in light of Wren being attacked in the past on a night just like this one, guilt twists inside me. "I'm sorry to have worried you," I say. "I shall return to the ballroom right away." I turn back to Alexander. "It was so lovely to make your acquaintance."

He gives a short bow, and just as I'm about to reach the threshold of the ballroom door, he calls out to me. "Miss Sinclair," he says, with a cautious smile, "may I seek you out for a dance?"

The pulse in my neck pounds an unsteady rhythm. I surreptitiously glance at my dance card. My brother is my next dance partner, thank heavens. "I would like that very much."

As I return to the ballroom with Wren, my silly smile of excitement dims when I think of Colin's reaction. I'm sure he will not be pleased. Even more surprising, though, is the next thought I have:

It's my ball, and I'll dance with whomever I please.

FIVE

I never imagined I'd find my own sister engaged in a tryst on the balcony," Wren whispers as we walk slowly toward Colin and Rob.

I suck in a breath in utter shock until I see the grin on her face. "Do not tease me so," I say. "We were only conversing. He is a most fascinating gentleman."

"Oh, he is indeed. I must confess, I've seen few gentlemen so *fascinating*." She places so much emphasis on the last word that I know she must be assigning a deeper meaning to it.

"Fascinating in what way?" I ask cautiously. It would be difficult to hear my own sister is prejudiced.

"What I mean is that he is handsome. Almost too much so."

"Though I cannot deny his fine appearance," I say with a smile, "I was actually referring to our topics of conversation."

"It seems you will be continuing your conversation sooner than you supposed," Wren says with a little nod to my right.

Alexander makes his way through the crowd, a polite smile on his face that does not quite reach his eyes. As he passes through, many turn to whisper, their eyes riveted on him.

He bows before us. A real smile replaces his earlier strained one as our eyes meet. "I hope you don't mind, Miss Sinclair, but I've come to claim that dance."

I dare not look at my sister, for I know my blush will be all too obvious. "I don't mind in the least."

He offers me his arm, and after only the briefest of hesitations, I take it. When he smiles down at me, an answering warmth spreads within. He looks at me as though no one else is in the room—not an easy feat since it seems as though everyone is watching, both openly and surreptitiously. But as soon as we assume the position for a waltz, all awareness of the rest of the room melts away.

His hand is warm on mine, and the skin on my back tingles beneath his other hand. Bows touch strings of their violins, beginning the waltz with a lilting melody. He moves first, and I follow.

Our movements are lively and surprisingly in sync. Each time we make eye contact I experience the unfortunate side effect of my breaths coming a little faster than they should.

"I'm sorry we were interrupted earlier—you didn't have the chance to tell me whether or not you paint," I say—both as a means of distracting myself from my heightened physical awareness of him and in a genuine desire to know.

He smiles, a flash of white against the bronze of his skin. "Not with any skill. But I have a great love for art. I once spent an entire week at the Louvre, wandering down its halls each day, only breaking for meals and sleep."

"How I envy you! Did you sleep there, too?" I ask with a teasing smile.

"I would have if they'd let me—I'd fall asleep staring at *The Intervention of the Sabine Women* or perhaps *The Raft of the Medusa*, though of course the latter might induce nightmares."

"*The Intervention* is one of my favorites, too, though I've only seen it in a book. I can only imagine how powerful the painting is in person." It had always reminded me of my sister—the woman in the center of the battle standing so defiantly, willing to sacrifice everything to protect her family.

"Powerful enough to spend hours in contemplation of it . . . and now you must think me terribly strange." He shakes his head, a self-deprecating grin in place as he continues to twirl me through the waltz.

"Not at all. Quite the opposite," I say, my coy words minimized by a flush I feel creeping up my neck.

"We have been talking entirely too much about me, and I'd rather learn about you," he says, his gaze warm. "All I've managed to gather so far is that you have a love for art, you are uncommonly kind, and you are almost blindingly beautiful."

By some miracle, my blush doesn't deepen. "Though I thank you for the compliment, I can't help but feel that would be a dangerous condition to be sure. Who would want to keep company with someone who blinds them?"

He laughs—a real laugh, the mirth reaching all the way to his eyes. "There are many who would. For doesn't the sun blind those who gaze too long at it? Yet, we all enjoy its company."

"Do you compare me to the sun? I have already been compared to a summer's day this evening, and I can only wonder if there is some conspiracy to tease me."

"Indeed there is no conspiracy, only two like-minded individuals."

Now it is my turn to laugh. "Oh heavens, you wouldn't speak thus if you knew him."

"I will take your word for it. But now you have succeeded in diverting me from my original goal. I still know almost nothing about you."

"You need only ask."

He twirls me effortlessly into the next move, and a breathy laugh escapes me. "You introduced me to your sister," he says. "Is she your sister by blood or by marriage?"

"By blood—my elder sister. She and my brother-in-law are kindly allowing me to stay with them for the Season."

"So you will be in London for several more months, then? This may seem strange to you, but though I've been to England many times, this is my first stay of any length in London."

"Oh! Well, I hope you have plans to visit all the lovely things London has to offer. Hyde Park, the opera, St. James's Street," I say in a rush. "There are many more that escape me at the moment. How long will you stay?"

The waltz comes to an end, interrupting our conversation. He bows before me and offers his arm. "I have yet to decide. At least another fortnight."

"Plenty of time then," I say with a smile.

He leads me back toward Wren, and with every step, I dread the moment we will part and I will have to resume my comparatively dull dances.

"Lucy," he says in a quiet voice, his eyes holding mine, "would you allow me to call on you later this week?"

"Yes, I would like that very much." I can barely keep the relief from my voice.

He smiles back at me until we're grinning at each other like fools. "I haven't many friends in London, so this means a great deal to me."

"No friends in London?" Colin drawls from behind us and I jump. I must have been so engrossed in my conversation with Alexander that I didn't notice his approach. "How lucky of you to find the one person who can befriend anyone."

Alexander's smile fades quickly, replaced by a wary expression. Colin's is just as suspicious, and nervousness blooms within me as I hurry to introduce the two.

"Alexander, hm?" Colin's face darkens. "Did you know I personally invited each guest at this party? The Devonshire I invited is three times your age, and I may not have memorized every member of the peerage, but I do know Devonshire's name to be William. You wouldn't be impersonating an earl, would you?"

"My goodness, Colin, don't be such a bully," I say as a gentle admonishment. Since neither even turns his head in my direction, I can assume my comment goes unheeded. With one hand gripping the side of my skirts in anxiety, I peer around for Wren. If ever a situation needed a mediator, it was this one.

"My father's name was William," Alexander says, his face void of emotion save for a slight tightening of his jaw. "He died a fortnight ago, so I accepted your invitation in his place."

At this realization, I have to curl my hand in a fist to keep from reaching out to touch his arm. "I'm terribly sorry to hear about your father."

A smile touches his lips. "Thank you for your condolences, Miss Sinclair," he says.

"Yes, the loss of a parent is a difficult thing," Colin says, and I can sense my brother-in-law's suspicion weakening. "I'm sorry to hear of it. I wonder, though, why I've never met you before."

"I am new to my title having spent most of my life in India."

I let out a little breath when I see Colin's expression soften. With an estate that is a miniature of the Taj Mahal, Colin and his family have long had a love affair with India.

"And your family?" Colin asks, though his tone is not so antagonistic. "Do they reside in India as well?"

"I have no siblings, and my stepmother resides in the dowager estate near Devonshire. I rushed home to England as soon as I received word of my father."

"Ah, I see," Colin says without a hint of regret over interrogating Alexander so abominably. "It's a pleasure to make your acquaintance then."

Alexander gives a nod in acknowledgment, his posture still on edge. I cannot blame him.

"Lucy," Colin says, "I sought you out because there is someone who has asked to be personally introduced to you."

The pleasantly diverted mood I was in evaporates. "Oh yes, of course," I say slowly, my tone reflecting my reluctance. I turn to Alexander. "I very much enjoyed our dance. I'm so glad to have made your acquaintance as well."

"You were the highlight of my night," he says, his eyes trained on mine. "How lucky I am that you discovered me on the terrace."

"The terrace?" Colin asks sharply.

I nearly groan in frustration. Just when I thought he might actually tolerate Alexander. "He happened to be escaping the crush at the same time I was," I say. My voice takes on the soothing tones I use when speaking to Izzie after she's taken a tumble.

Colin says nothing for a few painful moments. "How fortuitous for both of you," he says finally, the tension around his mouth still holding a hint of a warning.

"Shall I be introduced to your friend now?" I wish I could stay and converse more with Alexander, but certainly not under the scrutiny of my brother-in-law.

Colin gives a brief nod of his head. "Good evening to you, Lord Devonshire."

As I take Colin's arm, I meet Alexander's gaze and we share a hesitant smile. He will never come to call on me now—not when he must face such censure. This weighs heavier on my heart than I would have thought, and my shoulders slump a little in defeat while I let Colin guide me toward whoever is waiting to meet me.

"The gentleman I wish to introduce you to is an old friend of my father's."

"I believe my dance card is full." I try for a lighthearted tone but am dismayed to find that my words are sharper than I intended.

To my relief, Colin only smiles. "I deserve that. No, my dear sister, it's not the gentleman himself who would truly like to make your acquaintance, but his daughter instead. A girl your age, who I'm told spends nearly as much time as you do amidst paints and charcoal and paper."

Relief combines with piqued interest, and I let a true smile shine through. "How lovely. Why didn't you say so in the first place? I can't wait to meet her then."

"Unfortunately, she was unable to accompany her father tonight. He tells me she is of a frail constitution, but the more he described her to me, the more I thought the two of you would suit." He nods toward a steel-haired man watching the dancers with a nostalgic smile. "But I'll let Sir Thornby tell you himself."

"Lucy, my dear, how glad I am to meet you," Sir Thornby says, taking my gloved hand in his. "Rose was devastated she couldn't accompany me, but her lungs have never been strong, and her illness only worsens with the cold."

"Rose must be your daughter," I say with a smile. "Colin was only just telling me about her. I understand she likes to paint?"

"She adores it, and she's quite good at it, too." The pride on his face reminds me so much of Papa that I find myself instantly drawn to him. "But as I'm sure you know, such pursuits can be lonely ones, and she is doubly cursed by her lungs. I know she'd be overjoyed at the prospect of not only a visitor her age, but one who shares the same interests."

"Then I would very much like to meet her."

His smile brightened. "You may come to call any day you like. Thorne-wood, you still remember the location of our townhome, yes? I can still see you as a young man accompanying your father." He leans toward me as though imparting a great secret. "Do you know, his expression even at that young age was just the same as it is today? I never thought I would see such a haughty look on a child."

"You're mistaking my look for boredom, Thornby," Colin says. "As with any child, I found my father's conversations with other adults unbearably dull."

Sir Thornby lets out a laugh so loud many turn in his direction. "And still that remains unchanged! You are bored to tears by the conversations of those around you."

Colin's answering grin is wide and knowing.

Another waltz begins, and though I tell myself not to, I find myself searching for Alexander.

"Looking for me?" asks a voice that still sends a little thrill through me, much as I hate to admit it.

I smile as I turn toward James. "That depends. Are you next on my dance card?"

James's gaze slides toward Colin, who is still engaged in conversation with Sir Thornby. "What does it matter? Your nanny is otherwise occupied."

He holds out his arm, and with a sigh, I take it. The dance is another calmly twirling waltz, the music beautifully soothing.

"Did you enjoy your brief respite on the terrace?" he asks, and my gaze darts to his. At the absence of a smirk, I realize he's genuinely asking.

"Yes, thank you. You'd make a truly skilled accomplice."

He pauses in the dance dramatically, causing others to nearly collide with us. "Accomplice? Are you implying *you* would be the mastermind and I the lowly servant? I must say, I'm insulted."

I laugh. "All right, you've made your point. Might we continue our dance? Others are staring."

"Let them stare!" James says amid my embarrassed laughter.

I duck my head as he pulls me close again, and I don't need a mirror to know my cheeks are flushed. "Have I done something terrible to deserve every gentleman acting as though we were on the grand stage instead of a dance floor?"

"Very well, you've convinced me. I'll behave myself."

As we fall quiet and enjoy the music and familiar motions of the dance, my gaze wanders. I find Wren and Rob in one corner of the ballroom, talking with bright eyes and endless smiles while Papa lounges with a glass of scotch in hand. The plush leather chair in which he sits was clearly brought in from the library, no doubt just for him.

"Searching for someone?" James asks, and this time, his face wears a teasing smirk.

"Now who is playing the part of the overbearing nanny?" I counter.

His eyes brighten with mirth. "How I've missed this. Now that we've made friends again, you must agree to come for a drive with me. I think you'll quite enjoy it."

Echoes of the joy I would have once had over such an offer tease a wide smile from me. "I shall try to fit you into my schedule."

James laughs, the sound infectious. "Do. Shall I have my valet send my calling card to your room? After all, we're sharing the same house."

"It'll be rather hard to avoid you." I'd already learned that to be true.

As the waltz ends, and James leads me back to Wren and the others, I allow myself one glance around the room.

Disappointment sinks low within me. Alexander is nowhere to be found.

☥

THE night is clear and dark as Alexander Radcliffe enters his motorcar, bound for his father's—now Alexander's—townhouse. He settles into the buttery-soft leather seat. Outwardly, he is perfectly calm and still as deep water. Inwardly, though, his thoughts and emotions are violently at war with each other. And all because of that girl.

It'd been easy enough to find her. The moment he touched the invitation to the Honorable Lucy Sinclair's debutante ball, he knew. He thinks of it now: the creamy vellum lying undisturbed upon his late father's desk. He'd moved to throw it away, but once his fingers grazed its surface, he felt it: the intense tug within his chest, enough to confirm that she was one of the ones he was always searching for—one whose *prana* was so potent, he felt its echoes the moment he came to London.

And, possibly, one of *them.*

Her beauty he'd expected. The sparkling blue eyes, the blinding smile . . . he prided himself on being immune to such charms. What he hadn't anticipated was her being so kind, so intriguing that she managed to make his heart stop aching for India for an entire hour. He had wanted to spend the rest of the night talking with her. He wanted to see her artwork . . . to hear her opinion on the work of Pablo Picasso . . . to speak with her not as part of an investigation but rather because he wished he could be a suitor.

He closes his eyes for a second longer than a blink, his jaw tightening almost imperceptibly.

The problem, of course, is she may very well be the enemy.

The motorcar slows, drawing Alexander from his reverie. His features rearrange into a frown as he thinks of the reception he will most likely receive the moment he enters the townhouse, which now belongs to him.

The chauffeur comes around to open the door, and Alexander exits the cramped space. He takes a moment to straighten his tailcoat and sweep a lock of his hair from his face. The townhouse looms above him, the black door illuminated by soft gaslights.

His polished shoes scrape against the brick, and before he can touch the wrought iron door handle, the door is opened by Mr. Styles, the late Lord Devonshire's butler.

Styles gives Alexander a long look down the length of his hawkish nose. "Good evening," he says, pausing with a slight curl to his upper lip before adding the requisite, "my lord."

Alexander feels his skin prickling under the butler's disdainful regard. Though outwardly polite, the butler barely manages to hide his contempt for his new half-Indian master. Alexander hates him in turn, but not enough to deprive a man of a position he has held for nearly thirty years. Besides, he doesn't plan on staying in London long.

"I'll be turning in now," Alexander says, trying to banish the awkwardness from his tone. He is still uncomfortable with the notion of servants.

"I will send Smith up to help you change."

Alexander pauses on his way up the old, wooden staircase. "No. I don't need a valet's assistance." Especially not his father's valet. A man his father knew better than his own son. His regard for Alexander was little better than the butler's. This had been his father's townhouse, but these were his stepmother's servants, in truth. The cold reception he'd received here has made him terribly homesick, and he wishes he'd let Hansa, his nanny-turned-housekeeper, accompany him as she'd requested. Just thinking her name makes him crave sweetened *chai* and fresh *roti* bread—two things out of many he knows he won't receive here.

"How will you remove your formal clothes on your own?" Styles asks.

Alexander's mouth curves into a wry grin. "I shall manage." He turns his back on the butler and continues up the stairs, feeling the servant's disapproval follow him like a shadow.

He strides toward his room across plush red and gold carpeting, gilded paintings of his ancestors watching his progress. All have the same haughty looks he has come to expect from British nobility . . . *all except Lucy*, his mind reminds him, and he shakes his head.

Once inside his room, he shuts the door and begins the arduous process of removing his confining clothing. In India, his clothing had consisted of three parts: a linen or cotton tunic, trousers, and sandals. When required by cooler weather at night or by a visit from one of his few English friends, he wore a *sherwani*—a long coat.

He utters numerous oaths before he finally frees himself, missing the simplicity of his Indian wardrobe with every damnable button.

Knowing he is too tightly wound for sleep to come easily, he moves toward his writing desk with the intention of drawing until he is relaxed. His eyes land on three letters that must have arrived while he was out. The first two are business matters related to his father's estates and can wait for the morning, but the name on the third letter has him eagerly tearing open the ivory envelope.

> *Alex,*
>
> *I am writing to tell you that I will soon be in London—with any luck, at the same time as you.*

Relief pours over him, and he closes his eyes in thanks. He will not be alone in this country he has so little claim to. Not only is Richard like a brother to him, he is as English as ivy. He will serve as a guide to help him navigate twelve-course meals, arrogant servants, and gossip-hungry nobility.

He scans the rest of the letter quickly.

> *As for the other matter we discussed so briefly on the telephone, I have news that will interest you. Suffice it to say that you were right: there have been rumors.*
> *Until then.*
>
> *R.*

Though Richard spoke cryptically, Alexander has no doubt to what he referred. He'd ask Richard to use his considerable London connections to ferret out any leads. Common gossip rags have their uses, but nothing is better than a rumor flying mouth to mouth. And the rumors Alexander was particularly interested in were any to do with unusual activity—strange occurrences, mystical events, whispered rumors of power. Strangely, though, instead of the triumphant feeling he expected at the news, he feels a curious sinking in his chest.

After pouring himself a drink from the crystal decanter of scotch in the hopes of thoroughly distracting himself from his untoward reaction, Alexander pulls out the drawing he'd completed just before attending the ball.

The throne room of Buckingham Palace is beautifully rendered, though he's never set foot inside, but of greater interest is the subject of the drawing: Lucy Sinclair smiling a nervous smile as she curtsies before the king and queen.

SIX

THE next afternoon, I call on Rose, Sir Thornby's daughter. After a night of sheer mental torture, where my mind decided to remind me of every cringe-inducing moment with James, every word and glance shared with Alexander, and worst of all, Colin's embarrassing interrogation, I was desperate for an interaction that wouldn't result in a sleepless night. What is it about the dark that brings on such thoughts?

But today, the sunlight on my face is especially welcome, and London's weather cooperates for once with bright blue skies. Emily, my lady's maid, walks behind me in her navy blue dress and coat and her smartest hat. My own violet walking gown is a glorious complexity of silk, the matching coat beautifully tailored. My hair is styled in a pompadour beneath an elaborate hat for the very first time during the day—my debut allowing me to finally keep my hair pinned up rather than loose down my back like a young girl.

I may be exhausted from my late night with little sleep, but my beautiful frock lifts my spirits just as much as the sunlight renews my energy.

"We're to turn right at the next intersection, miss," Emily says, and I can tell from her relaxed tone that she is enjoying the chance to escape the house just as much as I am.

But the moment we turn onto the next street, my steps falter. The cobblestone path, the iron gates—I recognize these houses.

"Something wrong?" Emily asks.

Taken by surprise, I answer candidly, though it's a subject we rarely broach. "My grandmother lives on this street."

Emily's dark brown eyes widen before she manages to hide her interest. The grandmother I hadn't seen in three years, the one who'd been instrumental in nearly ruining Wren's life. After Papa and Colin had paid off Grandmama's many debts, she'd wisely withdrawn from society, and Wren and Colin had made it clear her presence in our lives would be unwelcome henceforth.

Nostalgia and an ill feeling of disgust war within me as I continue down the path. Memories of the first time we arrived in London flit through my mind—the awe and wonder I felt at being in such a bustling city, the envy of the beautiful hats and frocks the fashionable ladies wore, the hope I couldn't suppress that Grandmama would prove to be a loving grandmother. My hopes were horribly dashed, of course, but it's with a wry smile that I continue on my way. I now look the part of one of those fashionable ladies I so envied, but it's small consolation for the loss of a grandmother.

When we finally arrive at Sir Thornby's townhome, I pause at the iron gate for a moment, my attention secured across the street and down two houses. The red door of Grandmama's house taunts me—so close, and yet, it may as well be in China. I will never set foot in that house again.

I turn my back on her house and continue up the few steps to Sir Thornby's front door. A kindly older footman answers, and Emily and I follow him inside. It has the smell of an old house, the parquet floors worn, and yet by the burst of heat and bright lights that greets us, it's not without modern conveniences.

We're led to a bright, sunny room at the front of the house, a contrast to the somber masculine tones of the foyer. The room is small but comfortable, with two sofas done in a pale chintz and two armchairs in complementary colors. The walls are a pale blue, nearly white, but it's the paintings adorning them that draw my attention right away: vibrant landscapes from all around the world. A fiery Tuscan countryside, purple lavender fields of Provence, pale pink cherry trees from Japan, an English garden portrayed with a riot of color. My gaze darts to each one, and if it weren't for the young lady coming slowly to her feet to greet me, I would stand before each one to drink in the sights.

"The Honorable Lucy Sinclair to see you, Lady Rose," the footman says with the gentle tone of someone speaking to the very ill.

Though her skin has the pale sheen of illness, Rose is dressed impeccably in a pink silk afternoon dress, her dark hair in long curls down her back. She's so thin her collarbones are prominent above the neckline of her dress, but her smile is as bright as the room. "How good it is to meet you, Lucy. You'll forgive me if I don't shake hands—the doctor forbade me from any unnecessary contact." Her smile turns apologetic. "He'd keep me in a great glass bubble if he could."

"No need to apologize," I say with a shake of my head. "It's lovely to meet you, too."

"Won't you sit? This is a fresh pot of tea." She indicates a china tea service on the table. "The staff will just be sitting down for tea of their own in the kitchen if you'd like to join them," she says to Emily kindly.

Emily shoots her a grateful smile. "I'll do that, miss, thank you."

Rose sinks weakly onto the sofa behind her, and I take the plush armchair directly across from her. Rose's footman steps forward and pours us both a cup of tea, the porcelain appropriately featuring a bouquet of roses. He takes his leave after assuring himself that neither of us requires anything else. As I take a sip of the flowery tea, my gaze is drawn back to the paintings on the walls.

"I'm almost afraid to ask," Rose says, her tea cup clasped tightly between two hands, "but what do you think of my paintings?"

"Yours? Oh, but I should have known. Your father told me you were quite good, and I see he didn't exaggerate in the least. They are beautiful— truly. I can hardly keep my eyes off them. And such exotic locales!"

She beams at me. "I'm thrilled you think so. I'm absolutely terrible at portraits, but rather skilled at landscapes. I cannot travel, so I paint."

This last statement resonates with me so strongly I take a sip of tea to keep myself from spilling every thought in my head. For her words make me think: just what would happen if I painted an exotic locale and added runes from my mother's realm? Would I be able to transport myself to Japan? India?

I can feel the flush making its way up my neck, so I hurriedly draw her attention to the nearest painting. "This one is especially beautiful, though it's not such an exotic place."

She laughs. "Thank you, and I should say not. It's my grandmother's garden."

"I love the vibrancy of the colors, and the way the whole painting seems to center around those hedgeroses there."

Her eyebrows wing up. "I'm surprised you noticed. Yes, I made the hedgeroses the focus since my grandmother has always called me her Hedge Rose."

"How clever of you." A little pang runs through me as it always does at the mention of a loving grandmother.

Rose sets her tea cup down on the table and picks up a little brass bell. "Lucy, I know I invited you here for tea, and this is probably quite irregular, but would you like to draw together? I'd suggest painting, but neither of us is dressed for it."

"I would love it," I say even as my mind whispers warnings. I still haven't discovered just how I entered my last painting, and I certainly wouldn't want to do such a thing in front of Rose. Even still, I cannot resist the eagerness on her face, for it matches my own.

She wrings the bell and the same footman enters immediately. "Brownlow, will you bring us my drawing papers and pencils?"

"Right away, Miss Rose," he says.

"I so rarely get the chance to draw with others," Rose says with a small cough. "And I've heard so much about—" Before she can finish her thought, her cough escalates, deep and hacking, until she is bent over and gasping for breath.

I jump to my feet and press a cup of tea into her hand, patting her back as she takes a shaky sip. After a moment, the coughing spasm leaves her, her breath still a bit strained but not nearly as bad as before. A fine sheen of sweat covers her face.

"I am so sorry," she says. "How terribly embarrassing."

"You mustn't apologize," I say gently, my hand still on her thin shoulder. "It's not as though you can help it."

"I hate it—this weakness in my lungs, this uncontrollable cough. Now you see why I'm not fit to be seen in public."

"I can see how miserable it makes you. What do the doctors say?"

She glances down at her tea cup grimly. "Bronchial asthma, they call it. The cold and damp can aggravate it, and since it's been growing progressively worse, Father has been searching for a house for me in a warmer clime."

I think suddenly of Wren's healing powers whenever my debilitating headaches come on, and though I never have wished for the same burden of such an ability, I wish for it now. Rose's eyes and personality are bright with life, but I can see the effect her illness has on her body—the shadow that hangs over her head.

But I'm not completely useless in my capacity to help her. "I wouldn't mind a trip to Bath. Colin—my brother-in-law—even has a townhouse there."

Rose perks up for a moment before shaking her head. "Oh, but you couldn't leave in the middle of the Season—this is your coming out, after all."

"You underestimate how much I love to travel," I say, nodding toward one of her more exotic paintings. "We could go for only a few days—I'm sure my sister would agree. She loathes being in town."

Rose laughs. "Yes, I had heard that, actually. And you'd invite me, truly? We've only just met after all—what if you decide I'm an intolerable bore?"

"I don't think there's an intolerable bore alive who can paint such lovely exotic locales. Honestly, though, we have so much in common, I can already tell we'd get on famously."

She smiles brightly at that. "You're even kinder than my father described you. I thank you for the invitation. I shall speak to Papa, but I'm sure I'll be able to accept."

The footman enters then with the drawing materials, giving them to Rose. He pauses, taking in her face with a critical eye. "Shall I fetch your tincture, miss?" he asks, his voice quietly concerned.

"Yes, thank you, Brownlow." A blush colors her cheeks as she busies herself with her drawing supplies. My heart twists for her.

"You're welcome to anything in this box," she says, offering it to me.

It's clear from her hurried tone that she wishes to distract from any unwanted attention to her illness, and I jump to put her at ease. But the moment I get a good look at the red lacquered box containing rows and rows of pencils, charcoals, pastels, paint brushes, and little pots of paint, I needn't feign my enthusiasm.

"Where did you find this color?" I ask in a near squeal, snatching up an oil pastel in a warm mustard yellow. "And all of your supplies are in such pristine condition! By all your canvases adorning the walls, I can see that you are prolific." I think of my own pastels, worn down to near nubs. "You must have a steady supply of new ones."

She lets out a little laugh as she reaches back and pulls out two trays from behind her sofa. "You'd be amazed at what you're gifted with when you have a debilitating illness. And I'm afraid I shamelessly take advantage of their generosity."

"I can't say I blame you," I say as I take the proffered tray. "Just look at the results."

My comment brings a wry smile to her face. "These pastels were brought back from France by a kind gentleman who wanted very much for my father to like him, and these," she says, reaching for two ornately tooled leather sketchbooks hidden under the box, "were a gift from a gentleman who very much wanted *me* to like him."

I raise my eyebrows as I run my hand over the soft leather. "A lovely gesture, but was it successful?"

"In a way," she says, her tone overly light now. "Until I made it plain that I was destined to be an old maid—though of course, the 'old' is a mere token in my case." She must have seen the sympathy reflected on my face, for she quickly added, "But come, let us draw. I won't have you pitying me, Lucy Sinclair. I'm a realist, is all. I've found reality is always preferable to false hope."

"I don't pity you," I say quietly but firmly. "In fact, quite the opposite. I admire your strength."

She smiles at me then, a true smile, one that lights up her features. "You really are too kind." She rummages through the box and produces two pencils. "Now, shall we draw?"

"Yes, let's." In truth, I'm dying to see her technique. I can't remember a time I've had the opportunity to sit beside another artist and watch her draw—not since the half-hearted drawing lessons I was required to take in finishing school. I worry for a moment that I will feel self-conscious about my own technique, but soon enough, the familiar scratch of pencils on paper fill the small room and I relax.

I sneak glances at Rose's drawing as I sketch as innocent a scene as I can think of—the pond at my father's estate at Bransfield—something that has no connection to the Sylvan realm. She uses bolder strokes than I do, and she is on the whole speedier than I, but the results are incredible: a mountain scene that immediately reminds me of the Pyrenees. Her pencil strokes rapidly create contrasting shadows, capping the mountains in snow, adding wispy clouds in the sky.

"Drawing is the only thing that makes me feel whole," she says. "I can almost forget about the outside world when I draw—I just create my own."

Excitement bubbles up within me at the similarity of our thoughts. "I do believe we're kindred spirits."

She grins. "But that's not to say I'm not terribly fascinated by London society. Papa told me of your coming-out ball, but he is never detailed enough to satisfy me."

I put a few finishing touches to the trees surrounding the pond and put my pencil down. "I shall try to paint the scene for you, though I'm nowhere near as good at describing with words as I am with a brush. It was lovely, the type of night you remember with a hazy glow."

I describe everything I can think of—from my dress and the decorations of the ballroom, to the receiving line and dancing. She laughs at my description of Colin until she is breathless. Brownlow returns just then with the tincture, watching Rose like a clucking nanny as she drains the small vial.

I honestly didn't mean to continue—to tell her of my sudden meeting with Alexander, of our dance—but her rapt attention and obvious interest prove irresistible.

"So you've met your Prince Charming, then," she says with a wheezy laugh and a twinkle in her eyes.

I shake my head. "If I have, I'm afraid it won't result in a happily ever after for me—not with the way Colin doggedly interrogated him." I sigh. "Though Colin means well, of course."

Rose looks pensive for a moment. "What did you say Alexander's full name was again?"

"Alexander Radcliffe, Earl of Devonshire."

"Yes, I *have* heard of him—gossip though it may be. The Dowager Countess of Devonshire is not his mother at all, but his stepmother. She's said to be even paler and blonder than you and positively foul. Lord Devon-shire's father married while in India, and his wife lived long enough to bear him a son. Lord Devonshire is the true heir, but his stepmother delights in suggesting otherwise."

"How terrible," I say, indignation rising just beneath the surface of my skin. I cannot imagine the pain of having to deal with not only the derision of Society, but of one's own family.

"Fortunately for Alexander, his stepmother was never able to conceive, so there really is no contest." We both resume our drawings for a moment, and then Rose casually asks, "But did he ask to call on you?"

"He did, but that was before Colin treated him as though he might be a criminal."

"Well," Rose says with a final flourish to her drawing, "let us hope he's either very brave or very foolish." She holds up the sketch for me to see: a peacock struts among swaying palm trees, and a jungle of plants and flowers takes up nearly every inch of the white space.

I look at it in surprise. "Is that India?"

"It could be! I have a rare talent, you see, of drawing people their heart's desire."

"You were right," I say, grinning at my new friend, "I've always longed for a peacock of my very own."

We laugh, both delighted by our own cleverness. I end up staying long past proper visiting hours, both of us laughing and talking of everything from drawing to dancing. How lovely it is to find a kindred spirit, and love-lier still to find someone who knows nothing of my history—with James or Grandmama or anyone else. Someone with whom I can actually choose what I confide.

If only she weren't so ill.

SEVEN

MOST debutantes would have social events every evening, but of course with Colin and Wren in charge, I'm lucky to have something to go to once a *week*. After my visit with Rose, however, my social needs have been well met, and now I long to experiment further with my runes.

Rose's drawing inspired me. Before continuing to my room, I pay a visit to the Thornewood library. A miniature version of the one at his country estate, Colin's townhome library is still one of the biggest rooms in the house. All four walls are floor-to-ceiling bookshelves—including the wall with the door. The doorway is cut into the bookcase, surrounded on all sides by books. The slightly musty smell of old books, gleaming wood, and rich leather greets me the moment I step into the room.

I go straight to the thick, leather-bound volumes of distant locales. Just as I'm pulling out the book on the Himalayas, a voice calls out from one of the wing-backed chairs.

"How mysterious you are." James grins when I jump in surprise. I didn't notice him sitting there when I entered the room. "First, you're gone nearly all day, and then you go straight to the travel books. If I didn't know any better, I would think you were planning some sort of secret getaway. Have you met some wild-eyed gentleman who plans to sweep you away, Lucy?"

he asks, his smile teasing, but something about the seriousness in his eyes takes me aback.

I give him a withering look. "Of course not. Don't tell me you're turning into your brother."

He holds up his hands. "Heaven forbid!"

"If you must know, I've just been drawing with Sir Thornby's daughter, and I was fascinated by her paintings of far-off locales." I hold the book on the Himalayas aloft. "I wanted to try my hand at it."

"I didn't realize Sir Thornby even had a daughter. Is she terribly disfigured?"

"What a horrible thing to say!" I scold as his teasing grin widens. "Of course not. But she does have a rather debilitating illness—bronchial asthma. It's such a shame because she's absolutely delightful. We had so much fun drawing together."

"Well, now I'm jealous," James says. "Did you ever gush about me like that, Lucy?"

He may be teasing, but it doesn't stop the blush from spreading up my face like wildfire. He must take pity on me because he points to my book. "Do you intend to paint a mountain scene then? I should like to see that."

I smile, relieved by the subject change. "I'd be happy to show you later."

"I look forward to it."

I turn to walk away, but his voice stops me. "We're all to attend a ball tomorrow—did they tell you?"

I shake my head. "No, but they needn't. My sister knows perfectly well I'm always up for dancing."

"And would you allow me to escort you?"

I gaze into his, for once, serious green eyes. What I wouldn't have given for such an offer only a year ago. "I would like that, yes," I say with a wide smile.

He rocks back on his heels as though relieved. "Excellent."

"Though you may need your brother's permission. Who knows if even you will meet his list of approved contacts for me."

James laughs. "I'll get it in writing then."

We share another smile, which has the unfortunate side effect of making my knees feel rather unsteady, and then I hurry away to conduct my dangerous experiments with drawing and runes.

After poring over the book of the Himalayas, my mind is full of soaring heights and snowy white mountains. I begin a rough sketch of three majestic mountains overlooking a green valley below. All the while I tell myself it would be madness to try to enter such a drawing and that I'm only creating the sketch because I'd like another painting for my room.

But I know I'm only lying.

When the drawing is finished, I take a deep breath and add the rune at the bottom corner. The one Mama taught me when I was small and liked to look at her Sylvan book. The one that means "transport." With a shaky finger and a murmured prayer, I touch the rune, smudging the lead into the paper.

In a rush, my room disappears. The mountains loom before me in full color: white so blinding I squint, the sky painfully blue, the valley below a luminescent green. The beauty and shock of succeeding renders me incapable of doing anything but taking shallow, panting breaths. The view is *glorious*—spectacular in a way no landscape in England could ever be. But even more amazing is the fact that I drew something . . . and then transported my consciousness there.

As I look out across the mountains, I am struck by the faintest awareness of my room in London. The more I concentrate on the room, the more it comes into view: the messy floor, the soft lighting of the lamps, the smell of roses. I focus on the Himalayas and the green grass beneath my feet, and the room fades again to the very back of my subconscious mind. My brows furrow as I desperately try to puzzle out the meaning behind this.

When I entered my painting of my Court presentation, I'd been fully immersed in the memory. Here, before these great mountains, it's the same. I feel the grass sway beneath my outstretched hand, the smell of snow so real I can taste it, the wind a sweet song in my ear. But if I let myself, I can reach for that link to my room in London—stronger the more I think on it. When I entered my last painting, I'd panicked, believing myself to be trapped. But what if I'd always retained the link to the present time? Perhaps in my fear I'd been unable to find it until Izzie brought me back to myself with her calls.

These thoughts give me the permission to continue on, to explore where I might have turned back. I stroll toward the mountains, head craned back to take them in. The farther I walk, though, the more the scenery before me seems to shimmer. Puzzled, I walk closer.

Lucy, a voice calls, and I stiffen. It's not a familiar voice, and yet . . .

Lucy, it says again, and I slowly turn.

A snow-white fox watches me, its eyes the most beautiful shade of aquamarine, the tips of its fur shimmering silver. It's the color of the Himalayas, but one glance at the ethereal creature and I know it's from another world altogether.

"Are you the one who called me just now?" I whisper incredulously.

Its eyes seem to smile at me. *I've sought you at the request of your grandmother.*

"My grandmother?" I ask, thinking of my father's mother in London who had been haunting me ever since I saw her house on Rose's street. "But why would she—*oh*." My mouth forms a perfectly round *o* in my shock.

Again, the fox's eyes seem to shine with mirth. *Yes, your Sylvan grandmother. She has sensed your presence through your many travels to the In Between. You have drawn one portal to the Sylvan realm, but now you have discovered another.*

I look around at the breathtaking scenery, and it's hard to feel surprised. It would seem the perfect place for a portal to another world.

She invites you to speak with her.

I freeze, surprise and excitement racing up and down my spine. "I would love to! When?"

One day hence. The time of day matters not—she will sense you no matter when it is.

With my heart beating erratically in my ears, I nod. "And what must I do?"

Draw the rune for the portal just as you have today. She will help you cross over to Sylvania from there.

"Oh but I couldn't . . . I can't leave my sister . . . my family . . ."

The fox tilts its head. *Your physical form would remain behind . . . just as you're doing now.*

"I've separated my soul from my body?" I ask, my voice little more than a squeak.

Your sister had nearly the same reaction, if I recall, it says, its tone in my mind almost wry. *I used the same arcana on her once, to travel between realms.*

I fall silent, my mind going over everything the fox has revealed. I feel as though I'm a rowboat that's been set adrift in a turbulent sea. A thought strikes me then, almost frightening in its magnitude. "Do I also have the power to transport my physical body?"

The fox meets my eyes. *Yes.*

"I can completely enter my own drawings?" My mind strains beneath the weight of such a question.

In time. It is not for me to show you the way, but the ability is not beyond the realm of possibility for you.

I would ask the fox so much more, so many questions about my grandmother, but more and more, my room in London pulls me back. An awareness, perhaps; a change in the air.

"I must go," I tell the fox. "I—"

Whatever I meant to say slips away the moment my room comes into view again. My drawing is how I left it—simple pencil on paper rather than the vivid colors I witnessed when I crossed over—only the rune has disappeared.

"Auntie?" Izzie says, her eyes wide as she watches me.

"Izzie," I say with a laugh, "how is it you always seem to appear whenever I'm lost to my drawing?"

"I like the mountains," she says, her voice sweet and musical.

"Those are mountains! You are so clever—"

"The white fox was so pretty," she says, her eyes on the drawing.

I glance down at the sketch in shock, but there's nothing there. I take hold of my niece by her shoulders and look into her eyes. "Izzie, did you see a fox just now?"

She nods. "Can foxes talk?"

"White ones with turquoise eyes can." I hold out my hand, and she puts her small one in mine. "Come, darling, I think it's time we had a chat with your mama."

I'm not sure how Wren will react, but I can no longer avoid telling her, for it's clear that Izzie has the power to see within my drawings—to sense the In Between.

"Mama!" Izzie calls as we walk into the library downstairs.

Wren turns with a smile that lights up her eyes and then she scoops her up. "I'll never tire of such a greeting. I only saw her a moment ago," she says to me laughingly. "I hope she didn't interrupt your drawing."

"No, no, and even if she had, I wouldn't mind it at all." I glance around the room to be sure we're alone. "But I'm afraid I did come here to speak to you about Izzie."

"Oh, Izzie," Wren says in that stern motherly tone she cultivated the moment Izzie was born, "have you done something naughty? I do hope you didn't get into Auntie's paints."

Izzie grins. "I saw a fox."

Wren glances up at me, brows furrowed. "A fox?"

I meet my sister's gaze, suddenly reluctant to tell her. Still, I force myself. "She saw a snow white fox today that spoke to me from within my drawing."

Wren pales, her mouth frozen open as she takes in the many shocking things I just revealed. "Mama's spirit fox appeared to you? How could Izzie have seen it?"

Izzie squirms out of her mother's arms, clearly bothered by her stares, and begins to busy herself with the picture books at her level. "So her arcana is beginning to manifest, then," Wren says, "in spite of being only one-fourth Sylvan." She rubs her brow.

"Perhaps it's a dominant trait," I say weakly. "I'm not sure how to explain her seeing the fox. She must have seen my other drawing, too—she said the Court was pretty."

"And I brushed it off," Wren says with a shake of her head. "Do you think she enters the drawing with you? How do *you* enter it?"

"By leaving my physical body behind, apparently."

"The fox told you?" she asks, a wistful note in her tone. "What else did it say?"

"That our grandmother wishes to speak with me—our Sylvan grand-mother. It called the places I go in my drawings the In Between, and she was able to sense me. I was so surprised, and of course I'm terribly excited to meet her. Do you think she will be kind like Mama?"

Wren's expression is a world away, but she shakes herself back to the present. "Kinder than our earthly grandmother, I daresay. I know so very little about her—only what I gleaned from that tragic memory the fox shared with me. She was always on Mama's side. Her love for her was clear, but her power . . . it was nothing like Mama's—not gentle or healing in the least."

"Was it like yours?" I ask, thinking of the awesome destructive power Wren is capable of.

"More powerful than mine."

"Well, that's rather intimidating then," I say, and Wren grins.

"We have a powerful ancestry. I suppose I shouldn't be surprised Izzie has manifested it. I only wish she didn't bear our same burden."

"Perhaps it needn't be a burden. So far, it's nothing we can't keep hidden."

"Yes, but you and I both know it's difficult to keep such an inherent part of yourself hidden forever, and especially from the ones you love."

I think of my earlier desire to share my ability with Rose and nod slowly.

"Well, we mustn't tell Colin—not yet. If you think he's protective over you . . ."

"Izzie, you poor darling," I say, only partly teasing. Colin will scrutinize every single person his daughter comes into contact with—who can say if he'll even consent to her coming out years from now.

Izzie, lost amongst a great pile of colorful books, ignores us.

"Perhaps our grandmother will have answers when you speak to her," Wren says, and we both share a look of wonder.

Never before have we had the chance to talk to our Sylvan kin, and I can't help but think: why now?

EIGHT

COLIN and Wren may not often follow the rules of society, but that doesn't mean we aren't treated to a lavish, formal dinner every night. I should think Colin's London butler, Mr. Hale, would never allow otherwise. The table is set with crystal that sparkles in the soft light of the chandelier, the freshly polished silverware gleaming beside delicate porcelain plates. Two flower arrangements of purple hydrangea and leafy greens add welcome splashes of color.

With Rob and Papa still in town, six of us sit for supper. Colin and Wren sit at either end of the table, and I find myself seated beside James instead of Rob. As one, the footmen serve us the first course: a creamy watercress soup.

I take a bite, savoring the richness of it before the horseradish burns my sinuses and I reach for my small glass of wine. I inhale some of my wine wrong and try to suppress a choking cough. When that fails, a great hack escapes me.

James gives me a few helpful whacks between my shoulders until I can breathe normally again. "Good God, Colin, are you not making sure your sister-in-law is properly fed? She nearly inhaled her soup."

I laugh, shaking my head. "It was the horseradish. I assure you, I get plenty to eat here."

In answer, Colin merely gives his brother a long-suffering look before returning to his conversation with Papa and Rob on the newly established Territorial Force of the British Army—something neither I, nor James if his wandering attention is any indication, cares one whit about.

"Did you finish your painting?" James asks.

"I did—oh yes, of course. You wanted to see it. Forgive me, I . . . got distracted." I think of the conversation Wren and I had about Izzie and sneak a glance at her. After our talk, we'd both gone to change for dinner, and I'd forgotten all about James's interest in my drawing.

"Quite all right," he says with a smile. "I'm easily forgotten."

I snort into my soup, and the footman comes forward to sweep it away from me. They must believe I'm positively allergic to the horseradish by now. "Now you know that isn't true," I scold, but the double meaning of my words causes me to blush. "In any case, I'd be happy to show it to you after dinner."

"That'd be far more entertaining than anything these three could talk about," he says with a nod toward Rob, Papa, and Colin.

"Do you think they'd let me volunteer then?" Papa asks. "I could ride alongside you in the Royal Horse Artillery, Rob."

"I doubt they'd let you drink scotch and read books while doing so, Father," Rob says, and Papa harrumphs, but the hint of laughter in his eyes is inescapable.

I glance back at James with a smile. "I see what you mean." I open my mouth to say more, but then I hear Colin mention Sir Thornby. "Oh, I had such a lovely time with his daughter," I interject. "I must thank you for introducing us—however indirectly."

Colin grins. "Finally, I did something right." When both Wren and I give him matching withering glances he adds, "No, I'm glad for you, Lucy."

"Did you find her just as silly as you?" Rob asks as the entrée course is served: fowl au béchamel.

I huff good-naturedly. "She was both kind and a delight to talk to. We spent the day drawing and drinking tea."

Rob smiles. "A perfect match!"

"I'm so happy you've found a friend here in London, Luce," Wren says. "I found Penelope to be indispensable during my debut, and I'm sure you'll find Rose to be the same."

I think of Penelope, Wren's closest friend, and her bright smile. She had been married off shortly after Wren and Colin, and ever since then, Wren hadn't seen much of her. Many, including Wren, believed that to be because of Penelope's husband—a man who was chosen by Penelope's mother, but one who was known to be cruel. "How is Penelope? I miss her."

"I do, too. Well, I suppose. You know her husband passed? She's the Dowager Lady Brasher now."

"At her age? Goodness, how strange that would be," I say, though what I'd really like to say is "good riddance."

"Indeed, but I hope we might be seeing more of her soon. She wrote not long ago to say she will be in London next month. But what of Rose's health?" Wren asks after she pauses to take a few bites of her entrée. "Is it as bad as Sir Thornby led us to believe?"

Sadness twists inside me. "Worse, actually. She has bronchial asthma and sounded miserable when I was there—which reminds me! What say you to a short trip to Bath?"

"Oh," Wren says with a glance at Colin, "well, it would be fine with me, Luce. It's your coming out, after all. Do you mind missing even more of the Season? We've been abstaining from so many events during the week as it is."

"I wouldn't mind if it helps her. There would be room for her at Colin's townhome, right? Besides, I've always wanted to visit Bath."

"Yes, plenty of room. Rob, Papa," Wren interrupts, "would you like to accompany us to Bath?"

Papa hurriedly eats one more bite of his entrée before the footman whisks it away and replaces it with the second course of roast pork with apple confit. "I'm game for a visit. A spa village is more my speed than London anyway."

"I suppose I'll tag along, too," Rob says. "I could use a break from this grueling London schedule."

"Yes, I'm sure a ball every few days or so has been just exhausting for you," I say.

Rob looks at me, aghast. "You've been around your elder sister for far too long. Father, are you going to stand for her being so cheeky?"

Papa eyes him over his wine glass. "If you haven't learned how to manage both your sisters by now, Rob, then it's simply a lost cause."

I laugh at Rob's feigned look of exasperation and turn to James. "And as my instructor in self-defense, of course you should go, too."

"I accept your invitation, but only if you agree to start calling me *sensei*—that's what they call their teachers in Japan, and I rather like the pompous sound to it."

"It's only pompous when an Englishman insists on being called so," I say, and James barks with surprised laughter.

"I agree with Rob," James says, "you've become quite cheeky of late."

I laugh. "Well, I'm not sixteen anymore."

James meets my gaze, appraising me over a sip of wine. "No, you are not."

His tone sends a blaze of warmth from low in my abdomen all the way to my cheeks, and I take a bite of food to hide it, hardly tasting it.

Later, after we'd devoured our third course of quail followed by a meringue for dessert, we adjourned to the elegant drawing room. Because no guests were present, the men remained with us, which was just as well since I'd agreed to show James my drawing. After excusing myself to retrieve it, I was surprised that nervous anticipation made my knees shaky. It's not as though James had never seen my drawings before.

With a deep breath to steady my nerves, I pull James aside and thrust the paper toward him. He takes it from me gently, his eyes roving over the drawing. Uncharacteristically for him, he's quiet as he gazes at each detail. I have to bite my tongue to keep myself from asking for his thoughts.

After several moments of silent contemplation, he says, "I wonder if you might let me keep this?"

Taken aback, I cannot restrain the sudden smile of pleasure from my face. "You like it that much?"

"It's beautifully rendered, Luce, as all of your drawings are. The attention to detail is such that I can picture myself there, which is why I've made my strange request. This little valley here, well, it reminds me of the trip we took to India when I was a boy. Father was there . . . and Mama . . ." He trails off, his expression vulnerable for the first time in . . . well, as long as I've known him.

I'd forgotten how much we had in common, that we shared the loss of a beloved mother. Though for James it was much worse—for he had lost his father, too. In spite of that, he was always cheerful and good-natured, charming and mischievous to a fault.

"Then of course you should have it," I say, touching his hand. "If you'll allow me a little more time, I can fully bring it to life with paint."

He looks up, his smile almost sad. "I'd like that."

We hold each other's gaze for much too long, and I take a deep breath. "Well, now that you've made me feel like a proper artist, perhaps we should join the others?"

I turn to go, but he reaches for me. Before he can touch my arm in an overly familiar way, he seems to remember himself and withdraws at the last moment. "We have the whole day tomorrow before the ball—what will you be doing with your time?"

I think of the drawing and the fox's words and the possibility of seeing my grandmother. "Oh, this and that," I hedge. "I should look in on Rose to tell her the good news about Bath."

"Plenty of time then, for a training session with your *sensei*." He grins.

"Oh, I . . ." I struggle to think of an excuse, anything to avoid being alone with him again, but then I think of his moment of vulnerability and I find myself nodding. "Of course. When should we arrange it for?"

"Traditionally, we should meet just after dawn to start the day with vigorous exercise, but I suppose we can make allowances for breakfast."

I laugh. "Yes, I'm afraid dawn is out of the question. I'd be absolutely worthless."

"After breakfast then." He smiles and hands me my drawing.

I return the smile even as jittery nerves fill my stomach. I tell myself these are due to my meeting with the grandmother from another realm I've never even laid eyes on.

But of course, I'm lying to myself again.

With Monsieur Giroux so close to St. James Square and Colin's townhome, James and I elect to walk the next morning. Well, this is not precisely accurate. *I* decide to walk. James reluctantly gives in after trying several unsuccessful attempts to convince me to take a car or carriage or any other transportation, really, but walking. But with the sun still making a rare appearance, I hold firm.

We stroll arm-in-arm without the need for a chaperone since James has the benefit of being both friend and family. With my fencing uniform at

Monsieur Giroux's, I'm dressed rather smartly for our outing in a black-and-white striped tailored dress. My hat is fashionably wide-brimmed, so much so that I must tilt my head at an angle to be able to speak eye-to-eye with James. This impeccable fashion is largely wasted on the morning London streets, everyone still in their beds from late balls and dinners, but I don't mind. I didn't wear the dress for anyone but myself. It's my armor, my way of feeling beautiful and put-together and a lovely diversion from the roiling nerves at getting the one thing I always wanted: time alone with James.

Only now that I've gotten it, I find my fickle mind comparing him with Alexander. James is a delight to be around—now that I've moved past my embarrassment—but despite my nerves, I don't feel that electric jolt run through me when I gaze at him, that feeling like being out in a storm. An almost dangerous feeling that makes my heart pound and my breaths quicken. It's a sensation I have every time I think of Alexander, whom I barely know.

"What could you be thinking of?" James asks, his low, familiar voice bringing me back to the quiet streets in a rush.

I feel a flush coming on, so I keep the brim of my hat down so he can't see. "Forgive me. I'm being rather quiet, aren't I?"

"That and you seem to be having a quarrel with yourself—your eyebrows have been furrowed since the moment we left."

I laugh, and I feel the tension in my face melt away. "I was debating whether I'd have time to work on my painting before the ball."

James snorts. "You're a terrible liar, Luce, but never fear. I can see that you are trying to put me off, so I won't press."

"Perhaps I was nervously thinking of my training session with you." I tilt my face up at him so he can see my teasing smile, though I am partly serious. I still feel inept with a blade.

"As you should. This next session will be rather violent." I come to a halt to better stare at him. "Don't look so stunned. I'm convinced this will be a crucial skill for you, so I won't shirk my duty to impart everything I know."

"You're serious? What if one of us gets injured?"

He pats my arm—being deliberately patronizing—as we continue toward Monsieur Giroux's. "You have nothing to worry about in that regard. You're just not good enough to cut me yet."

I shoot him an incredulous look. "What a challenge! And how am I to respond? Deliberately aim to wound you?"

He shrugs as he opens the door for me. "If you can."

I sweep past him in answer, trying rather unsuccessfully to hide my grin.

A servant hurries over to me, ready to assist me in changing into my uniform. "If you're finished taunting me, I shall meet you on the floor shortly."

"Oh, I'm looking forward to it," he says with such a wolfish grin that, if it weren't for living my whole life with a teasing older brother, I would be quite undone by.

So with a seemingly nonchalant shake of my head, I turn to follow the servant to the changing room.

"I'm afraid you'll have to be more aggressive with me this lesson," James says.

We stand facing each other, daggers in hand. Sunlight streams in from the full-length windows—strangely out of place. It seems that knives and daggers are weapons for dark alleyways, not elegant well-lit spaces. We picked up where we left off last session—at least, James tried to. I'd forgotten nearly everything he'd taught me before, so he was forced to spend the first half hour or so refreshing my memory.

I furrow my brows as I stare down at the dagger. "I don't think I can. I'm used to the elegant dance of fencing . . . not something so . . ." I trail off, unsure of the word I seek.

"Vulgar? Uncouth? Yes, well, defending yourself with a dagger may be both of those things, but it may also save your life." He relaxes his grip on his dagger. "For anyone else in as lofty a station as you, training you in defense would be wholly unnecessary and perhaps even ridiculous. The chances of an average lady of noble birth encountering a situation dangerous enough to require a weapon to protect herself is laughable, but for you, the chances are considerably higher. Just consider what happened to your sister."

"You know I hate being reminded of that," I say softly.

"I wouldn't be a good friend if I didn't remind you," he counters. "I couldn't bear it if anything happened to you, Lucy." His eyes meet mine, intensely serious.

I sigh, knowing I've been bested. "Very well. What do I need to do?"

"We need to practice disabling your opponent."

"Disabling? Not disarming?"

He shakes his head. "You're not strong enough to wrest his weapon away from him—and there are far too many opportunities for that to go horribly wrong. No, you must disable your opponent's dominant arm—whichever hand is holding the weapon."

"Disabling it is, then." I glance down at the heavy dagger in my hand. "And . . . how would I go about doing that?"

"The best way is to sever your opponent's tendons in his arm, just above the elbow."

I feel the color drain away from my face. "You want me to *maim* him?"

"Lucy, your attacker will be trying to harm you or kidnap you. Yes, I want you to maim him terribly—so badly that he won't be able to lift his arm to wield his weapon." He takes a step forward and takes hold of my hand. Gently, he turns my wrist until the underside of my arm is exposed. He presses his finger onto a sensitive spot just above my elbow. "Here."

I shudder—but it's not a pleasant reaction. It's one born of imagining stabbing my dagger into that spot on another human being.

"I don't think—"

"You can," James says firmly. "I imagine there's little you wouldn't do to survive if you were in such a position. You and your siblings are the epitome of survivalists."

I let out a surprised laugh—more an unladylike snort if I'm truly being honest. "Oh yes, how hard we've had it as aristocrats born and bred."

"You've had to keep hidden essential parts of yourselves. I admire you for it."

His words bring a warmth to my chest, and I sink into the fighting position he showed me: balanced on the balls of my feet, ready to feint at the slightest provocation. "Come then, I shall try to dismember you."

James pales. "Good God. *Disable*, not dismember. I'm rather fond of all my parts."

He doesn't give me time to laugh, though, as he lunges as fast as a serpent's strike. I feint at the last possible moment, and he grins proudly.

"Now, next time you dodge me, I want you to come in close. Your attacker won't be expecting that—he'll be expecting you to flee."

He lunges toward me again, and I immediately dodge left. James comes up short, still holding his arm aloft. "You're in the perfect position now," he says, still holding his arm in the air as though he has been frozen in time.

"With my momentum carrying me forward, and you standing just there behind me, you can grab hold of me and disable my arm."

I take a step forward, and then another, so close now it would be scandalous in any other setting. So close I can smell the spice of his cologne. I reach out and grab hold of his shoulder, my dagger hovering just above his inner arm.

James lets out a hoarse shout, and I jump back and drop my dagger. "Did I cut you?" I demand, my voice so high with fear I'm sure he can barely understand me.

But then, of course, it's hard for him to understand me when he's laughing so hard tears are streaming down his face.

I press a hand above my galloping heart. "I hope you're happy," I say to him with a glare. "I don't think my heartbeat will ever slow."

"Forgive me, Lucy, but I couldn't resist," he says after he finally gets a hold of himself. "Shall we try again?"

I let him apologize a few more times before I finally relent, and we practice until nearly stabbing him in the arm becomes a natural motion to me. By the end of the session, I'm so weary and sweaty I never want to lay eyes on a dagger again.

"I'll ruin my dress should I put it on like this," I say forlornly.

James looks as though the thought never occurred to him. "Should I send for the motor car?"

I smile in relief. "Yes, that would be lovely, thank you."

"I'll give them a ring on the telephone—shouldn't be too long."

He strides away, and I walk over to one of the mirrors to frown at my wild hair. As I try several times to smooth it into something vaguely resembling a sane hairstyle, I hear voices coming down the hall. Monsieur Giroux's familiar accent is easily identified, but I don't recognize the other low voice. When it becomes clear they will soon come upon me, I turn toward the sound reluctantly.

"Mademoiselle Sinclair!" Monsieur Giroux calls to me. "You must make the acquaintance of my newest fencing pupil. Indeed, I was most pleasantly surprised by his skill."

"Actually, we've already been introduced," Alexander says, entering the room behind Monsieur. Though he's dressed in the classic white fencing uniform, his hair mussed as though having just removed the mask, he cuts as dashing a figure as he did in his tailcoat.

His smile is tentative yet hopeful, and I almost forget that I am a sweaty disaster in my fencing uniform instead of my beautiful black-and-white dress. "Alexander, what a lovely surprise—truly. I had no idea we shared an interest in fencing."

"Nor I, but I'm pleased to discover it. Perhaps we can even have a few matches against each other."

The thought of fencing against Alexander is such a heady one that I know I would be blushing if it weren't for having red cheeks already.

"The two of you would be well-matched," Monsieur Giroux says with a thoughtful nod.

"Forgive me for not having come to call yet," Alexander says. "I hope you will allow me to do so sometime in the next few days."

"Of course," I say, surprised but pleased. Perhaps Colin hadn't frightened him away after all.

"Is your schedule terribly full?"

"I'm to attend Lady Whitmore's ball tonight, but after that . . ." I trail off, suddenly remembering our plans to go to Bath. "Oh, forgive me, I'd nearly forgotten the short trip we planned—"

"Lucy, the chauffeur should be here any moment," James says, striding back into the room. His usually affable expression is wary as he takes in Alexander.

"James, may I introduce Alexander Radcliffe, Earl of Devonshire? Alexander, this is Lord Thornewood's brother, James Wyndam."

"Pleased to make your acquaintance," Alexander says and puts out his hand.

James hesitates for only a moment before taking it.

"Lord Alexander is my newest pupil," Monsieur Giroux says. "I was only just telling Mademoiselle Sinclair how well they'd do in a match."

For once, James has no witty retort, only an uncharacteristic frown. "Well, you must forgive me, but I believe our motorcar is outside waiting."

I shoot him a strange look, for when has he ever cared whether the chauffeur was kept waiting or not?

"If you'll excuse me, Monsieur Giroux," James says. "Lord Devonshire."

Monsieur gives a polite bow of his head, and Alexander nods tersely.

"Yes, do excuse us." I take a step toward James, eager to get him alone and determine why he is acting in such a rude manner, but I turn back. With a deep breath for courage, I manage to say, "Alexander, I do hope you'll come to call."

His answering smile is well worth it, his eyes warm. "I will be sure to. Enjoy the ball tonight—I only wish I'd known about it beforehand. I would have asked to escort you myself."

"And now I'm very disappointed," I say, my heart thudding wildly.

"Lucy," James calls from the doorway, his tone sharp. When I turn toward him with an incredulous look, he says, "We should go. I promised Colin we'd be gone only an hour."

I know this to be a lie for I heard Colin tell us to take our time just before we left, but I decide to not argue with him in front of Monsieur and Alexander.

"Yes, of course," I say. "Good afternoon, gentlemen."

I follow James out the door and will myself not to look back at Alexander longingly.

NINE

I hope you will explain your tone just now," I say to James the moment we are safely in the motorcar. "I should think Alexander will think you frightfully rude."

James shakes his head. "Lucy, honestly, I'm glad I walked in when I did. I was shocked to find you about to tell Lord Devonshire—Alexander, apparently, to you—that we are going to Bath."

"I'm sorry, James, but I fail to see how that would be wrong," I say, irritation turning rapidly to anger within me.

"What do you know of him? I myself know very little, and because of that, I dare say you shouldn't be telling him anything of your comings and goings."

I scoff. "You sound just like your brother. How could you assume anyone we aren't familiar with is the enemy? He's never done anything the least bit suspicious."

"Did Lord Blackburn?" James counters. "All I can say about this new Earl of Devonshire is that he suddenly appeared the moment you debuted, and no one can vouch for him. Reason enough, I think, to keep our distance."

"Then why aren't you suspicious of Rose? We know so little of her, after all. Perhaps it's all merely a ruse to get in close with me—perhaps she's even feigning her illness!"

"I'm serious."

I shake my head in disgust and turn toward the window. "So am I."

"I just . . . I care about you, Lucy."

The tone in his voice has me turning toward him in spite of my anger. I let out a sigh. "I appreciate your concern, James, truly. But I can only endure one overprotective gentleman in my life. It's not as though I've promised to go off alone in a dark alley with Alexander, for goodness sake. And even if he knew our plans to visit Bath, what of it? It's not as if I won't be surrounded by family at all times. Heavens, he'd have to fight his way through you, Colin, Robert, *and* Papa, after all."

James laughs reluctantly. "Yes, all right. You've made your point. Though I don't think you should discount your sister in that hypothetical battle— she'd probably be the most dangerous of all."

We share a grin, and I relax against the plush leather seat. And James is wrong—Lord Blackburn may not have acted suspiciously, but it wasn't long before Katherine became uncomfortable in his presence. The only thing I can think when I see Alexander is: how can I see more of him?

Later that night, after nearly two hours of preparation, we finally arrive at the ball given by the fashionable Lady Mary Whitmore. The gentlemen appreciate the famously delicious dinners she provides, and Wren finds her agreeable for the simple fact that she is eccentric enough to draw the attention away from everyone else—even the Earl and Countess of Thornewood.

As Wren and I alight from the motorcar we rode in—it takes two to transport us all—I run my hand nervously over the elaborate beading and embroidery of my blue silk gown. As soon as James exits his own vehicle, he strides over to me and offers his arm.

"You look stunning, as usual," he says.

I will myself to relax. This is James, after all—the man I just spent more than an hour profusely sweating with as we fought each other with knives.

"Shall we go in?" Wren asks, her hand resting on Colin's arm. The two of them make an incredibly handsome couple; Wren dressed in her beaded emerald chiffon and satin gown, and Colin in his tailcoat.

"Are we late enough to go straight in for dinner?" Rob asks.

"I hope so," James says.

Wren rolls her eyes at them both as she and Colin lead us into the elegant townhome.

A butler greets us as we enter the foyer, and my gaze immediately roams all over the marble columns, the sweeping spiral staircase, and the beautiful paintings. Our shoes ring out as we follow the butler across the polished marble floor.

"Welcome, Lord and Lady Thornewood," Lady Whitmore calls as we enter the drawing room. She holds her arms out wide, her tall, willowy body clothed in a Japanese kimono blooming with pink cherry blossoms. She presses a kiss to each of Wren's cheeks, and I blink rapidly as she does the same to me. "This vision must be your sister," she says.

"She is indeed," Wren says, her voice strained as though holding in a laugh. "Lady Whitmore, allow me to introduce the Honorable Lucy Sinclair."

Instead of the usual curtsy, she bows before me in the traditional Asian style. With her strawberry-blonde hair, freckled skin, and green eyes, her mannerisms seem wildly out of place. I widen my eyes at Wren over Lady Whitmore's head, and Wren quickly looks away, her shoulders shaking with mirth.

"Oh," Lady Whitmore says, when Colin and Robert join us. "I see you brought the whole family. Well, but not quite—it seems Lord Sinclair is missing."

"Papa rather enjoys his peace and quiet most evenings," Wren says.

Lady Whitmore nods somberly. "Yes, how well I understand. Oh, but how handsome these three are." She waves a lacquered black fan in front of her face. "Surely you will blind all the ladies here."

Robert snorts. "If they are blinded, it is only because of Lord Thornewood's terrible glower."

James snickers beside me.

"We thank you for your invitation," Colin says, offering his arm to Wren and obviously ignoring both Robert and Lady Whitmore's commentary.

"Oh, but he is famous for his glower," Lady Whitmore says, a wry smile on her face. "It is one of the reasons I invited him here. What better way to keep the other guests from becoming too haughty?"

Robert laughs, but I continue to stare, quite at a loss as to how to receive our hostess. She seems to be teasing, but she delivers her observations with such a serious tone that it's impossible to tell.

"Always glad to be of service, my lady," Colin says, and Wren shoots him an amused glance before they move toward a quieter area of the room.

"I hope you will enjoy yourselves," Lady Whitmore says to us. "I have the best cook in the world, I must say. Her pudding is euphoric. Perhaps it's laced with opium—it's simply that delicious."

"Ah, then we will certainly enjoy two or three helpings," Robert says with a wink.

Her eyes, thickly accented with kohl, narrow appraisingly. "I find I'm rather enjoying your company, Mr. Sinclair. Be sure to seek me out later for a dance. I'm a widow, you know, so we can completely enjoy ourselves without worrying what Society may say later."

My cheeks flame, and I give James a little tug on his arm to escape. Even more embarrassing than Lady Whitmore's proposal is Robert's response: "Oh, you can be sure of it, my lady."

She fans her face furiously and laughs. "Delightful." She turns her attention to me. "Your maiden sister is regretfully embarrassed by our bold flirtations. Ah, but your beau is just as handsome as your brother, my dear. It's a pity I can't have them both for myself, but of course that'd make me a terrible hostess. Perhaps you should both take a turn about the room? Go and enjoy each other while the bloom of youth favors you still."

"Yes . . . of course . . . thank you," I say, shock robbing me of the ability to make an eloquent response.

Her lips curve in an answering smile before turning her attention to another late arrival.

After Rob whispers God-knows-what into her ear, he turns to follow us.

"I cannot believe you behaved in such a manner," I say to Rob the moment the three of us are out of ear-shot. "I truly thought I would die of the shame."

"Come now, it wasn't that embarrassing." He shakes his head. "What did I do to deserve such overly dramatic sisters?"

"You're the one who flirted unabashedly in front of his own sister," I say, my blush finally receding.

Rob catches James's eyes, but James holds up his hand. "Don't look to me for solidarity. I suspect saying anything would be damning, so I won't say anything at all."

"A good strategy," I mutter.

Rob only grins in answer as we reach the sofa Wren has claimed for herself while Colin stands beside her, bored look in place.

"That is a perfectly mischievous smile you wear, Rob," Wren says. "You aren't teasing Lucy, are you?"

"No, indeed," he says with a little sideways glance my way. "She is the one who was teasing me."

I let out a little sigh of exasperation. Robert has clearly made his mission of the night to torment me. This situation requires an abrupt subject change, else he will carry on this way for the rest of the evening. "James, would you like to look at some of Lady Whimore's paintings with me? Her taste is rather . . . unusual."

"Diplomatic of you," James says with a nod as he eyes a nearby painting— one of a beautiful maiden floating fully dressed in a river.

As we walk closer to the painting, I see that it is *Ophelia* by John Everett Millais. It's a lovely painting, but morbid—Ophelia, the maiden in the water and a character from Shakespeare's *Hamlet*, later drowns in the river. "Goodness, I thought this painting was on display at Tate Gallery. However did Lady Whitmore get hold of it?"

"I can think of several ways," James says with a sly rise of his eyebrows.

"Don't be vulgar," I say, and he laughs.

"Well, it's a strange painting, but no one can say the landscape isn't stunning," a voice says behind us, and I turn.

"Rose!" I say, a delighted smile splitting my face. "You never said a word about coming."

"I wanted to surprise you." We share a brief embrace.

"You've succeeded." I hold out my hand toward James. "Allow me to introduce you to the Honorable James Wyndam. James, this is Rose Thornby. James has been kind enough to escort me to the ball this evening."

Her eyes widen. "Oh, I hope I'm not intruding."

"Not at all," I rush to assure her.

"No, indeed," James says. "I'm sure you have much more to say on these paintings than I could ever dream up. You're a welcome addition to our art critiquing."

She laughs, the sound much less wheezy than the last time I'd seen her.

"However did you manage to come? Did you get my note about Bath?"

"I have my good days every once in a blue moon. I did get it, which is partly why I willed myself better—I want to be able to enjoy a trip to such a relaxing locale." She turns to James. "Will you be accompanying us as well?"

He nods. "You'll find I'm rather difficult to be rid of, I'm afraid. Lucy travels with a small army as it is—I do believe the whole family will be in attendance."

"Even better," Rose says. "I rather like the idea of a large group of people surrounding me at all times—it'll make everything we do feel like a party."

"A party, or an insane asylum, depending on the day," James deadpans.

I shoot him a look. "Try not to listen to anything he says."

Lady Whitmore's melodic voice interrupts us. "If you'll follow me to the dining room, I have quite the treat for you tonight."

We process in with shared looks and raised eyebrows, since only a brief introduction to Lady Whitmore assures that anything she feels is "quite the treat" is guaranteed to be intriguing.

The table itself is elegantly set with silver urns and, unusually, cherry blossoms. We find our place cards, and I find myself seated in between James and Rose. She may be eccentric, but no one could doubt that Lady Whitmore is a superior hostess.

Lady Whitmore takes her seat, and the rest of us follow. Instantly, footmen appear with steaming bowls of soup.

"Tonight you will all be enjoying a traditional Japanese meal," Lady Whitmore says, and the bowls are placed before us. "Here we have miso soup."

"Oh, it's Japanese—you should love it then, *sensei*," I say to James, who promptly snorts into his spoon.

"This is delicious," one of the elegantly dressed ladies at the head of the table says. She must be someone with quite a bit of clout, for everyone else eagerly dives in and pronounces it divine.

"What do you suppose is her obsession with Japan?" Rose asks quietly as she takes small sips of the flavorful broth.

"I would hope that she's spent time there and fallen in love with the culture." I take a closer look at my bowl—a lovely Japanese scene is hand-painted in blue.

"What if she's never been and merely read a book or two on the subject?" Rose grins.

I stifle a laugh to avoid drawing attention to our conversation. "How awful it would be if that were true!"

"Lady Whitmore, what do you know of this new earl from India we have circulating about in London?" a rather rotund gentleman asks, his baritone voice easily carrying to my end of the table. Of course I perk up like a hound.

"Ah, you must be referring to the new Lord Devonshire," she says, a catty grin upon her face.

"I must say, he doesn't have an English complexion," one of the gentlemen says. "In fact, I suspect he may actually be a chee chee." The table erupts in laughter. I return my spoon to its bowl, a frown taking over my face. My military brother taught me lots of things over the years, and certain slang terms were part of that dubious lesson. I'd only heard the term *chee chee* one other time: when Rob explained that it was slang for half-British and half-Indian. I doubt that this round little man meant it as anything other than a slight.

"I should think he wouldn't be lily pale," Lady Whitmore says. "His mother was Indian, after all."

"Goodness, you say it so matter-of-factly," one of the ladies says.

"How else should I say it? It's all very legitimate. Lord Devonshire married her while living there—against his family's wishes, of course. Indeed, I doubt they even knew. But when he had to return to England, she refused to accompany him—or so the story goes. She's dead now, poor darling."

"Who raised him when she died?" I find myself asking—aloud—to my horror. I can feel James staring at me. Colin, too, seems excessively interested in the conversation.

Lady Whitmore shrugs one dainty shoulder. "I couldn't say. His mother's family, perhaps? Though I'd heard rumors that she came from nothing—she must have been divinely beautiful to snatch up an earl." Alexander's story becomes more and more tragic the more I hear of it, and I feel a shadow settle upon me at the thought of his trials. "My, you are a kind-hearted thing," Lady Whitmore adds when I fall silent. "You look truly concerned."

"It's a melancholy story." I lean back a bit to allow the footman to take away my half-finished soup. It's quickly replaced with a thin piece of bright pink fish atop a mound of rice.

"*Nigiri,*" Lady Whitmore announces, and I'm glad for the interruption.

"Is this *raw* fish?" a slim lady beside Rob asks.

Lady Whitmore smiles. "It is. And before you turn your nose up at it, you should all know that it's considered an aphrodisiac."

On the other side of the table, I hear Wren's unmistakable snort. Beside her, Colin affects an innocent look. I can only surmise he has said something vulgar—their favorite type of private joke.

"I don't think that's even true," Rose mutters beside me. "I think she has the wrong seafood in mind."

I laugh, but as I've never minded trying new and even exotic foods, I take a healthy bite. It's delicious, if a bit fishy. The sweetness of the rice balances it perfectly.

"Well, this new earl of Devonshire seems rather odd to me," the same gentleman who brought him up in the first place says. "I've seen him about town—walking everywhere he goes. Perhaps that's what browned his skin as dark as a farmer's."

Loud guffaws reward the man's extremely rude musings, and my hands curl into fists in my lap.

"If those are his only offenses—walking and being tan—then I'd have to say this conversation is the height of ridiculousness," Colin says amidst the laughter.

The room quiets.

Bless Colin for being able to say exactly what those of us who are decent are thinking. Wren smiles adoringly at him.

The rude gentleman puffs himself up. "What are you saying?"

"I'm *saying* 'cease and desist,'" Colin says, enunciating each word like the man is a child.

The rude man's face turns ruddy, but he's smart enough to keep silent.

"Although, I must say," Colin adds, swirling his wine nonchalantly in his glass, "your words have enlightened me. Lord Devonshire asked to come call on Lucy, and I believe I will allow it—if only to spite you all." With a wolfish grin, he drains his glass.

I glance down at my plate so no one will see my blinding smile, though beside me, I can feel disapproval coming off James in waves.

TEN

MUCH later that night, I sit on the floor with my drawing of the portal before me. I've drawn the rune; all I need do is touch it. But I must gather my errant thoughts first, and all I can think about at the moment is my deliciously fun evening. My mind has that silly golden haze it always does when I think of something delightful, and in spite of James's rather sulky mood after dinner, everything about the ball was a joy. The mention of Lord Devonshire seems to bother him, but I refuse to accept that he might be jealous, and there's a small, mean part of me that thinks it's good for him. I spent all those years pining for him, why shouldn't he do the same?

Oh, but I know such thoughts are terribly unkind. James is my friend, however else I may feel about him, and we usually have a lovely time in each other's company. Rose, too, danced as many dances as her lungs would allow. She only stopped to rest because I begged her to—her breaths were coming so shallowly I thought for sure she'd faint. Asthma and corseted dresses were never meant to go together but Rose is rail-thin and can get away with loose stays.

Aside from the dancing, the loveliest part of the ball was that Lady Whitmore had arranged for a beautiful Japanese lady—dressed in a full kimono—to play the Japanese violin for us. I want to pull the haunting sound straight out of my mind and onto a painting, but I haven't the time.

In truth, I'm procrastinating. I'm afraid to meet my Sylvan grandmother. I'm afraid she won't live up to my memories of Mama—that she will be nothing like her. But I'm even more afraid that I will love her, and then where will I be? I already feel the longing for the other realm. How much stronger might it be if I were to have someone there to visit?

I take a deep breath and close my eyes, steadying myself. Tentatively, I touch my finger to the rune, letting my arcana unfurl as my fingertip connects with the ink.

My room fades, and I stand before the portal my sister first discovered. A shiver races through me as the air around the portal blurs. No more glimpses and flashes of things barely seen—I will finally get to see what is beyond this pile of stone.

The moment I think it—think, *I want to see Sylvania*—the stones disappear, and behind them, I find a forest of such unimaginable beauty that I can do nothing but gawk as though struck dumb. The colors! I've never seen such color—more vivid than I'm used to, but also in unusual combinations. The leaves of the trees are the color of wisteria, and indeed, they remind me of it, only they tower above me. Some trunks are so pale they're almost white, and others are silver. I walk over to one and press the palm of my hand to the smooth bark.

My hand is ethereal, almost transparent, and the sensation of touch is not as strong as it is in my own world—presumably because I have only transported my spirit rather than my body. Still, I gaze up at the tree in wonder, purple leaves and silvery moss beneath my feet.

You must be positively ancient, I think to the tree, as wide as its trunk is.

Nearly as old as the sky, an old, deep voice responds in my mind, and I laugh in surprised delight.

I want to say more, but the fox appears. *Your grandmother awaits you.*

Excitement and more than a little apprehension races through me. *My grandmother.*

The fox leads me to a path of white stone, and we climb higher and higher, twisting our way amongst trees whose leaves make music like windchimes. Soon, the rush of water adds its own music, faint at first, and then slowly increasing in volume until it's an impressive roar. We reach the top of the path, and I suck in a breath and smile in wonder.

We stand upon a precipice. Spread before us in a valley are buildings made of stone, built into the cliff itself. The source of the roar becomes clear now: waterfalls pour from the foundations of the buildings. It's almost difficult to see them as separate from the mountain. Here, the sun is just setting, illuminating the white stone like gold. The cascading water sparkles, and the purple leaves of the trees turn such a vibrant shade of purple, I know I could never imitate it with paint.

"Will I be able to go there? To see the Great Hall as my sister did?" I ask, my voice hushed as though I'm in church.

"I'm afraid you'll have to settle for this view instead," a strong, melodic voice says behind me.

Goosebumps rise across my skin as I turn and lay eyes on my grandmother for the first time. "It was you I saw through the portal, not Mama," I say and then blush. What a thing to say for the first time! "Forgive me, it's just that you . . ." I trail off as she smiles kindly back at me, and my eyes immediately tear. It's like looking at Mama again, only the elegant woman before me has hair the color of a sunset. She is as ageless as a goddess, with skin as smooth as mine; the only sign of her age are her eyes. The moment I meet them—a clear, piercing emerald—I'm forced to look away again. There is so much ancient wisdom in those depths, it's like looking into a well one thought was shallow only to discover it goes so deep not even a rock thrown in has hope of reaching the bottom.

"The resemblance is uncanny, I know," she says, her smile turning melancholy. "Isidora always favored me. But looking at you, I feel my heart soothed—it's truly like seeing my daughter again."

"Oh, but surely I don't resemble her as much as Katherine does, though of course I take it as a great compliment that you should think so."

"I can't tell you how thankful I am that you agreed to meet with me. It's been far too long since I was able to gaze upon the faces of my grandchildren."

This captures my attention. "You've seen us before?"

She smiles. "Your mother found ways around her exile. Though all portals were closed to her, they were not closed to her children. She'd bring the three of you, and I'd get a few blessed moments to see that you were all well." Her face darkens. "That was, until your grandfather felt your mother's presence through the portal, and your mother decided it would be better not to risk it—she feared he would realize how much our realm is in need of a new generation and forcibly bring the three of you over."

Apprehension settles uncomfortably in the pit of my stomach, and I cannot help a wary look over my shoulder. "Does he know I'm here now?"

"Before I answer, perhaps I should explain how much things have changed." She holds up her hands, and I flinch, remembering what Katherine said of her power. Regret flits across her somber expression. "I would never hurt you, dearest one. Will you allow me to show you some of my memories?"

"Of course," I say, chastened.

She closes her eyes, and the air before her shimmers. Instead of the breathtaking scene before us, images appear, as though she painted them on the wind itself. Battle lines appear before me, with soldiers in gleaming armor and swords astride creatures that are like enormous elk. Mixed among the soldiers are as many animals, all predatory: wolves, eagles, lions, bears. The animals are as unusual as the soldiers' mounts—much larger and in varying shades of white and silver. The sight of them is like nothing I've ever seen, certainly like no wild animal I've ever learned of, nor seen in a zoo. They seem as ready and willing for battle as the soldiers, with patient anticipation. Spirit animals.

The scene shifts to one of frenzied battle: animals tearing into one another, soldiers cutting each other down from their lofty mounts. It's so chaotic, it's difficult to make out who's fighting who. Then, from the midst of the battle, strides a man clad entirely in gold. He does not ride, but he is accompanied by a great white bear who roars a deafening challenge as he steps onto the battlefield.

The soldiers and animals pause in their attempts to kill one another, their expressions wary.

The man in golden armor raises his hands, and a wave of power ripples through the soldiers and animals with such force, they are left utterly decimated. Cold fear paralyzes my limbs as I take in the carnage, done with ruthless efficiency. I let out a little whimper of horror, and the scene shifts, showing a great white tomb.

"Your grandfather stopped Lord Elric, the man you saw destroying both armies on the battlefield, but it was at the cost of your grandfather's life."

I'd never known the man, but I felt the sorrow circling my grandmother like a dark cloud, and I couldn't help but be empathetic to it. She waves her hands, and the transparent image disappears.

"How awful," I whisper. "I'm terribly sorry." I frown at my inadequate response—saying sorry doesn't nearly convey the horror I feel at such a loss.

"The battles were pointless—merely a power struggle between Lord Elric and your grandfather. Cascadia remains under our family's control—my control—but our population has dwindled to less than half." She steps forward, and after a moment's hesitation, takes my hands in hers. "I can't tell you how overjoyed I was to feel your presence, Lucy. I'd missed my chance when your sister so briefly touched our realm, you see. It was a relief to sense you not just once, but several times, and I knew then it would be safe to reach out to you."

"I'm so glad you did, Grandmother," I say, my throat tight. "I have dreamed of meeting you ever since I was a child, but I never dared hope it would be possible."

She smiles and squeezes my hands gently before releasing them. "In time, I hope to meet you all. I've sensed the presence of others—perhaps your brother and sister?"

My brows furrow as I puzzle out her words. "Sensed at the same time as me? Oh, but it must have been Izzie," I say almost to myself. "So she *is* sharing in my visions. Izzie is Katherine's daughter," I add.

A bird's cry interrupts us and draws our attention skyward. I'm sorry to say my mouth falls open like a commoner, and I'm struck dumb for the second time since arriving. The bird—if it can be called such an ordinary name—is larger than an eagle and like a blaze of fire in the sky. Its plumage is the color of a sunset—reds, oranges, pinks, gold. Its tail feathers cascade down beneath it as it descends; bigger than a peacock's. A name for this bird is tingling on my tongue, but it's one I've only read about in fairytales.

It lands on a low-hanging branch and dips its head daintily. *Forgive my interruption,* the deep, obviously male, voice says in our minds, *but Lord Titus has requested an audience with you.*

Irritation followed swiftly by a resigned sort of look flits across my grandmother's face. "I suppose I shouldn't be surprised. Thank you for coming to fetch me, then," she says fondly. She turns to me, one hand toward the stunning phoenix. "This is my spirit animal, Serafino."

Its golden eyes smile down at me from the branch above us. *And you are Lucy. Arria was correct in saying you look just like your mother.* His attention shifts to the fox, who has patiently sat through my meeting with my grandmother. *Does it pain you to see her, Rowen?*

"You have a name?" I burst out in surprise.

The little fox tilts its head. *You didn't ask.*

My face flames, and I look down in embarrassment. In truth, I hadn't even considered the fox might be called by a name, but by the way my grandmother addressed her own spirit animal, I realize my blunder was great indeed.

She doesn't know us well enough to tease in such a way, Serafino says, his voice mildly scolding. *Don't mind Rowen, his humor has always been as dry as ash.*

"My dear Lucy, I'm afraid I've called you here as a bit of a test," my grandmother says. She reaches out and touches my shoulder. "Though you see Sylvania before you, where we are now is the In Between—between your realm and mine. The ability to travel here is something all Sylvans learn when we are young, and I cannot tell you how impressed I am that you figured it out all on your own, but I'm also greatly concerned. You see, here, our spirit animals keep us grounded. They keep our bodies safe on the other side. You, on the other hand, have no spirit animal. Without a means of keeping your physical form grounded in your realm, your spirit—your mind—can become trapped within the In Between forever."

I think of all the times I've carelessly entered my drawings and feel my stomach drop in horror. "I had no idea—none at all. Am I in danger now?"

Grandmother shakes her head. "We will not stay long enough. The danger comes in the great strain your physical body must endure when you use arcana enough to transport your conscious mind."

"I've certainly experienced that before. Most recently, I entered a drawing without even meaning to, and then I couldn't find my way out. It wasn't until my niece called for me that I was even able to return."

Grandmother shares a look with Serafino. "I must ask you, then, not to attempt it again. It sounds as though little Izzie has an ability, similar to a spirit animal, to ground you. Even so, the risk is too great. Rowen will still be able to reach you through your drawings—he can safely travel to the In Between without you risking yourself." She reaches out to touch me, and though her hand doesn't actually connect with my shoulder, I can still feel her warmth. "There is more. I'm sure you knew your mother was capable of seeing the future, or at least, many different versions of it."

"Yes, though I only recently learned of it. She left behind a journal for Katherine."

Grandmother smiles and glances at Rowen. "I'm not surprised. She was always terribly brilliant." She returns her attention to me, her expression becoming more serious. "This ability was inherited from my lineage, and I come from a long line of Sylvans capable of foreseeing certain events, though it has its limitations. I can only see what my visions choose to show me, for one—I cannot forcefully scry into the future. I say all this to tell you that I *have* seen events pertaining to you, which is why I have had Rowen reach out to you. Darkness shadows you, Lucy, and though I cannot see how it will manifest, I am certain of one thing: you are in danger."

Fear turns my body cold, and I struggle to form a response. "But we've been so careful. What is it you see?"

"It's more what I sense. And what I sense is fear; fear and danger for not only yourself, but someone else you care about. Determination, too, as though you are prepared to do battle."

Now the fear turns to nausea. "Battle? Oh, but surely . . ." I think of James's preparations, then. Will I have need for self-defense? To defend myself and one of the many people I care about?

"I only wish I knew more. Send word to Rowen any time you have need—with anyone you find suspicious. We have ways of seeking more information on them." She glances at Serafino. "There is so much more we should talk of, but time runs short. I dare not keep you much longer."

And Titus awaits, Serafino adds.

"Yes, well, I'm afraid I will have to try his patience a little longer," Grandmother says with a tone so much like Wren's I smile. She reaches out for my hand again, and I can almost feel the touch through time and space. "Stay safe, dearest one. We are here if you need us."

She turns away, the scent of honeysuckle hanging in the air behind her. "Wait, Grandmother! Is it possible for me to cross over entirely, so that we may have more time together?"

Her eyebrows arch, and she shoots a sharp glance at Rowen. "I see you've been sharing secrets, little fox." Her tone doesn't sound angry, only cautious. "It's possible, but more preparation will be needed. Promise you won't attempt it without my guidance, Lucy. It can be dangerous if not done properly."

I nod somberly. "I promise. I am so glad to have met you, Grandmother."

Her smile is so warm and kind, it instantly reminds me of Mama's. Tears prick my eyes. "None of that now," she says, with a gentle near-touch to my cheek. "We'll see each other again soon. I can guarantee that. Rowen, will you help her return?"

Yes, Lady Queen. He gets quietly to his feet and trots away.

After one last glance at my grandmother, I follow, my heart so full it feels like a balloon within my chest. The longing to stay is strong; I am sorely tempted to ignore my grandmother's warning and explore, consequences be damned. But one look at Rowen's frequent glances over his shoulder tells me he would never allow it. So, reluctantly, I take note of all the fascinating flora and fauna we pass: the purple and silver trees, a pure white deer with sapphire blue eyes watching us with a silver fawn at her side, and birds of exotic color combinations only seen in the tropics.

As the path draws us deeper into the forest, I see movement flitting amongst the leaves—movement I initially attribute to birds. Until one appears directly in my path: a pixie the size of a hummingbird with a dress of silver leaves.

It's time, Lucy, Rowen says beside me.

I take one last long look at the beauty around me, trying to memorize every detail before returning to the mortal realm. Trying not to think about her dire warning.

How could I bring danger upon my family again?

☥

ALEXANDER'S pen skitters across the paper, leaving a trail of black ink. He feels it again—that pull of spiritual power like a cold douse of water over his skin. Goosebumps rise on his arms, and he lets his eyelids fall closed. The energy is stronger this time. As the minutes tick by, the doused-in-cold-water feeling remains.

He yanks open the drawer of his desk and pulls out a thick stack of drawing papers. Pencil in hand, he sketches the images that rise in his mind: ancient trees with wide, pale trunks; a white city atop cascading waterfalls; a fox who gazes out at him from the page with bold intelligence.

There is something about these images, and Alexander pauses as he takes them in, the end of the pencil between his teeth. A genuineness, he decides, despite the fantastical details. These were not things Lucy had drawn out of her imagination; these were things she had *seen*. The words feel right as he thinks them. He nods his head and leans back in his chair.

But at the same time, a feeling of profound disappointment washes over him. These drawings seem to suggest something far greater than spiritual power, and when Alexander considers the consequences—thinks of what they could mean for Lucy—he is taken aback by the vehemence of his body's reaction. He is almost sickened by the danger she may soon find herself in.

Still, he is committed to his cause. He swore long ago he would never let someone else go through the same pain he suffered as a child, and he won't falter now.

ELEVEN

THE next day, shortly after breakfast, the servants begin the process of sending trunks of our things to Bath. They will travel ahead of us today, and we will make the journey tomorrow morning by train.

I walk slowly down the stairs, hardly energetic enough to hold my skirt clear of my boots. This fatigue is bone-deep, despite my having slept all the way past noon. Grandmother had said traveling to the In Between would cause strain on my physical self, but I think I still hadn't anticipated the depth of my weariness—even after resting. Luckily Rose and I have plans to do a bit of shopping to take advantage of the sunshine and her continued good health.

I wander into the study, where Emily has agreed to bring me my tea and something light to eat. Light streams in through the windows, and the sweet mustiness of the leather-bound books mixed with the light fragrance from bouquets of yellow roses perfumes the air. It isn't until I've collapsed onto the nearest sofa that I see Papa watching from a wingback chair, book in hand.

"You look exhausted, my dear," he says, eyebrows furrowed in concern. "Did another headache keep you awake?"

He refers to my tendency to succumb to rather debilitating headaches—a condition I've suffered since I was a child. "No, merely a late night spent drawing." *And worrying over Grandmother's dire tidings.*

A footman enters with a tray of tea and scones, and I let out a happy sigh. Tea makes everything better.

"Is there anything else you'll be wanting, Miss Lucy?"

"No, I'm quite content now, thank you." I pour a cup of tea, the rich scent adding to the already relaxing smell of the old books in the study.

Papa watches as I take a sip. "I think it's a bit more than that," he says with a pointed look at my shaking hands. When I frown down at my cup in answer, he adds, "You'll find I'm a good listener."

I meet his warm, familiar gaze and know that I won't be able to keep anything from him. I've always been a terrible liar, for one, and for another . . . perhaps he of all people would like to hear about my mother's world. "I spoke to my grandmother last night." Before he makes the wrong assumption, I say, "My Sylvan grandmother."

Whatever he expected, it isn't this. His book slides out of his hand with a soft thump on the plush rug, but he doesn't spare it another glance. He almost stands out of his chair, but ends up sitting forward. "Here? In London?"

I laugh at the thought of my ethereal grandmother strolling the streets of London. "She was in Sylvania. I have this ability, you see, of entering my drawings with the help of runes." *And sometimes without them.*

His frown is so deep, every wrinkle on his face is shadowed. "Does your sister know? I must say, Lucy, this doesn't sound safe. Far be it for me to lecture you on the subject, but arcana does have its consequences, as both Katherine and your mother experienced."

"Of course I don't want to worry you, Papa. Katherine knows, and I must beg of you to think of the benefits to us! We've been without guidance regarding our Sylvan heritage, and now we finally have access to our family and the realm. Think what this can mean for us."

"Yes, but why now? Where has your grandmother been all this time?"

The series of battle images my grandmother revealed fill my mind, sending residual chills of apprehension through me. I decide to give my father the edited version. "Because my grandfather is no longer alive, and she felt it would now be safe to approach us."

His dark eyebrows rise. "They are immortal. How did he die?"

I glance down at my cup, cursing my father's good sense. "The result of a battle, I believe. I'm unsure of the particulars," I hedge.

"So now you're entering a war-torn realm?" he asks sharply. "Lucy, you cannot—"

"No, it wasn't at all," I say vehemently, thinking of the peaceful white city, the sentient forest. "The battle happened in the past—I'm not sure how long ago."

He sighs and leans back against his chair. "Well, I don't like this, but I can't pretend to know a thing about your mother's realm. But don't think I won't discuss this with your sister."

"Please do," I say wearily. "Only, if you could manage to do so without alerting Colin, I would be much obliged."

He smiles. "I shall try."

Our conversation thus concluded, I take a big bite of the buttery scone and wash it down with another sip of tea.

The door opens and Mr. Hale, Colin's butler, walks through. "Miss Lucy," he says, interrupting me as I take another bite of scone. "There is a Lord Devonshire here to see you. He says he was expected?"

My surprise is so complete that I do nothing but chew on my scone like a cow chewing cud. "Oh!" I say when I realize poor Mr. Hale is waiting on my reply. "Yes, you may send him in."

Papa eyes me knowingly while Mr. Hale leaves.

"My mouth was full," I mutter, but Papa's grin only widens.

Soon, we hear shoes echo dully across the marble floors, and I straighten my spine. Instead of Hale and Lord Devonshire, though, Colin strides in from the other entrance to the library, his eyes on the paper in his hand. He glances up to find us watching him, the air thrumming with anticipation.

"I daresay you cannot be waiting for me with such eagerness," Colin says. "Then who—"

The door opens, and Lord Devonshire enters, dressed splendidly in a dove gray three-piece suit, his Homburg hat held in one hand. My heart thuds painfully in my chest.

"Lord Devonshire," Hale announces and closes the door of the study behind him.

"Good afternoon," Lord Devonshire says, his eyes searching mine.

"I see you made good on your promise to call on Lucy," Colin says. "A bold choice," he adds, nearly under his breath, as he sits in the wingback chair beside Papa's.

I shoot him a pleading look to be on his best behavior. To Alexander I say, "Would you care for some tea?"

"I was hoping, actually, that you might join me for a tour of the National Gallery. I've never been, you see, and I can't think of anyone I'd rather go with."

"Pretty words and a respectable venue," Colin says before I can say anything. "Is your motorcar outside?"

"It is."

"I have an engagement with my friend Rose later this afternoon, but I would love to go with you," I say in the midst of the two men's staring contest. I can only pray that James doesn't suddenly join us. If only I weren't so weary! But I will just have to put on a good show of it—the thought of not going is far worse than any fatigue.

Alexander's eyes flick to mine, a warm smile lighting up his face. "I'll be sure to have you back here in time, then." He turns to Papa. "Do I have your permission, Lord Sinclair?"

Papa laughs. "Yes, yes, of course. If Colin here hasn't barred you from entering his home, then I'm sure I will find no fault with you."

I lean down and kiss Papa's cheek. "Thank you, Papa." To Colin I say, "You'll tell Wren where I've gone, won't you?"

Colin nods, still watching Alexander. "Have a good time," he says as we move toward the door. "Just not *too* good of one. Oh, and Lucy? Take Emily with you."

I roll my eyes as the door shuts behind us.

"Your maid, I presume?" Alexander says with a knowing smile.

"Yes, but we should be thankful he didn't insist on accompanying us himself."

"I'd like to say I wouldn't be bothered," he says, his warm voice just barely louder than our footsteps on the marble floors, "but I have to admit, I would hate to give up the chance to have your full attention."

I bite my lip at the corner to keep from grinning madly.

Alexander leans closer, smelling of cardamom and clove. "You don't have to do that, you know."

My gaze jumps to his. "Do what?"

"Hide your smile."

"You're too observant," I say with a blush. Before he can reply, I call out to the butler, who waits by the front door. "Mr. Hale, would you ask Emily to accompany me? She can play chaperone for Lord Devonshire and me at the National Gallery."

"Of course, Miss Lucy."

When he leaves, Alexander turns to me. "You address your maid by her first name?" His expression is a curious mix of genuine interest and confusion.

"I do—she's been with me since I was fourteen. My family and I tend to grow rather close to our servants." He seems to turn my words over in his head before nodding, but I can see he doesn't understand. "Have you never had any you were close to?"

"In truth, I've never really had servants," he says. I must look at him aghast because he laughs and says, "I'm sure you're imagining me living in a hut, only, now that I've experienced what it's like living with a house full of servants, I think I rather like having to rely upon myself. Though of course, I wasn't a complete barbarian. I had a housekeeper who was also a fantastic cook."

"No servants? How terribly independent of you." I grin.

His answering smile makes his eyes glow like topaz. "This is why I like you, Lucy. Not only do you not judge, but you make my ordinary existence seem dashing."

An electric joy fills me at his words, but two servants interrupt us before I can formulate a witty response. They carry trunks bound for Bath—mostly my clothes, I think with chagrin.

"Ah, this must be for the trip you mentioned the other day." Alexander gestures toward the trunks.

"Yes, and I'm sorry James was being so cryptic. We're only going to Bath for a few days."

He nods thoughtfully. "My father has a townhouse there, or so my solicitor tells me."

"Have you ever been?"

"No, but it's always appealed to me—I do enjoy hot springs."

Emily joins us just then, helpfully bringing both my hat and gloves, and smiles serenely at us both while I introduce her to Alexander. Emily is not much older than I am, but I've always been drawn to her calm, unflappable nature—which is probably why I usually take her into my confidence far more than I should. Still, the Sinclair servants are a different sort—chosen for their ability to maintain our family's secrets. Emily is kin to Mr. Baxter, my father's butler, who has been with the family for more than forty years now. A confidence shared with her is as safe as one shared with any member of my family.

With Hale watching from the doorway, Alexander leads us to his motorcar. His chauffeur opens the door, carefully avoiding meeting our eyes. I climb in and smooth my skirts while Emily sits beside me and Alexander takes the seat across from us.

The seats are black leather to match the car, and the interior smells like Alexander: cardamom and clove.

Conversation is limited in such a small space and with Emily beside me, but every so often, I catch Alexander's eyes studying me—leaving a little trail of warmth wherever they land. It makes me thankful I decided to wear one of the new beautiful frocks the French modiste designed. The entire dress is made of Irish lace and trimmed in satin ribbon. My hat is so wide and ornate that poor Emily must lean away from me to have a bit of room. The whole ensemble makes me feel terribly cosmopolitan. Wren may think a love for fashion is vapid, but I disagree. For someone who has to actively work not to be shy, a beautiful dress can be like a suit of armor, granting me the ability to smile back when Alexander and I lock eyes.

The car rolls to a stop in Trafalgar Square, just before the massive white columns of the National Gallery. As we alight from the car, my gaze is immediately drawn toward the impressive dome atop the building and the sheer magnitude of the Gallery.

"Well, this should keep us occupied," Alexander says, his eyes sweeping across the building.

"Oh, I could spend days here." My voice is hushed though we haven't even entered the gallery.

"Have you been here often?" He offers me his arm, and I take it, my ivory gloves bright against the gray of his jacket. Emily follows behind, her footsteps quiet. I know she is trying to be inconspicuous, and I love her for it.

"Several times, but the last was a few years ago. I see something different every time I come, so it's always a new experience."

"I look forward to hearing your opinion on the paintings," Alexander says.

"I can't think why," I say with a self-deprecating smile, "though I love to hear you say it. I'm no art expert, after all."

He shakes his head. "Let me be the judge of that."

We stroll toward the first exhibition room—paintings from the late sixteenth century. A hush falls over me as it always does in the presence of such beauty. Even the room itself is awe-inspiring, with marble floors and soaring ceilings. Alexander proves himself to be a superb painting-viewing partner, as he quietly takes in each painting, lingering over the brush strokes with what I recognize as a knowledgeable eye.

The majority of paintings in this room are portraits, and as we view each one in turn, my mind searches each for any signs that the artist was more than just a mere mortal. It's a game I've long played, for surely there must be others like us? My family cannot be the only half-Sylvan people in all of England. Lord Blackburn, for all his evil, did us one favor in that he proved that we are not alone—there have been others.

"What could you be thinking of?" Alexander asks quietly beside me. "Surely this gentleman's portrait cannot be as unattractive as all that."

I let out a tiny laugh as I relax the furrows between my eyebrows. "You're right; this painting hardly deserves such a scowl."

"Come, let us look at something that may bring a smile instead," he says and leads me to the next painting, aptly titled *Boy Bitten by a Lizard*. "What are your thoughts on this?"

My eyes take in the whole magnificent work, the lovely rich colors, the amusing subject matter—if only because it's so unexpected. As the title suggests, the painting is of a boy being surprised by a bite from a small lizard hiding amongst a vase of flowers. Caravaggio has captured the boy's combined look of surprise and pain mid-action, and I can almost hear the boy crying out. The longer I stare, the more I see: the boy's magnificent auburn bouffant hair, his rosy cheeks, the single white flower in his hair.

"Do you know what it reminds me of?" I ask in hushed tones. "It reminds me of the time a bee stung me."

"Of a bee stinging you?" Alexander repeats, confusion and amusement dancing across his face.

"Yes, I remember being very small—barely out of diapers—and my mother and I were in the garden. I'd just watched this beautiful yellow and black bee land upon a rose, and I reached out to touch it before Mama could stop me." I rub my finger absently through my glove. "I still remember the pinch and the surprising pain. It was the first time I experienced pain—or at least pain that I was cognizant enough to recognize. This painting reminds me of that—this boy expected the soft touch of a flower and got a bite from a cheeky lizard instead."

Alexander lets out a snort of laughter. He turns to me with mirth shining in his eyes, but his smile transforms into a more serious expression. "I don't think I would ever tire of your companionship, Lucy."

I can feel heat rush to my cheeks as I give him a quick smile before returning my attention to the painting before us. *Coward*, I chide myself.

We continue our perusal of the room, Emily following a few paintings behind, giving us a bit of privacy. When we come to yet another portrait, I pause, my head tilted to the side. The painting is titled *Portrait of a Young Woman*, but the artist has chosen to paint the subject with one breast exposed. Strangely, viewing this small bit of nudity beside Alexander doesn't make me as uncomfortable as I would expect—a good thing, too, since this is by far the least graphic of the nude paintings in the Gallery. Perhaps it's because of his quiet contemplation beside me—no sign of nervous fidgeting or furtive glances or anything so juvenile. I watch his eyes trace the artist's brushstrokes, and I see in his expression the appreciation of an artist.

When we move into the next room—works from the eighteenth century—my attention is immediately snared by the closest painting. I head directly for it, a smile sneaking across my face as I take it in. Though the landscape and colors are lovely, what I truly admire is the painting's subject: a young married couple about to go for a ride together. "I adore this one," I say. My hand reaches out toward the painting as if it has a mind of its own, and I feel a sudden tingling in my fingers. Hastily, I return my gloved hand to my side.

"*Mr. and Mrs. Thomas Coltman*," Alexander reads. "A quintessential conversation piece, to be sure. My father's estate has one or two like it."

"I love the familiarity and ease the couple shows with one another, so different from the stiff poses of portraits. Mrs. Coltman's horse, too, is delightful. See her ears back? I can practically hear her scolding the dog."

Alexander smiles. "I wouldn't be surprised if you could hear the horse's thoughts."

I glance up at him, expecting his attention to be on the painting, but a little shock runs through me when I meet his heady gaze instead. I'm sure his comment is meant to be innocuous, but I've been trained by both my sister and brother-in-law to be suspicious of everything. And the fact of the matter is, Wren *can* understand animals. My heart races as I stare back at him, my mind hurrying to catch up. Should I ask him what he means? But then he smiles, and the moment passes, and I berate myself for my nervous thoughts.

As we move to the next painting, footsteps ring out behind us purposefully.

"Lord Devonshire?" a deep voice calls, and we both turn.

A bear of a man stands before us in a dark suit, the silver strands in his black hair belying the smooth skin of his face. Beside me, Alexander stiffens as the man stares at me openly.

"Lord Wallace," Alexander says cautiously. "I'm surprised to see you here."

Slowly, Wallace drags his gaze to Alexander's face. "Are you? By all accounts you've been in London over a week now. I'm afraid when you didn't immediately come to call, I sought you out myself." Again, his focus shifts to me. "Your stay in India has dulled your social mores, Devonshire. You have yet to introduce us."

Alexander shifts his weight subtly so that I am behind him. "This is Miss Lucy Sinclair. Miss Sinclair, might I introduce to you Lord Tavish Wallace?" His words are brief and to the point, and he doesn't even enlighten me as to what Wallace is lord of. I find that I cannot bear to shake hands with the man. There is something about him—something that makes the arcana tingle just below the surface of my skin. A warning. Lord Wallace's lips pull back to reveal strong white teeth, and Alexander adds, "She is Lord Thornewood's sister-in-law."

The words hold a hint of warning, and for once, I'm thankful for my overprotective brother-in-law.

Wallace's expression turns cunning. "Are you telling me I should keep my distance, then, Devonshire? I have heard talk of Thornewood's intense scrutiny of anyone who comes near his family. Strange that he should allow you of all people to escort his sister-in-law." Alexander's shoulders tense, and I feel a ripple of anger go through me. Wallace turns and looks at Emily, who quickly looks to me for guidance. "And with only a servant for an escort. I'm impressed, Devonshire."

Alexander has gone as stiff as a threatening wolf, and I can feel the animosity coming off him in dark waves.

Before he can say anything, I speak my thoughts, "I do hope you aren't referring to his country of birth." My voice cuts through the silence of the Gallery, surprising us all. "It would be terribly small-minded."

"How pretty you are when your cheeks are flushed," Wallace says, and my eyes narrow at his condescending tone. "You must care for this man very much to defend him so ferociously."

His words cause my mind to flounder in surprise for a few moments before I can respond. "I would defend anyone in just the same way, because it is right."

"We must continue on, Wallace," Alexander says, his tone gruff as though his anger is barely in check. "We came to view the paintings, not to submit to an interrogation."

Before Wallace can respond, Alexander turns and offers his arm to me and leads me away.

"I'll come to call at a later time, then," Wallace says as we walk away, the amusement in his voice grating. Alexander ignores him and continues to another room.

We resume our tour of the Gallery, but Wallace's unsettling presence remains. We lose our easy banter, Alexander moving stiffly and silently beside me. Alexander's extreme reaction to this Wallace is both strange and worrisome. My instincts tell me Wallace is not to be trusted and that his notice of me is a decidedly bad thing. Worse, it reminds me of Grandmother's warning.

"How do you know him?" I ask Alexander after the silence becomes unbearable.

He takes a moment to answer, as though searching for the right explanation. "He is one of the few Englishmen I was acquainted with in India. With so few of us in the northern villages, we were often forced into each other's company—even when it was intolerable." I stay quiet to see if he will say more and am rewarded for my patience. "He also happened to be one of my father's closest friends, and he always had the unofficial job of keeping himself and my father updated on my activities."

I look at him aghast. "So he spies on you?"

He nods once. "How else would my father have known if I was behaving in a manner worthy enough to be his heir?"

I rub my arm, suddenly chilled. "Well, I must admit, I didn't much care for him."

"You're putting that mildly, I think." He sighs and hangs his head. "I cannot tell you how sorry I am that you were forced to meet. He has a nasty habit of showing up unannounced."

"It's not your fault, and I have been having a lovely time . . ." I trail off, my eyes shifting away from his.

". . . until he showed up," Alexander finishes for me. "No, I quite understand. I'll take you home now—you have a late afternoon engagement anyway, right?"

"I do, but I hate to end the day with you on such a note."

He takes my hand in his, warm through the kid leather of my glove. "Then think of this instead: this hour spent with you has been one of the most relaxed and enjoyable I can remember for a very long time. I could walk and talk with you for days. And it's because of this that I should take you home—I don't want thoughts of Wallace to overshadow that."

I smile as the warmth from our hands spreads throughout my body.

"I hope you will give me another chance to come to call on you," he says, his eyes intent on mine.

"Of course," I say, even as I know I may not be able to.

Perhaps our trip to Bath could not have come at a more opportune time.

☥

ALEXANDER makes it to his study before releasing a string of curses. His servants would gossip even more if they saw him so obviously agitated, but he can barely bring himself to care. He paces the room like a tiger, his body cutting through the swaths of light the windows cast upon the floor.

He growls in frustration when he thinks of his meeting with Lord Wallace. He knows Lucy could sense something was off with Wallace, and for good reason. He may be Lord Tyrell's right-hand man, but he is destructive and dangerous. Unbidden, thoughts of the last time he'd seen Lord Wallace rise to his mind, and his jaw tightens.

Alexander had sensed a surge of spiritual power during a trip to Bombay and had followed its glowing trail until he'd finally crossed paths with the prana wielder in the marketplace. He still remembers the vivid colors of her sari: reds and oranges that made her dark skin glow. Her arms were bare in the heat, and henna traced its way up her arms in vine-like patterns, and in her hands had been a stack of colorful silk. The moment her eyes met his, he knew she'd been the one he'd sensed.

He deliberately charmed her until she agreed to visit the marketplace stalls with him. It wasn't difficult—he is gifted with the ability to charm almost anyone. The sun beat down on them mercilessly, the air dry and hot, the roads dusty, but its heat never seemed to affect them. Her name was Nadi, and together they smiled and talked as though they'd known each other for years.

"What will you make with the silk in your arms?" he had asked.

"Saris for my sisters," she answered, looking down at the fabric shyly.

He gestured toward the sari she wore, so beautifully detailed. The paisley print was elaborate, and the closer he looked, the more he saw. A peacock hidden on the skirt, a tiger embroidered on her *pallu*. The fabric shimmered like a sunset, and he knew he'd found the object she'd poured her prana into.

This wasn't always the case. Not all the spiritual power users he found enchanted objects. He would know—he was one of the ones who didn't. But then, he wasn't looking for those like him.

He was looking for the one who had killed his mother.

Alexander convinced Nadi, the energy wielder, to show him the many beautiful temples Bombay had to offer. But just as he had today with Lucy, Lord Wallace had appeared suddenly. Then, Alexander hadn't known him long enough to know how deeply disturbed the man was, so he didn't respond with as much distrust and animosity as he'd showed today. Lord Wallace had insinuated himself before either Alexander or Nadi could realize the danger, and it wasn't long before Wallace tricked her into believing he was interested in the beautiful saris she created. She agreed to meet him, and though Alexander's instincts growled a warning, he did nothing. Lord Wallace was trusted by Lord Tyrell, after all, and Lord Tyrell had been like a father in India to Alexander.

But Alexander would soon find that Lord Wallace was a wolf masquerading as a dog, a beast that could never be trusted.

Alexander's hand shakes as he presses his fingers against his eyes, as though he could blot out the remembered images of Nadi. When next he saw her, her beautiful skin had turned ashy gray, her bright eyes opaque, her face caught in a permanent scream.

He thinks of Lord Wallace's gray eyes appraising Lucy, already surmising she was another energy wielder, and his hands curl into fists. Alexander doesn't doubt that Lord Wallace will find Lucy alone—even with as powerful a protector as Lord Thornewood.

After all, Alexander had gotten her alone.

As odious as he finds the man, he cannot ignore Lord Wallace's summons, not when he has the chance to prevent him from doing the same to Lucy.

The stench of cigar smoke mingles with the sweeter smell of smoke from pipes as Alexander is shown into the dimly lit gentlemen's club. Gentlemen in expensive tailored suits sit smoking and talking, or smoking and drinking, or smoking and playing billiards. The room is richly furnished in mahogany and leather; even the walls are wood-paneled. This is a club Alexander would never be privy to were it not for his newly acquired title.

He sees the man he seeks almost immediately, sitting near the fireplace alone with a cut-crystal tumbler of bourbon. Alexander's muscles stiffen the moment Wallace takes notice of him.

With a shark-like grin, he gestures toward the nearest leather chair. Alexander sinks into it reluctantly. A waiter comes and offers him a drink, but Alexander waves him off. He will need all his wits about him for this interview.

"So," Wallace says, pausing to take a puff from his cigar, "you came for a funeral and stayed for a Sylvani. One, I might add, that you have failed to report to Lord Tyrell."

Alexander forces himself to meet Wallace's gaze unflinchingly. "I haven't yet confirmed that she is Sylvani, only that she has an abundance of spiritual power."

Wallace releases a plume of smoke. "What further confirmation do you need?"

"I have spiritual power and use it to find others who have it, but I am not Sylvani." Wallace uses it, too, Alexander knows. It's how he drains the Sylvani of their spiritual power—their arcana, as they call it. Energy wielders and Sylvani both. Like Nadi had been.

"Perhaps I should interview the girl then," Wallace muses.

Alexander wills himself not to go perfectly rigid. He cannot give Wallace any indication of how much that would disturb him, or Wallace will certainly go after Lucy. "She is beginning to trust me," Alexander says calmly, "if you will allow me more time with her, I'm sure I can secure confirmation."

"I'm losing patience, and you are running out of time. My man says he saw trunks being carried out of the Thornewood townhouse earlier this morning. Do you know where they're going?"

The fact that Wallace already has spies on the Thornewood house makes Alexander's stomach knot. "I don't, but I can find out," he lies.

"See that you do."

When Wallace falls silent again, Alexander recognizes it as a dismissal and stands to leave.

"Oh, and Alexander?" Wallace calls just as Alexander has taken a step toward the door. "Be careful of the Lord and Lady of Thornewood, or you may find yourself going in the same way as Blackburn."

On that ominous note, Alexander strides away, eager to be free of Wallace's toxic company. At least one thing was made clear: Alexander has no choice. He'll have to go to Bath, even at the risk of Lucy believing he has followed her with an ulterior motive.

There is no doubt that now that Wallace has the scent, he will pursue her wherever she goes.

TWELVE

BATH is an absolute dream. Our first glimpse is of a picturesque village nestled in green, rolling hills. The buildings are all varying shades of yellow limestone, giving the whole town a lovely symmetry. Rising above it all is the Bath Abbey, its imposing gothic architecture somehow complementary to the town itself.

"I think I can breathe freer already," Rose says with a deep breath the moment we depart from the train.

"It's certainly warmer here," I say. When I breathe the air, it's lightly scented with the smell of sulfur, but not unpleasantly so. "Oh, what should we do first?"

"Why don't you go shopping?" Wren says, one hand tucked in the crook of Colin's elbow and the other grasping little Izzie's hand. "I know you love it, Lucy, and Bath has so many quaint shops."

I open my mouth to protest that I have trunks of beautiful new frocks and hats and gloves and shoes waiting for me at Colin's townhome, but then I realize my sister is doing this for Rose.

"And Rose, darling," Wren says, "you must allow all the bills to be sent directly to Colin and me. We wouldn't dream of having you here as our guest only to make you pay for every little thing."

Rose looks at both of them, aghast. "Oh but surely I cannot impose in such a way. Father did give me money to spend, after all."

Colin shakes his head. "I would be very insulted if you didn't spend my money instead, Rose. Katherine and I promised Izzie a long walk else I'm sure she'd accompany you as well—she does so love to spend money."

Wren gives him a long-suffering look. "Not nearly as much as *you* like to."

Rose casts around at each of our faces, searching for an ally. James smiles at her. "Don't be coy, Rose, they're practically begging you to spend their money."

"Well," Rose says, sharing a quick glance with me, to which I nod encouragingly, "if you insist."

"We do," Colin says. "I've been told I'm quite obnoxious in that regard."

"You're certainly skilled at it," Rob adds, joining the tail end of the conversation with Papa beside him.

James grins at Rob's quip, as he always enjoys a good dig at his older brother.

"Are we splitting up then?" Papa asks, one hand in the pocket of his waistcoat. "If so, then I should like to take the waters and relax. Let's see if this *Aquae Sulis* has all the magical properties it's touted to have. I expect to run circles around the whole town in a day's time."

"If it can do that, then it'll surely cure our lovely Rose here," Rob says with a wry smile. "Come, Papa, I'll help you in your endeavor. I'd like to have a rest for a while—not much else to do in a spa town, after all."

The pairing off leaves James looking very much alone and forlorn—something that has always twisted my heart. I simply cannot bear to see anyone left out. "James, why don't you accompany us? We could use your assistance carrying our packages home."

"Is that all I am to you, then? A glorified footman?" His smile is so bright, though, that I know he is pleased I included him.

"Perhaps you can also regale us with your wry sense of humor," Rose adds.

"That's something he'll do without having to be asked," Colin drawls.

"At least I *have* a sense of humor," James replies.

"As amusing as your teasing sibling banter is," Wren interrupts, "I think Izzie has been patient enough." Izzie's pixie face is screwed up in determination as she tugs her mother's hand, trying to inch ever closer to the street.

We part, then, leaving the little train station on foot. Rose and I lead, enjoying the relative quiet of the smaller town, the clean air, the rush of the River Avon. But as we reach a crossroads, I realize I haven't the faintest idea where I'm headed.

"We should go to the right," James calls from behind us, and I grin back at him sheepishly. "I seem to be earning my keep. The two of you would have found yourselves hopelessly lost without me."

"That's why I was clever enough to invite you," I say. "That, and your considerable upper body strength, which should come in handy when we're laden down with hat boxes and muslin and the like."

James shakes his head. "As your *sensei*, I thought I'd be treated with more respect."

Rose leans toward me conspiratorially, but her voice is loud enough for James to hear, "*Sensei*? What could he mean?"

"I train Lucy in self-defense," James says. "She's quite good at fencing, but only tolerable at best at daggers."

I shoot him a glare. Rose watches me with wide eyes. "I cannot deny that's exciting, but whatever for? Surely you don't imagine yourself in danger."

"You must forgive my family," I say, striving for an airy tone, "we're all a bit eccentric, I'm afraid."

"Which reminds me." James rummages around in his coat pocket a moment before pulling out one of the daggers we've been using for training. "You should keep this in your reticule at all times."

I scan the streets anxiously, my cheeks flaming as I think of the scene others may witness. I give a little shake of my head, but he only continues to walk after us, holding the dagger aloft.

"Give it here, then," I say in a hiss. "You could have waited until we arrived at the townhouse."

Once the dagger is safely hidden away in my reticule, I dare to meet Rose's face. To my surprise, she's grinning hugely. When I hesitantly return the smile, she bursts out in laughter so strong we're forced to pause in our walk until she can breathe again. "Oh no, no, I'm fine, I promise," she says when I pat her back in concern for her wheezing. "I always grow a bit breathless when I laugh too hard, but I don't mind—I love to laugh, and it's been far too long."

"I'm only glad it made you laugh and not run away from us screaming," I say. She shakes her head with another wheezy giggle.

The first shop we come to is a milliner with the most glorious array of hats I've ever seen. "Imagine finding such a shop here in Bath," I say as I drink in the luxe window display. "And Colin said this was practically a ghost town."

A little bell chimes as we walk in, and my eyes seem to dart everywhere at once. The shop boasts everything from turbans to elaborate hats so wide and filled with so many feathers that I doubt anyone wearing them would fit through the door.

"Oh, you must restrain me so that I don't flit about like a bird and embarrass us both," I say, gripping Rose's arm. The array of colors and textures are so deliciously displayed I ignore my own advice and wander about the shop, running my hand along an ostrich plume on one hat or marveling at the combination of lace and pearls on another.

"May I be of assistance to you, ladies?" a small, well-dressed lady asks. Her gaze shifts from Rose and me to James standing so casually behind us and back again.

"These beauties are in need of hats," James says with mock severity, his arms around us both, "and I am desperate to appease them."

The shopkeeper's eyes widen, and I cannot think what she must make of the situation. Over my shoulder, I give James a little warning look. He grins back widely. It's a game to him, of course. He finds nothing more entertaining than manipulating people of society, and if he can imply something strange or vulgar—or both!—while doing so, then all the better for it.

"Of course, my lord," she says, a little dazedly. "Do you have anything in particular in mind?" Her gaze once again darts from person to person, unsure which of us she should address.

I take pity on the poor thing and gesture toward a royal blue hat with a wide brim and a bright white ostrich plume that provides fabulous contrast. "Rose, that hat would look just beautiful on you, wouldn't you say?"

She pats her own hat with its modest brim as the shopkeeper hurries to retrieve it. "Do you really think so?"

I nod emphatically. "You could wear any of these hats, really—with your Gibson Girl brown hair and blue eyes."

I touch my own upswept hair. "Not like my unfashionable blonde." I wink to show her I'm only teasing.

"You know I think you're *both* staggeringly beautiful," James says, positively dripping with smarminess.

This time the shopkeeper manages not to stare at him in surprise, but I see the questions flit across her open face. She carefully removes Rose's hat and then secures the blue hat with a few strategically hidden hatpins. Rose tilts her head this way and that as we admire the transformation in a standing oval mirror.

James's hand is warm on my arm as he draws me away from the mirror. "What about this one for you?" In his other hand is a black hat with a curved brim trimmed in lace, pinstriped ribbon, and feathers. "May I?" he asks, cheeky grin in place.

"May you what, exactly?" I ask.

In answer, he gently removes my wide-brimmed hat—his fingers surprisingly deft—and places the black hat on at a rakish angle. One finger trails down the line of my jaw, and his eyes sparkle at me teasingly—but it's the heat I see reflected in them that makes the room suddenly feel much too warm.

"That one looks lovely on you, my lady," the shopkeeper says, and I jerk toward her terribly fast, as though we've been caught doing something—which, I suppose, we were.

James takes a step back, his expression pensive and admiring, as though he is viewing a painting in a gallery. He gives a terse nod. "Yes. We'll take them both." I give a little huff in warning—I can't stand when he tries to make decisions for me, and he's done so for years. "Unless, of course, there is anything else you'd like?" he asks Rose and me.

"I will be quite content with this hat, I should say," Rose says.

I inspect the shop's contents once more before answering. "Do you have any more of that violet-striped ribbon there?" I indicate a rather unattractive straw bonnet, save for its lovely ribbon.

The shopkeeper walks over and holds the bonnet in question aloft. "This ribbon? You have superb taste, my lady. I do believe I have more of the satin in the back. Shall I check for you?"

"I would appreciate it if you would. I have a violet-striped frock that I adore, but since I haven't had a hat to go with it, I haven't had chance to wear it yet. If I'd thought to bring it to Bath, I'd have you design a hat, but I'm afraid I'll have to make do with the ribbon instead."

She smiles. "Of course, my lady."

When she slips away to the back of her shop, I whirl on James. "I cannot believe you are teasing the poor woman so! She doesn't know what to make of us."

He grins. "You know you love it."

"And what of Rose? Did you stop to think she might not want to be embarrassed?"

Rose turns from admiring her new hat in the mirror. "Don't quarrel on my account. I'm afraid my expected lifespan is much too short to care what everyone thinks of me."

"Goodness, how could you say such a thing?" I demand, even as James nods at her encouragingly. I shake my head. "I can't take either of you anywhere."

Mercifully, the shopkeeper returns with the ribbon in hand—more than enough for a hat—and we make our purchases and leave.

"You're devilishly fun to be around, James," Rose says as we continue our walk.

"You see?" James says to me, eyebrows raised. "Rose at least enjoys my company."

"I do, too," I say. "You're carrying those hatboxes beautifully, after all."

Rose's hand is suddenly on my arm. "A bookshop! Oh, we must go in."

REED AND TAYLOR'S BOOKS OLD AND NEW, a sign proclaims in elegant gold lettering. The shop is small but welcoming with soft lighting and the comforting smell of books. James heads toward a section of books that are clearly very old, with yellowing pages and brittle leather covers.

"They have Bram Stoker's latest," I say with glee, snatching up the red cover of *Lady Athlyne*. "Did you read *Dracula*?"

Rose nods emphatically. "I read it in a single evening—I didn't sleep until well after dawn. Just as well, since it frightened me as much as I loved it."

I peek at the first few pages, savoring the sound the spine of a brand new book makes when first opened. I sigh happily. "And it's a romance!"

"Speaking of romance," Rose says with a little nod toward James, who appears to be shamefully haggling with the bookseller, "is he one of your suitors?"

"No." A line of heat travels down my jaw where James trailed his finger. "At least, I don't *think* so."

Rose watches me for a moment. "But you wish him to be?"

My mind instantly fills with thoughts of Alexander—his warm smile, his scent of cardamom and clove, his attentiveness. "I can honestly say I have no idea what I wish for."

She laughs quietly. "That's not a bad problem to have, but I sense a sordid past between the two of you."

My head whips toward her so fast she erupts into wheezy laughter, and I relax into a grin. "There's some truth to that, I suppose. He did kiss me, after all."

When I turn nonchalantly back toward the stack of books, she grabs hold of my arm. "You cannot just leave it at that! Promise me you'll tell me the full story."

I hand her a copy of *Lady Athlyne*. "I will, but I think you'll be rather unimpressed once you hear the whole of it."

James finishes haggling with the bookseller, and by his grin, I assume he talked him down. As he makes his way toward us, I abruptly change the subject. "Will you read *Lady Athlyne* with me? It's been ages since I've had the chance to read a book and immediately discuss it with someone afterward. My sister and I used to read books together, but she's usually too exhausted at night to read more than a chapter or two."

"Now, is that because Izzie runs her ragged . . . or Lord Thornewood does?" Rose says and then laughs when I make a sour face. "Forgive me, I shouldn't tease you. Of course I'll read it with you."

"A romance," James says when he sees the books in our hands. "Why am I not surprised?"

"I do hope you're not saying that because we are both female," Rose says. "That would be terribly dull of you."

"No indeed," James says. "I only meant that Lucy has a long history of only choosing stories with happy endings."

"That can't be true," I say. "I only just finished *Dracula*."

James smirks at me. "Yes? And what happens at the end, I wonder?"

I think of Mina's miraculous recovery and the note at the end of Jonathan and Mina's marriage and birth of their son. My face falls. "I did read *Wuthering Heights* years ago—"

"And loathed it," James adds.

"Well, what's wrong with wanting to read about something uplifting?" I demand.

James's eyes sparkle, clearly happy he managed to get a rise out of me. "Not a thing."

Rose remains silent through our little exchange, and when I meet her gaze, she only manages a wan smile.

"We're boring Rose," I say, linking my arm through hers. I hand both our books to James. "Could you be a darling and purchase these for us? I do believe Rose is quite fatigued."

"No, I'm well," Rose protests, but James does as I ask.

"Then perhaps it is I who am tired," I say with a little smile. "Or at least hungry. Shall we go settle in and pray the housekeeper can prepare us a late luncheon?"

"I certainly won't argue with you," Rose says.

"James, will you help us find the townhouse?" I ask when he returns with the books neatly wrapped in parchment and tied with twine. "You've already established how directionally challenged we are, and we're dying for a meal."

"Of course. Unless you'd rather we found a restaurant in town?"

I glance at Rose. "If you don't mind," she says, "I'd rather we went to the house since I'd love the chance to rest after luncheon."

"Then that's just what we'll do," James says.

He holds the door for us, and we walk through into the warm sunshine. I feel instantly rejuvenated despite my hunger. But the more we walk, the slower Rose walks, until it almost feels as though I am dragging her along.

"Rose, you should have said how tired you were," I scold gently, even as guilt at being so terribly blind to her discomfort tears into me.

Even James watches her with concern, his usual teasing manner gone. "Shall I continue on foot and return with a motorcar to fetch you both?"

Rose's eyes widen. "No, please. I wouldn't want to trouble you. How much farther?"

"It would be no trouble at all. We're not far—you can see the beginnings of the Crescent just there." He indicates a townhouse less than a block away.

She squints into the distance. "Is that row of townhouses curved or have I become confused?"

"No, they are," James says with a smile. "The architect, John Wood, was said to be rather fascinated with ancient stone circles."

"Oh, I cannot wait to see it up close," I say, my fingers already itching to draw the unusual semicircular Georgian architecture.

Rose takes a step forward determinedly. "I'm sure I can make it."

Our pace is slow, and though Rose tries to hide it, I detect the unmistakable sound of a wheeze with her every breath. A whisper of doubt takes hold of my mind, and I realize my new friend is a great deal sicker than I originally supposed.

A shadow hangs over her, and not even the beautiful scenery can detract from it.

THIRTEEN

MUCH later, after a filling luncheon of assorted tea sandwiches, smoked salmon, tea, and scones, and after most of us had a lie-down, a soft knock comes at my door.

"Come in," I say, and Wren enters, wearing a striking sapphire blue lace afternoon dress.

"I'm not disturbing you, am I?" she asks.

I glance down at my sketchbook, where I've been trying since I woke to sort out my thoughts. The results are a hodgepodge of half-finished drawings: James's warm eyes in one corner, a wilted rose, the hulking form of Lord Wallace, part of the columned townhomes of the Royal Crescent, Alexander's full mouth—the last has been nearly obliterated by charcoal, though.

"No, of course not." I put my charcoal down and turn toward her. "I'm only sketching."

Her skirts swish as she perches on the end of my bed. "Have there been any more incidents—traveling within your drawings?"

I shake my head. "None since my visit with our grandmother, and none that I haven't deliberately instigated myself. Although . . ." I trail off, thinking. "There have been times when I've felt arcana in the tips of my fingers without having summoned it." I catch her smiling. "What?"

"Just to hear you mention our Sylvan grandmother so casually . . . it's a little surreal."

"There has to be a way to bring you with me next time," I say.

Her eyebrows arch. "There will be a next time?" She smiles when I answer with a sheepish look. "And anyway, I swore to Colin long ago I would never cross over. I'll have to live vicariously through you."

Her smile fades, and I can see the longing in her eyes.

"You promised you'd never *physically* cross over," I say.

A surprised laugh escapes her. "Goodness, but you're sly!"

"It's taxing on our physical forms, but not if we stay for only a short time, and I'm sure Grandmother can help me."

She holds up her hand, but her eyes still shine with mirth. "All right, all right. I'll consider it. God knows I'd love to see Sylvania again." She sighs dreamily. "Anyway, James tells me you had a whale of a time shopping, but do you think you're rested enough now to go on a tour of the Roman Baths?"

I think of Rose barely making it home. "Oh I'd love to. I only hope Rose is well enough to go. She was rather tired out."

Wren must hear the note of melancholy in my tone for she searches my face for a moment. "Is she very ill then?"

The shadow I saw cast over Rose fills my mind, but I cannot bring myself to voice my fears. Perhaps if I don't, it won't give them the power to come to pass. "I think she tries to hide a great deal."

Wren nods. "I can certainly see that. She's drinking tea in the drawing room as we speak. Izzie just went down for her nap, so now would be the ideal time to go. Shall we see if Rose is up for it?"

I check my hair in the beveled mirror and move to follow her.

"Oh! Is this your new hat?" Wren asks, holding it aloft. I'd put it on display, thinking I might sketch its beautifully curved lines. "It'll look lovely on you."

"Thank you," I say. "I thought it would go perfectly with my black and white tailored dress—you know the one?"

"The one that makes your waist look nonexistent?" she asks with a wry smile. "I certainly do, and you're right, this will look divine. But you always did have exquisite taste—it must come from being a brilliant artist."

I loop my arm around her in a tight hug. "Have I mentioned lately that you're my favorite sister?"

She laughs. "You're certainly my favorite. You may even be my favorite sibling—it depends on whether or not Rob is behaving himself."

"Where is Rob?" I ask after we have walked quietly past Izzie's nursery. "Will he join us, or is he still resting up for tonight?"

"Speaking of tonight," she says, glancing back at me on the stairs. "I quite forgot to mention that Colin and I ran into Lord and Lady Sotheby in the park, and they invited us to the ball they're hosting this evening. The attendees will mostly be retired officers, so of course Colin was quick to say yes—" she pauses to give me a long-suffering look, "but I thought you might like the opportunity to dance—even if it's only with James and Rob."

"You know me too well," I say. "I'm certainly up for a ball this evening, even at the risk of Colin throwing every ancient and grandfatherly gentleman my way."

She laughs. "Good, because he will."

When we enter the drawing room, I find I was the only one who was unaccounted for. Rose looks wan still, but much more alert, and I go straight to her side.

"I'm sorry to have not come down sooner," I say, sitting beside her on the velvet settee.

"I've been perfectly content, I assure you," she says with a nod toward Rob and James, who stand nearby at the bookcases idly talking and browsing for books. I quite understand her sentiment, for together they truly could brighten even the most melancholy of moods.

"I'm glad to hear it. Are you feeling rejuvenated?"

"Quite so, thank you. I'm embarrassed I became so weary."

"You've nothing to be embarrassed about! We'd only just finished traveling. It was wrong of us to push you so soon. That's why I want you to feel no obligation whatsoever, but what say you to a tour of the Roman Baths?"

She glances down at her tea cup for a moment. "Would we leave now?"

"Or as soon as you're ready, but don't feel pressured in the least to go. We could always stay and read."

"No, indeed. We should take advantage of the sights." She leans a little closer so we won't be overheard by the others, who are all either teasing each other mercilessly or engrossed in their reading. "It shames me to admit this, but I don't think I have the energy to both tour the baths and attend the ball this evening—Lady Katherine mentioned it to me earlier. Would you be terribly disappointed if I only went on the tour? It's just that I've so wanted to see them—I've heard there are some incredible pieces of Roman art preserved."

A sense of obligation and guilt twist within me at the thought of leaving Rose behind this evening, much as I'd like to go dancing. "I've heard the same, but I'd be perfectly content to stay at home with you this evening if you'd like. I hate to think of you sitting alone while we're out enjoying ourselves."

"Don't be ridiculous. You mustn't stay here on my account—no, I insist," she interrupts when I open my mouth to protest. "I'll be going to bed straight after dinner, so there will be no reason for you to stay behind. Just imagine I am actually seventy years old instead of twenty—I think you'd be happier for it."

"How morbid!" I say with a shake of my head.

She laughs, which brings a bit more color to her face. "It's not morbid if it's the truth. I've accepted my lot in life. It does have some perks, after all. For example, I always have a brilliant excuse whenever I want to weasel my way out of something I'd rather not do."

"Lucy, are you ready?" Wren asks, Colin's arm around her waist—they're nearly always touching in some way, and apparently not even a houseguest is deterrent enough. Izzie, it seems, has actually been left napping with her nanny for once. "Rose, I hope you feel up to accompanying us."

"Yes, I'd love to," Rose says, getting to her feet.

"I'll be along in a minute. I want to bring my sketchbook."

Before I leave the room, James appears at my side. "I must say, I'm insulted. You didn't even ask if I was going with you. Is it because you have no need of my superior carrying skills?"

I laugh. "Of course not. I just assumed you were . . . just as I assumed Rob wouldn't." I give a little nod toward my brother, and he raises his tea cup in a teasing salute. "You'll join us, won't you?"

"Well, now that I've been invited, I daresay I will." He grins at me. "Besides, Colin and I were often dragged here as children for holiday. You might find I remember a thing or two about Bath's ancient history."

I can see where this is headed, and I give him a warning look. "Just don't antagonize the tour guide."

His eyes widen. "I would never."

"Hm, well, I'll be along in a moment." I start to walk out the door but then stop and turn back to him. "And, James? I am happy you'll be coming along."

"There is a legend that Bath was first discovered by a man with leprosy who watched pigs suffering from skin disease wallow in mud and be cured," our tour guide says, dressed head to toe in tweed. "When the man did the same, he was also cured. That man was Prince Bladud, King Lear's father, and the founder of Bath."

We stand in the restored Roman Baths, gazing down into a rectangular pool of water the color of jade—Mr. Sanders, our tour guide, assures us this is due to algae growth in the pool and that the water from the hot springs is actually colorless. Roman statues stand guard as mist swirls gently atop the pool.

"The Romans were fond of public baths, and hot springs in particular, and so it was that they built a temple here around 50 AD. But in reality, it was already known to the Celtic Druids, who considered this site sacred to the goddess Sulis," Mr. Sanders says, his tufts of brown-gray hair standing on end in apparent excitement. He leans closer to us. "This was a place where men could communicate with the underworld."

Something thrums through me at his words, and I glance at Wren. Confusion flits across her face. She felt it, too. On a whim, I take out my sketchbook and draw the geometric lines of the pool, the smooth columns surrounding it, as much sentinels to the pool as the statues that guard it. Arcana surges to my fingertips, and for once, I'm not surprised.

I fall behind so Rose has her back to me and mouth to my sister, "Arcana." She nods once.

My heart thumps rapidly in my chest. How I would love to hear from our grandmother what the significance of this place is.

"Beware the gorgon!" Mr. Sanders says, bringing me out of my reverie. He indicates a beautiful stone carving of a glowering gorgon, with a multitude of writhing snakes springing forth from its face. But upon first glance, the circular carving instantly brings to mind an ancient drawing of the sun.

In my sketchbook, I draw the snakes as points of the sun instead, and I can almost feel warmth traveling up my fingers from the pencil's tip.

Rose glances over my shoulder as I draw. "It does rather look like a sun, doesn't it?"

Her own drawing is an exact rendering as though the gorgon leaped directly onto her paper. "And yours is as accurate as a photograph," I say with a smile.

"Here we have the goddess Sulis," Mr. Sanders says, indicating a bust of an imposing woman. "The Romans decided this Celtic goddess was really just another manifestation of Minerva, so the Temple was dedicated to both Sulis and Minerva to appease both the Celts and the Romans who visited."

Next we travel down to the edge of the pool, where only stairs separate us from the jade water. James doffs his coat and moves closer to the edge. "Shall we all have a dip now?" he asks.

The poor tour guide's eyes widen comically. "Oh, no, my lord. That is, not here. There are more private opportunities to bathe in the hot springs, and we now offer the *Aquae Sulis* to drink."

"James," Colin says with a hint of warning in his tone, "kindly refrain from rattling our informative guide."

The tour guide lets out a little sigh of relief, his smile a little brighter. "If you'll follow me, my lord and lady, there are some beautifully restored mosaics of tritons."

Colin and Wren move to follow him, and James continues at a distance.

"Shall we follow?" Rose asks.

I glance up from my drawing of the main pool. "I'll be along in a moment. I only want to finish this sketch."

"I'll wait with you."

I could spend ages in this room, with the mist swirling above the water, and that tingle of arcana in the air. My pencil makes pleasant scratching sounds against the paper, and I glance up again to take in the view.

Movement catches my eye—a figure moving in the shadows across from us. I'm close enough to see immediately that it's not one of our party, and I freeze as prickling awareness creeps over my skin. A man with hair shot with steel and a broad face.

Lord Wallace.

Before I can even draw in another breath, he smirks at me and melds back into the shadows.

"Lucy, what is it?" Rose asks, her voice causing me to startle enough to drop my pencil. "Goodness, you look as pale as your drawing paper."

I open my mouth to reassure her, but I can't ignore the pin-pricks of fear chasing over my skin. It could be merely coincidental that he is here.

But I know that it is not.

"I only thought I saw movement across the way, but I'm sure I was mistaken. Shall we find the others?"

I start walking briskly in the direction I saw them go, and Rose hurries to follow me. The moment I reach my sister's side, I force myself to relax, smoothing the tension from my face. If I don't, she'll know instantly that something has spooked me, and I'd rather she carry on having a nice time.

He wouldn't dare attack us when we're all together, so I'll just have to spoil everyone's fun later when I tell them.

When I'm sure she isn't looking, I glance over my shoulder once more. The room is quiet, peaceful even. Yet Lord Wallace's taunting smirk haunts me still. Almost without thinking, I reach into my pelisse and touch the cold blade of the dagger hidden there.

⚿

ALEXANDER arrives in Bath by midafternoon and immediately takes a trolley to Richard's townhouse. Telling Lucy that his father held property in Bath was a lie, but a necessary one. It gave him at least a semblance of credibility for being in town. Perhaps he would only be seen as an overzealous suitor rather than the hunter he was.

As he steps out of the trolley and walks toward the easternmost townhome in the circular complex, an awareness enters his mind, ghostly fingers tingling over his scalp. He turns toward the source: to the west, toward the Roman Baths. The sensation ends as quickly as it came—a short burst of prana, then.

Sweat beads on his brow as he fights the urge to seek Lucy out immediately. The likelihood of Wallace taking her in broad daylight is slim. He is sadistic and cruel, but not foolhardy. No, Wallace will wait until nightfall, when Lucy will be at her weakest. Her sister and brother-in-law are formidable, but they won't be expecting an attack here in this sleepy spa town full of the elderly and the infirm.

Alexander shakes himself free of his worry and strides toward the door. After knocking once, the butler—a portly man with gray hair and small eyes—admits him.

"We've been expecting you, my lord. Lord Trawley is waiting for you in his office. Shall I show you the way?"

Alexander nods once, his mind still otherwise occupied. Every one of his otherworldly senses reaches out, searching for the barest hint of prana.

"Alexander," Richard says by way of greeting. His friend hurriedly scrawls something on a piece of paper and stands to clasp hands. "Your journey went well, I take it?"

"Yes, well enough. I'm surprised you arrived here before me. Did you take an earlier train?"

Richard nods, and a lock of dark hair falls across his forehead. He slicks it back impatiently. "I arrived yesterday evening. I wanted to have time to send my men out—get the word back on what the Thornewoods have planned."

"And?"

Richard gives Alexander a level look. "Your obvious concern for this woman is disturbing, Alexander. You know this cannot end well."

The muscles in Alexander's jaw tense. He hates to have these words—the very same words of warning his inner mind has told him—said aloud. "What would you have me do, Richard? It's one thing to seek out prana wielders and the Sylvani. It's another to let Wallace destroy the ones who may be innocent."

Richard appraises him silently for a moment. "You know that's not all this is about. What would Tyrell think?"

Alexander knows what Tyrell would say. Tyrell would say it's best to err on the side of caution, to treat Lucy as though she is Sylvan and not simply a prana wielder. To treat her like the danger she is.

There are two types of prana users, Alexander, Tyrell had said shortly after the death of Alexander's mother. Alexander can still see the tall, slim gentleman with jet-black hair sitting beside him on the wooden bench his mother had loved—the one where she could sit and watch Alexander play and see the mountains looming in the distance. *There are those, like yourself, who simply have an abundance of it. It's a beautiful but harmless gift.*

Tyrell had taken a breath and stared at Alexander, his eyes coal-black. *But then there are those who aren't even human like us, whose energy is too powerful to contain. Power-hungry and nearly invincible, these creatures are willing to kill to climb to the top of society. They call themselves the Sylvani.*

He took Alexander's hand in his. *They killed your mother, Alexander. Your beautiful, energy-wielding mother, because she got too close to one of them. She discovered the truth, and she was killed for it. But you can help us. You can help us find them and stop them before they take away someone else's mother.*

The rage had swelled within Alexander, drowning his grief. *Yes,* Alexander had promised, but that had been ten years ago.

Ever since Nadi's death, Alexander had feared some of Tyrell's men didn't make the necessary distinctions between the prana users who were dangerous and those who had a beautiful gift.

"She may not be a Sylvani," Alexander says forcefully. "She may only be a prana wielder like myself."

"Hm. And how many times have you told yourself that?"

Too many times to count. Over and over and over during the darkest part of the night. He always came back to the same answer: Lucy couldn't be dangerous. He couldn't accept that behind her kind eyes lurked a cold-blooded monster who wouldn't hesitate to kill. Wallace had been wrong about Nadi, and he was wrong about Lucy, too.

"I won't risk another Nadi." Alexander meets Richard's pale eyes with a challenging look of his own. "Is that what you would wish upon Lucy Sinclair?"

Some of the tension leaves Richard. "I wouldn't wish that fate on anyone, but that doesn't mean you have the right to make decisions for yourself. The protocol has always been to notify Tyrell immediately. He has limitless resources, and going off on your own is not only pointless—it's foolhardy."

Alexander straightens to his full height. "What will you do then?"

"What I've always done, Alexander. I'll give you my aid in any way I can."

"And you won't notify Tyrell yourself?"

"Against my better judgment . . . no."

Relief floods through Alexander's body. "Thank you, Richard."

"But you're running out of time. It won't be long before someone suspects."

"I suppose now is the time I should tell you that Wallace sought me out in London. I have no doubt that he has followed Lucy to Bath."

Richard closes his eyes and lets out an exasperated breath. "Blast that man. He has always had a sixth sense for where you will be at any given time. Has he declared himself your nemesis? It seems that he is in constant competition with you, but for what, I cannot tell."

"He has loathed me ever since I spoke against him to Tyrell."

"Then the plan is simple," Richard says. "You must get her alone, confirm whether or not she is Sylvani, and then immediately inform Tyrell. Wallace will prove a danger to her until then."

And perhaps even after, Alexander thinks to himself, but he dares not say it aloud. It is this irritating doubt which has wormed its way into his mind.

A knock comes at the door, and the butler enters. "Forgive the interruption, my lord," he says, "but you wanted me to inform you the moment a note arrived."

Richard strides over and takes the small square from his butler's gloved hand. "Thank you, Sanford." He opens the note and quickly scans its contents. "Good, good. Lady Sotheby writes to say she has invited the Thornewoods to a ball this evening. Just a moment, Sanford, and I'll pen a response."

"Then of course we must attend," Alexander says as Richard's pen scratches across the paper.

After handing the note to Sanford, Richard turns to his friend. "I knew I was right to take advantage of the Sothebys' desire to climb the social ladder. An earl and countess in this sleepy town are too exciting to resist. You have no formal suit, I presume?"

"No, but I can make do with whatever you have. We are nearly the same height."

Richard pats his more generous middle. "The same height, perhaps, but you are certainly more fit. I'll have my valet see what can be done."

Alexander nods dismissively, his mind already leaping ahead to other things. "If Wallace has followed her here, then he will almost certainly be there tonight."

"Then you'll have to attach yourself to her side—no hardship for you, I'm sure."

Alexander ignores the dig. An invitation to the ball may minimize some of Thornewood's ire and suspicion, but Alexander knows it will be impossible to avoid angering him at his unexpected presence. Even Lucy may be less than welcoming.

But surely Thornewood will thank Alexander one day for protecting his sister-in-law from the very real danger of Lord Wallace.

At least, until he discovers the truth about Alexander.

FOURTEEN

ARE you sure you will not go with us?" I ask Rose as Emily puts the finishing touches on my hair. Rose insisted that I get dressed in her room so that she may at least feel a part of the excitement of a ball, and truly, it is the least I can do.

"Oh no, I would never make it. I can hardly keep my eyes open as it is."

I turn to look at her and am dismayed to see she does look wan. "And you'd rather I didn't stay? Truly, I don't mind."

She laughs. "After Emily went to all that trouble? And what good would watching me sleep do?"

"Very well," I say with a defeated sigh. Pulling on my white evening gloves, I go over to her and touch her shoulder. It feels painfully thin under my hand. "Sleep well, then. I swear we'll have fun in the morning."

"I had a lovely time today. You needn't worry. Have fun with James," she says with a suggestive lift of her eyebrows.

I glance back at Emily, who hides a smile. "You heard nothing," I tell her with mock severity, for of course she knows all about my mixed feelings regarding James. She had been the one to listen to me cry over his rejection so long ago.

"Mum's the word," she says. "Is there anything else you'll need this evening, my lady?"

"No, you've made sure I'm quite beautifully turned out, Emily, thank you."

She smiles and turns to Rose. "Shall I help you change for bed, then, Lady Rose?"

"Go on, then," Rose says with a little shooing motion. "I'll live vicariously through your memories in the morning."

I smile and wish her good night before stepping out into the thickly carpeted hallway. Wren waits for me at the end of the hall, dressed in a deep purple beaded gown.

"How is she?" she asks quietly when I reach her side.

I think of the bones beneath my hands. "Frail and tired."

Wren looks back at Rose's door, face pensive. Finally she says, "Do you think I should . . . ?"

For a moment, I think of what she's offering. Of having her use her arcana to heal Rose of her illness. But in the next instant, I reject the idea. How could I risk losing my sister in place of my friend? "You cannot know how much that means to me, but no. It nearly killed you the last time you tried to heal someone who was dying."

Wren's gaze darts to mine. "You think she's dying?"

I can feel the color drain from my face. Just hearing it said aloud is horrifying. I press my lips tightly and shake my head, unwilling to answer. Wren reads this gesture perfectly, though, and pulls me in for a tight embrace. The familiar smell of her hair—like roses—brings me some small comfort.

"We shouldn't speak it into being," I say finally.

She touches my cheek with one gloved hand and nods, sympathy and understanding in her eyes. "Shall we go?"

"Yes. It would be better if she didn't find us out in the hall crying—I'm not the most skilled liar."

Wren snorts, the gesture perfectly unladylike, and so very her. "You're the worst liar. Your every little thought flits across your face. Thank God I didn't inherit such a trait, or all of London would loathe me."

She trails down the stairs, and I follow, grateful she has chased the shadows away—for the moment, at least.

The ball, as it turns out, is a gross exaggeration. It is barely more than a small gathering, really, with my family making up the bulk of the attendees—only twenty-two of us in all. Many of the gentlemen have already escaped to another room for cards, and there are few unmarried ladies from my brief observation of the room. Furniture has been moved aside for dancing, while footmen wander about offering glasses of champagne. Sir and Lady Sotheby are wonderfully gracious, though, and the musicians they've hired for the evening are as skilled as any I've yet encountered in London.

James is dancing with the only other lady remotely close to our age, and Rob joined some of the officers for a card game, so I've been keeping Wren and Colin company for the last set.

"I'm so sorry this is such a small party," Lady Sotheby says as she joins us.

"On the contrary," Colin says, "we prefer it to be small."

Lady Sotheby tilts her head, her dangling earrings catching the light from the chandelier. "More intimate that way?"

"Quieter," Colin says.

Wren smiles weakly, but Lady Sotheby only laughs good-naturedly. "I'm afraid I'm of the same mind, Lord Thornewood. It's why my husband and I spend so much of our time in Bath. But I believe a few more guests will be arriving—I hope it'll still be quiet enough for you."

"Oh, I'm sure it will be. My darling wife is my shield now from the matchmakers, so I can't complain."

"Really, Colin," Wren says under her breath, but I can tell she's hiding back a grin.

"Ah, now you shouldn't look down on matchmakers. You'll soon find yourself in such a position," Lady Sotheby says with a nod in my direction.

"Lord Thornewood believes I should have at least five Seasons under my belt before choosing a husband," I say, and Lady Sotheby's eyes widen until she realizes I'm only joking. At least, I hope I am.

"I should apologize for being a terrible hostess, then, Miss Sinclair. I had expected an even number of ladies and gentlemen, but there are a few who have yet to arrive. Perhaps I might show you a lovely Monet we have in the library? Your sister says you're an accomplished artist."

"Oh, I would love to see it! Though I fear my sister has grossly exaggerated my talent," I say with a glance at Wren. She shrugs shamelessly.

"Can I interest you in a viewing, Lady Katherine?" Lady Sotheby asks.

"I'm afraid she has promised this next dance to me," Colin says. "She promised to dance every dance with me for the rest of our lives, and I mean to hold her to it." He kisses Wren's gloved hand as she stares intensely into his eyes.

"Just us then," I say loudly.

Lady Sotheby snaps her mouth shut. "Of course. If you'll follow me?"

The Sotheby townhouse isn't overly large, but it is elegantly decorated. A mix of richly toned antique furniture hold carefully displayed bric-a-brac—framed photographs, tall vases with lovely flower arrangements, and porcelain figurines. The library is modest compared to any of Colin's, or even Papa's, the bookshelves lined with matching jewel-toned leather tomes. Not a novel in sight, which leads me to believe they aren't readers at all. A pity, that.

In a gilded frame hangs the Monet in all its beautifully subdued colors.

"*The Water-Lily Pond*," Lady Sotheby says beside me. "I just loved how peaceful it looked, and even more so that this is Monet's own pond. He wanted a traditional Japanese style bridge over the water, and he worked tirelessly on all the vegetation."

"It's so tranquil," I say quietly, thinking suddenly of Alexander and our trip to the National Gallery. Before it was ruined by Wallace.

Lady Sotheby watches me closely. "The colors are rather somber, though, aren't they?"

I force a cheerful smile onto my face, suddenly embarrassed that I descended into a gloomy mood. "Not terribly so—there are bright spots of sunshine on the water lilies, just there."

She nods when I point them out. "Like dappled sunshine through leaves."

We stare at the Monet for a while longer, both quietly contemplating it, when another painting catches my eye on the other side of the library. This one is a very different style from the impressionist Monet: a Baroque painting of a knight astride his charger. The rich colors of the oils give the horse a sleek appearance, and the knight's armor shines brightly even in the dimly lit room. I start toward it to have a better look, but stop when my arcana surges to life, tingling over my skin.

That's when I see the figure pass the doorway, as though he had only just been looking in. He is far bulkier than any of the footman or the elderly butler I've seen as of yet. A cold dread settles in the pit of my stomach when I think of who it might be. Perhaps I had been foolish to have left the safety of the townhouse after catching sight of Wallace?

"I hope you are not wearing such a horrified look because of the painting," Lady Sotheby says, her tone slightly alarmed. She indicates the horse and knight. "It's been passed down in Lord Sotheby's family for many generations, but they say the knight died a rather brutal death. The eyes are far too real for my taste."

I force a smile. "Oh no, no. I quite like it, actually. It's just . . ." I war with my natural tendency toward honesty and how paranoid I'm likely to sound. "It's just I thought I saw someone lurking in the doorway, and it spooked me a bit is all. I'm sure it was only a footman."

"Heavens," Lady Sotheby says, glancing toward the doorway in question. "Or perhaps a guest who was lost? My footmen would certainly approach me had they a need."

"I'm sure you are right." I force myself to relax the tension from my shoulders. I must look like a scared cat! "Thank you for showing me this—I didn't have a chance to see the Monets when last I was at the National Gallery."

"It was my pleasure. Shall we return to our makeshift ballroom? Perhaps more gentlemen have arrived. I invited a dear friend of ours, Lord Richard Borough, who is quite a bit older than you, but he's always a delight to talk to, and I understand he'll be bringing a dear friend of his own."

"I do enjoy someone with the gift of conversation," I say, though my mind is still occupied with trying to convince myself Wallace isn't stalking me. "I hope you'll introduce us."

"Of course," she says, leading me back to the ballroom. "Oh, it seems they've already arrived. Richard!"

A tall, blond gentleman turns toward us at Lady Sotheby's call, but it's his friend beside him who makes my mouth go suddenly dry.

"Claire, wonderful to see you again," Richard says, and Lady Sotheby leans in to give him a kiss on either cheek.

"Richard, you must meet the Honorable Lucy Sinclair," Lady Sotheby says, turning to indicate me, but I can hardly tear my gaze away from Lord Alexander. "Miss Sinclair, may I introduce you to Lord Richard Borough?"

"How do you do," I say automatically, even as my heart races.

Richard turns to introduce us to Alexander, who smiles cautiously at me.

I stare shamelessly into Alexander's eyes and let him take my hand in his in greeting. Was it he who was watching us in the library? But almost immediately I dismiss the idea. The man I saw was far larger.

"So this is the lovely debutante you told me of, Alexander," Richard says with a warm smile. "My dear Miss Sinclair, I'm very glad to make your acquaintance."

"Heavens," Lady Sotheby says with raised eyebrows, "you already know each other? What a lark!"

"They know each other well enough for Alexander to talk of nothing else," Richard says.

I blush as a burst of surprised pleasure races through me, and I try to dampen my body's response. It cannot be merely coincidence that both Alexander and Wallace are here in Bath. Alexander's smile widens—he at least seems unembarrassed by his friend's admission.

"Might I have the next dance?" Alexander asks.

"That would be lovely," I say. As fate would have it, one dance ends and the next begins—a waltz.

Gloved hand in his, we begin the dance, and I stare at him, so dashing in his white tie and black tailcoat. I pray that my suspicions are wrong.

"I'm surprised to see you in Bath," I say finally, forcing myself to stop staring and act halfway intelligent.

"You must think me terribly forward, but I confess it was all rather innocent—an invitation from Richard to stay at his townhouse." He leans close. "Though I would be lying if I said knowing you were here didn't factor into my decision."

I smile weakly. My emotions war with one another: logically, it isn't a good sign that Alexander has showed up unannounced and unexpected when Wallace has done the same. What it means, though, is beyond me. And yet, I feel myself being pulled toward Alexander, like he is the moon and I am the tide . . . no matter how much I should guard my heart.

In the end, caution will win out. I didn't almost watch my sister lose her life to a member of the Order not to have learned that not everyone can be trusted.

"I've upset you," he says after a moment.

My gaze jumps to his. "Oh, no. At least, not in the way you think. It's only just . . ." I stop myself, weighing the consequences of telling him about Wallace. In the end, I want to see his reaction. "Do you know that gentleman we came across in the National Gallery—Lord Wallace, I believe?"

His whole body stiffens. "How could I forget?"

"Yes, well, I've seen him, and it's just that—"

Alexander abruptly stops dancing. "*Here?*" His gaze sweeps the room.

I give him a little tug to continue dancing, and he does so, thankfully. The last thing I need is to draw Colin's attention—or worse, James's. "Not here—at least, I don't think so—but in town. At the Royal Baths, in fact." The wary look on his face is enough to confirm my own fears, so I begin babbling. "We were there for a tour, and he rather made an impression on me—it was the intensity in his eyes, I think—so when I caught a glimpse of him, I was sure it was him, though I couldn't see his eyes—he was across the pool from where I stood."

"Lucy, I can't explain right now, but would you believe me if I said he was dangerous?"

My heartbeat thunders in my ears. "Yes."

"What did you mean by you didn't think you saw him here?"

"I thought I saw someone watching Lady Sotheby and me when we were in her library, but I'm sure it was nothing," I hasten to add when his face stills. "Another guest, perhaps . . . or a footman."

He looks as unconvinced as I feel. "And your sister and brother-in-law, have you told them anything?"

I shake my head. "What would I tell them? I hardly know myself."

"You should stay close to them—don't go off on your own, even if you have your friend with you."

"You're frightening me."

"Forgive me, I don't mean to. I only want to impart to you how dire the situation is. I'd like to explain, if only we could steal a moment alone—"

The waltz ends then, and we both hear approaching footsteps. Fully expecting Colin, I glance up at James in surprise.

"You aren't upsetting my sister-in-law, I hope?" James asks with deceptive lightness to his tone. His eyes, however, say something altogether different.

"James, don't be silly." I inwardly curse my expressive face. "We were only talking."

"That's not what it looked like to me," James says, his tone inching closer toward belligerent.

I glare daggers at James, wondering why the Thornewood men have to be so overbearing. Alexander, however, looks entirely unaffected by James's threatening behavior. "I would never intentionally upset Lucy."

"But you managed to anyway." James turns to me, giving Alexander the cut. "Will you dance the next dance with me?"

"No," I say, feeling a rush of satisfaction at the surprise on James's face. "Not after such bullying. Alexander and I have more to discuss."

"It's fine, Lucy," Alexander says. "Another dance with me is against the rules anyway, yes? I will seek out that painting you mentioned in the library and find you before the evening is over."

He gives James a cold once-over and then turns and walks away. Stiffly, I move into position for another waltz with my new partner.

"Why must you treat him so unkindly?" I ask the moment we are out of earshot of the other dancers. This time I school my features to have an outwardly polite smile, else I will quickly earn the reputation of being foul-tempered with all my dance partners. "You say it is not because of his background, but I cannot see why else you would take such an instant dislike to a perfect stranger."

"You cannot?" James says with a snort. "Because he's an arrogant prig, and he was clearly telling you something distressing. What could he have said during an innocent dance that could upset you so? More importantly, why is he *here*?"

My temper flares. "He's here because he's free to do as he wishes."

"Lucy, do not be coy. It doesn't suit you."

My eyes narrow, and my face flushes. "You needn't dress me down like I'm a child. I hardly think you need to be privy to our conversation."

He glances away like I slapped him, and I hate the resulting guilt. "You may be right, but you cannot deny it's suspicious that a man none of us have even heard of turns up at not only your invitation-only debutante ball, but in Bath of all places."

His words resonate within me like the tolling of distant bells. They are my own thoughts, but I'm too angry to concede. "He had an invitation to my ball—"

"His father's."

"He still had an invitation, and his friend, who is well known to our hostess, invited him to Bath. Coincidences, all."

"Hm. And he wasn't aware you'd be in Bath?" I fall silent, and he nods. "Will you tell them, or should I?"

I know he's right, and knowing it causes frustrated tears to prick my eyes. I can only imagine what Colin and Papa's reactions will be. Forbidding me to see Alexander again—at least until Colin can have his man investigate him—is a given, but I fear Colin will decide my whole Season has proven to be too great a risk.

"I'll speak to Wren tonight," I say tightly. "If you'll kindly refrain from speaking to your brother, I would appreciate it."

"Please don't be cross. I only want to look out for you."

Thankfully, the dance comes to an end, and I pull away from him angrily. "And what makes you think I cannot look after myself?"

I turn and stride away before he can answer, but not before his expression of surprised hurt embeds itself in my heart.

FIFTEEN

IN the motorcar on the way back to the townhouse, Wren can sense my stormcloud of a mood, but she is careful not to say anything to Colin. Instead, she uses our silent code: a subtle tilt of her head, eyebrows raised in question. I nod once to tell her we need to speak later.

"I'm embarrassed to say I'm still hungry," Wren announces. "Lucy, darling, will you keep me company while I have some tea when we return?"

"Of course," I murmur, my gaze sliding to my brother-in-law's face. He seems faintly amused, but says nothing. James and Rob are, thankfully, in the other motor, so I don't have to endure any of James's knowing looks—at least until we arrive home. I've had quite enough of them both since they refused to leave my side at the ball, preventing Alexander from talking to me further.

The motor rolls to a stop, and the chauffeur hurries around to open our door.

"I'm rather tired this evening," Colin says as we make our way toward the house. "Would you mind terribly, my love, if I turned in?"

"Not if you don't mind that I will be taking tea with Lucy in the library," Wren replies as the butler takes our wraps.

He shakes his head and gives her a kiss on the cheek. "Good night, then," he says.

We watch him walk up the stairs for a moment, and then Wren turns to me and loops her arm through mine. "Shall we talk?"

"I think we'd better."

"Hale, could you have tea brought to us in the library?"

"Yes, my lady," he says.

The fire in the library is still crackling cheerfully when we enter—no doubt Papa has only just gone to bed. I have that bone weariness that only comes from a night spent on my feet, but my mind is too agitated to relax. Instead, I stand before the fire.

Wren crosses the room to the chair closest to me and sits. "Will you tell me what has you so overwrought?"

"It's probably nothing, but I thought you should know. Also, James has threatened to tell you if I don't—not that I wouldn't have told you, of course . . ." I take a steadying breath. My words always tumble out of me erratically when I'm agitated. "When I accompanied Alexander to the National Gallery, a man interrupted us there—a hulking, intimidating sort of man. He made a sort of veiled threat toward Alexander and seemed to be much too interested in me, but he left soon afterward. The trouble is . . . I saw him here. In Bath."

Wren's face stills. Before she can respond, Hale enters with tea.

He must sense the tension in the room, for he sets the tray down and quietly leaves.

"When did you see him?" Wren asks, her voice deceptively calm.

I shift from foot to foot. "At the Roman Baths. And perhaps . . . perhaps tonight at the ball. But I'm not at all sure about that, so—"

"Lucy! Why did you not *tell* me?"

"Because I didn't want to upset you over nothing—I only had suspicions. I *still* only have suspicions. It's only that Alexander confirmed them tonight."

She wraps her hands around her still-full tea cup, her eyes sad. "It pains me to say this, darling, but I have my doubts about Alexander as well. I know you found him intriguing. It's only that his appearance here, and his connection to this man you speak of, is suspicious. We cannot be too careful, after all. I learned that particular lesson for us both."

My first reaction is to deny that Alexander could be anything like the man who nearly ruined Wren, but of course I don't *know* that—not for sure.

I can't know anything for sure. And Grandmother had said I would be in danger. . . .

"You're right—I will endeavor to be more careful. Truly."

"I know you will," Wren says with a kind smile. "So what shall we do about this? The moment I tell Colin, he will whisk you away to the country and keep you under lock and key—the Season be damned."

I meet her gaze. "I think I should try to contact Grandmother again."

Her eyes narrow. "I trust you mean our Sylvan grandmother."

"Yes, of course. It's only that . . . you had Mama's guidance during your debut, and I know Grandmother could do the same for me."

"I don't suppose the Roman Baths helped influence your decision."

"It may have, though I'm not saying I should do anything so drastic as crossing over." *Not yet anyway.*

She looks at me sharply. "You think it was a portal?"

"I only know that we both felt the arcana, but of course I couldn't say for sure—it was something else I wanted to ask Grandmother."

"Lucy, your talk of portals and crossing over is making me nervous." Before I can protest, she holds up a hand. "But I agree with you. You should reach out to Grandmother and see what she has to say. Perhaps she will know just how much danger you face, and we can respond accordingly."

My shoulders relax with relief. I don't know why I thought she'd fight me on it. "You won't tell Colin?"

"Not yet, but I won't be able to keep it from him forever. I have a condition, though. I'd like to be with you when you draw the runes. It'd make me feel better to know I was there if you needed me—if anything should go wrong. Even spiritually crossing over has consequences."

"That's a condition easily met. Thank you, Wren. Are you up for it tonight? I don't want to waste any time."

"Yes, but we should let Emily and Devi help us prepare for bed first—then we can be sure we won't be interrupted."

We make our way upstairs after ringing for our maids, and dread weighs my every step. What will Grandmother say about Alexander?

If he isn't to be trusted . . . I almost can't bear to know.

Dressed in satin nightgowns and robes, our hair loosely tied back, we sit cross-legged on the floor just as we used to as girls. To avoid waking

Colin—or alerting him if he is awake—Devi helped Wren change in my room. Wren and Colin have never even entertained the idea of separate sleeping arrangements, and to their credit, none of the servants blinked an eye about it. It makes me smile whenever I think of it, though, not only because it's terribly romantic, but because of how horrified it would make Grandmama. How Wren would love to shock her.

I'm glad I had the forethought to bring some of my drawings—including the one of the Himalayas. Fitting, it would seem, since I am hoping Grandmother will enlighten me as to Alexander's true character.

All that's needed now is a fresh rune. I draw it carefully, a rune of my own creation. It is a combination of the swirling eye that means "homeland" and the tipped hourglass that means "portal." I've practiced drawing them so many times that I make the marks in just a few motions.

"There will come a time when I can bring you along," I say, more as a promise to us both. I cannot shake the feeling of guilt that I will be able to see Sylvania and our grandmother again without Wren.

She smiles beatifically. "Have no care for me in that regard, Lucy. Was it not I who was able to read our mother's journal entries? It's only fair that you should be privy to a piece of Mama's legacy."

"How do you always know the very thing to say that will make me feel better?"

"Because I'm your elder sister, and it's my job. Now hurry up and touch your finger to that rune. I'm exhausted already."

I take a deep breath and do exactly as she suggests.

The first moment in Sylvania is always the hardest. Along with the out-of-body experience, I am thrust into a beautifully alien world, and my senses are pulled in so many different directions: the fairy-tale loveliness of the trees, the glimpses of creatures so much like our own deer and squirrels and hares, and yet so much more, the awesome sight of the city of Cascadia down below.

I follow the little trail of stones the fox—no, Rowen, I remind myself—showed me before. I scan the line of trees as I walk, searching for a glimpse of white. Before long, the wind picks up, and the trees around me murmur, adding a music of their own.

Half-princess, one says, and the word travels from tree to tree, until they all repeat it.

Seeks the Queen's aid.

This message travels, carried on the breeze. I pause in wonder to watch them, to turn that word over and over: half-princess. How could that be when my mother was effectively exiled?

I continue on the path, wondering if it will be Rowen who will find me first or Grandmother. I have no doubt they know I'm here, but my stomach twists as I fret whether or not they will come quickly.

I reach the top of the trail that overlooks the city, glittering against the backdrop of the mountains. The roar of the waterfalls is loud, even at this distance, and I can only imagine the sound up close.

All the hairs on my arms stand on end, and I look to the sky. A fiery bird soars through the clouds, its red and gold wings cutting through the mist. It is much bigger than I remember from my first visit, and for a moment, I'm struck with a douse of cold fear.

Suppose this isn't Serafino at all?

But then I see a truly amazing sight: an equally fiery-haired woman upon the bird's back. Her golden gown trails behind them as the bird banks and begins its descent toward me. He hovers in the air a few feet away, his powerful wings beating the wind into a frenzy.

Grandmother dismounts elegantly, and Serafino shrinks until he is the size of a large hawk again rather than a flying pony. He perches on a nearby branch, watching with sharp gold eyes. As Grandmother walks toward me, I see that her gown is rather unusually cut. The chiffon fabric separates down the center to allow ease of movement—and, I assume, ease of riding or flying—revealing legs clad in golden leggings. The dress's bodice is intricately tooled leather and seems as though it was molded to her skin. Grandmother's eyes are awash with concern.

"I'm so glad you've come, dearest one," she says, holding her hand out to me in welcome. If I hadn't heard from you in the next day, I was going to send Rowen after you with a message. You're in terrible danger."

My stomach sinks. It was one thing to suspect, but another to have it confirmed. "Am I truly being followed then? Has the Order found us again?"

Grandmother's expression takes on a faraway look. "The Order. It's been an age since I thought of them. They are largely the problem of mortal Sylvani in your realm—"

"Well, they nearly killed my sister," I say, rather more sharply than I intended.

"You think I did nothing to help Katherine," Grandmother says, her tone one of surprise. "Ah, but you are wrong."

Rowen steps forward from the shadow of the trees, and I can't think how I must have missed the soft glow of his snowy white fur.

It was the queen who lent me the arcana to transcend the barriers of the realms and appear to your sister—and to you.

I look at them both agape. "But I thought it was part of Mama's arcana?"

"Her runes allowed the connection, but I was the source of the power," Grandmother clarifies. "Rowen came to me when he felt Katherine reach out to him, and I did the only thing I could to help. You must understand, though," she says, her voice softening, "that the Sylvani tend to handle strife differently here. We believe it does the other Sylvani no good to coddle them—even kin. We leave most of our difficulties to our own ingenuity and fate. What I did was nearly tantamount to holding her hand, and yet I know you both would see it as though I'd barely lifted a finger."

"You're right—I don't understand," I say and take a deep breath, "but I'd like to."

She smiles approvingly.

"Does this mean I shouldn't expect any help from you?"

Her expression turns wry. "I said we treat the *Sylvani* this way, but you are half-mortal." Her expression turns serious. "I didn't mean to imply the Order wasn't dangerous; they are. And the only way for you to be safe is to learn to defend yourself using the weapons that can defeat them: your arcana."

Strangely, I think of James and his self-defense lessons. He'd been trying to impart the same thing upon me. "If you think there are skills I can learn—I've never thought of my arcana as lending itself to defense."

"Shall I show you what you are capable of?" she asks. Above her, Serafino beats his wings as if in anticipation.

I nod warily and take an unconscious step back as Grandmother raises her arms.

With rapid strokes, she draws a symbol into the air. It shimmers and burns before us—a golden rune like wings in the sky. An instant later, the hair on the back of my neck stands on end as electricity crackles around us.

Grandmother points to a nearby boulder, and a bolt of lightning comes down from the cloudless sky, cleaving it in two.

My mouth dry, I can only stare at the blackened halves of stone.

"Using your arcana to draw runes can be just as powerful as commanding the elements themselves," Grandmother says. "I will lend you my aid with two conditions: I will not fight your battles for you—only give you the skills you will need to fight them yourself."

"What's the other condition?" I ask, my eyes never wavering from the cleaved boulder.

"You must cross over physically to Sylvania. Only then will you be able to learn how to manipulate your arcana into a force powerful enough to take down the Order."

The same breathtaking fear takes hold of my chest as it did years ago when Wren was nearly forced to cross over to Sylvania. I thought I'd never see her again. Convincing Wren I should do the same would be difficult. "You said once before that I would be able to make the journey from my world to this one, but will I be able to return?"

For once, she looks taken aback. "Dearest one, of course. I'm afraid it's in staying that you will have the most difficulty—you must stay long enough to learn, but not so long that you begin to crave the arcana of this world."

"Is the arcana of Sylvania so very different than mine?"

"It is more powerful, and not bound by the whims of your sun."

I glance at the spirit animals behind her and am struck by a poignant longing. "What must I do? My physical body is in Bath, and both Katherine and I sensed the presence of arcana in the old Roman Baths there."

Grandmother nods thoughtfully. "It is another portal to our world, built long ago by another Sylvani who chose your world over this one. The ancient peoples there believed her to be a sun goddess and worshipped her for her power—her arcana."

I smile, pleased my instincts had been right. "I hope she was a benevolent one."

Grandmother's eyes smile back at me. "Yes, I expect she was. Now, listen closely, for we are running out of time. Your body cannot tolerate the separation much longer. You must go to the portal under the cover of darkness and go to the great pool. There you must cut your hand and let the blood drip into the water. You will feel the change in the air, the thrum of power, and you will see a glimpse of our world. When this happens, you must step through immediately. Rowen will be there to guide you."

A shiver of excitement dances down my spine, but at the same time, I wish Wren could be with me. But I will have to be strong and go on my own. Not only would it be unkind to Colin—for I'm sure he would fear for her every moment she was away—but Wren would never leave Izzie behind.

I glance back at Grandmother, a half-formed idea in my mind. "Is it possible for Katherine and the others to come, too?"

"No, dearest one. Your father and your sister's husband are mortal and unable to cross into our realm, and much as I'd like to see my great-grand-daughter, the risk of bringing her over at such a young age is too great. Her arcana is still developing. To expose her to the arcana of this realm could change her irrevocably."

Confusion and surprise make my response slow in coming. "Mortals—humans—cannot travel to this realm?"

She shakes her head. "Only those with Sylvan blood."

Then Lord Blackburn's threat was empty all those years ago—he could never have followed Wren through the portal.

"And now, my dear, you must hurry back before the strain on your body is too great," Grandmother says, her expression kind but firm. She takes my ghostly hand in hers, and I feel nothing. "I look forward to the moment when I can hold your hand in truth."

"As do I." Another burst of excitement fills me as we share a smile. "Until then."

"Do not waste your arcana—I'll send you back," Grandmother says and leans forward to press a kiss on my forehead.

The Sylvan world melts away.

☥

Do you really believe he'd be so brazen as to call on her?" Richard says beside Alexander in his motorcar. They had been sitting outside the rear of the Thornewood townhouse in Bath since the ball ended. Alexander hadn't had the chance to speak to Lucy again—at least, not about anything of consequence. James and her brother had made it clear, as they flanked either side of her and looked down on him with matching looks of disdain, that getting her alone was out of the question. He had gritted his teeth in frustration, but in truth, he hadn't yet decided how much to tell Lucy.

Only enough to convince her Wallace was a serious threat.

The memory of Nadi creeps into Alexander's mind, and his jaw tenses. "I won't take any chances, but try not to insult my intelligence, Richard. Why did you think I had you park the car at the rear of the house? I don't believe he'd waltz in the front door, but what would keep him from going through the servants' entrance?"

Richard smirks. "No need to be cross. I only wanted to see if you were up to snuff on your English etiquette."

Alexander's face relaxes into a grin. "I'm not completely an ignorant savage, you know. And I wasn't cross—merely on edge." His expression sobered. "Lucy won't suffer at Wallace's hands as Nadi did."

A tingle of electricity spreads over Alexander's body, so strong he winces at the sensation, though it's not exactly painful—only intense.

"What is it?" Richard asks.

"She's using spiritual power."

Richard starts to open his door. "Do you think she does so defensively? Could Wallace have already entered the house?"

Alexander shakes his head. "Hand me my sketchbook."

As soon as Richard does so, Alexander begins to draw rapidly: a fierce maiden upon a fiery bird in the sky, a city at the foot of a great mountain, ancient sentient trees.

"She's not in danger," Alexander says, wondering at the drawings on the blank white page. "Merely drawing."

"Should we call it a night then?"

"No—I want to keep watch a little longer."

The two men fall silent, letting the darkness swallow their thoughts. The only sound in the quiet car is that of their breathing and the faint ticking of Alexander's pocket watch. And then, light spilling out from the servants' entrance draws their attention.

Alexander sits up straighter, leaning toward the window with squinted eyes. Two hooded figures come through the doorway, and it's obvious even from here that they are ladies. Behind them strides a gentleman in a black overcoat, and Alexander cannot decide if it's Lord Thornewood or his younger brother who accompanies them.

"Not Wallace then," Richard says beside him as he, too, watches the three of them get into one of the chauffeured motors. "What's the plan?"

"We follow them," Alexander says.

SIXTEEN

THE Roman Baths are eerie at night: dimly lit and ghostly quiet. The shadows are long and dark—setting my nerves further on edge. Wren is quiet beside me as we make our way to the Great Pool, but I should be thankful she came at all.

James walks behind us, practically seething. He was wildly against our plan, but we knew it wouldn't be safe to leave the house unaccompanied—not with Wallace on the loose—and he was the first able-bodied man we came across. Rob, as usual, was out seeking out the best card tables, and Papa was tucked into bed with a book. I'd almost preferred Colin, but Wren and I both agreed James was the lesser of two evils.

It'd been hard enough convincing Wren.

"Why should we trust her?" Wren had demanded when I returned and breathlessly recounted Grandmother's advice and instructions. "We were betrayed by the grandmother we knew, why not the one who is a total stranger?"

I had responded with calm patience, which I'd learned at a young age was usually the best way of dealing with Wren's knee-jerk reactions. She almost always came around after being allowed to bluster for a moment.

"How can we be sure you'll be able to return?" she'd continued. "That you won't be changed forever?"

"All we have is her word, Wren," I'd said, "but you were given memories of her by Mama's own spirit animal. Do you think she is untrustworthy?"

Her face had flushed as she grasped for another argument. In the end, though, she'd let out her breath in a rush. "Very well. You win. But I insist on accompanying you—at least as far as the portal. Beyond that, I'm afraid I won't be able to follow." She'd grabbed hold of my arm then. "Lucy, darling, are you *sure* you want to do this? I could speak to Colin right now, and we could be on the next ship to America."

"I won't be chased away from my home, and I certainly won't drag all of you down with me," I had insisted.

Now, in the darkness of the Roman Baths, fear struggles to take hold, but as I stare down into the water, I feel breathless with both anticipation and lingering fatigue from crossing over spiritually to Sylvania.

Wren, on the other hand, with her face so drawn and tense, seems to feel nothing but apprehension. "You *will* return—you aren't playing the martyr and merely telling me this, right?"

I smile and gently grip her arm. "You are the martyr among us, Wren, not me."

"Surely there is another option." James tries his argument again, his face pale in the dim light. "Don't you think this is rash? What of your papa and Colin? They will be furious once they find out you've taken such an enormous risk without their knowing."

Guilt makes me wince when I think of Papa. He doesn't mention Rob, of course—my brother would probably be the only one to encourage me.

"And they'll come to the realization, just as we all did, that this is the best option for me—the *safest* option," I say.

"*We?*" James says. "I don't recall signing off on this mad venture."

"You're here, aren't you?"

"Hardly voluntarily," he grumbles.

"I only ask that you make sure Rose enjoys herself before you return—I hate that I'm abandoning her."

"You're abandoning all of us!" James says, but relents when I stare him down. "Yes, of course, we will show her a good time. You needn't even ask."

"We'll tell her you've come down with something in the night, and we don't want to expose her," Wren says, and I relax at the mention of her plan.

If Wren has gone so far as to create an alibi for me, then she clearly has no intention of stopping me at the last moment.

I throw myself into her arms as I have ever since I was small, and she hugs me back tightly. "Take care of yourself," she says thickly.

"I will. I love you, and I *will* come back," I vow.

She pulls back and wipes away her tears in frustrated motions—Wren hates to cry. I let my own tears fall freely. It's always been hard to separate myself from my sister, and I don't try to hide it.

I take a few steps closer to the water, close enough to feel the mist coming off it. Before I can retrieve the dagger, James takes hold of my hand and pulls me to him. As I glance up, his mouth descends on mine.

I stiffen in surprise before melting into his kiss. It's nothing like the first time. Gone is the gentle hesitancy, though this, too, is meant as a good-bye. This kiss is urgent, his strong arms keeping me flush against his firm chest.

We break apart after a moment—he panting, and I in a state of stunned awe. Tentatively, I touch my swollen bottom lip.

"Stay," he says, his eyes lingering on mine. "I can keep you safe."

For a moment, I'm tempted. But then I think of my grandmother's words: *I won't fight your battles for you.*

No one should have to fight my battles for me. I have as much Sylvan blood as my sister—I *need* to be able to defend myself.

"I have to learn to keep myself safe."

His jaw tenses, and it seems as though he will force me to come with them, but then he nods. "Come back to us, then." He touches a stray lock of my hair. "Come back to *me*."

I nod and blink back tears before finally pulling my dagger free. With a shaking hand, I touch the blade to my palm and make a quick slicing motion. My blood beads up easily, and I hold my clenched fist over the pool, allowing a few drops to spill into the water.

The moment the first drop hits, the arcana hits me like a strong, sudden wind. The more blood spills, the more powerful the arcana becomes, tingling across my skin as though I'd touched a live wire. The mist clears, and then I see it: the white columns of Cascadia. I can hear the roar of the waterfalls in the distance, the sound of the birds calling; I smell the sweet exotic scent of the trees.

I can wait no longer; I must walk through the portal. I glance back at Wren and James once more. The portal pulls me forward as surely as though I have a rope tied around my waist. I take one step into the pool.

Footsteps ring out.

I turn toward the source of the sound, and when I see the dark figures beyond James and Wren, I struggle against the portal's hold.

James steps in front of Wren. The portal won't release me; it's pulling me through, carrying me under like the tide. I cannot see anything beyond them. It's hazy now, like they stand in the eye of a storm. Fear washes down my back. Has Wallace found me?

James's face is murderous, and Wren looks wary. The next instant, a fight breaks out—James struggling against some unseen opponent. Wren disappears from my view, and whether she is under attack herself or has gone on the defensive is unknown.

I struggle all the harder against the portal. "Wren!" I try to scream, but I cannot make a sound.

A shadowed figure appears, disrupting the waves of arcana pouring from the portal. The pull on my body becomes unbearable, and the next instant, I'm weightless and traveling at an impossible speed, too fast for my senses to register anything beyond flashes of light,

And then suddenly—surprisingly gently—I land on solid ground.

But my legs cannot hold me. I crumple to the ground, utterly drained. The sun above radiates a pleasant warmth, but nothing else. The arcana I used to travel between realms has left me weak, and the sun here is as useless to me as the light of a lamp. More, the sheer power of the arcana around me—like the pressure of the sea after diving deep beneath a wave—feels like a physical weight upon my chest.

I try to lift my head to get my bearings, to call for Rowen or Grandmother, but I can only remain prostrate. That's when I hear it—the groan of someone beside me.

I manage to move my head just enough to see out of the corner of my eye: a gentleman lying miserably upon the ground, dressed in a black tailcoat.

With my senses so disoriented, I can hardly bring myself to care—to even summon a healthy dose of fear. But one thing is clear:

I did not travel through the portal alone.

Ѽ

ALEXANDER winces as he hears someone groan. For a moment, he thinks it might be Lucy, and he wills himself to fight against the powerful weakness keeping him pressed against the ground. When he hears the groan again, he realizes it's coming from him. He grits his teeth to stop himself, embarrassed at the complete lack of control he has over his body at the moment. Horribly, it reminds him of when he was a boy and had nearly died of whooping cough. The pressure on his lungs is the same, as is the total inability to even lift his head.

I survived that, he thinks, *surely I can survive a trip to another world.* The thought is so ridiculous, of course, that he nearly laughs—or at least he would if he could do anything other than feel the soft, fragrant grass beneath his cheek.

He'd never intended to cross through the portal. The very existence of such a thing in Bath had shocked him, though he could feel the prana emanating from the place the moment he had set foot inside the Roman Baths.

But when he saw Lucy suspended above the water like some ancient goddess, he'd taken a step toward her as if in a trance, ignoring the very irate James Wyndam. Alexander's uncanny reflexes were all that kept him from being punched square in the jaw. Alexander had ducked and swung around him, and before he'd quite made up his mind, had jumped into the Great Pool after her.

It was possibly the most foolish decision he'd ever made in his life, and Richard, left behind to deal with both James and Lady Thornewood, would likely kill him the moment he returned—*if* he returned.

It'd been a long time since anyone had mentioned a portal to Sylvania to him, and really, Alexander had always had his doubts. He knew the Sylvani came from there, of course, but he always thought of it as a one-way trip. But as the powerful spiritual power in the air keeps him flat against the ground, he has to concede that he isn't in England any longer.

Instead of fighting the terrible pressure of the spiritual power, he decides to try a different tack through controlled relaxation. He methodically goes through each of the muscles in his body, relaxing each one while simultaneously taking deep breaths. By the time he reaches the muscles in his calves, his head feels clear enough to risk sitting.

The moment he pushes himself up and takes his first look around, he feels as though the breath is stolen from his lungs. The beauty and *otherness* of the landscape around him is astounding—from the trees and plants of such unusual color combinations that they hardly seem real, to the smells— like roses and hibiscus and lemon and verbena and yet none of those things, but rather a smell he's never encountered before. He hears the roar of a waterfall in the distance and feels the warm sun upon his face, the soft breeze ruffling his hair.

Then, suddenly, the landscape is alive with other sounds: sounds of the imminent approach of others. Panicked, Alexander wills himself to stand. Lucy is not far from him, lying in a small heap upon the ground, no doubt as weak as he.

"Lucy," he says, his voice coming out in a pathetic whisper.

He stumbles to his feet in a sheer burst of will, taking deep, restorative breaths. If not for his training, he wouldn't have found the strength to fight the pressure of the powerful spiritual power all around him. The more he opens himself up to it, the more he can sense the sources of it: the ancient trees, the grass and earth beneath him, the stones, the mountains and waterfalls in the distance. And of course, the Sylvani hurrying toward them.

Movement draws his attention to the skies, and his whole body stills. A massive firebird soars above him, its wings the many colors of a sunset.

But it's not the bird itself so much as its rider that ensnares Alexander in an awe-struck stupor: a woman with Lucy's eyes and mouth and hair so red and gold it looks like fire. The bird dives, and the woman's eyes narrow, piercing and threatening all at once.

Before Alexander can dive out of the way, the bird stops, its powerful wings buffeting Alexander and Lucy with wind.

So distracted by this awesome display, Alexander doesn't notice the advance of the other Sylvani until the sound of many men shifting in armor draws his attention away from the bird and the queenly rider.

Behind him stand twenty men and women dressed in armor so bright it's like platinum. Runes and knotwork are engraved in the metal, and each soldier carries a three-headed spear. But it's the enormous white wolves at their sides that exacerbate the fear already gripping Alexander's chest.

Both the soldiers and wolves stand at attention, watching the woman in the sky. She remains astride the bird, her green eyes fixed on Alexander's. With the armed soldiers and wolves at his back, and the obviously aggressive regal lady before him, Alexander suspects he may be in serious danger, though he does not yet know his offense. Still, his back is straight, his gaze unwavering.

A strange, sharp pain begins at the back of his head, quickly spreading to the front, until sweat beads at his brow. It increases in intensity as the lady's green gaze remains on Alexander's, and his hands clench into fists in pain. A torrent of memories flashes through his mind, things he never even knew he remembered: his mother singing to him as a baby of distant lands with tears in her eyes, the dark night after her burial, the many conversations he'd had with Lord Tyrell.

As suddenly as it had come, the pain stops. Alexander slowly unclenches his fists, though his attention never leaves the lady before him. He knows the memories were connected to the pain, and he knows neither of those things were coincidental.

"Arrest him," the lady says, and Alexander's fear becomes a metallic taste on his tongue. He pushes it away and resists the urge to fight or flee. Neither will save his skin.

"What is my crime, lady?" Alexander calls out to her.

She holds up a hand to the advancing soldiers. "Your crime is treason. You are a member of the brotherhood known as the Order of the Eternal

Sun, which has made itself an enemy of my granddaughter and her family. Thus," she says with a truly frightening smile, "you are an enemy of the Queen of Cascadia."

Her gaze shifts to Lucy, who has managed to stir but not yet speak, and his quick mind fills in the pieces. This woman who looks so much like Lucy is her kin, obviously a Sylvani queen, which means Wallace and Richard have been right all along.

Lucy is Sylvan.

SEVENTEEN

No! I try to scream when my grandmother's soldiers take hold of Alexander. Their wolves flank him ominously, and as they do, silver shackles appear, binding his hands and feet by long chains.

Grandmother must have thought he was Wallace after all I'd told her, and in my cursed weakened state, I couldn't tell her otherwise. I struggle wildly in my mind, but my body refuses to obey. Lifting my head has been the most I've managed to accomplish. I feel like I'm submerged beneath a turbulent sea—the very air filled with enough pressure to keep me on the ground. How Alexander has managed to stand, I don't know—though perhaps it's only I who feel the terrible press of arcana.

With sheer force of will, I push myself to my knees. "Stop, please," I manage weakly, but the soldiers take him away unheedingly.

Grandmother dismounts Serafino agilely and comes to me side. "Dearest one, I'm so sorry. I knew the transition to our world would be difficult for you, but I'm afraid neither of us was prepared for quite how debilitating it would be." Her gaze shifts to the retreating soldiers. "Rowen," she calls to the little fox waiting nearby, "will you come lend Lucy your aid?"

The fox pads over to my side and presses his soft fur against my leg. A burst of energy fills me, as though I'm finally breaking the surface of the sea, as though I stand in a beam of sunlight. I take deep, restorative breaths and get to my feet.

"You will need Rowen during your brief stay here," Grandmother says with a sympathetic look in her eyes. "Our sun is not your sun. It will not restore your arcana, but Rowen, as an unattached spirit animal, is the perfect solution."

Before I can address my many questions to the fox at my side, I jump to the most pressing matter. "Grandmother, that man you arrested, he's not the one I was afraid of. You must call your soldiers back, for I fear you've made a grave mistake."

The look in her eyes is one of deep regret. "I know who he is. Many times have I felt his presence attached to your arcana. I have seen the path he has chosen: he is a member of the Order of the Eternal Sun."

I feel all the color drain from my face. Every sound becomes muted until all I can hear is the throb of my own heartbeat. "No, it's Wallace who's part of the Order," I say. Tears sting my eyes.

You've always suspected, my mind whispers, and I squeeze my eyes closed as if I can block it out.

"This man you call Wallace is undoubtedly part of the Order as well," Grandmother says, not unkindly, "but the gentleman who followed you through the portal is, too."

My head jerks up at that. "Followed me through the portal . . . but I thought only those with Sylvan blood could travel between realms?"

She inclines her head, letting me come to my own conclusions.

"But . . . *why*? How could he be part of an organization that seeks out his own kind?"

"Perhaps he doesn't know," Grandmother says in a tone that suggests she knows the answer.

"How could he not?" I ask, but then I think of his family history—his mother dead when Alexander was a child, his absent English father . . .

"Later we will interrogate him," she says and I find myself grasping at that desperately. Yes, we will speak to him, and there will be an explanation for this, something that exonerates him from all blame . . . something that doesn't involve him belonging to the very brotherhood that means me harm. "For now, come, the hour is late in your world. You should rest—unless you'd care to eat first?"

I shake my head. "No, I'm afraid my appetite is quite absent, but I'll admit that rest would be welcome."

Who is Alexander? How could I let myself be so taken in? It is clear now that he followed me through the portal.

My mind chooses that moment to remind me of everything that transpired just before I crossed over, and I freeze. The kiss with James . . . the fight . . . Alexander crossing over alongside me. Are Wren and James all right?

As though sensing my distress, Rowen presses against me again. *The queen and I saw everything the moment you opened the portal. Your sister and her brother-in-law did not come to harm.*

Thank you, Rowen, I think to him, my shoulders drooping with relief, and he nods.

It's nice to feel useful again.

Grandmother walks to one of the ancient trees and touches its smooth, silver bark. With her head bowed and her eyes closed, her lips move but I cannot hear her words.

A whisper travels through the trees, the branches swaying and leaves fluttering as though in a strong breeze. The fine hairs on my arms rise as I sense a change in the arcana around us. And then two creatures step out of the trees' shadows.

The closest animal I can compare them to I've only seen in books on Africa: an antelope, though these are drastically different in both coloring and size. Both are a dappled silver, and their massive backward-facing horns are as white as ivory tusks. They are as tall as horses, and their eyes are kind and intelligent.

Grandmother walks up to one and gently strokes its nose. "These are oryx. They will carry us to the city below. Can you ride?"

I watch her with wide eyes. "I can ride *horses*, but . . ." I trail off as she grabs hold of one of the oryx's horns and swings astride. It prances in place, as if eager to be off.

The queen prefers the oryx *when not flying on Serafino. You will soon see why,* Rowen tells me, amusement clear in his eyes.

I approach the beautiful animal cautiously. Wren would adore them instantly, and probably be a natural rider, but I am not as skilled. I hold out my hand, and the oryx snuffles it gently.

"You must forgive me if I don't have a proper seat," I say, and it bobs its head, drawing a small laugh from me.

It lowers its horns, and I take hold of one as I watched Grandmother do. With a toss of its head and an awkward jump from me, I swing onto its narrow back. I pick up its silver reins, unsure what to do next.

"You're doing a fine job," Grandmother says encouragingly. "But you might relax your limbs and straighten your spine."

I realize I've been perched there like I fear being thrown at any moment and force myself to do as she suggests.

Grandmother nods approvingly. "Rowen, will you join Lucy? Lend her the arcana needed to bind her to her oryx."

Rowen leaps onto my mount lithely and settles into my lap like a cat. His arcana flows into me like warm sunshine. Soon, I feel the beating of my mount's heart through my legs, the soft warmth of his sides, the strength of his back. It becomes difficult to determine where his body begins and mine ends.

I smile in wonder as his thoughts trickle into my mind: how proud he is to be transporting the queen's granddaughter, the simple happiness of being useful, and the thrill of . . .

My head jerks up as I shoot a frightened glance at Grandmother. "Oh, but surely—!"

"Let's be off," she says with a smile and a pull of the reins.

Her oryx bounds away and mine immediately follows, his gait springy and breathtakingly fast. They approach the edge of the cliff that overlooks the city of Cascadia, and before I can suck in a breath to scream, we plummet over the edge.

I squeeze my eyes shut, but the wind wrenches them open again. The oryx's sharp hooves hit an outcropping of rock and spring away just as quickly. Only by the power of arcana do I stay on his back—the same arcana that keeps Rowen from flying out of my lap—as the oryx jumps from rock to rock, the city growing larger as we approach.

I risk a glance at Grandmother, and she's smiling widely as she leans back, keeping her center of gravity aligned with her oryx's. Serafino soars above us, back to his more compact size. Soon the rush of the waterfalls distracts me from our controlled plummeting, and I hold my breath in wonder.

The city shines like marble in the sun, no fewer than ten waterfalls cutting through the foundations of the buildings. The architecture reminds me of the Renaissance style, with dome roofs, eye-pleasing symmetry, and ornate columns. At the same time, it is rather organic, seeming to emerge directly from the rock, as though the mountain had grown a city. Though not all white-washed—the city is bursting with color, a riot of flowers and trees lend their beauty to pale stone in pinks and oranges and lavender. There are flowers I've never seen before—flowers so vibrant my eyes squint when I look at them, and so fragrant that I can smell them from here.

My oryx leaps one last time and trots over to the entrance of a wide stone bridge. Below us rushes the water from the waterfalls, sparkling like diamonds in the sun.

Grandmother dismounts, and I do the same. When my knees threaten to give out, I grab hold of the oryx's horn for balance. Rowen comes to my aid again, pressing close and allowing arcana to flow into me.

"What would I do without you?" I ask the fox with a sheepish grin.

"I'd love to give you the grand tour," Grandmother says, "but I'll show you to your room instead so you can rest."

The adrenaline from my frightening trip down the mountainside fades and fatigue sets in. "A pity, for I should love to see it all, but I know you are right."

She touches the oryx's neck and whispers a few words in another language. With a little snort, it bobs its head, and the bridle and reins disappear. She does the same to my oryx and both creatures incline their heads toward us before bounding off.

"Are all the animals here so intelligent?" I wonder aloud.

Grandmother smiles. "They are as they were in your world once, when man had no need of arcana to communicate with them." She gestures for me to follow and we cross the bridge toward the beautiful city. "Rowen will remain with you while you sleep to be sure your arcana does not fall to dangerously low levels."

I glance down at the fox gratefully. "And this won't change the way I use arcana? Here, or when I return?"

There is always that risk. We must take care to monitor your arcana at all times.

We fall silent as we approach the grand entrance to what can only be described as a castle. Sentinels with their white wolves guard either side, standing at attention as their queen passes through. I gaze up at the enormous doors—truly big enough to admit giants—and ornately carved with knotwork and runes. A rising sun shines at the pinnacle of the doorway, and by its glint, I think it may truly be gold.

But as we enter the castle, I realize just how foolish it was to stand and gawk at the doorway when such splendor awaits inside. The foyer is big enough for several carriages to fit inside with room to spare—the ceiling so high I have to crane my neck back to see the top. The floor is like white marble, only with shimmering gold veins that catch the light. Through it all runs a brook, which continues on and disappears through a hallway wide enough to pass three carriages abreast. I can only assume it ends in one of the waterfalls.

The hall is lit by countless floating orbs, their light as golden as the sun. Serafino flies ahead of us and lands on a white-barked tree sprouting from the middle of the foyer, its purple leaves hanging down like a willow tree. Massive paintings cover the walls in gilded frames featuring subjects I have only seen in mythology: a dragon soaring over a forest of unicorns, a harnessed gryphon perching in a tree above a cascading waterfall, its rider standing beside him, helmet in hand.

Grandmother leads me up a grand, spiraling staircase, and I continue to stare enviously at the paintings as we climb. Rowen stays quietly by my side, his energy becoming more and more familiar. When we reach the top, though, I come to an abrupt halt, my heart beating in my ears. Gently, I reach out and touch a painting, as though I could reach inside it.

It's a portrait of my grandmother holding what must be my mother as a baby. They are in a garden full of flowers of every color and more of the wisteria-like trees. The image of my mother holds me captive; even then, her eyes speak of the wisdom of the woman the infant will grow into. A baby snow fox curls at her side as Serafino watches from a branch above them.

"Later, dearest one," Grandmother says gently. "We will seek out every painting in the castle if that is your wish."

I follow her reluctantly, curiosity warring with my body's desperate need for sleep. This world has taken its toll on me, making every step heavy and slow.

We pass other lovely things—vases and more artwork and statues that look like angels—before finally arriving at ornately carved white doors.

Grandmother sends me a secret smile as she pushes the doors open. "I thought you might like to stay in your mother's rooms."

The sweet smell of flowers greets me the moment I step into the room—like peonies and roses—and I quickly find the source: robin's egg-blue vases overflowing with bright pink blooms. My feet sink into a thick cream and gold–colored rug, but before I can sigh luxuriously, my attention has already been diverted by the wall of bookcases.

"Oh," I say ineloquently as I run my hand along the edge of one of the jewel-toned leather spines.

"Tomorrow," Grandmother says with a smile in her voice, pushing me gently along to the next room—the bedroom.

My mother's room opens over the waterfalls, and all four doors—to her two balconies—are open wide to admit the warm sunshine, soft breeze, and the soothing roar of the water. *My mother once stood here*, I think as I look out over the waterfalls and the rest of the gleaming white city. It's a bittersweet sort of pain to see Mama's world, to stand in her footsteps, and I turn back to the room before the lump in my throat can devolve into tears.

The room is dominated by a large four-poster bed, the wood carved with knotwork in the most unusual color. I touch it to be sure it isn't paint.

"It's from the amethyst tree," Grandmother says. "The wood is dark purple in color."

"It's beautiful," I say and run my hands over the thick, downy coverlet. White with silver embroidery, it complements the furniture perfectly. "And this is divinely soft."

Grandmother smiles nostalgically. "Well, it should be. A bed could never be made plush enough to suit your mother, but we did our best."

I smile back, pleased at this small anecdote I never knew about Mama.

A knock at the door comes, and a girl with hair like black waves down her back enters. She's dressed in a white high-collared tunic and form-fitting breeches, the fabric shimmering like satin.

"This is Astrid," Grandmother says, and the girl places a hand across her chest and bows. "She'll be your handmaiden during your stay."

"It's a pleasure to meet you," I say truthfully.

Her answering smile is kind. "And I you, my princess. We've been waiting a long time for the chance to meet the children of Princess Isidora."

"Oh," I say in a surprised sigh of breath.

Astrid glances worriedly from me to Grandmother. "Have I said something wrong?"

I shake my head. "No, no. I'm a bit overwhelmed is all—I haven't quite wrapped my mind around the fact that my mother was a princess here."

"The fairest one I've ever known," Astrid says with a sad smile. "If you'll excuse me, my princess, I'll fetch a nightgown for you."

She strides away, her movements lithe and graceful—otherworldly, really. Like Grandmother. Like Mama.

"She was Isidora's handmaiden," Grandmother says when Astrid disappears into the adjoining dressing room. "It was hard on us all when your mother left." She reaches out and takes my hand. "But I understand why she did."

I glance down at Rowen, another who was abandoned by Mama for me and for my siblings, and swallow a lump of guilt.

"I'll leave you now to rest," Grandmother says. "Sleep as long as you like. It's best to begin your training with an able body and mind."

She turns to go, but I reach out to her. "Grandmother, if I may ask . . . where will Alexander—that is, the man who crossed through the portal with me—be taken?"

Her lips press together in an expression of regret. "Are you sure you wish to be troubled with knowing such a thing, dearest one? Why not focus instead on the happier parts of today?"

"I'd rather know."

"This castle is meant to be a fortress if the city were ever taken. And like most castles I'm sure you're familiar with in your world, it has a dungeon. This is where we hold any of our subjects who have committed the worst sort of crimes—like treason."

The word resonates within me. *Treason,* so very similar to betrayal. How could I have been so foolish? How had I not known he was a member of the Order?

"Any act of aggression against the royal family is considered treason," Grandmother continues, "and he is of Sylvan blood—no matter how diluted."

"I think—I should like to speak to him."

Grandmother's hard look is replaced by one of sympathy. "You may speak to him, if you insist. But it will keep until tomorrow."

I swallow hard, my eyes burning from unshed tears and too many emotions crashing over me at once. "Tomorrow then."

Grandmother gives my hand another squeeze before slipping out of the room.

I glance down at Rowen as Astrid returns with a long, silky nightgown to wear.

Not all hope is lost, Rowen says.

I nod, though all I feel is the crushing sense that everything I ever thought I felt toward Alexander was wrong.

He was my enemy all along.

☥

ALEXANDER runs a hand over the shimmering white wall of stone. It surrounds him on all sides; even the door through which the sentinels entered faded away again the moment they left. High above him, glowing orbs cast soft light in the windowless space. The room is without furniture, without even a blanket with which to sleep. When he closes his eyes and reaches out with his prana, he feels nothing. Not the faintest hint of the energy the Sylvani call arcana, nor any sense of Lucy's own power.

Arcana, he reminds himself. *Lucy is Sylvan. Her energy is beyond mere mortal prana.*

His hand drops away from the wall. He was a fool to think there was a chance Lucy wasn't Sylvan—when all the signs pointed to it. The Sylvani were beings capable of great evil, immortal creatures who thought nothing of killing a young boy's mother. But Alexander had convinced himself that Lucy was different. That Lucy couldn't have been Sylvan.

He was wrong.

And now he will likely be killed for his mistake.

Had he been wrong about Nadi? Had the girl who used her prana to weave beauty into cloth been a killer in disguise?

He remembers every one of the men and women he'd found for Lord Tyrell. The ones with an abundance of spiritual power—the ones suspected to be Sylvan. There haven't been many—only seven in the fifteen years he's been searching for them. All seven used their powers for evil, or if not evil, then at least personal gain: a hired killer; a seducer of rich, married women; a woman who was able to change the way she looked and who married man after man, killing each one; another who was such an accomplished thief that others just handed over their money; others who had profited from their abilities, amassing huge riches. And not a single one of them was the man he was truly looking for—the man who killed his mother.

But Nadi had been different. No matter how much he searched, he could find no sign that she was anything other than a good person. Poor, from a lower caste family, and the only daughter of parents who were servants to a wealthy merchant. She sold her saris to bring in extra money for her family.

Alexander's task had always been to use his excess of prana to find others with an abundance of spiritual power. With each new lead, he'd been filled with fervor, hoping *this* time he'd find the man who took his mother from him. So he'd seek them out, discover everything there was to know about them, and then bring them to Tyrell to be dealt with.

Alexander's jaw tightens as he stares at the wall. It wasn't until Nadi that Alexander felt the first inkling of doubt. He knew Tyrell had the Sylvans drained of all their power. Alexander never questioned it, and whether he was willfully ignorant or simply naive, he couldn't say. But he hadn't known draining them would end in them dying. He had stupidly thought their power was being harnessed for something good.

But then he found Nadi gray and lifeless, and that was when he'd begun to doubt.

He grips his head in his hands. Even thinking these thoughts feels like the worst sort of betrayal, though they've been whispering in his subconscious for months.

Unbidden, an image of Lucy smiling secretly at Alexander fills his mind, and his body tenses.

The worst of it was . . . he may have doubted, but if he had found anything suspicious with Lucy, he would have turned her over.

His physical reaction to her be damned.

EIGHTEEN

I awaken to the sound of birdsong and the roar of the waterfalls. A gentle breeze flutters the sheer draperies, bringing with it the clean smell of the water below. From the light pouring in, I'd say I've slept clear through to the next day. I sit up, pleased to see I feel refreshed rather than groggy from all that sleep. As I glance around the room—*Mama's* room—I see Rowen sitting in the doorway with his tail curled around his legs, gazing out toward the waterfalls.

As beautiful as the scene is, it also pierces my chest with sadness. This must be what my mother saw when she awoke, and how terribly I miss the woman I only remember in pieces. Small things will trigger my memories: the smell of lavender reminding me of her perfume (though now that I am in this exotic place, I wonder if that might be how she naturally smelled), a single note can bring forth a torrent of memories of her enchanting music, and the feel of a brush running through my hair—our nightly ritual. But I do not have as many memories as Wren and Rob do, though they have told me the stories so many times they have almost become my own.

Just as my nostalgia grows too great to bear, a soft voice interrupts my thoughts. "May I help you dress, my princess?"

Astrid stands in the doorway to the sitting room. She is dressed much the same as she was yesterday, only she wears a headband of silver leaves in her hair.

I smile gratefully. "How did you even know I was awake? Or have you been checking on me to be sure I was still alive? I cannot believe I slept so long."

A small laugh escapes her. "It's understandable to need rest when you travel between realms. But to answer your question, I have very good hearing—so good, in fact, that I have had to learn to block out most sounds, else I will hear the sound of someone breathing in the dungeon far below us."

I stiffen. The dungeon, where surely Alexander has spent a miserable night.

Good.

My mind had threatened to swallow me with worries—most notably, how had I let myself become so easily deceived?—but the exhaustion of traveling to another realm had won out. Now, clear-headed and fully awake, it all comes rushing back: Grandmother's guards surrounding Alexander, my fear for him turning to shock, the horror of realizing his true identity. For I've been a fool all along. I was afraid of what Wallace might do, while all the while, I was dancing with his compatriot. It sickens me that I've been betrayed.

For to be betrayed, I had to have believed him in the first place.

Astrid returns from the wardrobe with an outfit, and I am grateful for the interruption of my thoughts. "But mostly I can hear you're in desperate need to break your fast."

My stomach rumbles in response, and I press a hand to it as if to silence it. "I am rather hungry," I say as though we both didn't just hear my stomach's loud protest.

She holds up the emerald frock in response, and I see that it isn't a dress in the style I'm used to. Rather, it's cut in the same way that Grandmother's was when I arrived: a tight-fitting bodice with a cut-away chiffon skirt over breeches. It looks terribly daring and exotic. How Wren would love to wear such a thing.

I throw my legs over the side of the bed and stand, grasping the bedpost for balance. A day of sleep and no food or drink has made me lightheaded.

Astrid helps me out of the floor-length satin nightgown she'd given me yesterday, and then in no time at all, fastens me into the beautiful emerald green frock. The bodice is like a second skin, secured in the back with countless hook-and-eye closures. But much to my surprise and pleasure when I take a deep breath, I can actually breathe in it—unlike a corset. It's heavily embroidered with a swirling vine-like pattern of gold thread. The skirt is constructed of an airy chiffon, with golden threads that catch the light as I turn.

Astrid helps me into the breeches, and then I look at my reflection in the mirror with wide eyes. I've never been one to ride much—not like Wren and Rob—and so this is far more of my legs then I've ever seen. Soft leather slippers complete the ensemble, much like the ones Astrid wears, only gold.

The whole thing would be terribly scandalous in my world—my arms, décolletage, shoulders, and legs far too much on display—and yet, something about the outfit bespeaks royalty. I turn this way and that, puzzling over it. The lines, I decide. The tailored cut and the way the skirt billows out behind me like a robe.

"You look just as a princess should," Astrid says, smiling at me in the mirror. She runs a silver brush through my hair and pins it away from my face with golden hair combs. When I turn my head, I see a great soaring bird set in rubies on each comb. When Astrid catches me examining them, she says, "The queen's crest."

"Oh, I see it now. They look just like Serafino."

"The spirit animals of kings and queens become their emblems, for we believe the animal itself is the best representation of the person's soul." She glances fondly at her own owl perched on my wardrobe.

"Fascinating," I murmur, my fingers itching to draw all that I've learned.

Astrid makes a few more adjustments to the golden combs in my hair and leaves the rest in waves down my back, which must be the style here. She stands back to admire the results and nods approvingly.

"Thank you, Astrid—truly, this is lovely. I'm not used to dressing in such a way, but I adore what you've done. I love the freedom of movement, too—and being able to properly draw in a breath!"

"The clothes you arrived in *did* seem rather restrictive," she says with a smile, "but should you ever have need of them, you'll find them in your dressing room."

We hear a light knock on one of the outer doors of the sitting room, and then the door opens to reveal another Sylvani with a kind face and light hair dressed similarly to Astrid. She carries a tray from which the smells of delicious food waft into the air.

"The queen will be here soon," Astrid says as the other girl sets the tray upon a table in the sitting room, "but she thought you'd like to fortify yourself before seeing the rest of the castle."

"How thoughtful," I say, for she's right—the moment I left this room, I'd be consumed with exploring, hungry or not. As it is, it's hard to tear my gaze away from the books now that I've entered the sitting room. When I get a proper look at the food, though, I sigh with pleasure. "This looks divine!"

The girl with the tray beams, and a small, ferret-like creature crawls onto her shoulder to peer down at me. It, too, seems to be watching me with satisfaction as I take a sip of first the crystal glass of sparkling water and then the steaming cup of tea. Both are delicious—sweet and refreshing.

"This is Fianna," Astrid says, and the girl makes a short bow, "and her spirit animal Sophocles." The ferret's nose twitches at me merrily, and I smile.

"A pleasure to meet you both. Thank you for bringing me such a lovely spread."

Laid out before me is an array of fruits and cheeses, sweet-smelling breads, and pastries. I note a curious lack of meat, but as I gaze around at the three spirit animals in the room, I rather suspect why.

"If you need anything else at all, my princess," Fianna says, "you need only let Astrid know, and she will send for me."

With another bow, she leaves, and I waste no time trying every bit of food on my tray. I try a fruit as purple as an eggplant that tastes like honey and cinnamon; something else the color of a lime but with the texture and taste of a carrot; and the bread . . . the bread is so light and flaky it melts instantly in my mouth, yet is filling and satisfying at the same time. But even these delicious flavors cannot distract me completely.

I want to know the truth.

The thought makes me desperate to speak to him, but at the same time, icy prickles of fear take up residence in my stomach.

I want to know if he intended to drain my arcana just as Wren's was almost completely taken from her.

I drop the flaky piece of bread I'd been enjoying, my appetite suddenly waning. "Astrid," I say hesitantly, "you will think me mad, I'm sure, but do you think I might go and see him? There are things I'd like to say to him . . . to find out from him, you see . . ." I trail off before I start to go on and on.

Astrid's expression is sympathetic. "I'm afraid only the queen can take you."

"Oh, yes, of course," I say, trying rather unsuccessfully to hide my disappointment.

"But I do know she intends for you to speak to him today," Astrid adds, and I glance up hopefully. "She told me so herself."

I force down the desperate urge to interrogate Alexander. I must be patient. "Forgive me. Then I shall say nothing else about it."

Cup of tea in hand, I walk to the bookshelves, which have been calling out to me since the moment I laid eyes on them. I touch the jewel-toned spines, wondering which were my mother's favorites. After a moment, my gaze lands on a thick book the color of amethyst. I gently pull it free and find an unfamiliar golden rune stamped into the leather. When I open it, the smell of lavender rushes out and I close my eyes. *Mama.*

But it's the pages within that make me gasp with surprised pleasure. In vibrant colors and gold are elaborate designs and illustrations like that of a medieval tome. The first page is of a small unicorn, its legs curled beneath it, surrounded by curling vines with riotous flowers. The vines continue down the page, creating a border for the text.

I only wish I could read it! I can pick out a rune here or there, but not enough to understand the story.

Astrid must sense my confusion for she comes and peers over my shoulder. "You've found your mother's favorite," she says, her tone just a touch sad.

"I'm afraid I can't read the runes," I admit.

"You're in luck, then. Run your finger over the lines of text."

I give her a curious look but do as she asks. Instantly, the runes shimmer and blur before turning into English before my eyes. I laugh in delight. "*The Dragon and the Unicorn,*" I read.

She nods. "It's the story of a dragon prince falling in love with a unicorn maiden. It was once a children's tale, but this particular version is more about forbidden love."

"Mama always was terribly romantic," I say, though of course I don't know this from my own interactions with her—just from stories Papa and my siblings have told me. Is that how the Sylvani see love between mortals and their own people?

I turn to the next page with more beautiful illustrations—this time of a dragon hatchling—but before I can examine the drawings or the text, a firm knock comes at my outer door.

Grandmother enters, dressed impeccably in an ensemble similar to mine—only with tall leather boots. She grins at me, the look almost girlish with delight. "I trust you slept well?"

I smile back just as warmly. "I did, of course. I'm sorry to have slept nearly the entire time I've been here. It's shameful when you think about it."

She shakes her head, the soft lighting glinting off her sunset hair. "No indeed. Your body needed time to adjust. It's exhausting work, traveling between worlds." Her eyes shift to the book in my hands. "I see you've found your mother's books. I'm sure that one practically screamed for you to pick it up."

I look down at the book and then back at her in surprise. "It did, actually. I wanted to find a book that was one of her favorites, and this one seemed to call out to me."

"Our books tend to do that here. They have minds of their own."

I start to laugh but then realize she's serious. "Heavens," I say.

She turns and gestures toward the tray of food—what's left of it, anyway. "Did you find our food to your liking?"

"Oh, yes," I say eagerly. "In fact, I fear I will very much miss it when I return."

"Then we will have to send some along with you. I hope you've eaten your fill because there is much to attend to today. In fact, I'm afraid we'll have to postpone our tour of the castle, if you don't mind—though I tried to contain the news of your arrival, I couldn't prevent it reaching the ears of some of our kinsmen, and they are eager to meet you."

I stare at her agape. "I have other family members here?" Even as I say it, though, I realize that of course I must. The Sylvani are immortal.

She grins again. "You've already met one of your cousins."

Astrid smiles at me, and my eyes widen. "Distant cousin," she says.

"I'm so sorry, Astrid, I didn't know—" My face flames.

Astrid waves away my apology and laughs softly—good-naturedly. "I can see you're embarrassed, but you shouldn't be. How could you have known?"

But now that she's said that, I can see the family resemblance—willowy frame, big eyes.

Grandmother holds out her hand to me. "Come, now. No harm done. And anyway, you'll want to prepare yourself. Not everyone will be as charming as Astrid and I."

She ushers me out of the room and takes the lead once we're in the hallway. Serafino flies above, having waited for Grandmother just outside my room, and Rowen pads silently behind us. We pass a multitude of lovely things—fragile porcelain figures and crystal vases and abundant flowers, and everywhere, paintings.

Grandmother comes to an abrupt halt before an enormous painting of a girl of sixteen or so, waves of blond hair down her back and her hand outstretched toward a pure white unicorn. "Your mother's first encounter with a unicorn," she says, her eyes soft. "It's a rite of passage for the young girls here."

I'm so caught up in the vibrant painting that it takes me a moment to form a coherent response. "So there truly are unicorns?"

"As there were once unicorns in your world until they were nearly hunted to extinction," she replies bitterly. "Those who survived crossed over to our realm, and we Sylvani did our best to erase them from the mortal world's memory. We have one in attendance today, in fact, and you will have the chance to meet him."

Confusion flits across my face as I picture a horned white horse in the middle of the castle, but before I can question her, Grandmother strides on again.

We go down a spiraling staircase, which seems to be in an altogether different place from the one we used yesterday, and after a few more turns arrive in front of a set of massive double doors. Sentinels stand with their wolves on either side. The moment Grandmother inclines her head, they each pull door handles as tall as them and the doors groan open.

"Oh, heavens," I murmur, both because of the room itself and its occupants. The room appears to be a sunroom of sorts, with elegant sofas and chairs grouped in such a way to enjoy the views and converse. Wall-to-ceiling glass, the windows are so clear and sparkling they're almost nonexistent. Beyond, the sun is setting radiantly, streaking the sky with reds and oranges, pinks and purples. A garden waits just outside the glass, mimicking the colors in the sky before ending just before a waterfall.

A crowd of people awaits us, at least thirty, and their conversations die off the moment they lay eyes on us. Curiously absent, though, are their spirit animals. The weight of so many eyes falls upon me, and I resist the urge to wring my hands. My heart beats like a tiny frightened bird. There are just so many! And all so beautiful and otherworldly—their long hair tumbling down their backs in waves, their heavily embroidered clothing catching the light, gold and silver and jewels winking back at me. Many of the women are dressed similarly to Grandmother and me, but there are some dressed more simply in long tunics and leggings as Astrid wears. The men wear either adorned leather armor and breeches or long tunics not unlike those found in the east. They all appear to be the same age. No one, in fact, looks much older than thirty.

They are mostly here to satisfy their curiosity, Rowen says soothingly. *Save the man in the front with dark hair. He is your uncle on your grandfather's side. Take care in what you say to him.*

What do you mean? I demand, my heart beating all the louder, but the fox remains silent.

The people execute respectful bows toward my grandmother—arms crossed over their chests and heads inclined—and she dips her head in acknowledgment.

"How good it is to see all of you, and on a much happier occasion than last we met," Grandmother says. "As you now know, I've been successful in reaching out to the High Princess Isidora's children."

"In spite of King Brannor's wishes," a dark-haired man says. His eyes are dark as onyx as he meets my grandmother's gaze unflinchingly. He is the one Rowen warned me of—the one who is apparently my uncle.

Grandmother merely stares at him, almost wearily, as though this is an argument she has heard many times. She holds out her hand to me, and I step forward on shaky legs. "Princess Lucy, High Princess Isidora's daughter and my granddaughter, has come to learn more about her Sylvan heritage and to strengthen her arcana. She is your kin and your princess, and I hope that you will all welcome her as such." She scans the room with narrowed eyes. "Despite the king's opinion on the matter, there has never been a law banning the half-Sylvani from this realm."

"The King of Sentor has issued such a law," the man says, his whole bearing one of challenge. "He believes there are halflings who have joined forces with that ridiculous brotherhood."

"If they're so ridiculous," I find myself saying, "then why should you care?"

His expression darkens, and I try to channel my belligerent sister to calm my quivering insides. "Because they believe that a halfling is the same as a full-blooded Sylvani; they dare to think they could do the same to us, but of course, we would destroy them before they ever had the chance."

"Enough, Lord Titus," Grandmother says, quiet voice thrumming with warning. "An attack against a mortal is not only dishonorable, it's forbidden."

His stony face cracks into a smirk. "Is that why you're holding a being from that realm prisoner in your dungeon—because he's a halfling and not a full mortal?"

I can feel the tension between them mounting, but Grandmother only answers in a calm voice. "Imprisoned, yes. As I would imprison anyone who would threaten the princess." She meets his steely gaze with one of her own. "No harm has come to him." Before he can continue, her gaze turns away from him and onto the others. "The princess and I have much to do today. Anyone who would like to come and speak with her may do so for a short time. Otherwise, you will have your chance at the ball."

A ball? I think, and a little spark of excitement races through me. If even the trees here enchant me, then I cannot imagine how grand and wonderful a formal ball will be.

"I am not your kin, but I would dearly love to meet the princess," a male voice calls out, interrupting my inner reverie. I turn to see a figure of light step forward from the back of the room. My artist's mind immediately paints him. He is full of fascinating contradictions: he is pale and slight, yet radiates power as the crowd parts for him. His hair is long and blindingly white, though his face and body are young.

"Well met, my lord," Grandmother says with a warm smile, her shoulders relaxing marginally as though the man has brought a sense of peace with him.

As soon as my gaze meets his, I let out a breath as though I've been holding it all the while. And perhaps I have. A simple introduction to this man seems strangely inappropriate, and I have to fight the urge to drop into a curtsy.

"A pleasure to make your acquaintance, Princess Lucy," the gentleman says with a respectful bow of his head. This causes many in the crowd to whisper in excited tones, but of course I'm quite ignorant as to the reason. "I am Silvanus."

"*Prince* Silvanus," Grandmother adds. "He is prince of the unicorns."

Grandmother's words in the hallway return to me, and my eyes widen. Surely this isn't the unicorn she mentioned? Yet even as I think it, the image of the otherworldly man before me shifts in my mind . . . in his place is a pure white unicorn, its horn twisted and silver.

"It's a pleasure to meet you, Prince Silvanus," I say, even as my mind screams for pencil and paper with which to draw this stunning creature.

You have your mother's radiant soul, a clear, sparkling voice tells me in my mind, and Prince Silvanus smiles. Aloud he says, "Your mother and I were once dear friends, and I would like to extend the same courtesy to you."

The murmurs of the crowd seem to die down until everyone is once again staring at me. Even Grandmother looks rather stunned, and though I don't understand the significance of his words, I can see from their reactions that it must be important—or at least surprising.

"I'd like that very much," I say sincerely.

His smile widens, and a feeling of peace washes over me, like being bathed in the warmth of the sun. He turns and walks away, leaving the scent of a forest just after heavy rain.

The others swarm me after that. They introduce themselves and make polite conversation with me, and some even invite me to visit their estates. The whole thing is so similar to what takes place in every ballroom in London that it actually takes the edge off my nerves. I smile and nod and try to remember the names—so ancient and beautiful!—and thank heavens I had a governess and an upper-crust finishing school to prepare me. Though, of course, neither had anticipated I'd need polished manners to fit in with the nobility of another realm.

Lord Titus and a small group of other glowering kinsmen stand apart from the rest, watching me with serious, flinty eyes. Apparently the unicorn prince's approval doesn't change their opinion of me. I try to view this objectively—to perhaps try and understand the politics of it—but I'm afraid I'm too emotional of a creature not to take it personally. A *halfling* he'd called me, and I feel the prickling heat of embarrassment and anger spread through me.

I lift my chin and meet his gaze. He will not make me feel ashamed of my mother or my father.

Better a halfling than a creature with a heart twisted by malice and prejudice.

A hush falls upon the crowd. Every man and woman stares at me with surprised eyes or mouths agape, and Lord Titus turns on his heel and strides out of the room.

What just happened? I think desperately.

Rowen glances up at me, his thoughts pushing into mine. *You projected your thoughts onto us all.*

I erupt into flames as the embarrassment spreads like wildfire through my body. But it's tempered by one thought:

I regret that everyone heard, but I certainly don't regret what I said.

✟

ALEXANDER stirs and comes to his feet. He shakes his head groggily. He isn't sure what woke him—other than the unforgiving stone floor or the lack of blanket. Still, he'd been so exhausted he could no longer resist the siren call of sleep. He glances around the bare cell now, searching for any changes.

Then he feels it: a thrum of power. He has just a moment to step back before the doorway traced in bright white light appears in the wall behind him. His body tenses. It's almost shameful how badly he wants to see Lucy walk through that door. The words he has been rehearsing in his mind since he was thrown into the cell crowd his tongue.

But it's a man who stands before him—a man dressed in an oriental-style tunic and pants, his hair worn long down his back. His eyes are so dark Alexander cannot make out the pupils. Every instinct warns him that this man is dangerous, more so than the fiery queen or her sentinels. It's the same instinct that has whispered to him about Lord Wallace and in back alleys of Bombay late at night.

"So this is a member of the greatly feared Order of the Eternal Sun?" the man says with a mocking smile that heats Alexander's blood. "How quaint. And what is your dubious skill, I wonder? You are not one of the arcana drainers."

"I find it best not to lay all one's cards on the table. I'm already at the mercy of my captors; I should like to keep some air of mystery about me."

Instead of the fury Alexander expected, the man laughs. "Your courage does you credit. You may rest easy knowing I am not your enemy. On the contrary, you and your organization do a lot of good in the world." He smiles, though the gesture doesn't reach his eyes. "I am Lord Titus, brother to the late king."

Alexander suddenly feels as though he is a blind man set loose in an unfamiliar room. He can only fall back on his usual tricks: bluffing and wit. "I'm glad to hear it."

"Are you?" Titus responds with a smirk. "I suppose you are. After all, you are trapped in a room with someone who could kill you as easily as he breathes. But before you do anything that may change my mind," he says when Alexander prepares his body for a fight—balanced on the balls of his feet, arms loose at his sides, ready to evade until he's successfully measured his opponent, "I only came to thank you."

"For what?" Alexander asks, still wary.

"As I said before, your organization does a lot of good. You track down and eliminate halflings, who should have never existed in the first place. They are abominations, bringing shame to the true Sylvani. My people have become lax, allowing such beings to come into existence."

Ice water trickles down Alexander's spine. He doesn't quite understand the man's words, but something is trying to fall into place, something that has been chipping away at his mind ever since Nadi's death. "Halflings?"

"Half mortal, half Sylvani." He lets out a cold laugh. "You didn't think your Order was capable of taking on a full-blooded Sylvani, did you? No, you've been murdering the weak, pathetic half-human aberrations for centuries now."

Alexander feels the color drain from his face and his stomach drops like a stone. His mind replays that one word over and over: half-*human*. His rebuttal is on the tip of his tongue—that murder is an exaggeration, that the brotherhood only siphoned away the dangerous arcana from the volatile Sylvani—and up until a year ago, that would be true. But his eyes have been opened, and he knows now that his knowledge of the brotherhood was merely scratching the surface.

The human part, though, this is something new. The words hammer at the glass house of Alexander's beliefs until they crack: that the Sylvani are evil, that they walk among mortals to bring harm and bedevilment, that there are humans with spiritual power who were chosen to stand against them. If the Sylvani the brotherhood hunted are truly half-human, then what did that make him?

"I can see from your expression that you believe I'm here to seek retribution for your brotherhood's actions," the man says, "but I assure you, that is the queen's business, not mine. No, what I seek is information. You were hunting the princess; therefore, you must have some sense of her abilities. Tell me, and I can guarantee your escape."

The man's face is deadly serious, but as Alexander stares into his pitch-black eyes, he sees what lies beneath. If Alexander were to draw him, it would be of a shadow form filled with writhing snakes. There is no escape for Alexander—at least, not through this man. And though Lucy will no doubt forsake him, he would no sooner taint her by giving this creature before him any knowledge he may have on her.

But first, he will see what the man might reveal.

"What does it matter what her abilities are? She is one of these halflings you've mentioned, yes? Then what threat could she pose against a man of your stature?"

Lord Titus's lip curls. "She is no threat at all, you fool. But as I'm sure you've learned in your own pathetic realm, knowledge is power."

"A universal truth," Alexander says, still feeling like he's about to grab the tiger by its tail, but pressing on. "From what I've gathered, your desire for knowledge is in order to overthrow the queen."

It was a guess, really, just an instinct Alexander had. But his words find their mark: Lord Titus takes a step back as though Alexander struck him.

His features rearrange themselves into the same calculating expression, but Alexander's sharp eyes see that his own instincts have paid off. Titus is unsettled. "Keeping the princess's secrets won't help you. The queen is out for blood, and you will pay in full. You might remember my offer when they come for you with chains."

Fear whispers through him, but he stands unflinchingly before Lord Titus. "I'll remember, but my answer remains unchanged."

One last smirk, and then Lord Titus places his hand on the wall, filling the small cell with the almost electrical sensation of arcana. The doorway appears, and he steps through.

Alone again, Alexander gives into the adrenaline flooding his body and braces one hand on the wall while he fights to slow his racing heart.

NINETEEN

AFTER promising the visiting family members that they will have the chance to see me at the ball in just a few days' time, Grandmother gives me the grand tour she promised. The castle holds twenty-eight bedrooms, twenty bathrooms—with their own indoor plumbing thanks to the streams that run through the castle—two libraries, a massive kitchen the size of a ballroom, two dining rooms, and ten gardens. But what interests me most are the paintings: portraits of my mother, portraits of fantastical beasts, portraits of Sylvani kin—including one massively gold-framed portrait with my grandmother in an elaborate golden gown with yards and yards of train. She stands beside a dark-haired man in a long golden jacket and dark pants, a jeweled crown upon his head. Grandmother told me it was the portrait of her wedding day, and I spent long moments just staring at the many details in the painting—like Serafino and a big white stag watching the proceedings.

I try to memorize as much as I can. I want to be able to describe everything to my siblings, perhaps even draw it myself if I can. How I wish they were here.

Grandmother finally takes me to a room on one of the castle's top floors. Numerous easels with creamy white canvases stand waiting, begging for that first brushstroke. An entire wall is dedicated to art supplies, organized in jeweled boxes: pretty pots of paint, brushes from the thin and wispy to bulky and wide, charcoal, pastels, along with several things I've never seen before.

The ceilings are sky high, and this must be a place Grandmother spends quite a bit of time in, for there's even a silver and gold tree with branches for Serafino to rest on. The windows let in just the right amount of light, casting everything in a soft, afternoon sun glow. It's beautiful light to paint by, and as I look around, I realize that's the purpose of the room.

How Alexander would love to see this, I think before I can stop myself, and I stamp down on that line of thinking so viciously I nearly give myself a headache. I must acquaint myself with thinking of him as he truly is: the man who betrayed me, my enemy.

Rose, I correct myself angrily. *I should think of how much* Rose *would enjoy a room full of more art supplies than she could ever dream of.*

How I wish I could show her—the thought of her reaction to the many beauties of this world brings a smile to my face. Even the elegant scenes of Japan she painted would pale in comparison.

After a moment or two of internal debate, I realize I've remained silent for far too long. I struggle to form a coherent thought to express my excitement over this room. "Would you mind terribly if I spent the rest of my visit in here?"

Grandmother laughs, the musical sound filling the space. "I certainly wouldn't blame you. If I could, I'd spend every moment in here, painting."

"I always wondered where I got my love for art," I say with one of those unsteady smiles that could just as easily turn into tears.

"I'm sure you're quite gifted, as even mortals can be." She steps over to the wall of supplies and plucks a fan brush from a golden cup. After dipping it in a pot of azure paint, she moves it across the blank canvass in confident strokes, her hand moving so fast I only register the finished product: a bird in flight. "But there's so much more you can do."

I hold my breath. Grandmother sweeps one hand over the canvas, wiping the paint away. When she opens her hand, the bird from her painting bursts free.

I laugh delightedly as the bird flits from branch to branch under Serafino's watchful eye. "How wonderful—I always knew an artist could breathe life into her art."

"This is the least of what you can do—a child's trick." She hands me the brush and paint. "It's a good starting point for you, though, because the channeling of arcana is similar to what you must master."

I take the proffered supplies. "Will I truly be able to pull things straight out of the air?" I glance at my hands uncertainly. I have no doubt of my artistic talent, but what Grandmother did was so otherworldly it's hard to imagine ever channeling that much power.

"You can," Grandmother says with such confidence it is difficult to doubt myself. "It's part of my gift to know things about others, and I can say with certainty that I know this about you." She nods toward the canvas. "Paint whatever small, living object you'd like."

I glance back at her uncertainly. I'd been imagining trying my hand at something without a heartbeat—like a necklace. I turn back to the canvas, dip the brush in the paint, and do what I've always done when I need inspiration: let the brush paint what it will.

The first few strokes are a bit unsteady. Painting in front of an audience has never been easy for me, especially when it's someone as illustrious as my Sylvan grandmother. But as it always happens, I relax to the soothing sounds of the brush on canvas, the sweet smell of the paint, and the beauty of the creamy white turning blue.

In the end, my finished object has no heartbeat, but it's still alive: a blue orchid.

"Beautiful," Grandmother says approvingly. She takes a few steps forward and gently grabs hold of my hand. Placing it over my painting, she closes her eyes. After a moment, I do the same. "Do you feel that faint buzzing?"

I start to shake my head, but then suddenly, I can feel it. Vibrations beneath my fingertips. "Yes."

"That's the thrum of life, and all living creatures have it—even this orchid."

I open my eyes for a moment, confused. "But why should my painting be alive?"

Grandmother smiles. "Because *you* painted it. You set the groundwork without even realizing it. The next step is to harness it and set your orchid free."

"How?"

"Push your arcana into the painting. Use it to fuel the orchid and bring it to life."

I reach inside myself for the stores of arcana—like a spring of water bubbling just under the surface—only this time, the well is dry. I send a panicked look to Grandmother, but it's Rowen who answers my cry for help.

You are forgetting I am your source of arcana in this world, he says gently. *Bigger enchantments require more arcana than you have stored.*

Unsure exactly what I must do, I close my eyes and reach outside of myself this time—just as I'd draw on the sun's energy. Instantly, I'm flooded with arcana, and I clumsily transfer it to my orchid painting.

I try to mimic Grandmother's sleight of hand, transferring the arcana as I sweep my hand across the canvas, but when I examine the contents of my hand, my face falls.

Grandmother touches my shoulder as we gaze down at the sad, paper orchid in my hand. The electric thrum that was its life has disappeared.

"It wasn't bad for your first go of it," she says, and I wince. I'm used to succeeding on the very first try on anything having to do with art. "It's clear, however, that you're distracted."

I glance up at her in surprise. Am I distracted? I review my actions thus far—I thought I'd been concentrating—

Alexander's face fills my mind, his beautiful eyes intent on mine.

Grandmother nods. "I think it's time you got some answers."

I don't know what I'd been expecting, but it certainly wasn't this. Grandmother leads me down several stone staircases until we reach what must have been the very bowels of the castle. Above us, the waterfalls roar through the rock, and I glance at the smooth ceilings warily, afraid they may suddenly give under the weight of the water. The halls are dimly lit by just a few floating orbs. I don't see any doors, only unbroken walls, as though the dungeon has been carved out of rock by some enormous creature.

There is nothing frightening—no weapons or hulking armored men or lurking dragons—and yet, the fine hairs on my neck stand on end. I cannot imagine what it must be like to be hidden away down here, especially when one is a complete and total stranger to this world and its inhabitants.

Just when I think I will do something truly shameful—like actually pity this man who betrayed me—she stops in front of a blank wall. Much as she did with the canvas, she touches her hand to the wall and the bright power of arcana fills the air.

Blinding light fills the dim hallway, and after squinting and blinking through the pain, I see a doorway form. Grandmother steps to the side as the light fades.

"I'll be just outside," she says, one hand on my arm. "You should have the chance to speak with him privately, but I will insist that Rowen go in with you."

I nod numbly, so many conflicting emotions swirling within me they've almost rendered me paralyzed: fear that Alexander is truly my enemy, anger that I've been duped, and a burning curiosity to know the truth.

With Rowen comfortingly at my side, I cross through the doorway. The room I find beyond is a small, rounded cell, absolutely bare—no furniture or even a window. High above me, an orb glows dimly, the only source of light.

Alexander steps out of the shadows, his face just as achingly beautiful as it was the first time I saw it in my drawing.

"I wondered if you'd come," he says, his voice both familiar and strange in this otherworldly place. He shakes his head. "No, that isn't true. I begged and prayed to whomever would listen for one last chance to speak with you."

His tone is so resigned that I step toward him without thinking. But then I remember. "Are you really a member of the Order of the Eternal Sun?"

His jaw flexes once, regret flaring in his eyes. "Yes."

Pain ripples through me, surprising in its intensity. I'd been expecting this, and yet to hear him so readily admit it is a blow. "Did you seek me out so you could hurt me—take my arcana by force?"

He is silent for so long that I worry I will be sick all over the polished floor. "That's a question with a complicated answer."

"Is it? Because it seems rather simple to me. Either you were or you weren't."

"I sought you out because I knew you had an abundance of power," he says, "and I never intended to hurt you."

"*You* didn't, perhaps," I say, reading in between the lines.

"All research on your family pointed to the possibility that you held some power, but were no danger to anyone. For this reason, and for other, much more personal reasons, I didn't report your existence to my superior."

He looks at me, and I know he is willing me to understand, but I don't. I can't. "How can you be a part of such an organization? Of people who hurt people like me . . . people like *you*?"

His brows furrow. "It's true I have a large store of spiritual power, but I'm fully human, I assure you."

He doesn't know. I'm not sure if it helps his cause or hinders. "Only those with Sylvan blood can enter the portal."

Now it's his turn to look flabbergasted. He goes still and silent for a full minute. "You're sure? Perhaps because of my spiritual power . . ."

"Though I'm not entirely sure what you mean by spiritual power, I strongly suspect it has been arcana all along." His face looks even paler than it did before, but I refuse to pity him. "And what if you had found something about my family . . . about me? What if you determined I was a danger to others?"

He shakes his head. "You aren't. You couldn't be."

"Yes, but *what if*?"

He hesitates, and in that moment, I know the answer. I nod as tears prick my eyes.

"Lucy, wait! Please," he says, but I step through the doorway without a backward glance.

Rowen presses against my leg as the wall behind me closes again. Grandmother waits for me, her brows furrowed in concern.

"I'm not ready," I tell her before she has the chance to ask, and even I am not entirely sure what I mean. Not ready to listen to him? Not ready to forgive?

Grandmother reaches out and touches my shoulder. "No one is asking anything of you, Lucy. Certainly not me."

"I think I might return to my room for a moment—if that's all right with you?"

"Of course. Rest all you like. We don't have any commitments until dinner."

Rowen stays by my side as I make my way out of the dungeon, my footsteps heavy. It seems I didn't learn anything from Wren's brush with death at the hands of the Order.

Worse still, I had been falling for my own enemy.

☥

AFTER Lucy leaves, Alexander spends an embarrassing amount of time sitting on the cold stone floor with his head in his hands. He can still feel her energy even after she has gone, like the refreshing scent of lemons hanging in the air. Was everything he'd ever believed a lie? Lord Tyrell had told him as a boy that a Sylvani had murdered his mother. It was Lord Tyrell who'd always been quick to comfort a motherless boy, who always had wise advice when Alexander most needed it.

And Alexander had needed it often. Neither fully Indian nor English, he'd often faced animosity from both sides. He remembers one day in particular, when he was older than a boy but not yet a man, when the other boys in his school had destroyed one of his paintings. In bright red paint, they'd written "chee chee" across the painting.

Alexander's rage and sorrow had been blinding. He'd destroyed the painting himself, unable to look upon the hateful word.

He'd gone to Lord Tyrell's house that same day, as he often did, and Lord Tyrell was able to tell almost immediately that something had upset Alexander.

"You can tell me anything," he'd said when Alexander hesitated in sharing something so shameful. It was humiliating to be singled out, to be forced into the same schools as pale English boys who were just as privileged as Alexander, and yet, looked down upon him as though he were little more than a servant. It was why, even now, Alexander could only tolerate the help of a housekeeper and no other servants—his father's grand estates were torturous, but of course it would be far crueler to deprive them of their jobs.

When Alexander finally confessed what had happened to his painting, and all the taunts he'd been enduring at school, Lord Tyrell laid a hand on his shoulder. "It pains me that you must go through this, Alexander, but it's something that all men with talent have had to survive at one time or another. They sense your ability—your prana—even if they don't have a name for it. They see your incredible art, your resilience despite your hardship and loss, and they hate you for it. But *I* see your strength, your power, your way with people, and I have a job for you that will make you forget about the petty games of children."

Alexander had been inducted into the Order shortly after, swelled with righteousness at the thought of fighting back against the monstrous creatures who had murdered his mother—who had stolen his childhood from him.

What a fool he's been.

His father couldn't possibly have had Sylvan blood—he would have sensed it—nor any of his aunts or uncles or cousins. No, it would have had to be his mother, the woman with no living kin.

He struggles to recall everything he can about his mother—to remember her with this new piece of information—but he was only five years old when she died. His memories are like scattered shards of glass: the softness of her hair, the smell of cinnamon on her clothes, a few notes of the song she'd sing to him at night. He pushes his mind harder, tries to think of her in specific instances—like at bedtime. She would always come to tuck him in herself with a lullaby and a kiss goodnight.

And then, as though it has been waiting for him all along, his mind offers up a single memory in perfect clarity: he'd been frightened of going to sleep one night, even after his lullaby and having been tucked in. His mother had laid her hand across his forehead as though she was checking for a fever, the smell of cinnamon hanging heavily in the air. He can still see the slant of moonlight spilling across his room, his many toys lined up like little soldiers. His mother had leaned over him and whispered, "There is nothing to be afraid of. You'll dream of an enchanted jungle and all the creatures that once inhabited it." His mind had instantly filled with image after image of exotic trees and birds and lizards and even the hint of a creature that could have been a dragon. It was all so clear, as though he were looking at photographs of a real jungle, as if he'd really been there.

Remembering now, as a man, Alexander sees the truth: his mother had somehow pushed those images into his mind. She'd given him those happy thoughts, knowing his love for flora and fauna and jungles in particular at that age.

As though that one memory was the key to unlocking others, he remembers more: watching his mother paint a trio of playful tiger cubs for his room, and to Alexander's laughing delight, the cubs coming to life and bounding across the canvas.

Alexander sits now in a stunned silence, the cold stone against his back. His mother had abilities—abilities he might have once attributed to an abundance of spiritual power were it not for Lucy. His stomach churns with disgust as he thinks of just how wrong he's been all his life. But before he can mentally flay himself with thoughts of his every mistaken belief, the blinding light of a doorway appears.

He scrambles to his feet, daring to hope that it might be Lucy again, but it's the fiery queen who steps through, her hair dark in the dim light. The bird he'd seen her riding is now small enough to perch on her shoulder, and it does so with what can only be described as an arrogant look in its eyes.

The queen smiles, and though the gesture isn't overly warm, neither is it threatening. "Hello, Alexander." She waits until he gives a polite nod, but he draws the line at inclining his head—he may be imprisoned, but she is not *his* queen. "My granddaughter has spoken to you, but now I think it is time I presented you with an option." *Granddaughter?* Alexander thinks. *The queen doesn't look much older than I am.* "You can be useful to me, and if you are, then perhaps I will set you free." She tilts her head questioningly. "Would you like the chance to redeem yourself?"

"Redemption in your eyes or Lucy's?"

She smiles again—an expression that is almost amused but not quite. Alexander can sense the tension in the small cell. He knows that one wrong word may result in the queen locking him away forever. And yet, he has never been much good at total submission.

"Both, I should hope." Her eyes narrow. "I want you to help Lucy destroy your Order."

Alexander blinks stupidly. Whatever he expected her to say, it wasn't this. His mind fills of thoughts of Lucy, of her bright, gentle spirit—though even as he thinks of that, he remembers her standing so proudly in her fencing uniform. Still, the thought of her destroying anything causes so much cognitive dissonance that his head pounds. "Does Lucy have assassin skills I'm unaware of?"

Alexander speaks without thinking, the wry comment escaping his mouth before he has the chance to swallow the words.

"My granddaughter is capable of many things of which you have no knowledge," the queen says with a bite to her melodic voice. "Unsurprising since you didn't even know you were Sylvani. At least, that is what you *say*."

Her incredulous tone crawls under his skin. "I believed what I'd been told. You are right in thinking I was a fool, but I will not stand being called a liar."

She appraises him silently for a moment. "Your Sylvan blood is not as potent as Lucy's. By my estimate, you are at most only one-fourth Sylvan. I will therefore concede that it's possible you might not have known, though it's clear you still have the gift of arcana."

He turns this over in his mind. His mother had only been part-Sylvan, then. It seems that Lucy has more Sylvan blood than he and less than the queen . . . so she must be half? He knows that her mother, too, is dead, so she seems to be the likely candidate. As shocking as all this is, Alexander must admit that he is fascinated. "I was told all mortals have prana, or spiritual power, and I happened to have an abundance of it."

"Spiritual power? Yes, I suppose that's true, in a way. Though it's a little like comparing the strength of a summer breeze with the power of a hurricane."

A small smile teases Alexander's lips at this. He is not immune to a good metaphor. "And where does my power fall?"

"Somewhere between a strong wind and a gale," she answers readily, just a hint of amusement in her eyes. "Lucy and her siblings are unusual even for half-Sylvani. They have abilities that nearly put them in the same league as the pure-bloods."

"A tornado, then?" Alexander asks wryly, and she smiles. "So what is the plan for this tornado of power? How will she destroy an ancient order?"

"By cutting the head off the snake."

Alexander's expression darkens. He can deduce what she implies. "And if I refuse?"

"Then I will be forced to disappoint my granddaughter and keep you imprisoned until death comes to release you." She gives him the look of a queen unused to being thwarted. "I very much do not want to disappoint my granddaughter."

Though the thought of helping Lucy take down Lord Tyrell has Alexander feeling sick, he can see that he has no other choice. Even as he fears for the man who took him in as a child, his traitorous heart soars at the prospect of seeing Lucy again.

He meets the queen's intense emerald gaze. "What must I do?"

TWENTY

THE sun sets and the moon rises in its stead, and after my rather disastrous conversation with Alexander, Grandmother told me to rest again
before dinner. I tried to put aside all thoughts of him, but questions continue to swirl in my head. How had he not known he was Sylvan? What
must he feel now, knowing he had been hunting his own kind? A twinge
thrums painfully through my chest as I think about his words. He came in
search of me, and if he had found me guilty of whatever crimes the Order
accuses the Sylvani of . . .

I shake my head in an effort to banish the thoughts.

I lean on the balcony and gaze in wonder at the night sky. Here, the
moon hangs so low it looks twice as large as the one I'm used to. The stars
are bright and glittering, almost artificial in their intensity. I try to find
some of the few constellations I know—Orion's Belt, Ursa Major, and Ursa
Minor—but when I do find them, they appear to be the mirror image of the
ones I've always known. A little shiver runs down my back.

Rowen jumps up on the balcony beside me, balancing like a cat. I have
the strongest urge to pet him, but I restrain myself. We stare out at the city
below us together, a light breeze ruffling Rowen's fur, bringing the smell of
exotic flowers and the clean scent of the waterfall.

"I'm ashamed how easily I was taken in by him," I say to Rowen and to the night sky. "Even James had the sense to be suspicious."

Rowen glances up at me, turquoise eyes gazing straight into my mind. *And were you never suspicious?*

"Reluctantly," I say after a moment. "I'm still reluctant, and he's told me of his involvement to my face."

It isn't unusual for the mind and the heart to disagree—this is a fact that transcends worlds.

I smile down at him. "You are being too kind to me, I think."

He was foolish—no one should blindly follow another person in life—but I believed him when he said he had no intent to harm you.

"I only hope his generosity extended to others like me." A memory of Lord Blackburn, the odious member of the Order who nearly killed my sister, suddenly latches hold of my mind. I see myself standing at the top of the stairs at my grandmother's posh London townhouse, watching my sister leave with him—willingly, to keep me safe—and not knowing whether I'd ever see her again.

If Alexander has been responsible for even a fraction of that pain, I don't think I'll ever be able to forgive him.

"You won't have to forgive him," Grandmother says from behind me, "but you will have to work with him. You were projecting again, dearest one," she adds when I answer with a blank look. She wraps her arm around mine and draws me away from the balcony. "I'll explain it all over dinner. I'm sorry to have kept you waiting."

She starts to lead me out of the room, but I glance down at my frock with some alarm. "Shall I change?"

Confusion knits her eyebrows. "Are you uncomfortable in your gown?"

"Oh no, not at all—quite the contrary. It's only that we usually change into evening gowns to go down to dinner, but of course, this isn't England . . . this isn't even the mortal realm."

Grandmother still looks a bit confused. "And how many times do you change a day?"

I run the calculations in my head. "Perhaps . . . five or six times a day, depending on what activities are planned."

Her eyes widen. "How fascinating. Well, you'll find it a great deal simpler here. Although," she gestures to my elaborately embroidered golden gown, "I never thought I'd say that about our own clothing."

"The clothing here is anything but simplistic, but I quite like the freedom it affords. I'd never be able to wear something that bares my legs in such a way."

"I do remember that part of it, at least. It was I who helped your mother pack her things for her first visit between realms—though now that I know how often you change, I suppose I sent her with far too light of a trunk."

It's simple asides like these that I try to squirrel away in my memory—these brief glimpses of my mother's former life here.

"Now that we've agreed you are quite beautifully dressed, shall we go to dinner?"

"Dinner sounds lovely," I say as I follow her lead into the hall, Rowen and Serafino at our sides. "Will we be dining with anyone else?"

"Not tonight—I thought we'd dine informally if you don't mind."

I shake my head, thinking of my brief meeting with other Sylvani—including Lord Titus. "I don't mind in the least."

Grandmother leads me through a labyrinth of hallways, each with achingly beautiful artwork—still more fantastical paintings, but also spiraling glass work in many different shapes and sizes, so delicate I can't think how it doesn't shatter with our footsteps. Grandmother passes all of these by, as though immune to their splendor. My heart swells with every new thing I see, my eyes greedily taking everything in, and I realize with no small amount of dismay that I am rapidly falling in love with this castle and this world.

"Ah, here we are," Grandmother says as we arrive at a small outer door. When she pushes it open, it reveals a garden with a riot of color. "I'm afraid we won't be dining in the formal dining room as I'm sure you're used to. I can't stand taking my meals in the cavernous room unless I'm absolutely forced to."

"No, this is perfect," I say in a hushed voice as though I am stepping into a quiet church instead of a garden. Flowers of vivid colors—crimson, sunset orange, rich violet—tumble on top of each other, both exotic and familiar. The grass beneath our feet is plusher than the thickest Oriental rug, and my soft shoes sink into it pleasantly as I walk. A short distance away is a marble balcony, and beyond that, the waterfalls flow endlessly down from the castle and the other buildings in Cascadia. As my golden skirts trail behind me in this wonderland of color, I nearly feel like the princess they say I am.

In the midst of all the flowers and verdant grass is another ancient tree—this one something like a cross between a lilac and a weeping willow. Beneath its dropping branches of soft pink flowers is a black iron table with three chairs. A slender male servant, one of the first I've seen since I arrived, waits beside a tray filled with tantalizing food.

"Have a seat, my darling," Grandmother says, and the servant moves swiftly to pull out chairs for us both.

The servant places silver plates before us, and the fare is light and refreshing: fruits and cheeses and greens, crusty bread still warm, and goblets of wine that, when I taste it, explodes with flavor—honey and berries and something tangy. It's nothing like the heavy, decadent six-course meals I'm used to, but is delicious all the same.

Grandmother spends the first part of the meal in silence, eating her food slowly and mindfully, and I endeavor to do the same. The silence, while not unpleasant, is certainly nothing like what I'm used to. No forced small talk here. *Colin would enjoy himself immensely*, I think with an inner smile.

After a short time, Grandmother puts her goblet down gently. "I was a bit vague when I came to get you for dinner, and if you'd like, I can explain."

I swallow the bite of creamy cheese I'd been enjoying and nod enthusiastically. "Yes, I should be glad of that."

"Before I say anything of what transpired between myself and Alexander, I should make known one of my abilities." I perk up, giving her my undivided attention. Nothing is more fascinating to me than the many different shades of arcana. "I can search through someone's mind," she says, and a little jolt of surprise runs through me. I immediately try to control my run-away thoughts, but of course that only makes them even harder to rein in. "It's a fearful ability, as you can see from your own reaction, but know that I never use it on any of my kin or loved ones without their express permission. Enemies or prisoners though . . ."

I take her meaning perfectly. She'd no doubt dug through Alexander's mind as soon as she could, and though I know how terrible such a thing must be, I still find myself desperate to hear her findings. "What I can tell you is that he didn't know he was Sylvan, he's had suspicions about the

Order for quite some time, and most importantly, he never wanted any harm to befall you."

I am ashamed to feel my heart soften. "So what he told me was true."

Grandmother watches my reaction. "His innocence in that regard is why I enlisted his aid. He has information you will need in order to infiltrate the leader."

I stare at her, thunderstruck. "Infiltrate? But surely . . . you cannot mean . . . I thought you were going to instruct me in defense . . ." I trail off, too flabbergasted to continue.

"The quickest way to stop an organization such as this is to defeat its leader."

I pale. "And when you say defeat, surely you don't mean I should . . ." I trail off, unable to vocalize the word. I am no assassin.

Grandmother touches my hand comfortingly. "No, nothing like that, dearest one. To ask you to commit such an atrocity would be to blacken my own soul and yours. What you can do, however, is assist Alexander. Working together, the two of you can create a painting that will become a portal to Tyrell's very estate. Alexander will cross over, not you. His charge will be to bring Tyrell back through for trial."

"But how? Mortals cannot cross over into this realm."

She shifts her gaze to the falls, her expression darkening. "He isn't human. He's Sylvan."

Now even Rowen looks at Grandmother in surprise. For the leader of the Order to be Sylvan is the worst sort of betrayal for our kind. I think of Grandmother's earlier dismissal of the brotherhood, which is so incongruent with her obvious anger now. "So Alexander is innocent of knowing he was Sylvan and hunting his own kind, but the leader—Lord Tyrell—must be very much aware?"

Grandmother nods tersely. "I should have known, really. Your mother told me of the brotherhood long ago, but I dismissed it as a radical and relatively powerless group. It wasn't until I searched Alexander's mind that I saw the truth. I recognized this Lord Tyrell." I hold my breath, almost afraid to hear what she will say next. "He comes from a line of Sylvani with the power to drain arcana from others—a line so feared that most of them were wiped out centuries ago."

I take a sip of my wine, my mouth suddenly dry. "So you've met him then?"

"No. I've only seen his likeness in books. He is Centerius, the first Sylvani to be banished from our realm. He committed an unforgivable offense—he took another's life by draining him completely of arcana." A terrible sense of foreboding takes up residence within me. "In truth, he should have been executed, but his sister pleaded for him. She claimed the man he'd killed had attacked her, and her brother was only coming to her defense. It was one of my own ancestors who searched her mind and found the truth buried there, and so Centerius faced only exile."

"I am confused, though, how Lord Tyrell—Centerius—survived this long. I thought once a Sylvani crossed over to the mortal realm, they gave up their immortality?"

"I'm afraid the answer to that is what makes this whole affair so disturbing. Centerius did lose his immortality upon his exile, but he found a way to preserve himself. We know that their ability to drain another's arcana results in greater power and vitality for the caster, so it doesn't take much to assume that's exactly what he did when he crossed over to the mortal world. He sought others like him—and then descendants of others like him—and drained them of arcana. He founded this nefarious order to continue his goal, using men and women with Sylvan blood to track other Sylvani descendants or to drain them of their arcana."

My mind works through everything I've known about the order, about men who have the power to drain us of arcana—Lord Blackburn, who stole my sister's arcana, and Lord Wallace, who has drained at least one girl to the point of death. These men were monstrous creatures in my mind, but even more so now that I know the truth. "They're all Sylvan," I say, the words filling me with horror. "All our enemies are Sylvan."

Grandmother nods sadly. "Your mother must have known they had Sylvan blood, of course, but she didn't know the truth about Centerius."

Even this comes as a shock to me—how much Mama must have known. "Why wouldn't she have told us the truth?"

"You were isolated enough without knowing that the enemy who threatened you was also Sylvan." Grandmother nods toward the fox sitting quietly next to me. "Think how it would have affected your sister when she most needed Rowen's aid. Katherine may not have trusted him, may not have even considered coming to this realm—she never needed to, but it was important she had the option. The same line of thinking applies to you. It would only hurt you if you were to think Sylvani were your enemy."

Her words resonate. Wren and I were terrified enough about crossing over to the Sylvan realm, simply because we had no real knowledge save Mama's bedtime stories, nor did we know if one could easily return. It would have been that much worse had we thought there were real enemies hidden here.

"I know Alexander lost your trust—and rightfully so—but he will be the one who provides us his physical abilities for this venture. His abilities as a fighter are impressive; if it hadn't been for the effect of this realm on him, I suspect he would have seriously injured more than one of my Sentinels."

Surprise and grudging respect mingle closely within me. "Can't you just send your Sentinels through the portal to apprehend Lord Tyrell?" I ask, a little irritably. Working beside Alexander is the last thing I want to do, but not for the reason she thinks. Already my heart is moving rapidly toward forgiveness, and though I'm often seen as excessively compassionate, at this moment, I only find it to be a frustrating and unwelcome trait.

She smiles tolerantly. "It's against our laws to send a military force through the portal. Not only is it difficult for so many to blend in with the mortals, they cannot bring their spirit animals—can you imagine the reaction to armored men with white wolves at their sides? Even if it weren't for our laws, I told you once before that I wouldn't fight your battles for you, dearest one." She touches my arm gently. "You will never be in any danger. The aid you will provide is spiritual. It will be Alexander who will assume the risk. Still, I know what I am asking of you is no small thing."

I rub my arm uncertainly. Is it fair to ask such a thing of him? *Stop sympathizing with the enemy,* I chide myself harshly.

There is no shame in empathy, Rowen says in my mind. *It's important to understand the emotional state of everyone involved—even your enemy.*

I smile at him gratefully, only slightly unnerved he'd detected my thoughts. "But why should Alexander help us at all?"

"I sense in him a change in heart, a desire to right some wrongs," Grandmother says, but her expression turns calculating. "In truth, though, I have the means to drag him back to his dungeon cell should he think to defy me."

A surprised laugh escapes me. "Heavens. Remind me never to cross you."

"I'm only frightening when it comes to protecting my family," she says, smiling though I know she is serious. "So, knowing now the truth about Centerius and his nefarious Order, will you help apprehend him?"

All I'm being asked to do is create a portal from my drawing, something I've already begun to do, and something I'm sure I can perfect now that I'm here. Still, this is much more of a serious undertaking than I had mentally prepared myself for. When first the concept of self-defense lessons came about—both from James and from Grandmother—the danger to my person or anyone I cared for had been an abstract concept. But deliberately attacking Lord Tyrell is very different. The mere thought of it, and the fear that if anything should go wrong, it will be my fault, has my stomach rolling.

And yet . . . what choice did I have?

"Of course I will help in any way I can."

Grandmother nods approvingly. "I'm relieved to hear it."

"Then shall we begin our lessons again in the morning? I confess I feel quite anxious to continue knowing just how much is at stake now."

"Of course. But this time, Alexander will join us."

I slosh a bit of my wine. I hadn't expected to have to see him again so soon.

Grandmother takes a sip of her own wine. "Dearest, if only you'd realize that he is the one who should be nervous around you—not the other way around."

TWENTY-ONE

I concentrate on the painting before me, adding more details to the blue-bird until it looks real enough to fly off the canvas. I take a step back to appraise my work. Sunlight streams through the windows, making the blue paint shimmer. It looks almost like light reflecting off shiny feathers, and I tilt my head to see if there's anything that needs to be added. I think of the difficulty I had before, and suddenly I wonder if I should add a rune to help. Grandmother never said I couldn't, and I'm more familiar with bringing my paintings to life with them.

I take a clean brush, dip it in black paint, and make a swirling symbol—the one for life. I've used it before to make certain things jump off the page—twirling dresses, galloping horses, trees blowing in the breeze—but never as lifelike as Grandmother did. Compared to her arcana, mine is a cheap parlor trick.

I set the brush down carefully and hold my hand over the painting as she showed me. I hesitate, glancing at Rowen. "Perhaps I should have tried something a little less full of life," I say nervously.

You were wise to add the rune. Don't doubt yourself now.

I nod and close my eyes. I search for that thrum, that hint of life Grand-mother taught me to look for. With a little inhalation of surprise, I realize I not only detect the thrum, I can hear the bird's heartbeat, the beating of its tiny wings. Quickly, before I can lose the sensation, I reach out for Rowen's bright energy—like a little glowing sun beside me. Taking his energy and transferring it to the painting must be something like a circuit feels when electricity travels through it.

Deep inside, I know I was successful, but even so, my hand shakes as I reach into the canvas and retrieve the bird. It takes a full breath before I realize I can feel the soft feathers against my palm and the beat of a tiny, frantic heart.

I let out a little *yip* of surprise and nearly drop the poor creature. It bursts out of my hand in a flurry of blue feathers, darting toward the window with surprising speed. Just before I'm sure it will bash its tiny head against the glass, it veers right and flits about the room. I watch it in awe—not just because I actually succeeded, but because the bird is acting like any other. Who would think that a creature that started its life as a pot of paint would have the same basic instincts as a wild songbird?

"I'm so happy to see you were successful," Grandmother calls from behind me, and I turn with a bright smile . . . which fades the moment I see Alexander.

"I used a rune," I say woodenly, staring at Alexander. He's dressed in a long white tunic with a simple embroidery of golden thread, plain white slacks, and shoes that look more like slippers from *Arabian Nights*. It makes the rich color of his skin look divine, and I hate myself for noticing. He avoids my gaze—his eyes everywhere but me.

Grandmother's eyebrow arches. "Did you now?" she asks, her tone impressed. "How clever. Did it help?"

Even with Alexander distracting me from the doorway, I cannot help but answer her with more than a little excitement. "It made it so much easier—I don't know why I didn't think of it in the first place. I'm much more comfortable using runes to transfer arcana to my drawings." I risk a glance at Alexander to see how he's reacting to my frank discussion of Sylvan things, but he would make a superior card player—I can tell nothing from his expression, and his eyes are on the bluebird flitting about the room. I nod to the little bird. "I'm surprised to see it behaving like any other bird," I tell Grandmother.

"It's understandable once you know where it really comes from," she says. "As powerful as our arcana is, we never create something out of nothing. The painting you brought to life is a real bird—one that comes from the world around us. You simply transported it here."

I watch the bird with a frown. "So I've stolen this bird from its nest somewhere? That seems a little sad." I feel the press of eyes on me and turn to find Alexander staring. A flush creeps up my neck.

Grandmother nods solemnly. "Then perhaps you should learn how to send it back."

"What must I do?"

"The easiest and most direct way is to catch it again and draw a rune of transportation above it." She smiles as she watches the flitting bird. Serafino watches, too, from his perch high above us all. "But of course, first you must grab hold of the little thing."

The bird must sense us discussing it, because it renews its efforts to find the way out—flying from wall to wall erratically. I watch in dismay, knowing my chances of catching it are slim, and I don't relish looking the fool in front of Alexander.

Any advice? I think to Rowen.

He glances up at me with a wry expression on his face. *I suppose you are asking me because I'm a fox.* I smile sheepishly. *Unfortunately, I am not a* real *fox. I don't hunt, and I don't have a single natural instinct.*

I move toward the frantic little bird—perhaps I can corner it?—but before I can grab hold of it, a blur of movement races by me. As fast as a cobra striking, Alexander's hand darts out and captures the bird.

I stare at him with my mouth gaping as though I am very ill-bred indeed. He walks over to me, the bird held gently in one hand. When I manage to close my mouth and meet his gaze, I'm surprised to see a hint of pride in his eyes. *He's enjoying how shocked he's made me.*

"Very neatly done," Grandmother says, voicing my thoughts. "Lucy, do you know the rune to send it back?"

"I think so."

I take a step closer to Alexander until I can smell his familiar scent of cardamom and clove. As scents often do, it sets up a chain reaction of associated memories: meeting Alexander for the first time on the balcony, dancing with him, touring the National Gallery together. But most of all, it resurrects my emotional state during that time, leaving me feeling giddy and hopeful and ridiculously attracted to the man who shares so many of my interests.

Desperate to take back control of my emotions, I draw the rune in the air without thinking: two parallel lines, which represent transporting. At the same time, I draw heavily on Rowen's arcana, just as I would if I were painting in the bright sunshine.

The rune bursts into life above the bird in a flash like a camera's bulb, and both Alexander and I jump back in surprise. He opens his hand, and the bird is gone.

"*Beautifully* done," Grandmother says with real feeling as Alexander and I stare at each other. "You didn't hesitate."

I let out a relieved breath. "Thank you, Grandmother." I turn to Alexander to thank him, too, but stop myself at the last moment.

"If that is what your arcana looks like, then I have been wrong indeed." Alexander's eyes are full of regret, his voice with its slight accent drawing me in almost against my will. "You brought your painting to life."

I glance between the two of them in surprise. "I had no idea you both were watching."

"I didn't want to disturb you," Grandmother says unapologetically. "I could see that you were deep in concentration."

"I'd never seen a more lifelike bird," Alexander says, his voice unmistakably full of awe. "And that was before you made it fly around the room."

Warmth spreads through my chest, and I make the mistake of looking directly into his tawny eyes. And then I remember what was left unsaid in the dungeon, and my heart hardens.

"Lucy," Alexander says, my name a plea on his lips, "might we talk for a moment?"

I glance at Grandmother. "I will step out and give you some privacy," she says, but I wish she wouldn't.

I'm afraid to be left alone with him. Afraid to forgive him.

She leaves the room despite my internal protests, and Alexander turns to me. "You gave me much to think about during our short conversation, and as I contemplated the fact that I am Sylvan as you say, I realized how very wrong I've been. Not only that, but I realized that no matter what, I couldn't have hurt you."

"And I'm to believe the Order isn't really out to hurt any of us, I suppose."

Shame floods his face. "There was a time I would have told you that the Order only wanted to neutralize Sylvani who are dangerous—but that was before I'd personally witnessed what Wallace could do."

"Dangerous!" Anger ignites within me, flushing my cheeks and clenching my jaw. "How could you possibly think such a thing? If anyone, it is *you* who are dangerous."

He stands unblinking in the face of my rage, even though I can feel the beginnings of that shaky-desperate feeling I get when I'm about to dissolve into bitter tears. "Because one of them killed my mother."

I suck in my breath, my anger dampening ever so slightly. I try to hold on to it, even as my mind betrays me by sympathizing. How would I feel if my mother had been murdered by a group of strangely powerful beings and I didn't have a loving papa or siblings to raise me? *I wouldn't bloody go around attacking innocent people*, I growl back at myself.

"Even if that's true, your argument is still weak. This spiritual power . . . is that how you found me that first night?" Before he can respond, I continue, confiding in him the one thing I've always wanted to. "I saw you before I ever met you . . . in a drawing I'd made of my debut. Of course I'd wondered how that could be or if I had truly seen such a thing, but now that you're here, I see that it was all entirely possible."

"It's true," he says, his eyes still full of disbelief. "Part of my ability is that I can sense others with strong spiritual power around me—I can track them. But with you, it was different. I could see your drawings as clearly as though I watched you make them right in front of me. This must have been what you saw in that first drawing: the moment we connected."

"Then you were lying the night you met me." Pain blossoms at this lie more than any other. "You acted as though you hadn't seen me before, but you *had*." I pause to think, remembering that drawing in particular. It was the first one that had pulled me within—that had created a temporary portal without my consciously calling forth arcana. "I was pulled into that drawing of my debut, pulled and nearly trapped."

He looks surprised for a moment, and then thoughtful. "I sensed a powerful burst of your spiritual power that night, and when I sat down to draw, it was a throne room that filled my paper, and a beautiful woman in a white dress who captivated me." He pauses. "It may have been our connection that pulled you through, especially knowing what I do now—that I am part Sylvan." He says the words with some element of disbelief.

"Did you come to England just to find me?" I ask quietly, my whole body tense as I wait for his answer.

His gaze jumps to mine. "No, I swear it. I came because of my father's funeral—just as I said. It was only while I was in London that I felt it—felt *you*."

"So you tracked me, spied on my drawings, came to my debut ball— why? To report back to the Order that another evil Sylvani had been found?" He winces as my words and tone turn sharp.

"I never told the Order about you. I should have, I might have eventually, but I hadn't yet. There was still too much I didn't know, but I never thought you were evil, Lucy. Never."

"How comforting," I snap.

He sighs, rubs his face with his hand in frustration. "Once, I would have reported my findings immediately to Lord Tyrell—the head of the Order and the man who took me under his wing in India. He has been like a father to me. But ever since I saw what Lord Wallace was capable of . . . what Lord Tyrell sanctioned . . . I've had doubts about everything. Enough so that I wouldn't risk your safety until I'd gotten to the bottom of them."

"You keep mentioning Lord Wallace. What is it that he did?"

He shifts his gaze to the wall behind me. "There are those in the Order who have the power to drain away arcana from the Sylvani."

My eyes narrow. "You think I don't know that? One nearly killed my sister."

He looks taken aback at that, but gamely presses on. "Lord Wallace is one of these, but I'd always been led to believe that draining away arcana never hurt the Sylvani—only rendered their power impotent." He pauses, a haunted look entering his eyes. "I believed that right up until I found a girl dead—her face so ashy gray that I knew every drop of arcana had been drained from her until she died. It was Lord Wallace who'd killed her, but Lord Tyrell swore to me it was an accident. I couldn't get Wallace's expression out of my mind, though—that look that said he'd done it on purpose. That he'd *enjoyed* it."

Great spiders of fear creep across my skin, and I rub my arms vigorously. I think of meeting Wallace's cruel eyes across the pool at the Roman

Baths, of how close I'd come to the same fate as the poor girl Alexander described.

"When Wallace confronted us at the National Gallery," Alexander continues, "it was all I could do to stop myself from simply spiriting you away. I was terrified he'd get to you before I found the opportunity to warn you. I knew you were always surrounded by family, but I had no way of knowing if they'd be on their guard for such a threat."

"And then you followed me to Bath . . ."

A ghost of a smile crosses his face. "I did. Wallace made it clear he had no intention of leaving you alone."

Silence descends, thick with the weight of the many emotions hanging between us. I hate that my heart is thawing, that I so desperately want to believe him. *He betrayed you*, I remind myself aggressively. *He is your* enemy.

"It seems that I should be thanking you, then, for being a secret knight in shining armor. Unfortunately, I cannot ignore your involvement in a brotherhood that tried to murder my sister, nor have you even denounced them in our conversation today—merely that you have doubts. Not only that, it seems to me that you led Wallace—whom you've freely admitted is dangerous—right to me." I shake my head, my throat feeling uncomfortably thick. "And most of all, I cannot forgive you for making me believe you were someone who might understand me, for someone I might even . . ." I trail off, unable to finish. Even what? I cannot bear to hear myself say the words.

His face is stricken as I meet his eyes. The lump in my throat grows until I fear it will choke me. "You have no reason to ever forgive me," Alexander says, "and yet I cannot stop myself from hoping one day you might."

But the truth is, he's right: I have no reason to forgive.

And yet, I fear that's exactly the direction my traitorous heart is moving.

"I should call for Grandmother," I say abruptly. "She's waited outside long enough."

I walk away before he can say another word, and Rowen joins me from the corner he'd exiled himself to.

There is no shame in forgiveness, he thinks to me.

Not even when the man is your sworn enemy? I think back.

He doesn't reply, only leaves me to stew in my own thoughts darkly. The fact that Alexander's mother was killed by a Sylvani has changed everything for me. It's made his quest . . . almost understandable. Almost.

Except for the handing over of innocents to monsters.

Except for the fact that there is no proof he wouldn't have done the same to me if given the right circumstances.

After sending Rowen to Grandmother to inform her that our conversation has come to an end, she has us meet her in the training grounds. They are like the rest of the castle: sky-high ceilings, bright sunlight spilling in, and organic—carved from the rock itself, with a little stream running through it. The water disappears below the window, and when I walk over to peer out, it seems we are directly above one of the waterfalls.

"It's time we discussed what you must do to apprehend Centerius," Grandmother says. By Alexander's reaction, I can see that she has already told him the truth about Lord Tyrell. "This realm has less of an effect on you, Alexander, but Lucy does not have many more days before she'll be forced to go back."

"I will aid you in any way I can," he says resolutely.

"Can you truly turn against the man you said was like a father to you?" Disbelief peppers my tone.

"Even if draining people to the point of death wasn't enough," Alexander says quietly but firmly, "discovering the truth behind his sickeningly cannibalistic and selfish actions is enough to sway the hardest of hearts. And mine had never really been in it."

I glance at Grandmother, who gives me the smallest of nods. She has combed through his mind, no doubt. He speaks the truth. "Well said." I try not to sound resentful. "What must we do, Grandmother?"

"Lucy, you will open a portal directly into Centerius's estate through your drawing—into his library where he keeps rings containing the arcana of fallen Sylvani. Alexander will be the one to step through and apprehend him."

"But how am I to paint his library in such detail I can transport anyone there?"

"That is a valid concern," Grandmother says, "but rest assured, there is a way for you to see it before you paint."

I've come to know her well enough to know her cryptic answer will be revealed in time. "Still, it cannot be so simple," I say, glancing between the two of them.

"No, I should think not," Grandmother says. "You will need to provide Alexander with anything he should need to protect himself, for he cannot bring anything from this realm. As it is, we are skirting a serious law on a technicality." She glances at Serafino for a moment, as though lost in thought. "No Sylvani may open a new portal to the mortal realm; furthermore, nothing but the clothes on our backs may travel to the mortal realm. Since neither of you are pureblooded Sylvani, we are following the letter of the law—if not the spirit. But there are those who would see this as a breach either way, and thus, I must bind you both to silence."

"Of course," I say instantly.

Grandmother nods and turns to Alexander, where her gaze lingers for a moment.

"You have my word," he says.

"I'm glad to hear it," Grandmother says with a sharpness in her eyes. "Now if you're both willing, let's move to some physical training. You are both familiar with swordplay, yes? Lucy, if you are to anticipate what Alexander may need in any given situation, you need to familiarize yourself with how he fights."

My mind immediately jumps to fencing with James and to our short-lived self-defense lessons. I miss the familiarity of sparring with him, the comfort of doing something we both enjoyed. I glance at Alexander, and the image of him as he looked at Monsieur's—dressed so handsomely in his bright white fencing gear—sticks in my mind. And in that instant, I realize I'm still attracted to him in spite of everything. What sort of person am I then? To be attracted to a man I haven't decided to trust?

He catches my eye, and my heart beats a little faster.

I'm a terrible person.

"Lucy," Grandmother calls. She has moved to stand in front of a wall of weapons of every sort—swords and lances and spears and daggers. Some which I have no name for. "Which weapon are you most familiar with?"

"Foil swords, mostly," I say, a little intimidated as I stare at the vast array. "And James was trying to teach me to defend myself with a dagger."

She nods approvingly. "I'm surprised, actually. I was afraid you'd say nothing at all, though I suspected your sister would want you to have some skill after her close call." She pulls down a sword with a slim blade and hands it to me. The hilt is silver with a subtle knotwork pattern, and though the weapon is light, I can feel that it is well balanced. "This should do nicely," she says, and I nod my approval.

Alexander remains quiet throughout this exchange, his eyes on the wall behind us.

"Which weapon are you most drawn to?" I ask, and we both look at each other in surprise—I suppose because I've hardly said anything to him at all.

"I'm comfortable with anything," he says. "If you would like to start with swordplay, then I will be happy to do the same."

He strides forward and removes one of the swords from the wall, one that is longer and heavier than mine—a rapier. He holds it balanced on the flat of his palms for a moment, as though testing its make. Then in one smooth motion he transfers it to his right hand. Immediately it looks like an extension of his arm—his body makes subtle shifts until I can see the strength in his back and arms, the solidness of his legs, the power rolling off him in waves. I'm simultaneously impressed and intimidated. This won't be like fencing with James at all.

Grandmother watches, too. "I may have come at this the wrong way." When I glance at her curiously, she waves me away. "Never mind. You should have the chance to practice with each other at least once, and then we will talk."

I almost ask for a fencing uniform, but then I realize my current dress, with its split skirt and form-fitting leggings, will be more than adequate.

After a brief salute, I get into position. The weight of the sword and the tension in my muscles is all blessedly familiar, but with both Alexander and Grandmother watching, I feel distinctly uncomfortable.

Please let me not make a fool of myself.

Alexander returns the salute, but he remains upright, sword held loosely out before him. Thinking it is perhaps a difference in styles, I advance first.

He parries fluidly, almost lazily, as though batting aside my sword.

Surprise nearly causes me to lose my footing, but I manage to remember my steps and advance again. The result is the same: a lazy batting aside of my sword.

Again and again we repeat the pattern, until I begin to have the distinct feeling I am nothing but a mouse being toyed with by a very large cat.

And then, suddenly, everything changes.

I advance, and he parries so fast I can barely track the movement. Next I know, he is behind me, the tip of his sword a hairsbreadth away from my back. A crawling sensation raises the hair on the back of my neck just knowing how close I am to the point of a blade. Before I can decide whether to truly be afraid, Alexander moves gracefully away until he's standing before me again.

"How did you learn to fight like that?" I ask, my breaths coming faster both from my nervousness and from the quick footwork.

His gaze drops to his sword, and a hint of a smile comes to his mouth. "I spent two years training at a *kalari*—a fighting school in India. I continue to practice it daily." His gaze returns to mine. "You move well. Monsieur Giroux did not lie when he said you were one of his best students."

"I may be accomplished at fencing, but you're as graceful as a dancer," I say. "I rather had the impression you were toying with me."

He bows. "Forgive me. I wanted you to be able to know that I have some skill so that you might put your trust in me."

Trust—if only I could trust him. And though I am eager to bring an end to the Order, thinking of Alexander coming up against a full-blooded Sylvani makes me think of a zebra trying to attack a lion. Centerius will be much more powerful, and the only real advantage Alexander will have is that of surprise.

"I think it may help if you see what Alexander is truly capable of," Grandmother says, stepping away from the wall. "Centerius may be strong, but I think the two of you working together may be stronger."

She gestures toward Alexander to come closer. He puts the sword back on the wall and then does as she asks. Grandmother draws a rune in the air before immediately placing her hand on Alexander's temple. Images spring to life in front of us, just as they did when Grandmother showed me the long-ago battle.

The visions are of Alexander, clad rather scandalously in only a pair of white flowing pants, his body balanced on one foot. The real Alexander holds very still as he watches these images—the shock at seeing memories of himself playing out before us more than evident.

They show Alexander going through a series of motions—the muscles of his body rippling and contorting—but always there is the utmost control.

He makes it look fluid, easy, as though he is not a man of flesh and bone at all, but rather of air and water.

The images of the controlled movements fades away, replaced in its stead by a clear memory of a rocky beach, the waves crashing against the shore under a gray sky. Again Alexander is dressed in nothing but loosely flowing white pants, but this time he holds a scimitar in his hand.

He faces off against a man dressed exactly the same and wielding the same wickedly curved blade. Through some unseen signal, they begin to spar, and I suck in my breath—how will either of them keep from getting slashed to pieces? It seems insanely risky to spar with no armor and with blades that are clearly sharp.

Alexander takes a running leap at the other man, his entire body bowed back, lending power to the blow of the sword. The other man somehow manages to parry the move, and then the two of them continue their fight in increasingly impossible leaps and contortions. Not once do they harm the other—not once do they even impart so much as a scratch. Their moves are fast but efficient, and I can sense the power and control behind them.

I glance at Alexander, still standing with Grandmother's hand upon his temple, but a look of fascination has replaced his earlier shock.

The sparring match between the two men repeats itself with several different weapons—daggers, swords and shields, a dagger worn over the knuckles—and all end the same way, with no blood shed.

And then, the memory shifts, changing to a moonlit nursery. A riotous jungle can be glimpsed just outside the window—vibrantly green plants with thick leaves, brightly colored flowers, enormous trees.

Grandmother glances at Alexander in obvious surprise, but his expression looks determined.

The memory shifts from the window to a small bed, surrounded by mosquito netting. A woman stands over a boy, singing softly as she tucks him in. She is beautiful, her hair spilling down her back in thick waves, her sari the color of persimmons. The love in her softly rounded face for the tiny boy makes my heart ache.

When I glance at Alexander again, tears fall down his face unchecked, even as a soft smile touches his lips.

All too soon, the image fades.

"I never thought I'd see my mother again," Alexander says, and though I already suspected, I still feel a jolt of surprise.

I think of the small boy, transposing his image on the man before me. He once had a mother who loved him—a half-Sylvan mother—who was later killed. Though my mother didn't die in such a violent way, I still can't help but see the parallel.

"She was beautiful," I say, "and I could see she loved you very much."

"Both are true," Alexander says, a shadow crossing his face, "but I fear that I haven't been worthy of her love for some time now."

"Stopping the man who manipulated you into hunting your own kind will go a long way toward redemption," I say, and this time, I mean it. "I've never seen anyone fight the way you do—some of it doesn't even seem possible! And you fought without armor, without any means of protection."

"Your good opinion means a lot to me." His smile cautiously grows wider, as though afraid I will suddenly take back my praise. "It's called *kalaripayattu*. We fight with no protective clothing because we have total control over our bodies—we know our limits, and we know our range. We can safely spar without injury."

Grandmother has allowed us to speak to each other uninterrupted thus far, but now she steps forward. "I am glad you could see Alexander's abilities for yourself, Lucy. It's important to have trust in your partner, and you will have to rely on him greatly in the days to come." She turns to Alexander. "But I must confess I am surprised you had the ability to control what was revealed just now—you shifted the memories to one of your own choosing."

He nods. "And forgive me if I overstepped my bounds, but once I realized what you were doing, I had an overpowering desire to see my mother again."

"There is no need to apologize, but what I *am* interested in is the fact that you managed to change the memories. It takes great strength of mind to resist me, and even greater to wrest back control of your own mind once I have infiltrated it."

I feel some of the color drain from my face to have it discussed in such terms. What power! It's frightening to imagine someone with such a gift; the mind is such an intimate thing—memories, even more so.

"It was always obvious to me that you had Spiritual arcana," Grandmother continues, "but I hadn't expected it to be this strong." She falls silent for a moment, her eyes sweeping over him as if appraising him. "You will make a better partner for Lucy than I had imagined."

Though she must mean our shared objective to stop Lord Tyrell, an almost indefinable feeling comes over me—like the primal awareness of an oncoming storm. Her words have a greater meaning, and the hair on the back of my neck rises even as my chest lightens at the thought.

But then, I'm struck by a realization so stirring I cry out, "Grandmother! Does this mean I may see images of my mother—perhaps even your memories of her?"

Grandmother turns to me with a slowly widening smile. "You can, dearest one. And we have Alexander to thank for the idea."

TWENTY-TWO

GRANDMOTHER and I spent hours watching memories of Mama. I had so few of my own that the vast majority came from Grandmother, and tears spilled unchecked as I saw aspects of my mother's life I never even knew about: her brief stint as a dragon rider after healing a hatchling dragon princess, her time spent in the ancient woods riding the oryx with Rowen by her side, and when she and Rowen were both young and small and would spend almost all their time swimming in the crystal blue lake.

But my favorite memory of all, the one I replay nearly all night long, is the moment when my mother returned from meeting my father for the first time.

"We danced all night," Mama said to Grandmother, her voice so joyful it brings a smile to my face.

She is much younger than I have ever seen her, and yet she doesn't look very different. Her eyes are a little less worldly, perhaps, and her mannerisms more enthusiastic and girlish. She's still dressed in a gown from my own world, one I remember from her trousseau because it's breathtakingly lovely. With a plunging neckline, wide skirts, and miles of satin and lace, the sapphire blue dress makes her eyes seem almost violet.

The skirts hang over the edge of Grandmother's bed, where Mama rests at the foot. Grandmother smiles at Mama encouragingly.

"From the moment I touched him, I knew." Rowen looks up at her from his spot between Mama and Grandmother, and the two of them share a wide grin.

"You had a vision," Grandmother says knowingly. She leans forward, and it takes me a moment to realize that my unflappable grandmother is excited.

Mama nods. "I saw children—blonde-haired, blue-eyed children." Her eyes fill with tears. "Not just one, either. A son and two daughters. They looked like me." She whispers the last almost reverently.

Grandmother leans forward and takes hold of Mama's hand. "My darling. There is no greater news you could have brought me."

Now Mama cries in earnest. "Truly, Mama? Do you mean it? I thought you would be . . ."

Grandmother shakes her head. "You know the plight of our people. The struggles we have had to bear children. How could I wish that for you? No, my wish is for you to bear me many grandchildren, to live your life with someone you love, and with children you adore."

Mama grips Grandmother's hand. "Even if it means I must leave Sylvania? Leave you and . . ." She looks down at Rowen and loses the ability to speak.

"Your visions should not be ignored, especially if the fate of future children hangs in the balance. They will only be half-Sylvani, but it has been done before. Our bloodline will continue, and it's your happiness that's most important."

"But Father . . ."

"Your father will be furious," Grandmother says, her eyes intensely focused on Mama, "but even his anger will fade in time."

"Then I will return to Robert as soon as I can and give him my answer," Mama says.

"It will be unbearable without you, and yet I will endure it for the chance of one day meeting grandchildren," Grandmother says.

Mama throws herself into her mother's arms, and I think I can feel a little bit of what she must have felt: joyful hope, anxious fear, desperate love. But there is no greater gift than seeing how truly, madly, hopelessly Mama loved us all.

I fall asleep finally, thankful beyond words that my mother chose to put aside everything she'd ever known just for the chance to bring us to life.

And for her mother, our grandmother, who stood by her side and encouraged it.

Lucy.

   Lucy.

   "Lucy!"

   I wake up with a jolt, my heart doing that horrible thing it sometimes does when I'm awoken suddenly where it threatens to burst from my chest. I look around my dark room in utter confusion. Moonlight spills in from the open windows, and then I see the ghostly image of my sister.

   "Wren! What—?"

   "Forgive me, I didn't realize it would be in the middle of the night here."

   "Yes, but . . . Wren . . . how *are* you here?" I ask, still in that sleepy-bewildered state.

   "Ah, yes. Well, we've had some surprising news that apparently lets me travel between realms."

   I sit up in bed at that. "Are you here only in spirit then? I should hope so anyway, otherwise you should know you look positively ghoulish."

   Wren laughs. "How kind of you," she deadpans. "My goodness, I shall refrain from waking you in the middle of the night in future."

   I cover my mouth. "I'm awful. Of course you look beautiful as always. And what is this surprising news? Nothing bad I hope!"

   She shakes her head. "No, no. Nothing bad. Well, at least, *I* don't think so. Colin may have a different opinion altogether . . . right, I shouldn't keep you in suspense," she says when I give her a look that says she's galloping away on a tangent. "I'm here because of Izzie. She can do as you do—transport my spirit to this realm."

   My mouth falls open in shock—I hadn't expected her to be so powerful so soon. "How did you discover this?"

   Rowen pads over silently at my outburst of a question, returning from the balcony where he spends the majority of the night. *Katherine,* he projects into both of our minds, *you found a conduit to transport you here? Is there urgent news? I can fetch the queen.*

   "Oh, hello to you, dear fox. No, I don't think it's quite so urgent as that." Wren's image seems to flicker, as though she's fading. "I'd very much like to see my grandmother," she answers him wistfully, "but I fear I won't be able to maintain my presence here much longer. Izzie missed you terribly, Lucy, and I kept finding her in your room. She'd always been interested in your paintings and things, and tonight I found her with a drawing of the portal. It was quite by accident that I touched her shoulder just as she touched the drawing, and the next thing I knew, I was here in your bedroom—which is just beautiful, by the way," she adds as she turns to take it all in—the balcony and waterfalls and the lovely room itself.

"This is our mother's room," I say thickly, nostalgic longing crashing over me like a wave.

"Is it?" she says in a reverent whisper, her gaze darting about the room as if she wishes she can memorize ever corner. "Oh, but I'm so relieved to see you! We were worried, of course, after that rather disastrous meeting with Lord Devonshire and his friend. After Lord Devonshire followed you through . . ." She shakes her head. "James beat the living daylights out of the other man—his friend, apparently. He swore up and down neither of them meant you any harm, that the real danger was Lord Wallace, so we weren't out of our minds with worry, but still, it was all rather suspicious."

"I'm terribly sorry, Wren," I say, guilt settling uncomfortably in my stomach. "I should have tried to contact you right away to send word that no harm had come to me. I wish you could truly see this castle . . . Mama's library, the paintings of her, even the smell of the flowers is almost beyond words."

"I'm so happy you've been able to experience so much of her realm," Wren says sincerely. "Has Grandmother been keeping you busy?"

"Yes, and also, so much has happened since I arrived . . ." Wren raises her eyebrows expectantly, and I can feel my mouth run away with me. "Alexander—that is, Lord Devonshire—followed me through the portal, and Grandmother had him arrested for treason against me. He—" I stop myself just in time before I reveal anything else. I don't want Wren to know the truth about him yet. I can hardly face it myself, and she will never forgive him. She must be told in the right way when we have more time. Nor can she know our true plan to take down the Order. She would never allow me to risk myself in such a way, even if it is Alexander who will be in the most danger. I have no other option but to lie, and I can only hope her spirit form won't be nearly as intuitive as her physical self. "It was a bit of a misunderstanding," I say weakly. "But the short of it is that Grandmother has agreed to tutor him on defensive arcana as well."

I can see the confusion on her face. "But why would he follow you through? Did he know where he'd end up?"

"We're still trying to determine that," I say weakly, and her eyebrows furrow even more. "But how is everyone?" I ask, in the hopes of distracting her. "Did Rob and Papa understand? What did you tell Rose?" I wince. "And how did Colin take it?"

She grows suddenly still and glances behind her, and I know she's seeing our own realm. "I haven't much longer, I'm afraid, Lucy darling. Everyone took it well enough, though they're concerned. Rob is fascinated by the idea of our Sylvan grandmother, and Papa is both afraid and angry about the Order finding us. I told Rose that you'd come down with something terribly contagious and we didn't want to expose her to you." She sighs. "I'm nearly positive she knows we're lying, but she's kind enough not to pry. And as for Colin, well . . . he took it like I'm sure you expected him to."

"Heavens," I say, wincing again. "And are you still in Bath?"

"We are. We saw no reason to cut our visit short and inconvenience Rose, and in fact, we've extended it. We want to be near the portal for when you return." She glances behind her again, and her image flickers. "I really must go, darling, but before I do, will you do me a favor?"

"Of course—anything."

"Will you tell Grandmother about Izzie? Ask her if this is normal . . . what we can expect . . ."

"I will. I'll ask her everything and write it down. What does Colin think? Is he terribly worried?"

Wren looks sheepish. "I haven't told him yet. Oh, don't start," she jumps in when she sees my expression. "I've heard enough from Rob on the subject. Colin is near his breaking point over you in Sylvania and the Order sniffing around. If he should know his daughter has manifested abilities strong enough to be targeted . . . well, I don't even want to imagine his reaction to that."

"I shudder to think of it, actually," I say, and we laugh.

"I love you, Luce," she says, her eyes shining.

"I love you, too, Wren. I'll be home soon."

When I wake up—rather groggily, I'm afraid, after all that happened last night—I ask Astrid to take me directly to Grandmother. Guilt chips away at me, hurrying my steps. I've been here for three days already, and I haven't once asked her about Izzie as Wren requested so long ago. The thought of my niece's power has me rather dumbfounded. She is only two years old and only part-Sylvani instead of half, and yet she can perform arcana on the same level as me. What will she be capable of when she comes of age?

Astrid leads me to a room I suppose would be considered a sitting room in my own world, but unsurprisingly, it's completely different from any sitting room I've ever seen. The soaring ceiling is glittering mosaic—small white unicorns facing off against a bright crimson dragon. The floor is white marble, and at one end is an indoor waterfall cascading into a dark pool. Serafino perches at the very top of the waterfall, letting his wing feathers dangle into the water. Grandmother sits upon a chaise lounge, drinking a cup of tea, when Rowen and I enter. She stands when she sees me, her eyebrows rising.

"I didn't expect you up for hours," she says.

I feel heat on my cheeks. "Contrary to my behavior here, I don't usually sleep until the afternoon, though I didn't get much sleep last night—my sister came to visit."

She looks surprised for a moment before nodding to herself. "I thought I'd felt a disturbance in the air. Serafino assured me it was nothing to worry about, and I knew Rowen would have come to fetch me had there been a need."

I offered to, Rowen projects into our thoughts.

"It was my niece, Izzie—Isidora," I correct myself, and Grandmother smiles a pleased smile at the name. "She transported Katherine's spirit simply by touching one of my drawings of the portal."

"Our blood is strong," Grandmother says with pride, and I think of the memory I witnessed between Grandmother and Mama. Our Sylvan bloodlines *were* strong.

"That's just it—Katherine wanted me to ask you if it's at all unusual. You see, Isidora is only two."

"Is she? My stars." The proud smile slips from her face as her expression turns introspective. "That *is* rather unusual, I must admit. Her father is entirely mortal?"

"As far as we know."

"Hm." Grandmother glances back at Serafino, who has stopped washing his wings in the water to attend our conversation. "The child must certainly be made to rest after such a powerful expression of arcana. I hope Katherine knows this."

I nod, feeling fairly confident that Wren would insist on sunlight and rest for Izzie—whether she appeared to need it or not. "I'm sure she will. I think she was most concerned about the future. If Izzie is this powerful now . . ."

"She will be no doubt powerful, but I should think her arcana will be as easily hidden as yours. Her abilities are Spiritual, after all, as opposed to Corporal."

"I'm relieved that you should think so, though I'm afraid I'm unfamiliar with those terms—I know you said yesterday that Alexander used Spiritual arcana."

She nods. "We call the abilities that directly affect the body—such as healing or any of the explosive offensive and defensive arts—Corporal. Your sister's abilities fall into that category, while yours are Spiritual—though you can produce some tangible things, the majority of your power lies in the abstract, the spiritual realm. Most Sylvani have an affinity for either Spiritual or Corporal arcana, but your mother was unusual in that she had an affinity for both."

I know my understanding of her explanation is elementary at best, but my chest swells with pride when I think of Mama's power. "We always knew Mama was amazing," I say with a smile.

"She was one of a kind in many ways," Grandmother says with a sad smile of her own.

"Which category does your arcana fall into?" I ask, though I'm fairly certain I know the answer.

"Spiritual, just like you, but I've been gifted with a broad range of abilities—from pulling objects from the spirit realm to various aspects of prophecy. You grandfather had Corporal abilities. Generally, Sylvan unions are chosen this way—joining Spiritual and Corporal in an effort to continue the line. It was an incredible blessing when your mother developed both."

I think again of the memory Grandmother allowed me to see. "And you still let her leave."

Grandmother smiles and touches my cheek. "For you, dearest one—and for your brother and sister. Your mother and I both saw it as a fair trade, though I'm afraid your grandfather disagreed until the day he died."

"Well, I think I can safely say we all thank you for it."

She smiles. "Actually, your concern over little Izzie makes me think it's time to test you on a portal."

I look at her in surprise. "So soon?"

"We haven't much more time. We'll send for Alexander, and then you can open a portal to your sister's house and send him through."

I think of Colin's reaction and shudder. "Oh, Grandmother, I'm not sure . . . Katherine's husband might not—"

Grandmother waves her hand. "Her husband is the least of my concerns right now, Lucy darling. There's no reason you cannot perform arcana of this magnitude, and I'd like for you to have one practice run before the real thing."

"Very well, of course I cannot say no to you."

Though I hope I'm up to the challenge of both opening a portal and sending Alexander through. I think of Colin happening upon him and barely suppress a shudder.

So many things could go wrong.

♀

ALEXANDER cannot help but smile the moment he sees Lucy. He'd been summoned to meet Lucy and the queen in a room of wild, natural beauty. A waterfall cascades at the far end of the room while the ceiling has been created with countless mosaics. But Alexander doesn't waste time staring at the room around him when Lucy is around—something about her draws the eye, a light within that's difficult to ignore. He was right to think her beauty blinding during that first fateful night, or if not blinding, then at least thoroughly distracting. And here, in this setting, she seems so at ease, so at one with her surroundings.

When she meets his eyes, she even returns the smile, and Alexander feels an answering lightness in his chest. She's still guarded around him, and her smiles aren't what they once were toward him, but they are steadily growing friendlier.

His overall mood has much improved since moving out of the godforsaken cell, though the queen still keeps him under guard. After yesterday, though, he feels as though he can endure anything. Seeing his mother again was an unexpected and supremely welcome gift. Her memory had been fading in his mind as memories do—he'd often had to refer to the one photograph he had of her to remind himself of the exact shape of her eyes—and to see her again, not only in color, but in *moving* images . . . it was almost more than he could bear. But the fact that he had passed on such a gift to Lucy—allowing her to see her own mother—was the greatest gift of all.

The Sylvani were never evil, he thinks to himself. *Not when such women of character like Lucy and her mother,* my *mother . . . even the queen . . . exist. Lord Tyrell has led me astray, and he must face the consequences for his actions.*

Thinking of Lord Tyrell reminds him of the truth the queen imparted—the story that was almost too impossible to believe. That Lord Tyrell is actually an exiled Sylvani named Centerius, and that he created the Order expressly to drain other Sylvans of their arcana to maintain his own immortality. Many times has Alexander reviewed this in his mind, searching for any indication that it may be true. He thinks of Lord Tyrell's walk-in vault, a room dedicated to everything he has confiscated from captured Sylvani: enchanted rings, paintings, elaborately embroidered fabrics, jewelry and gemstones. But there is a case he keeps with rows of identical rings resting on black velvet, rings shaped as ankhs—the secret symbol of the brotherhood. These rings are given to members of the Order who have risen in the ranks. They are a closely guarded secret because of their own unique ability—they store arcana, thus giving their wearer increased longevity of life.

Alexander owns such a ring, but from the moment he touched it, he couldn't wear it. It had brought a sense of unease with it, as though he wore something that belonged to a dead man. With a grimace, he realizes just how accurate that may be.

"Alexander," Lucy calls, and he is instantly pulled from his reverie. It's not often that Lucy addresses him directly. "Grandmother has asked that I practice transporting you, and so I am to open a portal and send you to my sister's house in Bath."

He winces. "That's nearly as bad as sending me straight to Lord Tyrell's."

Lucy laughs—laughs!—and Alexander grins back at her, enjoying the sound. "I daresay you're right." She sends the queen a pointed look. "And I told her as much."

The queen shrugs unapologetically. "Then send him to an area of the house least likely to be frequented by Katherine's husband."

Lucy looks thoughtful for a moment. "Rob's room!" She laughs. "Oh, what I'd give to see his reaction when you pop up in the middle of the room. It's a cruel prank, but I'm sure he'll appreciate it after he gets over his fright."

"Just as long as he doesn't hit me in surprise."

Lucy shakes her head. "He's far too lazy."

"I can handle lazy. It's your hot-headed brothers-in-law who take a little more finesse."

"Yes, well, I'm afraid they *were* right about you," Lucy says, but though her words are antagonistic, her soft smile is anything but.

Thoroughly confused now, Alexander tentatively smiles back. "Then I shall have to change their opinion of me along with yours."

Something sparks in her eyes, and he knows he's said the right thing. The relief weakens his limbs.

"Well, let's send you into the lion's den, shall we?" Lucy asks.

Alexander crouches down in the unfamiliar room, his heart rate elevated just slightly. He knows Lucy said her brother wouldn't react violently, but Alexander has trained too long and too hard not to be cautious upon entering a new environment. He is impressed as to how quickly and easily Lucy sent him through the portal. It took her no time at all to draw the room belonging to her brother, and her attention to detail had been enviable—the painting on one wall of a hunting scene, the particular pattern of the oriental rug upon the floor, even a silver dish her brother keeps his cufflinks in.

Her confidence in transforming the drawing into a means for transcending realms seemed to have risen greatly after successfully bringing the bird to life, and more so after sending it through its own portal. He smiles inwardly when he thinks of how she was a touch more anxious over sending Alexander through—a human is certainly different than a bird.

The sound of deep breathing tells him the occupant of the dark room is asleep, and by the tone, he can tell the occupant is male.

Alexander straightens, every muscle in his body under his complete control, making each of his motions silent. He moves toward the sleeping man in just this way, carefully listening for any change in breathing patterns. When he reaches the side of the bed, he sees what he's looking for: blonde hair.

In a blur, Alexander's hand darts out and covers the man's mouth, bringing him to a hasty awakening.

"I'm not here to hurt you," Alexander says in a rushed whisper to the wide-eyed Mr. Sinclair. "Your sister Lucy sent me through a portal from Sylvania, and if you will agree not to alert the others, I will release you."

Mr. Sinclair nods after a moment, and Alexander quickly removes his hand. He sits up in bed, eyeing Alexander suspiciously.

"Lucy sent you, did she?" he asks. "Well, of all the people in this house to wake, I suppose I was the best choice."

Alexander grins. "We agreed you were the least of all the evils."

"So why are you here? Did Katherine get word to Lucy?"

Alexander nods. "About your niece's arcana? Yes, and she asked me to pass on a message: her arcana is Spiritual, meaning it will be easier to keep hidden, and though it's surprising it's manifesting at such a young age, she comes from a powerful bloodline. Lady Thornewood should be sure to give her adequate rest."

Mr. Sinclair looks distinctly confused as he gets out of bed—curiously, he's almost fully dressed instead of wearing the usual pajamas. "No, no—not about Izzie. About Lady Rose."

"Lady Rose?" Alexander scrambles to place the name—he does not like being unprepared. In his experience, it can be dangerous. "Lucy's friend?"

"Yes, she's taken a turn for the worse, I'm afraid," Mr. Sinclair says, his whole expression shadowed. "Her father has been sent for."

"She's dying," Alexander says, as a dull horror grips him. He can almost feel Lucy's pain.

"The doctor says she doesn't have long. It's why I've gone to bed in my day clothes—my sister sits up with her now, but I told her to call me the moment she needs anything. Lady Rose has been an absolute saint about it all—it'll be a dark day when her gentle soul leaves this world."

"Lucy loves her," Alexander says, more to himself than to Mr. Sinclair. He can't bear to think of Lucy in pain—and he knows how much pain this death will bring her. "What is the cause of her illness?"

"Weak lungs—the doctor says pneumonia has set in. Apparently she's been at risk of dying from it since she was born."

Alexander's mind races through possible treatments. He'd had some training in the art of using herbal medicine—he'd found it both necessary and convenient when he was hundreds of miles from the nearest doctor, and he'd become so skilled that many turned to him as a healer—but he has to think what may be available here. His mind flips through the catalog of known treatments for inflammation of the lungs. Suddenly, he lands on the answer. "Is there a way to get pleurisy root?" he asks sharply.

Mr. Sinclair shakes his head. "Pleurisy root?"

"It's also known as milkweed."

"Oh yes . . . I'm not sure. We could send for a gardener. Why?"

Alexander doesn't answer for a moment—he's remembering other treatments. "Turmeric? Garlic? Both of those things could help for now—if you mix both of them with fresh lemons and raw honey."

Mr. Sinclair strides over and pulls a long velvet rope to summon a servant. "The cook should have those ingredients, I should think. Are you experienced in medicine?"

"I have some working knowledge of herbal treatments," Alexander says. He's willing to try anything if it prolongs Rose's life. Lucy should have the chance to say good-bye properly. Because of her chronically weak lungs, Alexander knows the herbs won't save her, but they can give her time, and hopefully, a more peaceful death.

The servant arrives—a harried-looking valet. "Can I be of some service, my lord?"

"Will you wake the kitchen maids and ask for a paste of garlic, turmeric, and honey? It should be given to the Lady Rose." The servant looks distinctly confused, especially when he sees Alexander standing near the fireplace, but he nods willingly. "And I don't suppose a gardener might be awoken at this hour?"

"A gardener, my lord?"

"We are in desperate need of milkweed," Mr. Sinclair says.

"If it's milkweed you're needing, my lord, I can get it for you."

Mr. Sinclair perks up at that. "You can? Good man!"

"Yes, my lord, my grandfather worked as a gardener, you see, and I learned quite a lot from him. I've seen some growing beside the bridge out of town."

Alexander and Mr. Sinclair share a look of profound relief. "Though I hesitate to send you on such an errand in the middle of the night," Mr. Sinclair says, "it's for the Lady Rose—it could help her greatly."

"I'll fetch it then, my lord," the valet says.

"Thank you, Holt. Quick as you can."

The valet leaves, and Mr. Sinclair turns to Alexander. "I don't dare hope this will save her, but if it will give her a few more days of life, it'll be well worth it. Her father is due to arrive late tonight, but even then, he may be arriving just as she breathes her last."

"Will you show me to her room?" Alexander asks. "There may be still more I can do."

Mr. Sinclair hesitates. "I cannot promise you will not encounter the Thornewoods on your way there. My sister has been maintaining a vigil over the girl, and the others may be asleep now, but I have no way of knowing."

"I'd rather not spend the rest of the night cowering in your room," Alexander says.

But as he moves to follow Mr. Sinclair, he feels a pulling in the center of his chest, like a thread being tugged. The sensation strengthens until it seems to squeeze his lungs. *Lucy*, he thinks. She must be summoning him back—it's the agreed upon signal, and Alexander need only draw a rune to allow the connection. Should he try to contact her? But every nerve in his body is tingling with the awareness that he doesn't have long. He must go to Lady Rose now if he is to give her any aid—even a few minutes more delay may be too long.

His decision made, he strides after Rob and into the darkened hall.

The smell of death is strong in the room—sour and almost cloyingly sweet. But the girl continues to breathe, though each breath is clearly a struggle. Alexander's heart feels like lead in his chest as he watches her, her face so pale, her lips with a bluish tint from the lack of life-saving oxygen. Her lungs rattle in her chest.

Too weak to rouse herself, she makes no sign of knowing the two men and Lucy's sister are in the room.

"She only just fell asleep," Lady Thornewood whispers, her own face drawn and pale. "It was . . . she was suffering terribly."

Mr. Sinclair puts his arm around his sister. "There's nothing you can do, Wren." He eyes her meaningfully, and Alexander realizes he must mean with arcana.

Lady Thornewood looks up at Alexander for the first time. "I dearly hope Lucy sent you, for if you are an assassin, I think I hardly have the energy to fight you."

"She did send me, my lady, and the queen—your grandmother—did as well." He pauses, unsure how much else to say—he's unsure if Lady Thornewood knows the extent of Lucy's plans. "She wanted me to ease your mind about your daughter. The girl should rest, but she's in no real danger. Her arcana is Spiritual, which means she can hide it as easily as Lucy does." He glances at Rose again. "But I'm also here because I can help."

"Well, that's a relief," Lady Thornewood says.

Mr. Sinclair nods. "He has Holt fetching various herbs—I thought anything would be worth trying. Her father still hasn't arrived . . ." He trails off as everyone in the room becomes painfully aware of Rose's labored breathing.

"I agree," Lady Thornwood says softly. "If you have the means to help her in any way, Lord Devonshire, please do."

"I will. But please, call me Alexander."

She gives him a ghost of a smile. "Then you must call both of us by our given names, for it wouldn't do for all of us to be working together as nurses in a darkened room and maintain ridiculous formalities."

"Well said," Rob says, and Alexander gives a single nod.

He moves closer to the bed and holds his hands above Rose's frail form, fingers splayed and palms down. He lets his eyelids fall closed. When he opens himself up to sense her prana—her life force—he frowns when he finds how faint it is. He knows her levels will never be on par with his—and certainly not with Lucy's or Katherine's—but all human life has at least a soft glow simmering beneath the surface. Rose's is like a single candle in a cave. Still, he will do all he can to fan the flames into greater life.

He brings his palms together and brings them to his chest. Rapidly, he forms hand motions: hands clasped, then index fingers steepled then clasped again. He learned these hand signals long ago in the *kalari*. They are a way to physically connect to spiritual power, and now that Alexander has seen Lucy utilize runes, he thinks they may be similar.

The candle flame of Rose's prana flares with the coaxing of Alexander's hand signals, each motion acting like a gust of wind. A fine sheen of sweat breaks out across Alexander's face as he keeps up the motions, but he's rewarded by Rose's face blooming with color. A little more, and her breaths come easier—the death rattle disappears.

"She looks so much better!" Katherine says, her voice still quiet but excitement shining in her eyes.

Alexander finally releases his hands, the muscles in them sore from his intense efforts. He lets out a breath of relief. If she responded to this, she may respond equally well to the herbal medicine.

Rob claps him on the back. "Well done."

Just then, Holt enters the room with the mixture of garlic, turmeric, and honey. His cheeks are streaked with dirt, and he's panting for breath. He holds an uprooted scraggly plant in his hand—the milkweed. "Forgive me, my lord, but I wasn't sure what part of the plant you'd be needing, so I brought it all."

Alexander takes the plant from Holt. "Thank you, Holt. You were right to do so—it's the root I'm after. Katherine, if you'd be so good as to assist Lady Rose in taking a spoonful of the mixture in that bowl, then I will prepare the pleurisy root. Holt, would you mind showing me the way to the kitchen? I need access to a mortar and pestle, water, and a kettle."

"Right this way, my lord," Holt says.

He leads Alexander back out into the darkened hall and down a wide staircase. Once on the main floor, Alexander is led to yet another staircase and down into the bowels of the house. It reminds him uncomfortably of the dungeon in the Sylvan castle, and a sensation rather like an elephant sitting on his chest descends upon him. Steadying himself with a few deep breaths, he follows Holt into the kitchen, where a tired-looking kitchen maid waits for him.

"I thought you might need something else," she says with a resigned sigh. "What can I get for you, my lord?"

"A mortar and pestle, boiling water, and a tea cup."

If she thinks the requests are strange, she says nothing of it, and hurries to retrieve the necessary items. When the kettle is on the stove, and the pencil-thin roots have been thoroughly washed, Alexander gets to work. He cuts them all into uniform lengths and then separates out some to be ground into a paste and others to be made into a tea. It may be overkill, but the poor girl is so far gone that the extra dose may help pull her back from the brink.

When the roots are thoroughly ground to a white paste, he scoops them out and puts them in a bowl. "You can take this up to Lady Rose directly," he tells Holt. "Tell Lady Thornewood that it should be spread across her chest."

"Yes, my lord," Holt says and hurries away.

The kettle whistles, and the kitchen maid anticipates Alexander's need, bringing it swiftly to his side. He takes it from her and carefully pours it over the roots in the tea cup. "This can steep while I carry it up to her. Thank you for your assistance."

"I'm happy to help, my lord. We haven't known Lady Rose for long, but we do care for her."

Alexander nods once and strides away, careful not to spill a drop. After two sets of staircases, he turns down the hall and nearly strides headlong into James Wyndam.

"What the devil?" Lord Wyndam shouts, his expression darkening so fast Alexander realizes violence will be unavoidable.

If he causes me to spill this tea, I shall kill him—consequences be damned.

It seems to only take an instant for James to make up his mind, and Alexander recognizes Lord Wyndam's decision to stop Alexander forcibly before he even takes the first swing.

Lord Wyndam's fist flies straight for Alexander's jaw, but for Alexander, it may as well be in slow motion. Alexander neatly dodges. He glances down for a fraction of a second to be sure the tea hasn't spilled. It hasn't.

When his punch connects with nothing but air, Lord Wyndam is thrown off-balance, and Alexander gets behind him. With his fingers pressed together and his hand flattened to a knife-like edge, Alexander delivers two swift blows to two pressure points on Lord Wyndam's body. One-armed, he helps Lord Wyndam sink to the floor.

Alexander feels a twinge of guilt over the unconscious man, but he ignores it. He knows it wasn't just the threat of his being a potential intruder that made Lord Wyndam attack—he has hated Alexander from the moment he sensed his interest in Lucy.

The room smells strongly of herbs when he enters, but the Lady Rose is still sleeping. Rob and Katherine turn to him as he carries the tea over to her bedside. He uses a spoon to pull out the roots, and tests the liquid on his wrist to be sure it's not too hot.

"If you will help her sit up, I'll pour a bit of this down her throat," Alexander says, and Rob and Katherine both jump up to help.

Cupping the back of Lady Rose's head in his hand—and with Rob and Katherine supporting her back—the three of them manage to dribble the warm tea into her mouth. With effort, she swallows, and they let her rest again.

Alexander leans down to listen to her chest, hovering just above her frail breastbone. Her lungs sound a good deal clearer—the wheezing still present, but much less of a death rattle. He lets his own breath out in relief.

When he steps back, though, he notices a darkness hovering just about Lady Rose. His muscles tense, prepared to attack if need be, but then he recognizes what it is. He's seen it before—many times on the poor streets of India.

The shadow of death.

So it is but a temporary reprieve, he thinks, his chest filling with a heavy sorrow. *Still, it is time she needed most, and time I have given her.*

"She just needs a good deal of rest now," Alexander says, and Katherine nods eagerly. "Shall I relate to you how to prepare more tea and the paste for her chest? It can be repeated in the morning, or if she happens to wake in the night, she may have more of the tea and another spoonful of the garlic and turmeric mixture."

"Yes, please do explain it to me." She reaches out and touches his arm. "You cannot imagine how grateful I am that you have helped her so. It will mean so much to her family, of course, but we have grown fond of her as well." Her eyes fill. "And I couldn't bear for anything to happen to her while Lucy is away."

"Don't cry all over the poor man," Rob says, wrapping his arm around his sister's shoulders. "No gentleman should be rewarded for his efforts with a crying female."

She laughs tearfully. "You are perfectly awful, dear brother."

After Alexander dictates all the instructions to make the tea and other herbal mixtures and Katherine carefully writes them all down, he finally gives in to the urge of Lucy calling him back. "I should leave from Rob's room, if you don't mind," Alexander says. "I think it'll be easier for her to summon me that way."

"Of course," Rob says. "I'll show you the way."

"I should warn you, though," Alexander says, suddenly remembering the mishap with James. "I had a bit of a confrontation in the hall—"

Katherine sucks in a breath. "Heavens! I hope it wasn't my husband. He swore he was going to bed—I had to force him to leave since at least one of us should have the energy to function tomorrow."

"No, it was his brother, I'm afraid. He must have taken me for an intruder—perfectly understandable, really—but I must apologize for the way I handled it. If I hadn't been in such a hurry to bring the tea, I would have tried to talk him down. Unfortunately, all I could do was render him temporarily unconscious."

Katherine's eyes widen, and she lets out a little squeak. "Unconscious? Good Lord. Did he attack you, then?"

Rob looks surprised for a moment, but then bursts into riotous laughter, to which Katherine immediately shushes him. "Is he just slumped over in the hall, then? For all the servants to step over?"

"Yes, but I assure you the effects are not long-lasting. He may be a little bruised in the morning, but I dare say he shouldn't be in any pain."

"This I must see," Rob says and strides out of the room and into the hall.

Alexander and Katherine follow, and they quickly come to where James lies.

"Not a hair out of place!" Rob says. "He looks like he simply couldn't make it to his room after a long night of drinking and debauchery." Rob laughs again, and Katherine shoots him a warning glance. "You must tell me how you did it."

Alexander shifts his weight, distinctly uncomfortable. Now that he sees the man lying unconscious after the heat of the moment has long since cooled, it seems like a rather extreme reaction.

"There are certain pressure points on the body that will render one unconscious should they be struck in just the right way. I hit two of these spots."

Now both brother and sister watch him with a mixture of bewilderment and wariness.

"And you're sure he'll be all right come morning?" Katherine says slowly.

"Yes, he'll be quite well. The worst he may have is a headache."

"Let's not interrogate him, Wren." Rob's wry smile returns. "The man was just defending himself, after all."

"So he says," Katherine says, her intensely blue eyes suddenly piercing Alexander's. "I do appreciate everything you've done for Rose, but I would also like to caution you when it comes to our sister. She told me that you will be assisting her in her . . . goal . . . but none of us can deny that there is much about you that is highly suspicious. If you hurt Lucy in any way—"

"Yes, yes," Rob interrupts. "You'll kill him in some horribly painful way, etc., etc. Come now, old chap, before she threatens you further."

Alexander allows himself to be shepherded back toward Rob's room, but before he walks through the door, he turns back to Katherine. "I would gladly lay down my life to keep your sister from harm. Though she'd hardly believe it herself, she is the dearest person in my life. I will stop at nothing to keep her safe."

She looks surprised, but not as surprised as he, for he meant every word.

TWENTY-THREE

I pace the floor, incapable of staying still. It feels as though it's been ages since Alexander left. "What could he be doing?" I ask Grandmother. "Why is he ignoring my summons?"

"I'm sure there is a perfectly reasonable explanation," Grandmother says with her implacable calm.

"Suppose something went wrong, though . . . or I sent him to the wrong place." My voice is taking on a tremulous quality the more I think of all the devastating possibilities. Since that first moment he didn't respond, my stomach has been a pit of snakes. It shouldn't have taken him long to speak to Rob. My instincts tell me something is wrong, and I simply cannot listen to reason.

A comforting warmth presses against my leg, and I look down to see Rowen gazing up at me in concern.

"There's no need to panic," Grandmother says. "The fact that you can still feel a connection to him when you reach out means he was successful in crossing over."

"Perhaps he has forgotten how to draw the proper rune. Should I follow through and help him?"

"You cannot," Grandmother says firmly. "It doesn't work that way. Once a connection has been established, you cannot simply follow through to the mortal realm. The portal would collapse. You must remain here so that he may find his way back."

Just then, the connection between us thrums, as though a cord has been struck. Bright light fills the room, blinding in its intensity, and when I can see again, Alexander stands in our midst.

"Alexander!" I cry and then race toward him before I even know what I'm doing. I come to an awkward stop just in time to keep from throwing myself in his arms. I'm so relieved to see him, so relieved I was able to send him through to the other side in one piece, so relieved that something didn't go horribly wrong. And then I flush with embarrassment at the strength of my reaction. "Why were you gone so long?" I ask, and my tone is sharp to make up for my enthusiastic greeting. "It was horrible of you to make us worry so."

Grandmother makes a face that clearly says she was never worried at all, but Alexander apologizes to us both nonetheless. "I do appreciate your concern, though," he says, and his eyes shine with a vulnerable hopefulness that makes me have to suddenly look away. "I was away so long because your brother and sister were filling me in on what has transpired since you left, and of course, I had to pass some rigorous interrogations." He smiles to show he's joking, but I can see that there may be more to it than his light tone implies.

"And what have I missed since I've been gone?"

Something flickers across his face, and I find myself tensing for a blow.

"Lady Rose had taken ill," he says, "but she is recovering well."

I suck in my breath. "Oh, poor Rose! It's her lungs again, I suppose. And I had hoped Bath would be so good for her!" I glance at him sharply. "But she's recovering?" I think of the shadow I've seen hovering near her, waiting to prey on her weakness. "She's not . . ." *Dying?* I think but cannot will myself to say. I am a coward and don't want to hear the answer.

"She was recovering well when I left. They had the very best doctors attending her, and your own sister hasn't left her side."

There's something about his tone, something that makes me carefully scan his features to see if anything is amiss, but his expression is as it has been lately—guarded.

"I also passed on your message to Lady Katherine about your niece," he continues. "I think she was rather relieved to hear it."

"I'm glad to hear it," I say. "Thank you."

"Well, now that you've returned safe and sound," Grandmother says, "we should have a late luncheon, for I'm sure you're both famished, and then we can work on some of the runes you might need—but not for terribly long. The ball is tonight, and I suggest you both train early so you can rest, for the dancing will go on all through the night."

"That sounds like a dream come true," I say. "I do love to dance."

"And when will we infiltrate Lord Tyrell's estate?" Alexander asks.

"Tomorrow morning—when you will have the cover of darkness in the mortal world."

"So soon!" I say, my heart galloping about in my chest. "Are you sure I'm ready?"

Grandmother smiles at me, the gesture so like Mama's when she was particularly proud of us. "My dearest one, you've always been ready. I only had to show you the way."

☥

EARLY in the evening, Alexander walks over to the onyx-framed mirror in his room and stares at the formal clothes the manservant brought for him. Used to the rather monotonous black and white for evening attire—at least in England—he cannot help but admire the colors of the garment he now wears. The long, heavily embroidered coat is like a *sherwani* worn in India, the color a blue he's never seen before—like the deep blue of sapphire but darker, like it's being viewed only in shadow. Gold paisley covers the fabric, shining when it catches the light. Underneath he wears a shirt made of an impossibly soft material—like silk, but of a heavier weight. His pants are the same midnight sapphire color and somehow tailored perfectly to fit him. Soft, buttery leather shoes complete the ensemble.

His thoughts stray to Lucy again, and he unnecessarily straightens the standing collar of his coat. He lied to her about Rose. It had been a split-second decision the moment he came back and found her overjoyed to see him.

She cannot know how close Rose hovers near death, he had thought at the time, *for she will abandon all our goals and return to Bath straight away.*

He told himself he was just thinking about the success of their shared objective—not that her response to his return hadn't given him a selfish burst of hope, one that he was loath to abandon. Leaving this enchanted world seems like a death sentence to the possibility she may forgive him.

He scrubs his face with his hand as his conscience peers back at him in the mirror. He should have never been dishonest with her—not when her trust in him was already so fragile.

I'll tell her the truth tonight, he thinks.

A knock at the door shakes Alexander free of his thoughts. "Yes?" he calls, inwardly chastising himself for being so lost in his own mind that he didn't hear someone outside the door. Being aware of one's surroundings is one of his most sacred rules he lives by.

"Lord Alexander?" the manservant who helped him dress says through the door. "I've been sent to bring you to the ball."

Alexander strides to the door and opens it. The servant, dressed in an ivory tunic and pants much like Alexander was wearing earlier that day, waits politely in the hall. But Alexander barely spares him a glance—not when Lucy stands only a few feet away.

"I thought we could go together," she says with a shy smile that makes Alexander want to gather her into his arms. She is hauntingly beautiful, dressed in a gown fit for a queen. The skirt is so long it drags behind her, and the color is like her eyes at sunset—a deep, mesmerizing blue. Clear gemstones glitter across the swirling embroidery, and Alexander suspects they are diamonds. The bodice hugs her breasts in a way that makes it difficult for him to look away. But it's the look in her eyes that has him captivated: a flare of interest hidden in their depths, hesitant, but still there.

"I'd be honored to escort you," Alexander says, his mouth suddenly dry. "I've never seen a woman more beautiful."

Her cheeks flush, and Alexander's mind immediately fills with other reasons that might bring a rush of color to her cheeks. A hunger stirs within him. "I thank you for your compliment," she says with a pretty smile. "You look dangerously handsome tonight."

He offers his arm to distract himself from the almost overwhelming need to kiss her. It will be his goal tonight—to find a moment to steal a kiss—before he has to tell her the truth about Lady Rose. Doing so will almost certainly break the spell.

She takes his arm, perfuming the air around her with the delicate scent of jasmine. The white fox stays close to her side, watching Alexander with its intelligent turquoise-colored eyes.

"Do you know where we are to go?" he asks.

Lucy shakes her head, long diamond earrings catching the light. "All I know is the ballroom is located outside." She glances down at the fox. "I was trusting Rowen to lead me there."

"An outdoor ballroom? How curious," Alexander says, though in truth, he's relieved. There's nothing so stifling and claustrophobic as a ballroom, and he suspects this sensation may be even worse for him after being locked away in the Sylvan dungeon.

The fox trots a little ahead of them, and they follow down the corridors of the castle with its enormous paintings and floating lights.

Lucy looks up at him with a blinding smile. "I should think you would enjoy an outdoor ballroom—it was on a balcony that we first met, after all."

"You were so beautiful that night, and always," he says, but he didn't mean to voice his inner thoughts. "Like a moon goddess, all dressed in white." And like the tide, he'd been pulled toward her. He'd felt her spiritual power, known this was the woman he sought, but all he felt at the time was a deep and abiding need to talk to her, dance with her, *know* her.

"Heavens, how can I respond to that?" Lucy demands with a teasing smile as they arrive at an outer door. "I've been compared to the sun before, but never a goddess."

He grins, pleased she remembered their conversation from so long ago. "In some cultures, the sun is a god, so I daresay I wasn't far off the mark."

Lucy blushes prettily and glances away. "I have enough difficulty accepting I'm a princess here—a goddess is much too far out of the realm of possibility."

Alexander holds open the door for her, and together they emerge into one of the outer gardens. With the moon high above them, and the heavy scent of exotic flowers lending a sweet perfume to the air, Alexander pauses and turns to Lucy. She gazes up at him with an open expression, more so than he's seen yet since the horrible night she spoke to him in the dungeon. And before he can stop himself, the thoughts that have been crowding together inside his mind burst free.

"It was kismet that we should meet, Lucy. You helped open my eyes to the truth around me, to the truth about my heritage. I was wandering a dark path before we met, and you came with your beauty and gentleness and light and showed me the right way—the way my mother would have wanted me to travel. Our destinies are intertwined, but I want to travel the same path as you." He takes a ragged breath. "You have every right to spurn my words, but I wanted you to know how I felt. I've tried not to fall in love with you—for your sake—but I cannot control it, just as I can hardly stop myself from relating to you the depth of my feelings."

Lucy's expression rapidly changes—from stunned stillness, to surprised hope, to something that Alexander cannot even begin to describe.

Her eyes soften, her lips just barely part, and Alexander can resist the urge no longer.

He leans down to touch his lips to hers—lightly at first, slowly gauging her reaction. When she takes a tentative step toward him, her body so close he can feel the warmth of her skin, Alexander wraps his arms around her and pulls her flush against him. Her response is instantaneous: her lips parting and her body melting into his. His first taste of her is like the sweetest wine.

He knows the manservant is looking on—the fox, too—but he cannot help himself. He touches her silken hair, which tumbles down her shoulders in wild abandon, with only a small silver diadem to pull it back from her lovely face. Her breathy sighs fan the flames, and he feels desire surge within him.

It's several minutes before he can come to his senses, to realize he is kissing the queen's granddaughter shamelessly—the very same queen who had only days ago locked him in a dungeon. With reluctance, he slows his sensual assault on her, pressing gentle kisses on her swan-like throat, her regal cheekbones, her smooth forehead. He dare not kiss lower, though her curvaceous décolletage is tantalizingly close.

She smiles at him beatifically, and Alexander realizes right then in that very moment:

There is nothing he won't do to make her his.

TWENTY-FOUR

MY knees quiver as I meet Alexander's heated gaze. This kiss is nothing like the one shared with James—the moment our lips touch, I lose track of time, my surroundings, my propriety, everything but the feel of Alexander holding me close. But as I melt into him, images flash in my mind, as vivid and real as though I am seeing them with open eyes: Alexander cradling a baby with dark hair and wide eyes the color of the sky—the color and shape of mine. *A boy*, I think and know, and the baby smiles at me, his mouth a perfect cupid's bow like Alexander's.

I take a step back, my heart hammering away. I think of Mama's excitement after meeting Papa, of her immediate acceptance of the future she glimpsed, but I feel as though I'm torn down the center of me. How can I marry a member of the Order, no matter how reformed? I can't imagine my family ever agreeing to it once they know the truth—and as I think of the disappointed anger in Wren's eyes, I find myself forcibly pushing the image away.

I don't see visions of the future, I tell myself, but then I think of the sweet, plump baby and his blissful smile, and I want to weep.

Alexander watches all of these emotions flit across my face with growing concern on his. "I've upset you," he says quietly. "Forgive me for taking such liberties."

"No—I only realized we've been here for quite some time, and I don't want to be late."

"Of course," he says with a forced smile. "I'm afraid my skills as an escort leave much to be desired."

I take his proffered arm again with a terrible, sinking feeling in my stomach. I can see that I've hurt him, but now I don't know how to make it right. Rowen leads us to where the servant waits beside a path through the hedges, and my face flames when I think of all he must have witnessed. I don't know enough about the mores of Sylvan society to know if we had made as potentially disastrous mistake as what would have been in London—kissing brazenly in plain sight of whomever should walk by will generally result in either ruin or marriage.

Have I done something scandalous? I think to Rowen, and he twitches his tail to show he heard me.

You are not the first Sylvan noble to be found kissing amongst the hedges, he thinks with what I sense is a wry grin.

So Grandmother will not mind?

Not in the way you're implying. You will not be reprimanded. I know such a thing is frowned upon in your world, but here, it's simply a part of life.

His words erase some of the tension from my muscles, though I dare not think of the true scope of the freedom that implies.

Silence descends upon us as we walk in the soft glow of moonlight, and it suddenly occurs to me that we should hear the sounds of music and dancing by now. All I can hear is the roar of waterfalls and a silver stream at our side.

We enter a clearing, and before us is a wide lake, still and quiet. The moon hangs in the very center, floating effortlessly and surrounded by dancing stars. As we draw closer, a little jolt of awareness goes through me: the moon and stars in the water are not celestial beings at all, but lights. Golden light surges up from somewhere below, illuminating the water around it.

But before I can ask after its source, the servant continues on to a covered doorway built into the side of the lake. I glance up at Alexander, but he looks as curious as I do. The servant holds open the heavy metal door for us, and when I peer down, I see a spiral staircase lit by the same golden light. Laughter and many voices drift up to us.

"Does this lead beneath the lake?" I ask in awe.

The servant smiles. "It does, my princess. The ballroom is below, the lake above."

"How enchanting," I say with a smile up at Alexander, and he returns it. Even my unease over my vision has faded in light of this amazing development. For some reason, a ballroom hidden beneath a lake seems more fantastical to me than a unicorn prince.

The staircase is narrow, so Alexander goes first, and I follow, holding my skirts aloft carefully so I don't trip. The steps lead to a narrow hallway, but the ceiling is higher than I would have expected—at least a head taller than Alexander.

The voices and music grow louder and louder, until finally, we arrive at an arched doorway. The servant slides past us to open the door, and golden light spills out.

Alexander smiles back at me just before walking through—his face lit up in excitement and wonder—and I follow.

"Oh," I say in a breath—the most inadequate thing I've ever said.

The ceiling soars above us, made almost entirely out of glass, and through it, the clear water of the lake is illuminated. Fish in a dazzling array of colors pass by, swimming languidly, decoration unto themselves. The light is created by at least a hundred floating orbs, at the center of which is an enormous crystal chandelier that glitters like diamonds—considering my gown, they may well *be* diamonds. It's suspended from nothing, hanging in the air impossibly, yet no one pays it the slightest bit of attention.

A full orchestra provides the music, and dancers turn effortlessly on a floor of creamy marble with a golden mosaic sun inlaid in the very center. The people are every bit as fascinating as the stunning ballroom and nothing like what I was used to in a typical London setting. Most notable is the diversity of fashion, as though many come from different parts of the Sylvan world: velvet trimmed in snow white fur, satin in impossibly bright colors, even a full mantle of swan-like feathers. Their features, too, suggest they are all from different cultures—they run the gamut from delicate, almost porcelain-like, to beautifully dark. The only thing that unites them is the fact that no matter the differences in fashion, their frocks are clearly ones of the very rich—with gemstones and gold and silver embellishments.

Though the news that Alexander has been freed from the dungeon must have spread by now, we are not greeted with whispered asides or outward stares—only welcoming smiles. It seems Grandmother is respected enough not to be questioned.

Grandmother comes to my side the moment she sees me. Serafino flies nearby and settles on a branch of a golden tree wrought from metal. Rowen goes to join him, wrapping his tail around his haunches neatly as he sits. A cursory glance around the cavernous room shows that only Grandmother and I have spirit animals in attendance, which I find disappointing. I should have liked to see what creatures these exotic and beautiful people have as their spirit animals.

"What do you think of our secret ballroom here?" Grandmother asks with a bright smile. Her gown is like nothing I've ever seen—thick emerald green satin with intricate black lace and what appear to be real diamonds and emeralds scattered throughout the bodice and skirt. Her sunset hair cascades down her back, and a tiara with emeralds and diamonds glitters in the midst of it. The skirt trails behind her, but she makes it look effortless. She looks regal and beautiful without seeming remote and unapproachable—so different from when I debuted before the queen of England.

"It was a fantastic surprise! I couldn't quite accept what I was seeing when I saw the lights in the middle of the lake—I mistook them for the moon and stars at first. This is by far the most gorgeous ballroom I've ever been in—and that includes the ones in Buckingham Palace."

"A compliment indeed. I remember your mother saying the entire palace seemed to be made of gold."

I laugh. "Not quite so grand as that—but close." I turn to Alexander naturally, without thinking, but as his beautiful eyes meet mine, I think of the kiss and feel warmth spread throughout my body. "Have you ever been to the palace?"

"Only in a dream," he says and grins.

I remember the vision we shared—the drawing that took place in the throne room—and smile back at him.

Suddenly, the music changes from a violin-heavy classical piece to something heavily dominated by drums. The sound is primal, irresistible, and instantly quickens my blood. The thundering beat would so scandalize London society that even the tango would look as innocent as a game of Ring around the Rosey. Surprisingly, this only makes it all the more enticing.

The other Sylvani in the room seem to be just as affected as I—moving toward the dance floor with fluid grace. Then, as though following some unseen guide, they begin to move as one. Their steps are fast—moving in time to the music—their bodies pressed close to their partners. It's shockingly sensual, and I can't help but stare.

Alexander moves closer to me. "Care to dance?" he asks, his hand outstretched, his eyes hungry.

I take his hand but send a quick glance at Grandmother, suddenly unsure. "I wouldn't know how."

She laughs. "You will as soon as you join the others on the dance floor—you'll see," she adds when I open my mouth to question her.

Alexander gives my hand a little tug, and I follow him toward the dance floor where the beat of the drums gets into my blood, primal and irresistible.

He pulls me close—much closer than I've ever been to a man. Heat comes off him in waves, and I run my hands tentatively up his arms, marveling at the strength of his body. The others dance around us, and we are like the eye of the storm.

I'm not sure if he moves first or I do, but then we join them, the drums moving us, guiding us, telling our bodies how to move. It's chaotic and free and dangerous, and all I can see are Alexander's luminous eyes and the shape of his full mouth and strong jaw.

The drums beat louder, faster, and somehow we keep pace. Orbs of light pulse around us, keeping time. The more I focus on them, the more I see something hidden in their depths—images coming to light.

I see Alexander and I see myself; I see infants who look like their father, and I see children who resemble us both; I see our children frolicking in verdant meadows, and I see them walking hand-in-hand beneath swaying trees with lavender leaves. I see a beautiful girl with flaxen hair and tawny eyes debuting in a white dress in Buckingham Palace, and I see her dancing in a ballroom hidden beneath a lake.

The drum beat slows incrementally. I hardly notice until we all come to a shuddering stop, cheeks flushed, eyes bright. I am panting for breath, but the others are smiling and laughing. I glance up at Alexander, and he looks at me like he's been waiting for me to meet his eyes. He looks at me like a drowning man looks at his rescuer—with a desperate sort of adoration.

His warm hand cups my cheek, and as he leans down to press his lips to mine, he murmurs, "I saw it too."

ALEXANDER knows the tribal drum beat has lowered their inhibitions as effectively as a glass of strong scotch, and with Lucy gazing up at him like he holds the key to her soul, he cannot help but kiss her—even in front of so many. Surprisingly, though Lucy is by all rights the granddaughter of the queen and a princess, no one pays their embrace the slightest bit of attention. In fact, many others are doing the same.

He thinks of the images he saw in the floating lights, of children like him and Lucy, children of both worlds who fit into each one seamlessly. Seeing that both terrified him and gave him such a surge of hope that he's afraid to think on it further. But the truth is, it's difficult for him to imagine himself with such a charmed life—to be so forgiven for his sins that he's rewarded with someone like Lucy.

Lucy's eyes flutter closed, and Alexander feels an answering surge in his own body. When he begins to picture taking her to a remote corner of the room, he decides it's time to resume control of himself.

"Shall I fetch you something to drink?" he asks, trying not to let her eyes—which have changed from a cerulean blue to a deep sapphire—suck him into their depths.

"That would be lovely, thank you," she says, her voice still a little breathy from the dancing.

Alexander tears himself away and goes in search of a refreshments table—not easy to do when the room is both crowded and unfamiliar. He weaves through amorous couples, groups in intense conversation, and others who appear to be playing a game with golden coins and pieces of ivory instead of cards. He wonders, distantly, where the servants have all gone to—and then he sees them: interspersed amongst the guests. It's then he realizes he saw them dancing alongside him, dressed in their creamy white tunics and pants. They look natural and at ease—no sense of discomfort at having to mingle with their masters. The scene is so different from one he'd find anywhere in Europe—almost anywhere in the world, really—that he just stands and stares for a moment.

"Looking for something?" a voice asks—a voice Alexander, unfortunately, recognizes. Lord Titus, the shadowed man.

"Only for refreshments."

"So the queen has released you—for now," Lord Titus says.

Alexander prickles at his knowing tone. "As you see."

Lord Titus steps closer. "My offer to assist you still stands. The queen has you fooled if you are to believe you can stand against Centerius. My spies tell me her hope for the outcome is that you weaken Centerius while he succeeds in killing you."

Alexander struggles to prevent the seed of doubt from germinating within him. The queen has never given him any reason to doubt her word, while Lord Titus is the complete opposite. "If her plan is so set, then how could you be of any help to me?"

Lord Titus smiles, the gesture anything but comforting. "You have only to tell me the details of the plan—I know the princess will be aiding you in some way—and I will guarantee your safety."

Alexander scoffs. "And why should you care for my safety? Why help me at all?"

"Because you have an ability I covet," he says, and his eyes flash with an eerie intensity.

Alexander's only ability, besides his proficiency in the fighting arts, is to detect others who use Spiritual power. The mere thought of this man having such a power disturbs him so much he takes a step backward in distaste.

"I'm afraid the details are not mine to share," Alexander says, and Lord Titus's face turns hard. "You'd have better luck asking the queen herself. Now, if you'll excuse me, I must find the refreshments table."

He turns away before Lord Titus can respond, letting the anger get the better of him, but when he glances back again, Lord Titus has moved away.

The crowd parts, and Alexander finally catches sight of a table laden with drinks and food, but his mind is no longer on the task at hand. The snakes he'd once seen within Lord Titus have taken up residence within Alexander, churning within him with a deep sense of foreboding.

He doubts very much Lord Titus will drop the matter so easily. He must warn the queen.

TWENTY-FIVE

AFTER dancing until my legs ache, and a sort of delightful bone-weariness settles over me, I pull Alexander aside. He's been my partner for nearly every dance—save one where the unicorn prince led me through an intricate and elegant waltz—and I've been reveling in the freedom of dancing with whomever I choose, for as long as I want. Something about the dances here loosens all my English reservations and almost makes me forget myself . . . makes me forget everything but the sound of the music and the feel of Alexander's body.

"Shall we go for a walk?" I ask as he leans closer to me so he can hear above the music and laughter. "I would love to see the lake again from above, and I think I cannot last much longer here. I'm worn out, I'm afraid."

"It would be my pleasure to escort you," he says with such warmth in his voice that I feel a soft fluttering in my stomach in answer. "I've wanted to speak to you about something."

I meet his gaze, but swallow any teasing response when I find it troubled. "I'll speak to Grandmother then."

As I go in search of her, I ponder what he could want to discuss. Surely he cannot have any more terrible secrets—not after discovering so much about him already. Despite my dismay, the image of that baby boy—the one I know is mine—takes hold of my mind. I think of rocking baby dolls as a child, of cradling an infant Izzie in my arms, and my heart swells. I want this baby, want it as much as I would if I discovered I was already with child, and suddenly, I understand how my mother felt. How she was willing to sacrifice anything.

A vision changes everything, Grandmother had once said to Mama.

I find Grandmother seated upon a golden throne on the far side of the ballroom, Serafino perched on the arm of the chair and Rowen at her feet. All three turn in my direction when they see me approaching.

"You've finally stopped dancing," Grandmother says with a wide smile. "I thought we'd have to carry you out when the night was done."

"You may well have if I don't stop now." I smile as the music swells again into another furious dance—like an Irish jig. The dancers fly around the room, their footsteps so loud and furious it sounds like thunder. "I came to ask if I may have a walk around the lake with Alexander before I turn in for the evening."

Grandmother searches my face for a moment, and I blush. "It seems you've been able to forgive him of his involvement with the Order. I couldn't help but notice how the two of you have been nearly inseparable this evening."

"Forgive me, Grandmother," I say in a rush. "I hope I have not shamed you—I didn't think it was frowned upon to dance with the same partner here."

She reaches out and touches my hand to calm me. "You misunderstand me, dearest one. You've done nothing wrong. I'm only curious as to the reason."

Her question takes me momentarily aback. It happened so gradually—this softening toward Alexander—that I hadn't pinpointed the exact reason for it. But now that I do . . . I think it's been so many things: his agreement to help us defeat the Order, his memories of his mother, but most of all, the vision I saw the moment we kissed.

"You've seen something," Grandmother says in that knowing way of hers, and my gaze darts to hers.

"A baby," I say, as a sense of déjà vu settles over me, as I remember Mama's words. "I saw a baby. Children, actually."

Grandmother laughs delightedly, which takes me by surprise. "Oh, I should have known. I'm surprised I didn't predict it myself, really." When I only watch her with an undoubtedly confused look upon my face, she squeezes my hand. "I'm afraid I wasn't entirely truthful about Alexander's arcana."

"His . . . arcana? You mean that he uses Spiritual arcana like me?"

She nods. "He does—but it is not his greatest ability. His true skill lies in his fighting arts, his total control over his body."

"So he's Corporal then," I say, but she shakes her head.

"No. Something else—a Warrior class. A rare form of arcana that manifests when a Sylvani has the right combination of Spiritual and Corporal."

A warrior—that seemed to fit Alexander after seeing from his own memories what he's capable of. "But what does this mean?"

"It means, dearest one, that you are extremely compatible. When the Warrior class was more plentiful, they were almost always married off to members of the Spiritual class. This baby will have a serendipitous fate indeed; his lineage will be powerful beyond imagining."

"His," I say quietly, in a stunned sort of way. "You said 'his.'"

Grandmother smiles. "A beautiful baby boy. I saw the same vision when I first searched Alexander's mind."

I shake my head in wonder. "You never said."

"No, I wouldn't have. Visions are best experienced for one's self." She stands and embraces me. "Go for your walk." She pulls back and looks me in the eyes. "Go, with my blessing."

Her words are heavy with meaning, but I am too embarrassed to discern it. I turn to Rowen. "Will you be joining me?"

There is far too much amusement in his eyes as he answers. *No, I will stay here. However, I won't be so far away that you will begin to feel the effects of this world's arcana.*

I nod. "I shall see you later in the evening then?" For some reason, I feel almost naked without the little fox, and the more I think of being without him, the more I realize I will be entirely without chaperone.

I have slept on that balcony for nearly fifty years, and I don't intend to change that now.

I smile one last nervous smile at Grandmother before turning away in search of Alexander.

When I weave back through the crowded room, I see Lord Titus watching me, and a little chill sneaks over me. In some ways, he reminds me of Lord Wallace, and once I've thought such a thing, I find it so disconcertingly true that I catch myself reaching for the dagger I still keep on my hip—the one James gave me what now seems like a lifetime ago. A different time, a different place.

The metal is coolly reassuring, though, and the warm smile of Alexander's greeting even more so.

"After you," he says, holding the heavy door open for me to pass through. I see the muscles of his arm flex effortlessly and think of Grandmother's revelation.

"Grandmother said something interesting to me just now," I say as we make our way back down the tunnel outside of the ballroom. I have to glance back to see if Alexander is listening, for the tunnel is so narrow we must walk in single file.

His eyebrows raise. "Did she? I imagine she said she will be sending sentinels to track our progress and that I should deliver you straight to your room."

I laugh. "No, not at all. That must be only your guilty conscience." He laughs, the sound easily filling the small space. "She said that you do not have only Spiritual arcana, but you are also of the Warrior class."

He seems to be mulling over my words as I start up the metal staircase that will take us above ground. "So I use my prana—arcana, I should say—in my fighting arts?" I nod. "Interesting."

I push open the metal door and step through into fresh air. When he emerges, I surprise him by reaching for his hand. "That's not all she said. Apparently the Warrior class was once always partnered with the Spiritual class."

He glances down at our entwined hands and squeezes gently. "I'm not at all surprised."

His gaze drops to my mouth, and I think, *I want to kiss him again.* The moment I think it, I realize I want so much more from this man who was first a friend and then a supposed enemy and now . . .

He leans down and presses his lips to mine, just once, gently. He pulls back almost immediately. "I must confess something to you, Lucy, before we take another step."

I nod reluctantly. I'd almost forgotten his earlier request to speak to me about something. "What is it?"

"I should have told you right away, but I wanted you to enjoy yourself at the ball, and now I have only selfish reasons to keep from telling you, so I am forcing myself to put them aside. I'm afraid I wasn't entirely truthful about Lady Rose's condition. She is gravely ill and doesn't have long to live."

Of all the things he might say, I never expected this. A cold fear grips me as I think of that dark shadow I'd seen hovering over her.

"What has happened?" I ask, wrapping my arms around myself as though I can chase away the coldness of death.

"She contracted pneumonia. This is why I was away for so long when I crossed over. I know of some ways to treat disorders of the lungs—herbal teas and other things—and I wanted to try everything I could to prolong her life."

I clutch my stomach. How could I be making merry all the night long when my poor friend lay dying? "Did they help? Will she live long enough for her to say her good-byes? For me to see her again?"

"Yes, she responded well." I sag in relief. "But," he says and reaches for my shoulder, "they are not a cure. She will eventually succumb to it, but for now, I am confident she will survive long enough to see you again. Her father was arriving that evening, and your sister was maintaining a constant vigil at her bedside."

"That sounds like Wren," I say, still torn and feeling rather guilty. "Ought I not return tonight? What if she should die while I'm here?" My throat constricts at the thought, tears suddenly leaking from my eyes. "I couldn't bear it."

He shakes his head. "I won't advise you either way, for *I* couldn't bear it if I encouraged you to stay or go and it was the wrong choice—I can only say that she had improved remarkably when I left. In my experience, such ongoing treatments will buy her several weeks of time—if not months."

"I'll stay—of course I'll stay. I should see this awful mission through, after all. But tomorrow—tomorrow, we must return." My tears are running unchecked down my cheeks now—I can't stop thinking about Rose. About her frail body lying there, dying when there's still so much life in her eyes and in her heart.

Alexander wraps me in his arms, and I allow myself to be held for a moment. When I'm able to compose myself again, I take a step back. "Shall we have a walk?" he asks, his expression and tone still soft. "The moon is so bright we haven't any need for a lantern."

He offers me his arm, and I take it. "Thank you—you've been so kind to me, even when I was rather waspish toward you."

He snorts. "Waspish? Your reaction was just—you had every right to be angry."

I did have every right, but now . . . now everything has changed. My instincts when I first met Alexander were that he was someone like me, someone with the same interests and maybe even some of the same struggles—he had secrets to keep as did I, though of course I had no way of knowing what his were. Now that I know, though, I realize I have already forgiven him. He was a lonely and grieving child who had just lost his mother—his only loving parent—when Lord Tyrell swooped down on him. What would I have done if I was all alone without my father and siblings after losing Mama? His only real crime was not realizing sooner that the brotherhood was hurting people—killing them, actually. And now that he knows, look what he's agreed to: to fight against the man who raised him. Surely not even Wren and Colin will be able to argue against such selflessness.

"I hope I have not reminded you of your anger toward me," Alexander says after I've been silent for a few minutes. The lake glimmers softly under the light of the moon, golden light at the center of it.

"No, indeed—quite the opposite. I was thinking of how quickly my anger disappeared—if it was ever truly there at all."

He comes to a halt, and I turn to face him. "I cannot tell you how relieved I am to hear it. I care so much for you that I would never want you to believe I was capable of betraying you."

I take a deep breath. "Alexander, that vision . . . I was shocked at first, but now . . . now I think I very much want it to come true."

He smiles down at me and tucks a wayward strand of hair back behind my ear. I shiver at his touch as his fingers brush the sensitive skin of my neck. When I meet his eyes again, it's like I'm seeing two Alexanders: the one before me with an intense longing on his face, and another only slightly older Alexander with love in his eyes as he gazes back at me. The sensation is disorienting, but not frightening. Was this how it was for Mama? Did she see my father's future love for her, his undying devotion to her, the moment they first touched?

And then Alexander closes the distance between us and takes me in his arms, and I can no longer think of anything but the feel of his lips on mine, the way the mingling of our tongues unravels something within me. The proper English Lucy separates from the Sylvan Lucy, and I clutch him desperately as his hands plunge into my hair, then skim lower, tracing my curves through my slim gown.

The moonlight reflects off his dark hair, and a soft breeze makes the tall grass at our feet undulate like waves. His mouth moves down my neck, each kiss making me tighten a little more, wanting something I don't dare voice. And yet, in this enchanted place, it's easy to believe we exist outside of time—outside of reality. All of my objections blow away like sand in the wind—I cannot grasp a single one in my mind.

So I give into my instincts and ignore everything I've ever been taught about the way a lady should behave.

I pull him down to the soft grass beneath us. The smell of cardamom and clove is intoxicating, and the warmth emanating from his body makes me want to pull him still closer. He stares down at me in silent question, but before he can voice any objection and break the spell, I kiss him until neither of us can speak.

☥

ALEXANDER tries to get himself under control—never before has he given into his body's wants and desires so completely—but he cannot stop himself. Lucy has made it clear that she doesn't wish him to, and he tries to berate himself, to tell himself that he should be the one to stop this before it goes too far, but then she writhes beneath him again, her breath coming in little pants, and God help him, he cannot resist.

He reaches out to touch her again, and her bodice slips low enough to bare more of her décolletage. Her hands clutch at him, and he pulls back for a moment to remove his jacket and shirt. When her gaze sweeps over his naked chest, that appreciative artist's look entering her eyes, it's nearly his undoing.

"Lucy, my darling," he says raggedly, "you must know how desperately I love you, but we don't have to do this here and now." He takes one of her slim hands and puts it over his rapidly beating heart. "I want to marry you if you'll have me. I want to spend every day of my life drawing and painting with you, enjoying the beauty of this world, and atoning for my involvement with an organization that has brought you such pain."

She's quiet for so long that Alexander's stomach drops in anticipation of the worst. "And the vision? What of children?" she finally asks, her expression turning intensely serious.

"Do you think ten children would be too many?" he asks in turn, and she dissolves into relieved laughter as he grins back at her.

She tentatively moves her hand to his upper arm and gives him a gentle tug. When he acquiesces to her unspoken request and lowers himself to her, his chest mere inches away from her tantalizingly soft breasts, he locks his gaze on hers.

"I love you, Alexander. And of course I will have you," she says, pulling him ever closer. "You and your ten children."

And then they succumb to the enchantment of the Sylvan world, of the freedom of being together without chaperone, of the exquisite discovery of each other's bodies.

My wife, Alexander thinks. *She will be my wife.*

TWENTY-SIX

LUCY, a voice calls, pulling me from sleep.

Lucy, it's time.

I open my eyes to find Rowen's turquoise ones staring down at me. As I shift in bed to sit up, I find I am rather sore in unaccustomed places, and my cheeks flame as I remember everything that brought that about. The beauty of Alexander's body in the moonlight, the intoxicating feel of his touch, the contrasting hardness of his muscles and the softness of his lips—his lips that left no part of my body unexplored.

But most importantly: his proposal and my acceptance.

In the light of day, my actions seem rash, even shameful. Not only did I act wantonly, I accepted a proposal without giving it a moment's thought. I hide my burning face in my hands. What possessed me to do such a thing?

Whispers of the vision I saw last night sneak to the forefront of my mind, but I push them away. Mama had seen a vision of children, too, but I'm sure she didn't lose her virginity the first chance she could! I touch my flat stomach gingerly. The vision never said *when* I'd become pregnant—what if life already bloomed inside me?

I peek through my fingers to find Rowen still watching me. With a groan, I flop back against my bed. "How could I be so foolish?"

Foolish? Rowen tilts his head.

"Never mind. Has Grandmother sent for me?"

Rowen jumps down from the head of the bed to the floor. *Yes, and Astrid waits to help you dress.*

Still blushing, for I'm certain both Rowen and Grandmother had antici-pated such a thing happening between Alexander and me, I gingerly get out of bed. My embarrassment and discomfort does well to mask the nervousness that buzzes in the background of my mind, but the moment Astrid strides in purposefully, her hands full of a pale blue gown, the buzz turns into a dull roar.

"Good morning, my princess," she says. "I've brought you tea and something you can eat quickly, for I'm afraid the queen has requested your presence in her art studio right away."

I nod. "Of course. I'm sorry if I overslept."

"No one blames you, at all—it's to be expected with such a busy evening." I quickly look away as she laces me into my bodice, willing my cheeks to stop blushing. "The Lake Ball always lasts until dawn," she adds, and I find myself relaxing.

And what did you think she was referring to? I ask myself reproachfully.

After she dresses me quickly and efficiently in the open-skirted gown with leather leggings that I will miss terribly when I return to England, she pulls my hair into a knot at the base of my neck.

"I thought you might like it out of your way," she says when I reach back to feel it neatly bound.

"That was thoughtful of you," I say with a smile. "Thank you."

She leaves the room for a moment and returns with a steaming cup of tea contained in a cylindrical container with a lid and a handheld pastry of some sort. "So you have time to eat." She hands both to me, and I smile gratefully. "Lord Alexander is awaiting you outside this room—he will escort you to where your Grandmother waits."

The thought of seeing Alexander again after our night spent together so distracts me that I take a few steps forward in a daze. But before I leave, I turn back to Astrid. "I want to thank you for helping me during my stay here. It's been so wonderful to know you."

She smiles softly and reaches out to touch her hand to my arm. "I'm glad to have helped you. May arcana favor you this day."

I return the gesture as Rowen joins me at my side. At the door, I hesitate for a moment with my hand on the latch. A jittery fear jolts through me as

I imagine seeing him for the first time since our night spent together—is he having the same fears as I? Do I *want* him to feel ashamed? But when I open the door, and he smiles warmly at me in welcome, reaching toward me for an embrace, which I return gingerly.

"You look beautiful," he says, and he kisses me on the cheek, lingering there for a moment. He touches the knot at the base of my neck. "Though I think I'll miss being able to run my fingers through your hair."

I force a smile and try to ignore my own embarrassment. We haven't the time to discuss what happened last night. "It's strange, but wearing it up feels odd to me now. Truly, though, that's the least of what I'll miss."

He offers me his arm, and we walk down the hallway in the direction of Grandmother's art studio. "There is something about this world that makes you feel as though it's a part of you—like arriving home after a long journey. Though I think we will be seeing much more of it in the future—" he glances down at me, and I feel pinpricks of emotional tears "—if our shared vision is any indication." He stops, watching me more closely. "Is something wrong? You seem . . . distant this morning."

"Just worried about what lies ahead." *In more ways than one.* "I want to feel like my family is safe again."

"Destroying the Order should go a long way toward that end."

"I hope that isn't your only reason for going through with this," I say, starting down the hall once again.

"I am doing this because I believe it is right." He offers me his arm again as we walk. "Everything else is secondary to that."

We fall into a thoughtful silence after that, but the closer we get to Grandmother's art studio, the more anxious I become. What if I cannot create a proper portal? Or worse, what if something goes terribly wrong once I do? As I steal a glance at Alexander's handsome profile, I feel a twist of unease low in my stomach. I'm generally an optimistic person, but still I fear something terrible will befall him before this is done.

The door to her studio stands open, and we walk through, my heart beating so loudly I fear everyone must hear it.

Grandmother comes and presses a kiss to my cheek. "I have everything ready for you, dearest one." She turns and places a graceful hand on Alexander's shoulder. "Is there anything you need, Alexander, to make ready?"

"Only a warning: Lord Titus has sought me out twice now, and it's clear he is in league with Tyrell—or desires to be."

I shoot Alexander a surprised look, though I suppose I shouldn't be. Titus made it clear from the very beginning he was no ally. Grandmother's reaction, however, is much milder.

"It is true," she says with a glance at Serafino. "He will try to join forces with Centerius, but it does not change our goal here today: to stop him."

All the pieces click together. Titus's clear hatred for all half-Sylvani, his flagrant disrespect for Grandmother's authority, his eerie interest in me at the ball.

With a step back, Grandmother gestures toward the blank canvas. "What I thought would make this easier on you, Lucy, would be if I simply showed you Alexander's memories of the place Centerius is most likely to be."

"His library," Alexander says decisively. "If it will be late evening when I travel through the portal, then he will be found there."

"Very well. His library, then." She holds out her hand to Alexander. "If you would be so kind . . ."

He acquiesces, moving closer to her so that she may touch her hand to his temple. Instantly, images are projected before us of a cavernous library filled with countless books tucked safely away in mahogany bookshelves.

"Draw what you see, dearest one," Grandmother says, and I retrieve a pencil to do just that.

As the images move to give us the full view of the room, I pick the best entry point for Alexander: the corner farthest from the door and steeped in shadow. My pencil moves over the canvas, and I infuse arcana in it as I go, paying particular attention to the details that make the room unique: the fireplace with the carved sun on the mantle, the leather furniture—two wing-backed chairs and a sofa from this vantage point, and the strange decorations—like the skeletal remains of some large sea creature mounted just to the left of the window.

I concentrate so hard on each stroke of the pencil that my knuckles turn white and a fine sheen of sweat covers my body. When at last I've filled every centimeter of paper, when even the spines of many of the books have tiny titles, and each bone of the skeletal creature has been faithfully recreated, I take a step back to compare my drawing to the images suspended before me.

"A perfect rendition," Alexander says with so much awe in his tone I blush.

Grandmother nods, and lets the images fade away. "I quite agree. As accurate as a photograph."

Relieved by their good opinions, I look over the drawing critically and pray it's detailed enough.

Now for the runes.

I approach the canvas, the shakiness of my limbs spreading throughout my body until I'm a mass of jittery nerves. Beside me, Alexander is the eerie calm just before a storm—tension seems to swirl just beneath the surface of his skin, and yet outwardly, he seems almost peaceful.

I pick up the paintbrush and dip it in golden paint. Before I can touch it to the canvas though, I turn to him. "I'm afraid to send you through. After everything we . . . after last night . . ." I trail off, unable to finish. How can I send this man I love, one I want to spend the rest of my life with, into such danger?

He takes the paintbrush from my hand gently and sets it down. And then, before Grandmother and Rowen and Serafino, he gathers me in his arms. I stiffen at first, expecting an immediate rebuke, but a sneaked glance at Grandmother shows she's turned away. "I love you, and I will come back," he says into my hair. "You said yourself my arcana lends itself to my fighting abilities. Let me do this for you, Lucy. Let me atone for my mistakes."

I nod into his chest, fighting tears. This reminds me too much of being forced to stay behind while Katherine sacrificed herself to keep me safe. And the memory is too much. I may not be able to sort out my feelings toward him right now, but I won't stand by this time, not when I can help. "No," I say and take a step back. "You won't go alone."

"Lucy," Grandmother says, taking a step toward me, "I cannot allow you to risk your safety against Centerius. Alexander must go, and you must stay to keep the portal open."

"My *body* must stay, but I can and will transport my spirit."

I look at Alexander, fully expecting an argument from him, but to my surprise, he remains silent. He nods, as though in approval, pride shining in his eyes.

"I will concede that is an option," Grandmother says. "Though it's not without its own dangers—the strain on you will be great."

"But can I withstand it?" When she nods, I press on. "Will I be able to draw runes in my spirit form?"

She looks momentarily taken aback at that—glancing at Serafino for a moment as if conferring. "I think that you will be able to, yes. Spiritual arcana is fueled by the spirit."

A relieved sort of determination washes over me. "Then it's settled. We will go—together."

"I couldn't ask for a better partner," he says, and I feel a new flood of confidence.

He picks up the paint brush and hands it back to me, and I stand in front of the canvas once again. I take a deep breath, reach for Rowen's store of arcana, and draw the rune with bold strokes. A burst of shimmering light fills the room, and the painting looms larger and larger before us. It has a hazy quality to it, like we're viewing it from underwater—the leather chairs and bookshelves and fireplace nearly transparent. When every element in the room is life-sized, the portal stabilizes, standing open with golden light.

Alexander glances back at me just once and then steps through. Immediately, the painting shrinks back to size until it is only paint on canvas once again. I move to make another rune, the one that will allow me to transport my spirit, but Grandmother reaches out to me.

"Do you remember that first time I showed you the power of drawing runes?" she asks. "When I called forth the lightning?"

I nod warily. "It's a difficult thing to forget."

"And do you know the rune for lightning?"

"I do."

She reaches out and touches my cheek. "Do not hesitate to use it, if it should come to that. Centerius is one of us, and by law he has the right to a trial by a council of his peers, but I don't want that to be at the cost of your safety. Or even, in light of recent events," she says pointedly, and I blush, "at the cost of Alexander's safety."

"Thank you, Grandmother—for everything," I say, and she pulls me to her and presses a kiss to my cheek.

"Be safe, dearest one."

☥

THE library is dark when Alexander arrives, lit by only the soft glow of a fire, which does little to illuminate such a cavernous space. Alexander keeps to the shadows while he appraises the situation, listening carefully for any sign that Lord Tyrell is here. When it seems the room is empty, he relaxes a fraction but remains attuned to any noises beyond the room. Alexander remembers Tyrell to be a creature of habit, almost to an unyielding degree. He never deviates from his routine, which he treats as sacred. And in the late evening, Tyrell always enjoys a glass of brandy by the fire. The only potential hitch, the one that Alexander has no control over, is whether he has arrived on the scene too late. He will have to wait here, in the dark, until he can make that determination. He would rather have the element of surprise on his side when he encounters Tyrell, rather than the very real danger of searching his house—parts of which Alexander has little familiarity with.

His decision to stay thus made, he moves silently about the room, searching for the best vantage point as well as any hidden weapons. When he opens one of the desk drawers, he breathes in the lingering sweet smell of pipe smoke, and he is instantly transported back to so many memories from his childhood: evenings spent reading with Lord Tyrell by the fire, Lord Tyrell teaching him how to use his spiritual power to sense others like him, and learning for the first time in his young life that he was something extraordinary.

His memories are all positive ones, which only serve to taint his mind with feelings of betrayal.

But it is Lord Tyrell who is the betrayer, he chastises himself. *Lord Tyrell who formed an organization to hunt his own kind.*

He has only to think of Lucy, of this all-consuming desire to keep her safe, and he knows no one will stop him from his goal—not even the man who helped raised him.

Alexander moves silently to the bookshelf. One of the books catches his eye—an old copy of a collection of Arabian tales. As a boy, Alexander had read it many times, and now, as a man, Alexander relives the memory of evenings spent reading here. He wishes, suddenly, for the queen's power to show memories as moving images. For, looking back, he realizes his time spent with Tyrell is missing a vital aspect of a young boy's life: an emotional response.

Though Tyrell is present in so many of Alexander's memories, and took him under his wing when he joined the brotherhood, there was a distinct lack of any sort of humanity—no sympathy, no kindness, no signs that he cared at all beyond the fact that Alexander was another member of the Order to do his bidding. If it weren't for his loving nanny-turned-house-keeper, Alexander might be as cold and unyielding as Tyrell himself.

Like a strong wind, the dark mists of guilt are blown away. Alexander is not betraying a loving father figure; he's bringing justice to an ancient being long lost to evil. Thus freed, Alexander's gaze sweeps the room with renewed energy. He notes the single entrance, the serving cart with a crystal decanter of an amber-colored drink—freshly prepared, as though waiting for the master to return, and the few options for weapons in the room: a letter opener, an iron fireplace poker, a table that can be easily overturned and broken.

The darkest part of the room is a niche flanked on both sides by book-cases, and Alexander moves there in just a few quiet strides. He has no need for the weapons right now; his goal will be to incapacitate Tyrell as silently as he did James Wyndam. But as Alexander has found, it's best to be pre-pared for anything—especially when dealing with someone who is clever and powerful.

He watches the clock on the mantel with growing unease: Lucy still has not joined him in her spirit form. If she should join him at the wrong moment, it could jeopardize the element of surprise. But almost as if his thoughts summoned her, a soft glow appears before him.

Her back is to him, her beautiful hair ghostly pale. Softly, he calls her name, and she turns. Seeing her here, in this place of danger, makes every nerve in Alexander's body stand on end. He has to remind himself firmly that she is insubstantial—Tyrell will pose no threat to her here.

She moves toward him without a word, clever enough to stay silent, and Alexander reaches out to touch her—as a reassurance to himself and to her—but then he remembers he cannot. It has the strangest effect on him— like being suddenly deprived of sunlight. He pushes away the worrisome thought.

They wait together without speaking, Alexander's eyes on the clock. Much past midnight, and Tyrell will be turning in. It's half past eleven now.

A noise comes just outside in the hall, and Alexander shifts his attention to the door.

Lord Tyrell enters with confident strides and moves toward the serving cart. There, he pours himself a brandy in a crystal glass. He swirls the liquor around pensively for a moment. As he walks fully into the light of the fire, Alexander can see that he is still dressed in a formal tailcoat as though just returned from dinner. He looks as he always has: tall, imposing, and not a day over thirty-five.

The signs had always been there, it seems, if Alexander had ever chosen to make himself aware of them.

"I had wondered if it would be you," Lord Tyrell says to his glass, his familiar baritone of a voice having the very unfamiliar reaction of curling both Alexander's hands into fists. Alexander steps out of the shadows to meet his gaze, and Lord Tyrell smiles. "Wallace told me to expect a traitor to reveal himself soon and was adamant it was you."

His words both take Alexander by surprise and send the first icy whisper of warning into his mind. By all accounts, Tyrell is dangerous and powerful—an arcana drainer, one of the first. Alexander's advantage was in his personal relationship with him. He had hoped he could talk to him, catch him unawares. But now that Tyrell is clearly already on guard . . .

Alexander knows the tide could easily turn against him.

"And?" Alexander says evenly. "Did you believe him?"

Tyrell smiles and takes a drink from his glass. "I think I've always known." His gaze shifts to Lucy's ghostly form behind Alexander, and Alexander tenses. "You are in good company, though, my boy. You are not the first who betrayed another on behalf of a woman."

"He is not acting solely on my behalf," Lucy says, taking a step forward. Alexander feels a surge of protectiveness within him, and he has to remind himself that Tyrell cannot hurt her. "He is acting on the behalf of all those you have wronged, including those you coerced into hunting their own blood."

Tyrell swirls his drink around and around, the amber liquid catching the light. "How righteous you sound. Alexander, did you ever feel wronged? If it were not for me, I daresay you'd be little better off than an orphan."

Before the barb can find its mark in Alexander's heart, Lucy says, "Raising a child to be your own personal hound to track down the Sylvani is hardly a loving situation."

Her words seem to break free the last link of the chain that binds Alexander to this traitorous man. "For once in your life, Lord Tyrell, tell me the truth. Because here is how I see the situation: you found a boy who had lost his mother, who had no father to protect him, and you knew that boy was part Sylvani with the arcana capable of finding others like him—like you. You made him think you were taking him under your wing, but in actuality, you were turning him into a minion to do your bidding—to find you more arcana to keep you alive so far from Sylvania."

Tyrell smiles, the gesture more threatening than friendly. "Figured it all out, have you? I suppose you think yourselves terribly clever. If you know so much about me, Alexander, then I wonder if you know who I really am?"

"Centerius," Alexander says, the name still strange to his ears.

Tyrell closes his eyes for a moment. "Ah, it's been a long time since I heard that name." When he opens them again, his expression turns dark. "Then you must also know the arcana affinity I have been gifted with."

Alexander's lip curls at the use of the word *gift*. Draining another of their life force didn't seem to be a positive thing in any stretch of the imagination. "I know of your power—the power Wallace has always abused."

"Wallace's arcana is anemic compared to mine. Do you take my meaning, Alexander? If you persist on your current path, I will not be held responsible for the consequences. You may try, but you will fail."

Alexander knows all too well this is not false bluster. He may die in this encounter, and as he thinks of Lucy behind him, he is relieved beyond words that she is not here physically. It's a cause he's willing to give his life for. Tyrell must be stopped no matter the cost, and one life is nothing compared to the hundreds it may spare. Still, Alexander is not defeated yet. He has one advantage left to play: he is deadly fast.

Tyrell moves to take another swallow of his drink, and Alexander strikes. He hits Tyrell just above the heart, the center of his chest, and the middle of his abdomen in rapid succession and with complete and total precision. Only one of these pressure points will render him unconscious, but Alexander doesn't take any chances.

After such a powerful attack, Alexander allows his own momentum to carry him away. But instead of the crash he expects to hear as Tyrell hits the ground, Lucy screams a warning. Alexander spins back toward her. At the same time, he sees movement out of the corner of his eye. He dodges, crouching low to keep himself a smaller target.

Tyrell is not only still conscious, he's still on his feet. He dashes the glass in his hand against the fireplace and moves toward Alexander purposefully.

Alexander's mind races ahead. He knows if Tyrell touches him, it will give him the chance to drain his arcana. Alexander must keep moving.

As Alexander evades, he moves steadily toward the fireplace—keeping furniture between himself and Tyrell. When he earlier scanned the room, Alexander noted all possible weapons. The iron fire poker is his best choice.

Alexander grabs hold of the poker just as Tyrell arcs a jagged piece of glass toward Alexander's throat. Alexander contorts away and then immediately goes on the offensive with a weapon in hand.

Alexander wields the poker like a spear with deadly force, but Tyrell manages to evade him. Thrust and evade, thrust and evade, until they are caught in a grim dance.

Tyrell knocks one of the armchairs aside and comes at Alexander with the piece of glass. Alexander takes advantage of his close range and raises the poker—if he can, he will bludgeon him and render him unconscious. The piece of glass arcs toward him again as the poker falls, and seemingly in slow motion, Alexander watches Tyrell drop the glass and grab hold of the poker instead.

Alexander prepares to release it, for he does not want Tyrell to pull him off balance, but then his chest erupts in excruciating pain. Alexander cries out, and distantly, he hears Lucy calling his name, but he cannot even look at her. It feels as though every drop of prana is being pulled forcefully from his body, surging outward from somewhere deep inside him. In its wake, a wrenching pain, like his heart is being slowly cut from his chest.

How? he thinks through the haze of pain. He was so careful. Even now, there is no physical contact between Tyrell and Alexander. But as he tries once again to release the poker and fails, he realizes the truth: Tyrell has used it as a conduit.

Alexander summons what's left of the prana in his body just to have the strength to let go of the makeshift weapon. But as his energy rises within him, Tyrell's power grabs hold and siphons it away. After several attempts, Alexander grasps the true depth of the dilemma, but rather than give into the fear, he thinks of how helpless he was when he first entered the realm of Sylvania. Then, he hadn't had the ability to even lift his head. He thinks of what Lucy told him: that he is Warrior class. If he can break free from Tyrell's hold before he can drain him completely, then he may stand a chance against him.

Perhaps prana or arcana isn't the answer at all—perhaps he must rely entirely upon the strength of his muscles. He tries a different tactic. Instead of trying to release his hold or pull back on the weapon, he shoves it forward with all the considerable power of arm muscles honed by years of daily training.

Tyrell stumbles back, and the poker clatters to the floor. Much too soon, though, he rights himself. Power is radiating from him in waves—like black flames, visible to Alexander as surely as if the man had been lit on fire.

Faster than Alexander would have thought possible, Tyrell lunges toward him, and though Alexander dodges agilely away, Tyrell's hand grasps hold of Alexander's arm.

Bloody hell, Alexander thinks.

TWENTY-SEVEN

I move toward Alexander as if to help him, intending to wrench Tyrell's hateful hand off his arm, but then I remember I have no substantial presence. Before me, Alexander's back is bowed in obvious pain, his mouth open in a silent scream.

Desperation rises within me, and I know if I don't do something to help him, Tyrell will drain him completely. In my mind, I see Grandmother drawing the rune—the one that called down lightning. In this small space, though, I see the possibility of more harm than good coming from such reckless action. I rack my brain, running every rune I've ever seen through it. No weapon can help me—I can neither wield it nor expect Alexander to be able to. Again and again, my thoughts return to forces of nature. Typhoons and hurricanes and tornados. But again, to release any of them in the confines of this room . . .

If only I'd had more time to train! Still, I must do this.

And then the solution comes to me, so suddenly it must be divinely inspired. I've always had the ability to combine runes, and in this case, it can mean the difference in destroying the room and everything in it with lightning, and sending a bolt directly into Tyrell's heart.

The rune for lightning is a short, jagged line. The rune for a sword is a single slash of ink. If all goes well, I will wield the summoned lightning like a sword. I raise my hand and try not to think about the implications—that I'm about to make an attempt on someone's life. He may be evil, and this is in clear defense of Alexander, a man I clearly have strong feelings for no matter our differences, but murder rests uneasily on my shoulders.

I draw the jagged line in the air, pulling arcana from Rowen through the portal's connection to my physical self. It shimmers brightly, but just as I add the line that will transform it to a controlled bolt, I feel a fierce pull from behind. It disturbs the flow of arcana, and the rune fades harmlessly.

I raise my hand to try again, but the pull comes once more, insistent this time. The library and Alexander's struggle for his life begin to fade, and I cry out as fear grips my insides painfully.

"No!" I shout, struggling against the pull, but the library fades still more, until I am thrust back into my body in Grandmother's art studio.

Before I can demand what has happened or try to send myself back, the words die on my tongue. A battle rages here in this room.

The sound is terrible: the roar of a bear, the screeching cry of Serafino, the buffeting winds of a conjured hailstorm, in the center of which is Grandmother, locked into battle with Lord Titus and two others—sentinels by the looks of them, though they wear red uniforms instead of the silver I've grown accustomed to.

Titus slips past Grandmother before I can make a sound, striding right for me. "Let me through the portal," he says, his dark eyes flashing. "Let me through, and I promise not to kill you."

I'm so desperate to return to Alexander, I almost do as he says right then.

"You cannot, Lucy!" Grandmother calls in a strained voice as she and Serafino hold off the other two sentinels with whirlwinds that imprison each of them. "You know what he plans to do."

"I want to wipe you all out," he says with such malice in his face and in his tone I take a step back. "I want to do what should have been done long ago."

Again, I think of Alexander—is he still alive? How long have I been gone? Fear and desperation claw within me like a frantic animal, and suddenly, I realize the solution to the current crisis. A way I might be able to solve two problems at once.

"If you swear not to harm Grandmother or me, then I will take you through," I say.

Grandmother's eyes widen in horror. "Lucy, no!"

Titus nods once. "You have my word."

I have a plan, I tell Rowen, and he nods that he heard.

The paints and paintbrushes have been strewn around the room in the chaos, and I scramble on my hands and knees to grab hold of a brush. I dip it in a pool of spilled golden paint and slash the rune messily across the bottom of the canvas. The drawing of Lord Tyrell's library yawns before us in perfect detail—save for the two people currently locked in battle.

Please be alive. Please, please, don't die. I'm coming.

Titus steps through confidently, and the moment the canvas returns to normal, I draw another rune and send my spirit through after him.

☥

ALEXANDER knows that Lucy's spirit form is no longer in the room with him, but all he feels is calming relief. The queen must have sensed the danger here, and the very real and almost certain possibility that Alexander will die at Tyrell's hands. Twice Alexander has broken free from Tyrell's hold only to be caught again, more and more energy and prana draining from him with each contact. Alexander's body has been trained to fight and maintain control in reduced circumstances: fasting, lack of sleep, extreme thirst, extreme cold or heat. But even his otherworldly ability to control his body is slipping.

He stumbles instead of dodging, and Tyrell nearly lands a solid blow with the iron poker. "There's no use running from me, Alexander," Tyrell says with a taunting smile on his face. "I know everything about you. Your strengths, your weaknesses . . . who really murdered your mother."

Stunned, Alexander misses a step, and Tyrell scores a glancing blow off Alexander's ribs.

Tyrell stops his pursuit, staring Alexander down. "I did tell you the truth, you know. It *was* a Sylvani who killed her." His smile widens, and the blood pounds in Alexander's ears. He already knows what he will say. "It was me."

When Alexander thinks of all he has trusted Tyrell with, how he's looked up to him, joined his brotherhood, believed him to be a father-figure—this man who is actually his mother's *murderer*—it snaps something inside of him, something that must have been holding him back. He feels a surge of renewed energy, fueled by hatred and vengeance.

I'm so sorry, Lucy, Alexander thinks. He removes the letter opener he pocketed. If he cannot complete his mission to bring back Centerius alive, then he will kill him and end his terrible crusade against the mortal Sylvani.

But before Alexander can make that first move that will most likely be Tyrell's last, a bright light blinds them. Both men freeze in place, and though Alexander doesn't dare to hope the light is a sign of reinforcements, he is also terrified it will be Lucy returning. Instead, the light solidifies into a figure of a man, and as the man's features become recognizable, Alexander's stomach drops.

Lord Titus.

TWENTY-EIGHT

SEEING Alexander still alive in the library brings such profound relief that if I were in my physical form, I think I may embarrass myself by sinking to my knees. As it is, I feel boneless with thanksgiving as his eyes meet mine across the room, though with both Titus and Centerius here, we are by no means out of danger. I pray that Alexander will intuit my plan—that he will recognize the gift of Titus arriving here, without his spirit animal, still unused to the lack of arcana in this world. He will be at his weakest, while Centerius will be thoroughly distracted.

Titus sweeps into a bow. "My lord Centerius, I had to stage a coup to get here, but I assure you, if you agree to take me on as your partner, then it will be worth it for us both."

Centerius says nothing for a moment, his attention focused entirely on Titus just as I hoped, and Alexander moves by small increments out of his range. "I'm flattered that you've heard of me," he says, his expression still unreadable, though a faint thrum of tension still hovers in the air, "and though I can clearly see what benefits our partnership would provide for *you*, I'm afraid I can't see how it would be helpful to me."

Lord Titus smiles wolfishly. "I can see from the dangerous scene I've arrived upon that you will soon be in need of another Sylvani with tracking abilities. This boy with tainted blood has abilities that are nothing compared to mine."

"How kind of you to offer such arcana to the service of the Order. I wonder, though, why you've decided to do such a thing."

Hovering here like a ghost, I can see the players in this room from a completely different perspective. I see Lord Titus sneering like he knows he has Centerius convinced. I see the tension that has never left Centerius, that seems to be growing exponentially. And, most importantly, I see Alexander slowly moving into a position that will hopefully prove fatal to one or both of them.

Titus's eyes glitter with malice. "Because I want to erase all the impurities from our bloodlines; I want to wipe the mortal Sylvani from the face of their earth."

Centerius smiles, and if I had my body here, the hair on the back of my neck would rise—there is no joy in that gesture, only the smile of a predator who has decided on its prey. "As noble as such a cause may be, I'm afraid I must disagree. You see, if you were to wipe out all the mortal Sylvani as you so elegantly put it, then I would no longer have a source for harvesting the massive amounts of arcana I need to keep me immortal. So in threatening them, you threaten me."

Before Titus can respond or backpedal, or do anything that may stop the fall of the axe, Centerius lunges forward and grasps hold of his neck. With his mouth yawning open, he seems to call the arcana from Titus's very depths, and it answers, streaming from his own mouth and into Centerius like golden smoke.

Alexander leaps forward at the same time, his movements sure and graceful as a tiger's. I watch the sharp end of a letter opener plunge into Centerius's side. Even so, Centerius releases one hand from around Titus's neck and wraps it around Alexander's instead.

Everything slows down until it's just image after horrible image:
Titus's body crashing to the thick, crimson rug—
—his face the color of ash—
—Centerius with both hands now wrapped around Alexander's neck—
—Alexander mouthing, *Run.*

I lift my hand. I will do what I failed to do before. I draw the runes faster than I ever have—lightning and a sword to guide it with. A bright light fills the room, as the sword of pure, raw electricity manifests into my ghostly hand.

His heart, I think, and the sword obeys.

Spitting and glittering and filling the room with the smell of a thunderstorm, the lightning plunges into Centerius, my hand at its hilt.

Alexander falls to the floor as Centerius's grip on him releases. I try to catch Alexander, but my hands can no longer grip anything but the phantom sword's hilt.

Centerius convulses so violently I hear numerous cracks as his bones give way under the assault. When at last he is still, lightning still gently moving through his body in bright blue waves, his mouth gaping and his eyes rolled back into his head, I make the rune that will take Alexander back to Sylvania.

Later, I will examine this and remember the horror, the fear, the terrible, soul-bruising knowledge that I took another's life. But for now, in this moment, I feel only relief.

TWENTY-NINE

THE moment I return to myself in Grandmother's now-familiar art studio, I rush to Alexander's side. He lies prostrate on the floor, completely unconscious.

He is nearly drained of arcana, Rowen says, materializing by his side.

Grandmother and Serafino join us, with no sign of the sentinels who had tried to aid Titus in his coup, though her own guardsmen are here—dressed in their silver uniforms, wolves at their sides. "He will never recover here," she says brusquely. "Every moment spent in this realm will only drain his depleted supply. We must go, but before we do—Rowen? If you would be so kind as to transfer arcana to Alexander. It needn't be much—just enough to stabilize him for our journey between realms. Lucy, too, could use a touch."

Rowen moves toward Alexander and presses his soft fur against his side. Afterward, he moves to me, and my body fills with the warmth of the sun.

It is done, he says after a moment.

"You have my undying gratitude for all your help," Grandmother tells him.

It's only then that I really look at what she's wearing: a very modern traveling gown in a deep emerald green. "I don't understand—are you coming with us?" She only smiles at my incredulous tone and makes a little wave of her hand. Instantly, Astrid appears from the doorway, my dress in hand.

"We thought you'd be needing to return in a hurry," Astrid says with a sad smile.

"I'm thankful someone is thinking," I say with another anxious glance at Alexander, "for I'm afraid I feel as though my mind has been siphoned away."

With a gesture from Grandmother, the sentinels turn away, and Astrid strips me down right there in the art studio. I help her as best I can with shaky hands and eyes searching Alexander's chest, terrified it will stop rising at any moment.

"Astrid, I cannot thank you enough for all you've done for me," I say when she's dressed me in record time. "It's been such a pleasure to know you."

Grandmother laughs. "She sounds as if she'll never return when we both know that's quite far from the truth."

"Truly?" I ask, thinking of the visions I saw of future children, ones who played in the mortal realm and this one.

"I'll miss you, my princess," Astrid says, touching me gently on the shoulder.

Grandmother takes my hand and leads me to Alexander. "Stand beside him, dearest one, and we shall return as quick as we can."

And good-bye to you, Rowen, I think as Grandmother draws the rune that will return us to the mortal realm. *I can't think how I shall sleep at night without you standing guard over me.*

We'll see each other again sooner than you think, Rowen says. *And don't fear for your Alexander. His body is strong, and his love for you even stronger.*

I smile as Grandmother's powerful rune transports us body and soul to another realm.

With Alexander safely hidden in the shadows of the Roman Baths, his chest rising and falling much more easily, I take my first deep breath of English air. I'd become so used to the heaviness of arcana in the air in Sylvania— like the oppressive feel of humidity or fog. Now that I'm home again, my lungs revel in the freedom of taking an easy breath—well, as easy as can be expected now that I'm wearing a corset again. Lucky for us, it is full dark here, not a soul to be seen, only the gentle sound of the water lapping at the sides of the pool.

Grandmother stands tall as she ever did—none the worse for the wear, even in a foreign realm. "I will go and seek out your sister to help us with Alexander," she says, "but before I go, there is something I must say to you." Her eyes seem to well with emotion, and she surprises me by embracing me tightly. "Lucy, my dearest one, it was a terribly noble and clever and foolish thing you did. I could see Titus's intent for a coup, and I even saw that he would be defeated, but I failed to see who would stop him. Had I known, I'm not sure I could have borne risking you. It could have ended so very badly. I must ask you, though," she says as I pull back to look at her, "if Titus and Centerius still live, or if Alexander was able to complete his mission."

Still tired and a bit dazed from all that conspired, I have difficulty following her question. "Was not Alexander's mission, per se, to bring Centerius back here to be imprisoned?"

She shakes her head. "I only said that, I'm afraid, because it would be illegal of me to suggest otherwise. But I knew what the outcome would be when I sent Alexander."

"Centerius killed Titus the moment he suggested taking away his sources of arcana. But it wasn't Alexander who killed Centerius. I did." Confessing it for the first time makes the whole thing so very real, and my body shakes as though I am in the middle of a snowstorm. "He was going to kill Alexander—he had already drained Titus—and I knew I had the power to stop him."

"You've done both our worlds a tremendous favor," Grandmother says and touches my cheek. "There is no shame in defending someone you love—even to the death."

Even still, it does something to the soul to take another's life—no matter how evil that someone is. For me, now that I think about it, it feels as though a terrible weight has been chained to me.

"I will go to fetch your sister now," Grandmother says as I wrestle with my internal thoughts. "Will you tell me the way?"

After I give her detailed directions, I turn back to Alexander. Thoughts of how Colin and James will react to the sight of him—badly, violently—swirl in my mind, but I push them away. I'll have to face them both soon enough. Better not to fret over it now—it'll only result in my being reduced to a jittery basket of nerves.

I sit down beside Alexander and circle my knees with my arms. His warmth is comforting, his deep, peaceful breaths even more so. I have seen a body recover from a massive loss of arcana once before, and I myself have experienced a bit of it. Thus, I'm not nearly so frightened to see him still unconscious.

"They will love you," I promise him. "Perhaps not right away, but you will win them over as you did me."

Besides, I think to myself as the vision of a beautiful baby fills my mind, *they may not have a choice in the matter.*

The moment Wren arrives, Rob striding just behind her, I can read all over her face that something has gone wrong. I run to her and hug her tightly, and she lets out a weary sigh into my hair. Rob puts his arm around my shoulder, his expression tired.

"We're so relieved you're home," Wren says, taking a step back. She looks over at Grandmother. "And the fact that you brought our grandmother along with you is more than we could have anticipated. We're so terribly sorry not to have received you properly, Grandmother."

She shakes her head. "Seeing the three of you is all the reception I need."

"Will you help me with Alexander?" I ask Rob, anxious to get him to a comfortable bed instead of the hard floor of the Roman Baths.

Rob strides over to take stock of Alexander's injuries. "Is he safe to manhandle a bit? I think I can carry him easier over my shoulder."

"If you're terribly careful," I say, wringing my hands. "He's not injured physically—only weak and drained. He needs sunlight, really, but as it's the middle of the night, I don't expect we can do anything about that."

"That's the thing, Lucy," Wren says with a pointed look. "How *did* he get injured? Grandmother was terribly vague."

Rob joins her in staring me down until I shift uncomfortably, a blush creeping up my neck. "I'll explain as soon as we get home."

"Yes," Wren says, "you will."

Rob stoops down and grabs hold of one of Alexander's arms. When he stands, he pulls Alexander neatly over one shoulder. "Something you learn in military school," he says at my impressed look.

He heads outside with his heavy, unconscious burden, and Wren, Grandmother, and I follow.

"One of the maids will have a room prepared for you when we return," Wren says to Grandmother, and as we enter the light of a street lamp, I see how terribly shadowed her eyes are. "I hope you'll find it to your liking."

Grandmother smiles. "Don't worry about me, dearest. Not when there are so many others to concern yourself with tonight."

"Wren, you must tell me what's wrong. I can't bear it another moment."

She opens the car door for Rob to help Alexander in before turning to me. "I'm so sorry, Luce, but it's Rose. In spite of Alexander's treatments, which helped her at least regain consciousness to say her good-byes, she is very near the end now."

In spite of Alexander warning me of such an outcome and sensing such a thing myself, it still hits me like a physical blow, forcing tears out of my tightly clenched eyelids. Wren rubs my back comfortingly, but it only makes the lump in my throat grow. I take a deep breath and swallow my sob—there will be plenty time for that later, and I'd rather not go to Rose's bedside weeping openly. "So her father is here?" I ask after a moment when I'm sure my words won't end in a sob.

"He is—he's been here for a little over a day now," Wren says, ushering me into the car. I move to where Alexander is awkwardly laid out on one seat. I gently lift his head and place it in my lap as I sit beside him. Grandmother, Wren, and Rob squeeze together across from us. Rob raises his eyebrows at me but doesn't say a word.

"We owe much to your Alexander," Wren says softly as the motorcar jolts forward. "The night Rose's father was due to arrive, we were afraid he'd never make it, but then Alexander came and worked up some potions and pastes and did something rather amazing with arcana and her breathing came much easier. Later, when her father arrived, she was able to wake up and speak to him."

I glance down at Alexander with awe mingling with deep gratitude. He used abilities in front of virtual strangers to him, alone in a house without me there as a mediator, and he did it all without demanding even the briefest thanks from me. I cannot help myself and lean down and press a kiss to his cheek.

"James will be thrilled to see this," Rob mutters, but of course I hear him in the close confines of the motor.

"You owe more to Alexander than you think," I say, struggling not to snap at him. Since when had James lay claim to me? We had entered no formal agreement. "So much has happened . . ." I stop, unable to put everything into words: learning the truth about Alexander, dancing at the ball, the powerful vision, our night spent together, and of course, defeating two evil men who had been bent on destroying everything I love.

Grandmother leans forward and takes my hand. "Later, Lucy. I may not have much arcana here in this realm, but I have enough to show them what they have missed."

I nod slowly, eyes wide. The thought turns my stomach into knots, and at the same time, brings a profound sense of relief. Seeing everything play out for themselves may make all the difference in the world when they learn the hardest truth about Alexander, though I think he has more than redeemed himself.

That's what I tell myself, anyway.

Rob is kind enough to give Alexander his room so that he may have a bed to lie in right away, though when Rob and his valet carried him up the stairs, he was beginning to stir. After Alexander is comfortably settled, I go to Rose, my heart pounding in my throat, joining the lump that has already taken up residence.

The moment I see her, I freeze in the doorway. Fragile before, she is skeletal now. Every bone protrudes from her nightgown, and I can hear her audibly gasping for breath. The room smells pleasantly of an herbal mixture, but underneath it is that unmistakable smell of sweat and death. Sir Thornby rests his head on Rose's hand, the one he clutches so tightly. I almost back away, then, to give his grief privacy, but then I realize I won't get another moment to say my good-byes.

I take another step into the room, and Sir Thornby glances up, his eyes haunted. "My dear Lucy," he says, the depth of despair so clearly audible in his tone that tears immediately prick my eyes. Shared grief erases any awkwardness I may feel, and I walk forward and put my hand on his shoulder. "I'm so glad you are here," he says after a moment. "So glad you could return from . . . where did you say you had been?"

I shake my head. "It doesn't matter now. It's far more important that you were here, my dear Sir Thornby, but I am relieved to be here now, with you both."

"She would be very glad to know you're here, I think," he says, and guilt stabs low in my heart that I hadn't been here when she was lucid.

I squeeze his shoulder and move closer to her side. "Oh my dear friend," I say, and then I must pause for my words are mangled on a sob. "I haven't had the privilege of knowing you long, but you brightened my life so very much in that short time. Your soul is too much for your fragile body to ever contain, and I know that you will find more happiness in the next life, unbound by sickness or pain."

Her shortness of breath seems to worsen, then, her gasps becoming more desperate as her body tries to give oxygen to her drowned lungs. Sir Thornby wraps an arm around me as we watch in pained silence, so helpless to give her any relief.

A soft noise comes from the doorway, and I turn to find Grandmother there, so lovely and otherworldly even in her modern gown. "May I be of any assistance?" she asks softly, her eyes full of sympathy for Rose.

Sir Thornby can hardly tear his eyes away from his daughter, who even now coughs and gasps and grabs hold of his hand.

I'm about to tell Grandmother that I'm not sure how she can help, but I can no longer speak. The tears fall unchecked now as I watch my dear friend struggle desperately for every breath, her face ashen.

Grandmother moves forward and places her hand on Rose's forehead. Instantly, Rose calms, her breathing slowing, her body relaxing. Rose's eyes flutter closed. Sir Thornby is weeping now so powerfully that I think he does not realize what Grandmother is doing, for in truth, I'm not sure I do either.

Peaceful now, no clawing or fighting or gasping for breath. The worry lines of her face have smoothed, and she almost appears to be sleeping, if not for her terrible complexion.

"She deserves a peaceful death," Grandmother says quietly. "I can give her that—an escape for her mind from the trappings of her body in its final moments."

I watch as Rose's thin chest rises once and then exhales. Seconds go by, and her chest finally rises again shallowly. Once more, and then she breathes her last.

"May you finally have rest, my dear friend," I say, and Grandmother wraps her arm around me as I give in to my grief.

THIRTY

THE night of Rose's death, after checking on Alexander and seeing him to be recovering well, I spend the rest of the night in my room sobbing until I feel as though I am nothing but an empty husk, dried up and hollow. So when the first rays of morning light peek through my window, I'm desperate to feel the sun on my skin and be rejuvenated—at least enough to face the day.

The whole house is shadowed by death—the late night spent tending to Rose in her final hours and grieving her loss has resulted in a heavy veil of silence come morning. Everyone seems to still be abed, including the servants. Wren, in all her thoughtfulness, most assuredly told them to sleep another hour or two.

I tread quietly down the hall, pausing only when I get to Rose's door. I think of her father, his face awash with grief, still refusing to leave her side. I expect he slept there, and the thought sends another stab in my heart. He is without wife or daughter now, but I shall adopt him into my family. In no way can I replace his Rose, but perhaps I can ease his lonely grieving.

Once downstairs, I linger for a moment in the foyer, undecided. If I were in London, I'd go straight to the small garden there, but here, I don't have that option. However, just outside is a lovely park—not one hundred feet from the front steps of the townhouse. Just a moment spent on a bench there will go a long way toward rejuvenating me.

There is still so much I must face this day: showing my family the truth about Alexander and what happened with the Order, Rose's funeral plans . . . James. I touch the inside of my jacket where I've hidden the dagger he gave me.

Strangely, when I think of what I'm dreading the most, it's facing James. I wince as I close the door behind me, imagining the look on his face when he sees the truth laid out before him in Grandmother's clear, moving images. As the crunching gravel under my feet turns to springy grass, I touch the tips of my fingers to my lips. Twice he's kissed me now—both times just before we were to be separated. Dare I hope it didn't mean anything to him? The thought of wounding him as he once did me brings me no pleasure. I may not love him as I do Alexander, but I still care for him as a dear friend and the brother of my sister's husband.

I sit heavily on the bench, my sorrow and worry weighing my shoulders down like a yoke. Just as my mind turns to thoughts of Rose again, the clouds part, and sunshine splashes onto my face. I close my eyes for a moment and drink it in. After spending so much time without it in Sylvania, it feels as rejuvenating as a cup of tea after a day spent outside.

Much of the weariness I've been carrying melts away, leaving me refreshed, and I stretch languidly and open my eyes. A few puffy clouds cross over the sun, dimming its rays momentarily. Innocuous as it is, it raises the hairs on the nape of my neck. Feeling rather silly, I scan my surroundings for anything out of the ordinary.

Just a few more minutes, I think, *and then I shall face the day.*

With my face tipped up to the sun, I let my eyes fall closed again even as my mind keeps worrying at a teasing question: what was it I sensed just now? Why should I be afraid?

A shadow passes over me, then, like a cloud suddenly hiding the sun from view, and I open my eyes.

My scream is strangled instantly by a thick hand.

Too late, I remember: Lord Tyrell had not been the only threat.

There is also Lord Wallace.

☥

ALEXANDER awakes to a strange bed and a strange room, though as his vision clears and he takes a second look, he realizes he's been here before. Rob's room at the Thornewood townhouse in Bath.

He carefully lowers his shaky legs to the floor and holds on to one of the bed posts to stand. Across from him, morning sunlight streams in from a window, and he walks over to it slowly. After fighting with the jammed frame for a moment, he finally wrenches it open. Warm sunlight kisses his skin, and he rolls up his sleeves to admit more of it.

He can feel the sunlight's effects almost instantly, and, combined with his deep, restorative sleep from the previous night, he finally feels restored— at least enough to go seek out Lucy. The velvet rope that Rob pulled to summon his valet hangs a few feet away, but Alexander decides against it. Relying on servants is still too much of a foreign concept to him—he would feel far too uncomfortable doing it in another gentleman's home. With a passing frown at his rumpled appearance in the mirror, and consequently a minute or two spent making adjustments until his gray suit is a bit more presentable, he walks into the hallway.

The first thing that strikes him is the complete silence of the house. As he moves past the other doors toward the stairs, he senses the spiritual power of the people behind them—all except for two rooms: one that he knows belongs to Rose, and another that seems to be empty. The more he reaches out, the more he begins to suspect neither Rose nor Lucy seem to be here at all.

And suddenly, he realizes Rose must have succumbed to her pneumonia—perhaps even the night they arrived. Though he hopes he's wrong. He hopes she made a miraculous recovery and is out with Lucy at this very moment.

He comes to a halt in the hallway, his heart hammering in his chest. Is Lucy out of the house? With all that happened with Lord Tyrell and Lord Titus, they'd both forgotten the other threat—the one that chased them from this realm in the first place.

Lord Wallace.

Striding purposefully now, Alexander pounds down the stairs, his own fear nipping at his heels. When he reaches the bottom, he finds the queen standing in the foyer, watching him with concern.

"Where is Lucy?" he asks abruptly.

"I don't know, but if you are this agitated, then you must have reason to suspect something."

Alexander appreciates that the queen does not waste time with inane questions, and her directness goes a long way to soothing his desperate need to lash out. If anything happens to Lucy—he cuts off that line of thinking savagely, refusing to even consider the possibility.

"The man who posed a threat to her when last she was here—Wallace. He could still be in town."

She nods her understanding. "Can you sense her?" When he starts to shake his head in frustration, she interrupts, "Try harder."

He closes his eyes and does as she says—expanding his mind beyond the house, beyond the immediate vicinity, and finally, there, he finds a pinpoint of the bright light he's come to associate with her.

"I found her—not far, but she's moving away," he says in a rush.

"Then let us go to her."

THIRTY-ONE

THERE is no one to see him drag me away. The sleepy spa town is no bustling London; no carriages rolling by, no farmers bringing in their wares and livestock, not even a single paperboy. I try to fight Wallace, but his strength is far greater than my own, and worse still, he is slowly siphoning my arcana—just enough to weaken me.

Fear crashes over me like waves breaking on rocks. The need to escape is so great that my steps are stilted, energy zinging through my body like lightning, only to be siphoned away again by Wallace's arcana.

"You may not know this yet," I say as I try again to free my arm enough to reach inside my jacket for the dagger, "but the leader of your brotherhood is no longer even alive."

Wallace says nothing, only continues to drag me toward some distant point.

"Worse still is the fact that he *was* Sylvan, just as you are at least part Sylvan. You're hunting your own people," I shout when he doesn't respond to my words.

He smiles a slow, mean smile. "I would hunt you down if you were my own sister," he says, and I flinch at the venom in his tone. "It's clear that Alexander cares for you, and I've made it my life's goal to destroy everything he cares about in this world. As for Lord Tyrell—good riddance, I say. More for me," he says, flashing gleaming white teeth like a wolf.

"How could you hate Alexander so much? What could he have possibly done to you?"

He answers me with a rough jerk of my arm that sends a shooting pain through my shoulder. As I grit my teeth against the pain, he changes direction, leaving the cover of trees in the park for a side alley.

But it's when I see the end destination—a gleaming motorcar—that I begin to fight in earnest. His grip only tightens on me like a vise, and the panic rises within me, nearly blinding in its intensity. I try to calm myself, try to remember some piece of advice James once gave. Arc the dagger out, don't stab . . . how to dodge . . . how to *feint.*

On that last thought, I think of James pivoting away so smoothly on his heel, and suddenly, I know what I must do.

Instead of fighting against Wallace, I throw myself toward him. Surprised by my sudden change in direction, his grip loosens, and I free one of my hands. With a speed I hardly knew I was capable of, I pull out my dagger. He dodges away as I slash violently—just as James taught me.

But before I can pivot again, his meaty hand closes on my wrist again. He squeezes so hard I feel the bones grind together, and I cry out even as my grip on the dagger loosens. I hear it fall to the ground with a resounding *thunk.*

"You want to know why I hate Alexander?" he asks in a near growl. "He betrayed the brotherhood, he threw everything aside for you, and for what? I warned Tyrell myself—I was always his most faithful disciple—but always he showed preference toward the weak-willed chee chee. You say Tyrell is dead? Good," he says savagely, his eyes flashing. "It's no less than he deserves."

He pulls me closer, then, and I struggle wildly.

No, no! *I will not let him take me away and drain me.* I think not only of myself, but of the life that may be growing inside of me, and I feel my determination renew.

A dagger is far from the only means of defense I have.

But I need to free my hands first.

I'm not strong enough to yank them free, and I doubt he'll fall for a feint again. And then, suddenly, I think of Alexander fighting, using his whole body to defeat his opponent. Using Wallace's own hold on my hands, I pull back and launch myself up enough to kick him soundly in the groin. With a grunt of pain, he moves to protect himself, and my hands are freed.

I could call down lightning here and now, just as Grandmother showed me, but I have a much better fate in mind for him. I make the runes quickly, without hesitation.

Two parallel lines to represent transporting to another location.

A broken circle to represent the dungeon located in the bowels of my grandmother's castle.

Golden arcana flows from my fingertips in a brilliant display, the runes illuminating the air around us. Wallace makes a move toward me, but the runes snare him as easily as a net catches a fish—he thrashes against it for a moment, and then in a flash like lightning, he disappears.

I bend over at the waist, shaking violently, my breaths coming so fast I fear I might faint. The adrenaline leaves my body in a rush, leaving me as weak as an infant.

And then strong arms wrap around me, surrounding me with the smell of cardamom and clove.

"Alexander," I say in relief. He only holds me tighter.

"I was terrified I wouldn't make it in time," he says, and when I look up at his face, it's awash with fear.

"You did well, dearest one," Grandmother says, walking up and placing her hand on my shoulder. "You proved you were perfectly able to defend yourself, and that our mad dash here was superfluous indeed. But I must ask—where did you send him?"

Alexander glances over at the empty space where Wallace once was, and I do the same. "To your dungeon. It's what I should have done against Tyrell, only it seems that when someone I love is threatened, I choose the most violent resort."

Alexander gently turns my head toward his. "No more guilt. You've done nothing wrong."

"I agree," Grandmother says sternly. "I would have been equally approving had you decided to defend yourself to the death against Wallace—your life has far more value to me than his."

"Nor would he have shown you the slightest bit of mercy," Alexander adds with a flex of his jaw.

I think of the terrible draining feeling of having my arcana taken from me, of the weakness I still feel, and shudder. "What will you do with him when you return?" I ask Grandmother.

"I will search his mind and discover the depths of his wrongdoing, and then the Council and I will determine his fate."

She says all of this matter-of-factly, though I know it's no small matter to dig through someone's mind, and Alexander shifts slightly as though uncomfortable. He knows firsthand what it's like to have one's memories pillaged, and it makes me regretful such a tactic was used on him—even if it did allow me to trust him again.

"Lucy," Alexander says, taking my arm, "do you think I might have a word with you alone?"

"Of course, only . . ." I glance over at Grandmother, and she nods in understanding.

"Take your time," she says. "I wanted to walk through and examine the flowers of this garden anyway."

"Thank you, Grandmother," I say with a relieved smile.

Alexander waits until she has moved away, and then pulls me into the shelter of a small copse of trees. The town still hasn't stirred to life; the park is still empty. Ironically, where only a short time ago the lack of people around was a terrible thing, now I am celebrating that fact.

Alexander tucks a stray lock of my hair behind my cheek, the love in his eyes plain to see. It makes me feel as beautiful as a goddess, though I'm sure I must look a fright. Lack of sleep and no time to be properly outfitted ensures that I'm by no means presentable. But when he leans in to kiss me, I return it eagerly. After nearly losing him to Centerius, I find I feel none of the shame and worry I felt this morning—only a calming sense of rightness, like I've found the one person who can understand me.

He gathers me in his arms. "Lucy, darling, I don't regret a moment we spent together the night of the ball, but I am afraid you do. I feel as though I was a cad to share such an intimate moment outside in the grass like . . ." He shakes his head. "Forgive me, for I simply couldn't resist you."

His words resonate within me—had I not had the same worries?—but after seeing him in the light of day, I've never been more sure. "You didn't lead me to do anything I didn't already want to do," I say firmly. "Rest aside any fears that I hold any regrets, for it's quite the opposite." I touch his cheek. "Alexander, I love you. That fact won't change for the rest of my life, much less only a few days later."

He laughs and hangs his head. "Of course you're right. I didn't mean to suggest your heart was fickle." I meet his gaze, and the smile drifts off his face as he leans down to capture my mouth in a kiss. "I love you desperately," he says after a moment. "Do you think your family will ever accept me? I do so want things to be perfect for you."

I smile a little sadly and kiss him once, softly. "I think in time they will. Once they come to know you as I do, I don't think they'll be able to help it."

"I think it would be easier for you if I stayed at my own townhouse here. You're under enough duress with the loss of your friend, and I don't want your family to have to deal with my arrival as well. For now, only your siblings know I was even there. I should also see about my friend Richard, since I believe I owe him an apology for abandoning him when I went through the portal."

"I don't want you to feel as though you aren't welcome," I say, even as I try to hide the real reason I don't want him to leave: his presence is a comfort to me now, and I crave it. Without him, the idea of facing Rose's funeral alone seems daunting.

He grins. "Welcomed by you, perhaps. But even I know encroaching upon Lord Thornewood's territory is no way to court you. I want to do it properly—I want to have the chance to speak with all the protective men in your life."

"Speak to them about what?" I ask, almost teasingly, though my heart pounds as rapidly as a bird's in my ears. He'd said he wanted to marry me in Sylvania, but now that we've returned to our own realm, it seems as though it was only a night spent in enchantment—like being whisked away in some faerie wood.

"I want to marry you, Lucy Sinclair," he says, his gaze swallowing mine. "If you'll still have me."

I don't need a vision to tell me that I'm madly in love with Alexander, that perhaps I have been since the moment we first spoke on the balcony together. A glimpse into the future only solidifies that knowledge in my mind. I chose to be with him the moment I gave myself to him in Sylvania, and despite my initial fears, I know it was right for us both. "There is no one I'd rather spend my life with," I say firmly. "Who else would spend hours painting and discussing art with me?"

He laughs and gathers me into his arms again. "I love you as you are right now in my arms," he says, his words warm in my ear, "and I love you as I saw you in the future, with our children surrounding you."

A baby with dark hair and blue eyes, I think as his mouth descends on mine, as I give into the heady sensation of being kissed by the man I love . . . the man I first saw in my own drawing.

The man I must convince my family is the best for me . . . no matter his previous ties.

THIRTY-TWO

ROSE was buried, two days after her death, in a small church just outside of London. She was laid beside her mother in the church in which both of them were baptized. The sky, contrary to our mourning clothes and tears streaming down our faces, was a bright blue with plentiful sunshine. I think Rose would have much preferred it to a gloomy thunderstorm, though.

I sent for the most exotic hothouse flowers for her in deference to her love for faraway places, and so I was able to throw a large bouquet of orchids, hibiscus, and birds of paradise on her casket beside all the roses and peonies.

Alexander came and was well-received by Rose's father, who thanked him profusely for intervening and helping her to survive until he could say a proper good-bye.

"She had a beautiful aura," Alexander had told me as I tried unsuccessfully not to weep all over his beautiful black suit. "Nearly as bright as yours. I have no doubt her soul is free now, no longer tortured by the pain of a dying body."

"You can see auras?" I'd asked, intrigued despite my grief.

"I believe it's part of my ability to sense a person's prana, for the aura has much to do with that, both of them being an aspect of one's spiritual form."

I'd tried to maintain a respectable distance from him, but I craved his closeness and couldn't resist looping my arm through his, though James narrowed his eyes at us from afar. "Will you come speak to them tonight?"

"Tomorrow," he had promised.

So now we are all assembled in the library, a party of seven with Izzie gone to take her afternoon nap. Only Rob and Grandmother seem at ease; everyone else is tense as we await Alexander's arrival.

"Darling," Wren says as she joins me on the couch, her voice barely above a whisper, "would it not be better for only Papa to be in here when first Alexander comes? Surely we shouldn't *all* be lying in wait for him." Her gaze shifts to Colin and James, who wear matching scowls as they lean against the bookshelves ominously.

No doubt Wren has guessed the true purpose of Alexander's visit, but I still shake my head obstinately. Better to have Grandmother reveal the full truth to us all, rather than having to repeat it to each individual person. It will be like tearing off one giant bandage at once.

I can only hope I don't hemorrhage.

A sound comes at the door, and Wren and I jump. Hale enters with Alexander on his heels. "Lord Alexander Devonshire," he announces.

I stand to greet him, and he comes over and takes my hand. "Lucy," he says in greeting, his warm eyes instantly relaxing my tense shoulders.

After a brief exchange of pleasantries with everyone else—though his exchanges with Colin and James could hardly be called *pleasant*—he sits down on one of the leather chairs adjacent to the sofa.

Grandmother takes that as her cue and moves to the front of the room. Seeing her dressed with her sunset hair pulled up and outfitted in a modern frock with a full skirt is something I think I'll never get used to, though she looks every inch a queen. "I know Lucy and I have mostly kept you in the dark about what you can expect from me today, and that's because it's far better to show you than to attempt to explain. However, if you will give me permission, my dearest Katherine, I would like to provide a demonstration."

Wren glances at me, but I shake my head. I'm not sure where Grandmother is going with this either.

"Of course," Wren says, joining Grandmother by the fireplace.

"Thank you, my dearest. Now, if you will recall one of your fondest memories for us—perhaps your wedding day, or the moment you held Izzie in your arms for the first time—something you wouldn't mind sharing with us all."

Now I know what she has in mind, and with a shared glance at Alexander, I think I agree with her methods. My family will need a way to know that what Grandmother shows them is the absolute truth—that there is no possibility that Alexander somehow deceived us all.

Wren smiles at Grandmother curiously as she takes her hand, and then the smile rapidly fades into a look of pure surprise and awe when her memories flicker before us in moving images.

A gorgeous Wren dressed in an ivory satin wedding gown gazes up at Colin adoringly. A much younger me stands to one side, dressed in a beautiful violet satin gown with lace trim, and James stands beside Colin as his best man. The bishop pronounces them man and wife, and then Wren and Colin are kissing far too passionately for church.

The images fade immediately after that, and Wren stares at Grandmother in a stunned sort of silence.

"That was incredible!" Rob says. "I have a memory for us all to enjoy."

"Heavens, no," I say. "I doubt very much whatever you want to show us is appropriate for one thing, and for another, our grandmother isn't here to entertain."

"Does it mean we can see memories of Mama?" Wren asks, her eyes shining with hope.

"I'd be happy to show you Isidora," Grandmother says. "I'm afraid, though, that I have a finite amount of arcana stored within me, and it may require a brief trip back to Sylvania to replenish my supplies. I want to be sure I have enough to show what has been asked of me. Later, I can show you any memories you so desire. For now, though, let us start at the beginning."

Grandmother draws a golden rune in the air, and it shimmers and fades into a bright white light. I'm not sure what I was expecting, but it wasn't for Centerius to suddenly appear, dressed in what I've come to recognize as Sylvan clothing—an elaborate embroidered long jacket and fitted trousers. Grandmother reveals enough of the surroundings as to leave no doubt he is Sylvania, and then we are subject to image after image of him draining other Sylvani.

I reach for Wren's hand, and she grips it tightly, both of us flinching as we think of the terrible sensation of having arcana drained away against our wills. Colin comes and puts a hand on his wife's shoulder comfortingly, though his own face is grim. A glance at Alexander shows his jaw tight and his face pale. He knows what Grandmother will show next.

After the terrible battle with Centerius and his resulting exile, the images change abruptly to a young Alexander crying on a stone bench of a cemetery. Dressed all in black, he holds a picture of his mother, and my own heart twists. But when Centerius appears, dressed now in modern attire, a ripple of tension moves through the room.

We watch him take the boy in, offer him the one thing he's always craved: a father. We watch him convince the boy the Sylvani are evil, that they are responsible for the death of his mother—a fact we will later learn is true, but not the way he always portrayed it.

I flinch at the cruelty Alexander endures—from other children at school, from his own father and stepmother, from grown men and women. *Chee chee* they call him, and worse names still.

And though I know it's coming, it still twists my stomach in painful knots to watch him be inducted into the hateful Order, to use his arcana to find others like him—like us—and hand them over willingly to Centerius.

"You can't be serious," James says explosively as we see more of Alexander's involvement in the Order. "Why is he still here?"

Grandmother doesn't stop though, doesn't even acknowledge his words, and the images keep coming.

The Alexander in the images meets a beautiful Indian girl in a marketplace, but before a stab of jealousy can rip through me, the next image shows him finding her dead—her face so ashen there can be no doubt she was drained of arcana.

The images move through Alexander meeting me, his confrontation with Wallace, his decision to follow me to Bath, and his split-second decision to follow me to Sylvania. Once there, the images move through everything we went through in that beautiful other world, including our joint effort to defeat both Centerius and Titus.

"Oh Lucy," Wren says with a shake of her head, "how could you put yourself in such danger? And here we were . . . with no idea. I should be furious with you if not for the gift you've given us of ridding the world of such evil."

I thought the images would stop there, but they continue to the night of the ball, culminating in the vision Alexander and I shared.

The final image is of children who look remarkably like Alexander and me, playing in a Sylvan field. When it fades away, the room is left with a pregnant silence.

"This, as you can see, is a story of redemption," Grandmother says. "Alexander is not blameless in all this, though he was taken in by Centerius at a very young age directly after the death of his mother."

Alexander sits like a man on trial, silent but tense. Wren is the first to speak, her hand still gripping mine. "I know you probably worried about my reaction the most, dear sister," she says, "but I do not see in Alexander's character the same darkness that Blackburn had. I think he has more than proved his loyalty to you, and more importantly, redeemed himself of his participation in an evil organization."

"Well said," Rob says from somewhere behind me, but I'm too busy throwing myself into my sister's arms to see.

I shouldn't have doubted my siblings' support. When it came to it, we were thick as thieves.

"Though I do worry," Wren says, glancing at Grandmother. "Is this truly the end? Does killing Centerius ensure the rest of the brotherhood will fall apart?"

"Defeating the leader will have an enormous impact on the brotherhood, but you are right to stay on your guard—only time will tell how much the threat has been mitigated." Grandmother turns to Alexander. "How fortuitous for you that you have a former member in your midst. He, more than anyone, will be able to ascertain how safe you will be in future."

"I will keep this family safe," Alexander says, his eyes darkening. "This I swear to you."

"You cannot be serious," James says, glancing from us to Alexander indignantly. "It's not as though the chap belonged to the wrong sort of club. He was caught up in a brotherhood that *murdered* people. Namely, *your* people. He may have sought vengeance upon the man who killed his mother, but I daresay that doesn't make him an acceptable part of our family now—or even society!"

I feel the heat rising to my face in the onslaught of James's words, though not at all because I am ashamed. Rather, I've never felt angrier. "Thank God you are not judge and jury of us all, James Wyndam, for I should think no man would be capable of redemption in your eyes."

"I can only assume," Colin interrupts, walking around to the front of the sofa before James can respond to me, "that we have been shown this because Alexander would like to become part of this family." He turns, then, and stares at Alexander, who meets his gaze unflinchingly.

"I've come here to ask for Lucy's hand in marriage from Lord Sinclair," Alexander says, his gaze shifting to Papa, who has not uttered a word yet. "I consented to all of you viewing some of the darkest and most shameful parts of my life because I believe there shouldn't be any secrets between us. I know Lucy wants the approval of her family, and her happiness is worth sacrificing any fleeting embarrassment or shame I may feel in sharing this with you."

I stand and go to Alexander's side. "Papa?"

My father seems to rouse himself from a deep thought. "If the decision lies with me and me alone, then I fully give my permission. One thing I learned from my beloved wife is that she could be trusted implicitly, particularly where visions were concerned, and I daresay her mother has the same ability." He turns to Alexander. "Yes, Lord Devonshire, you may take my youngest daughter as your wife, but I expect that all will be done as it should be—the banns to be read and so forth."

James seems to be struggling to hold his tongue, but I admire that he does so. His brother, on the other hand, shakes his head. "If my opinion counts at all, then I must say I think your turning against the man known as Centerius shows an astounding lack of values."

"Colin, for heaven's sake, what are you even saying?" Wren demands. "That he's unscrupulous for fighting against an evil man?"

"No, I'm saying it seems to illustrate that he doesn't know his own mind. He couldn't recognize the evil until it was beating down his door."

Again, I feel that rising anger within me, and my cheeks instantly flush. "He was only a child—"

"He has every right to say such things," Alexander interrupts, coming to his feet to face Colin. "You are right, Lord Thornewood, I didn't turn against the brotherhood until the facts of their evil deeds were staring me in the face. For this, I blame my loyalty. Once given, it's nearly impossible for me to rescind it. But you are right—failing to leave the brotherhood immediately is something I will carry with me for the rest of my life. The fact that Lucy has chosen to love me in spite of this brings me inexplicable gratitude, and I know I may never be able to atone for my misdeeds."

Colin says nothing to this, but I can see a shifting in his expression, a reluctant respect.

"I do love him," I say quietly but firmly. "I love him and I will marry him—regardless of anyone else's opinions on the subject. You are all my family and I love you, and so I also want your acceptance and support, but ultimately, I do not need it."

"You need it if you want to marry," James says obstinately.

"Papa gave his permission freely, but even if he hadn't, I would elope."

The words hang in the air for a moment, and just as I feel myself start to pull away from my family, Rob laughs. "Good God. What would you have Father do? Sign for his permission in blood? You will have your wedding, little sister—no need for a sordid trip to Gretna Green." He comes over and claps a hand on Colin's shoulder. "Colin and James will accept Alexander eventually. Neither of them likes anyone upon first meeting, so I hardly think they are a good judge."

Colin's expression darkens at my brother, but he thankfully says nothing more.

"Then it's time for supper, is it not?" Rob asks. "Grandmother, you must be famished, shall I escort you in?"

"You may indeed, but just a moment." She comes over to me and touches my arm. "This is but a small trial in a very long future of happiness," she whispers.

I nod and give her a kiss on the cheek. "Thank you, Grandmother."

"The gong for supper should have been rung ages ago," Wren says, getting to her feet and linking her arm through Colin's. "Shall we go, darling?"

With one last glance at Alexander, Colin smiles down at Wren. "We shall." Before he leaves though, he turns to Alexander and me. "Lord Devonshire, you are welcome to join us for supper. We cannot be the only ones hungry."

"I thank you for the invitation," Alexander says formally. "I think I will take you up on it."

As the others begin to leave the room, however, Alexander and I hang back to have a moment alone. James is last to leave, and I can see the tell-tale tension in his back and shoulders. "Might I have a word, Lucy?"

"Of course," I say, though it's honestly the last thing I want. I know he will only rail against Alexander, but I almost feel as though I owe him an explanation.

"I'll just wait over here," Alexander says and crosses the full length of the room—a considerable distance since ten bookcases and two fireplaces stand between us.

"How kind of him," James says with a wry smile that doesn't reach his eyes. "Moving across the room to allow me a moment to say good-bye to my friend."

"There's no need to be unkind," I say, my frustration with him quickly negating all my good intentions. "And why should we not stay friends?"

He shoves a hand through his hair. "Because I love you."

"Oh, James, that cannot be true. I think you do love me, but not in that way. If you did, then you would want me to be happy." When he lets out an explosive sigh and shakes his head, I press on before he can argue. "I know you don't understand, but I know—I think I've always known—that my path lies with him."

"So because of some *vision*," he says with a distasteful curl to his lip, "this is why you want to be with him—with a man who only just recently belonged to the Order?"

"I want to be with him because I love him," I say, trying rather unsuccessfully to keep the edge from my tone. "The vision is merely confirmation of things I already know."

James shakes his head, frustration and anger darkening his usually carefree features. "Is this revenge on me, Lucy? For passing you up when I had the chance?"

The idea is so absurd I almost laugh—until I see his expression of complete despair. "James, no, of course not. I was sixteen then, and I've long since made amends with you. I'm not so cruel as to devise some elaborate punishment."

"I can see that I won't change your mind on this, but at least I can tell myself that I tried," he says, pain evident in his voice. Before I can say anything, he turns and strides toward the door. At the last moment, though, he stops. "In answer to your earlier question—we will stay friends, I'm sure. If only because I can't help myself."

With that, he leaves the room, and I already know—without the gift of a vision—that he won't be at supper, nor even in London after tonight. The thought bows my shoulders with regret.

"Everything all right?" Alexander asks, coming quietly to my side.

"I hope so—in time," I say, still watching the doorway where James exited sadly. I turn to Alexander and place my hand on his arm. "But you were kind to let him have a word with me."

He pulls me close, and I suddenly find myself rather distracted. "It wasn't easy," he says. "I could see you were upset, but I also would hope I'd be given the same courtesy were I the one to lose your affections."

"That," I say as I wrap my arms around his neck, "is a problem you will never have to face."

He smiles just once before pulling me flush against him and kissing me until I forget my conversation with James, my own name, everything but the feel of Alexander's body against mine.

"I love you desperately, you know," Alexander whispers huskily into my ear.

"I love you, too," I whisper back. "And I do know. It only took a visit to another world to realize it."